Bayou Sweetheart

C

Lexi Blake

JOVE
New York

A JOVE BOOK
Published by Berkley
An imprint of Penguin Random House LLC
penguinrandomhouse.com

ISBN: 9780593439555

First Edition: July 2022

Printed in the United States of America
1   3   5   7   9   10   8   6   4   2

Book design by Alison Cnockaert

Bayou Sweetheart

chapter one

Brynn Pearson took a deep breath and soaked in the morning light. The world seemed softer here, the green of the trees above in stunning contrast with the blue sky and puffy clouds. Their trunks seemed to come straight out of the water, their limbs bending and twisting.

But what she really loved about Papillon, Louisiana, was the quiet.

She sat on the back porch of the small cabin and stared out over the water, her corgi resting contentedly on her lap. She absently ran her hand along Duke's fur and felt him yawn. Even her dog was at peace.

She could think here. How long had it been since she was still? She'd forgotten how good it felt to know she had a whole day with nothing planned. No agenda items. No meetings. No rehearsals or interviews. She'd been staying in the cabin on the grounds of the Butterfly Bayou Bed-and-Breakfast, owned and operated by the cutest family she'd ever seen. From what she could tell, no one even recognized her here. If the owners of the B and B did, they gave her absolutely no clue. Maybe it was the new hair and the lack of makeup.

Or maybe not everyone had watched her grow up on TV, and wasn't that the coolest thing?

Duke's head came up and swiveled.

"Hey, I've got your lunch along with some water and a couple of snacks."

She glanced up. One of the proprietors stood there with a big German shepherd and the little boy who'd been introduced as Luc. Harry Jefferys was a handsome man with a ready smile. He was one of those guys whose obvious goodness shined through.

He could have killed in Hollywood, had every casting director in the world at his feet. But she got the feeling the man was happy right where he was.

Duke jumped down and greeted the newcomers.

Brynn stood and offered to take the backpack from him. "Thanks. I can't tell you how much I appreciate your wife's cooking."

If she didn't watch it, she would be in trouble when production started up in a couple of weeks. Papillon was playing hell on her diet. When she'd decided to come out early to prep for her role, she'd banished her personal chef/sadistic purveyor of all things kale. Her character wouldn't have a chef. Or an assistant. Or a chick who walked behind her with a compact to make sure her skin didn't shine.

"She's the best, but if you want to try some real gumbo, you might want to go to her brother's place on the bay. It's called Guidry's," Harry offered.

"And bread pudding." Luc wore a Spider-Man T-shirt and jeans, his dark hair adorably messy. He knelt down to pet Duke. "Uncle Remy makes the best. And French fries."

"I'll have to give it a try," she promised. It all sounded good, and really, how much damage could a week off her ridiculous diet do?

Harry nodded. "There's a chicken salad sandwich in there, along with potato salad and some brownies. I also snuck some of last night's pork chop leftovers in a baggie for Duke."

The B and B was a pet-friendly place. Besides the big German shepherd named Shep, there was a pretty tabby cat who wandered the grounds. There were all kinds of what Harry called "critters." She was pretty sure last night she'd seen a group of raccoons running around. Or maybe it had been possums. "Thank you. He'll love it."

"I also packed some supplies you might need. Be careful out there. It's been raining the last week and the mud can be dangerous. All kinds of animals get stuck and can't get out. The trail you're going down takes you around the water. That little thing right there could get sucked right in."

Luc frowned up at his dad, a hand still on the corgi. "Brynn won't let her doggie get hurt."

"I'll stay on the trail. Promise." She looked back at Harry. "You said the light was good on the dock, right?" She wanted to spend the day sitting on that dock, sketching and soaking in her surroundings. She would take pictures so she could remember the details when she went to paint.

Harry frowned. "Well, the light is pretty much the same everywhere, ma'am."

Ah, the non-artist. They thought light existed merely so they could see and be warm. She knew light played all around her. Light illuminated far more than the way. "It's pretty?"

"Oh, yes, it's gorgeous, and you should be alone at this time of day," Harry agreed. He held out the keys. "All you have to do is go back down the drive, hang a right, and you'll see the turnoff about a mile down the road. The trail will take you to the dock."

"And I will be sure to avoid the mud."

Harry grinned. "You should. That mud is serious. Suck a

man right down. We'll be back later this evening. You sure you don't want Sera to leave some dinner for you?"

"That's okay. I can pick up dinner. Maybe I'll go to Guidry's." She wanted to hang around the town, soak it in. If Harry and Sera were any indication, no one would bother her. She might even be able to blend in.

Maybe she would get to feel normal for half a second.

"Be careful out there." Harry put a hand on Luc's shoulder. "Come on, son. Let's go find Momma and Ella."

Luc gave her a heart-stoppingly sweet smile. "Bye, Brynn. See you tomorrow. Momma's making pancakes."

She'd had breakfast with the family this morning because she was their only guest for a couple of days. The production crew had bought the place out for three months. She'd sat down in the dining room all alone and thought about taking the food back to her room, when Seraphina asked if she wouldn't mind eating in the family kitchen since it would be easier for her to serve there.

"I'll be there, buddy." She'd loved it, loved the camaraderie and the way Harry and Sera worked together to take care of their kiddos. She'd enjoyed hanging with Luc and watching baby Ella laugh.

Breakfast at home usually consisted of making sure she didn't get a single extra gram of fat while her mom was on the phone with her agent or one of her other clients or whoever had gained her ire overnight and her sister prepared for yet another audition.

All in all, she liked pancakes and baby spit-up and a big German shepherd who waited patiently for one of the kids to drop food.

She waved good-bye, picked up her pup, and then headed into one of the three cozy cabins located around the grounds of the gorgeous B and B. She and Duke were in the one closest to the water, and she'd gone to sleep the last couple of nights to the sounds of the bayou. The noises of the bayou were for the most part charming and lulling. They only once made her wake up in fear that there was some kind of wolf outside her door. But that was crazy. It had probably been a dog. Maybe Shep liked to howl at the moon.

She gathered up what she needed and headed for Harry's truck. Brynn had been thrilled when he'd offered her his truck for the day. The car she was owed by contract wouldn't be delivered until the actual film production started, though honestly, her mother and Ally would likely drive her to the set each day and then use the car as their own.

Freedom. That was what that banged-up Ford represented. She had a few weeks of freedom before the production team landed and she had to be Bria Knight again. For now, she could be Brynn.

She settled Duke into his safety seat, got into the truck, her lunch and sketchpad tucked away in the backpack Harry had given her, and started down the road.

It wasn't their first adventure. Since she'd gotten Duke as a puppy four years ago, he'd been her constant companion. He'd traveled with her to Europe when the show filmed there. She remembered a time when she hadn't had a dog and she'd been lonely on set. Duke had changed that and she viewed being able to have him with her as a new stage in her life, a better stage.

Now she was on the cusp of another change. This new project was supposed to catapult her past her childhood stardom and into full-fledged adult movie star.

The trouble was, she wasn't sure she wanted it.

Brynn took a deep breath and turned where Harry had told her to. The truth of the matter was she didn't have much of a choice. This had been her path for a very long time, and her family depended on her. Unless she found a way to make her paintings sell for what she made per movie, she was out of luck.

Her cell trilled and Brynn barely bit back a groan as she pulled over to the side of the dirt road. Harry had suggested parking here and hiking the rest of the way. This had to be the place since there was already a big SUV parked on the other side. It was black and white with police lights on top. Emblazoned on the side were the words *Papillon Parish Sheriff*. She hoped there wasn't trouble.

She glanced down and realized she couldn't avoid this call. If she did, the person on the other end of the line would call the governor of Louisiana and send in the guard to find her. So she answered. "Hey, Mom."

"Did you look at the scripts I sent you?" Her mother rarely wasted time.

"Not yet." She unclipped Duke from the safety harness, exchanging it for his leash. He was a wanderer, and that could be dangerous here. He wasn't used to the terrain, and apparently there were gators who would think her sweet baby was a light snack.

She put her mom on speaker. If she didn't get moving, she would miss the good light because her mother could talk forever.

An impatient huff came over the line. "Why? I thought you were going to read them on the plane."

She'd meant to but then she'd started a book and the hours had flown by, and when she'd gotten here she'd realized she simply needed a break. Not that she could tell her mom that. There were no breaks in her mother's world. "I got caught up replying to some emails. You know what a time suck that can be."

She felt only a little guilty about lying. If she didn't, she would get a long lecture on how she should never stop hustling. She grabbed the backpack and Duke hopped out of the truck, eager to get going.

"Yes, I do, but I need an answer on those scripts or they'll send them to someone else," her mother insisted. "We need to lock down projects for next year or it will look like no one wants to hire you. I don't want anyone to think that the big directors are waiting to see how you pull off this project. It could set you back months."

That didn't sound so bad. Would it be wrong to take a couple of months off? She'd been working almost nonstop since the age of five. A couple of months to enjoy the fruits of her labor didn't seem like a crime. But again, she was trying to avoid the hustle lecture that would inevitably lead to some story of how her mom had to work twenty-two-plus hours a day while wearing hot designer clothes and six-inch heels right before walking a runway for some dastardly designer. "I'll have an answer for you tomorrow."

She could read the scripts tonight. After she got in some sketching time.

"I think you should consider the romantic comedy. They're talking about casting Stephen." Her mom's voice had gone low, coaxing. Like the idea of working with Stephen would change everything.

Stephen Cane was a dear friend. She'd worked with him many times, but the love connection her mom had always hoped for had never panned out. "I'll think about it. If the script's good, I'll say yes."

"It's adequate, and that's all that matters. You know it's likely to change five times before you actually film the damn thing. The important part is that they want you for the lead, and working with Stephen would make a good story."

Her mother was very concerned with a good story, and not the kind that was in a script. She wanted the press to pay more attention to her daughter. She wanted Brynn to be this generation's Julia Roberts or Reese Witherspoon. America's new sweetheart. She wanted the next decade to be about banking as much money, power, and influence as possible.

She wanted to ensure her daughters would never, ever find themselves in the position she'd been in after their dad died.

"Mom, it's not happening between me and Stephen, but I promise I'll pick between these two projects." Her mom had been forced to go from pampered trophy wife to drowning in debt with two children and no husband. They'd gone from living in a mansion to homeless almost overnight, and her mother had hauled them out of poverty, and for that Brynn would always respect her.

"Honey, you know you don't have to actually care about him," her mom said, voice softening. "Just give the press something to write about. If you don't, they'll start questioning why you're not dating."

Harry had been right. The trail was easy to find. Someone had cleared a walkway through the trees and brush. She could hear the sound of water gurgling nearby and for a moment she was in the shade, the trees above forming a canopy. "I'm not dating because I have no time to date. I've gone from project to project for years."

"Another reason to have someone like Stephen around," her mom replied. "He's attractive, talented, and he already escorts you to the red-carpet events. All you need to do is have a meal with him every now and then and those lesbian rumors will be gone."

She rolled her eyes. "I told you I don't care about those. I have lesbian friends. They're awesome. If someone wants to confuse my sexuality, they should go for it. I don't owe any-one an explanation." A thought hit. "Hey, by your reckoning, I could fake date one of them."

A low growl came over the line. "You're impossible, Brynn. Pick a project. I'll see you soon."

The line went blissfully dead, and Brynn slid her phone into her back pocket.

She hadn't seen any evidence of a sheriff being out here. She hoped he wasn't fishing.

Correction. She hoped he or she wasn't fishing. It was awfully sexist of her to think whoever had driven that SUV could only be a dude. It could totally be a woman.

Duke trotted beside her, and she was glad she'd put him on his leash because the trail did get close to the water. She couldn't see the mud Harry was talking about, but she believed him.

In the distance, she heard the sound of a dog barking.

Duke stopped, his whole body tensing up before he barked back.

The barking in the distance became desperate, and Brynn started to jog toward it because that dog sounded scared. She'd grown up around dogs. Two of the series she'd been on had "family" dogs, and she'd learned how to work with them. Hanging out with the dogs and their handlers had been one of the best parts of her job. She knew what a fearful bark sounded like, and this dog was scared.

She would also bet the dog was big.

"Hey, calm down, girl." That was a human voice. A deep, masculine voice.

She rounded the curve on the trail and stopped because a big, gorgeous man was standing thigh-deep in the water, and he wasn't alone. He had a terrified pit bull mix around his shoulders, clinging to him. The dog had obviously spent some time in that water because she was wet, covered in mud to her hindquarters.

"Sweetie, if you don't stop moving, I'll drop you, and I really don't want to drop you," the man said. He was in sweats and a soaking-wet T-shirt that clung to his very muscular chest. He'd obviously not gotten Harry's memo about staying away from the water.

Duke barked and his stubby legs moved, stretching the leash to the max, because despite the fact that he was a little dog, he firmly believed he could handle anything. She was sure his doggie brain had plans to save everyone.

The man's head came around at the sound of the bark and his eyes flared. "Hey. Wow. Hello. I could use some help here if you don't mind."

He was stunning, and she'd been around a lot of attractive men. But there was something about this one. Maybe it was the fact that he was trying his hardest to comfort a frightened dog. Or it could be the chiseled jaw and that bit of scruff that made an almost-too-pretty face rugged.

He was in trouble, and she was almost drooling. This was not who she was. She was practical and tactical, as one of her old directors liked to put it. She got the job done.

"Of course. Let me take off my shoes and roll up my jeans and I'll help you with her." She would have to secure Duke, too, or he would go right in that water.

"Absolutely not." He nearly shouted the words. "I'm sorry. I don't want you to join me. I'm stuck."

"Stuck?"

He nodded. "Yeah. We were on our daily jog and Dolly here decided to try to play with the fish. She got stuck in the mud. I got her out and, well, I'm worried I live here now. And it's not a good place after dark, if you know what I mean. The neighbors have lots of teeth."

"I can call 911."

"Please, don't. I'm a deputy for the local sheriff's department and honestly, I would rather die here than listen to the crap I'll have to take for the next . . . well, forever. It'll become a whole urban legend." The gorgeous man sighed. "How about you save Dolly and if anyone asks, a gator got me."

So, he was a very dramatic man. She'd dealt with the type. She also got the whole saving-face thing. "All right, then I'll have to fashion something to get you out of there. I have this guy's truck, and there was some lumber in the back."

"Wait. Are you staying at the B and B? You're one of the production crew?"

He asked the question like her saying *yes* would give him some hope. "I am."

"Yes," he said under his breath. "You've got Harry Jefferys's truck. Drive the truck down here. He's got a winch."

She wanted to make a joke about winch versus wench, but she actually knew what he meant. She'd grown up around a whole bunch of production crew who'd adored a little girl who'd wanted to learn what they did. "All right. Hold on. I'll be back soon."

It looked like her sketch time would have to wait.

Major Blanchard was having a rough day.

It had started with his father forgetting who he was and arguing that they were actually living through the 1950s again. And now it looked like it would end with a slow death by mud.

Oh, and he'd lost his damn cell phone, and he was pretty sure he hadn't paid that sucker off yet.

He'd managed to rescue his rescue dog. He'd had her for two months, and she was a never-ending ball of energy. Zep Guidry had brought her into the station house and loudly told his wife, Roxie, that he feared the poor puppy would have to be put down because her breed was misunderstood and feared, and wasn't that sad because she was such a sweetie.

Yeah, he'd taken the dog home because she'd looked at him with big puppy eyes and basically begged him to save her from death.

It was only later that he discovered Papillon's animal services had a no-kill shelter.

Of course, by then he was half in love with the pit bull mix. He was fairly certain that Dolly was half sunshine, because she always made him smile. Though he was not smiling today. Nope. Today she'd chased butterflies, and butterflies had led her to the water, and then she'd obviously decided that it would be fun to catch a fish, but oops, the mud was bad news.

He knew better than to get in the bog. Intellectually, he knew it was a terrible idea. He'd been out on calls to this very spot and had to help dumbass mudders get their vehicles out of the sludge, or the occasional deer who wandered in and couldn't escape. He was fairly certain lots of animals got stuck and became an easy meal for the gators.

He hoped the cute blonde hurried before he became one of those meals.

Dolly whimpered and seemed to try to wrap her body more closely around his neck and shoulders.

"You know you're supposed to be a badass dog who everyone fears, right?" She'd obviously not gotten that note. Dolly was the sweetest dog he'd ever had.

His dad thought she was Rufus, the dog he'd had while growing up. She didn't look anything like Rufus, who'd been a smaller hound, but that didn't stop his dad. Major didn't look much like his long-dead uncle, but his father had no problems calling him Henry and talking like they were brothers. Like they were brothers and it was 1954.

His father was losing his grip on reality, and Major was doing everything he could to keep him in the here and now. If that rope came completely loose, his father would be lost to a sea of memory. The doctors didn't hold out much hope. He'd sat down with them the day before and gotten the hard talk about what was likely to come in the near future. After the fifth time his dad had wandered off and nearly been killed, Major had to accept the fact that he couldn't take care of his dad the way he needed to. His stepmother had fled the minute the diagnosis had come down, and now he had to be the asshole who'd put his father in an assisted living home.

He was pulled from those dark thoughts by the sound of a vehicle moving slowly and carefully down the trail. Normally he would tell anyone that driving down here was a bad idea, but he desperately needed that truck, or he could be in this horrific position for hours.

Was that a snake?

Dolly barked and bounced. He definitely would not need to work on his shoulders and arms this week. Maybe ever again.

Thank god the blonde seemed competent. She was driving that truck with a careful hand as she turned the front of the vehicle toward the water. He could see the winch and the chain that would pull him from his folly.

Hopefully he'd be able to keep all his limbs intact, though he'd consider giving up a few to get on dry land again.

She put the truck in park and climbed out. "There's a large piece of what looks like siding in the back. I think Harry was planning on a trip to the dump later on this week. I thought we could use it to get your dog on dry land. I think it's long enough that she should be able to walk to the shore."

"I promise she won't bite."

A brilliant smile lit the woman's face. "She doesn't look like she bites. You're a sweet girl, aren't you, Dolly?"

Dolly's tail thudded right against his face. "Yep, she's a sweetie. And she's heavy. Really heavy."

The woman nodded and disappeared behind the truck.

He probably shouldn't notice that her backside was as pretty as the rest of her. He should have his brain firmly focused on being rescued and not on how hot his rescuer was.

But it had been a long time since he'd thought about how hot anyone was. Despite the fact that he'd been on twenty-two blind dates in six months, he had not clicked with a single eligible woman. Some had been pretty or funny or kind. Some were all three, but he hadn't connected with any of them. He'd gone on more than one date with four of the women, but each relationship had fizzled out before they ever got to a place where he might have thought about sex.

He hadn't thought about sex—*really* thought about sex—in months. But given the way that pretty woman's backside swayed, he was thinking about it now.

He didn't even know her name.

"I'm Major, by the way," he called out. He was so dumb. He should only be thinking about getting his ass out of this situation. She was a pretty tourist, and he didn't do brief affairs.

Also, she probably wouldn't want an encounter with a dude she had to pull from the earth.

"Well, I didn't think you were minor."

She came around the corner of the truck, hauling the big piece of what used to be Remy's awful siding. Major recognized it from the apartment located over Guidry's.

Her little bit of a dog was standing in the cab, his paws on the dashboard. He looked out as though checking on her, his head swinging between where Major and Dolly stood and her.

It was not the first time someone had pointed out how weird his name was. He'd had to get through years in the Army with the name Major.

"Major Blanchard," he corrected. "It's an actual name."

"Interesting." She tentatively came to the edge of the mud and started to ease the siding down. "I've never met a Major before."

Almost no one had. "And you're?"

She flashed him a smile. "I'm Brynn Pearson. I'll be your rescuer today. My partner is Duke. He's the beauty and I'm obviously the brawn of this operation. Okay. I think this will hold her weight if you want to ease her down. Is that your SUV back there?"

"Yes. I bring Dolly down here a couple of times a week. There's a trail that's usually a nice jog." The siding was the tiniest bit short, but it would have to do. He twisted slightly, leaning over so Dolly could ease down onto the board and then make her way to dry land.

Except she wouldn't. She dug in, whimpering and trying to wrap herself harder around his neck.

"Dolly, come on, sweetie." He couldn't dump her. She would slide off and they would be right back where they started.

"Hold on." Brynn moved to the truck and pulled out a backpack, her hand disappearing briefly before she came back, kneeling at the other end of the siding and offering the one thing that might make Dolly overcome her fear. "Want a treat, baby?"

Dolly practically jumped onto the board, trading her fear of death for what looked like dehydrated beef. Before Major could take another breath, she was over the siding and on dry land, that treat halfway down her throat.

So at least the dog was all right.

He tried to move and managed roughly half an inch before he felt the mud try to suck him in deeper. Damn it.

He caught something moving out of the corner of his eye and barely managed to not scream like he was the prettiest girl at prom and there was a serial killer coming. That had definitely been a snake.

He was going to die here, and beyond being a cautionary tale for all future Papillon Sherriff's Department recruits, no one would really care. It was depressing. Dolly would find someone new to love her and give her treats. The house he'd worked so hard on would be sold, any profits given straight to the assisted living facility, and his father would probably forget he'd ever been born.

He was not in a good mood.

"You're a sweet baby, aren't you? Such a good girl." Brynn ran a hand over Dolly, offering the dog comfort.

He was the one who needed comfort because he was the one who was about to die. "Hey, uhm, I don't know if you've ever been caught in a coastal bog, but it's pretty gross, so if we could get this rescue going, I would appreciate it."

She looked up, her eyes widening. "I'm so sorry. Of course. Should I leash her so she can't get back in the mud?"

He sighed because he didn't think that would be a problem. "She's no longer interested in me."

He nodded toward her truck. Dolly had already inhaled the treat and now had her big paws on the driver's side door. She was staring in at the corgi like he was something magical. Naturally, the corgi was barking.

Chaos. He seemed to be surrounded by chaos lately.

Brynn worked the winch, drawing the chain down to where the siding still sat. She started to gingerly walk toward him.

His breath nearly caught because one wrong step and she could end up in here with him. "If you fall, try to get your body as flat as possible. Keep your feet up."

She stopped and one hand went to her hip. "You are not

a very positive person, Deputy Major. You can't get through life with a frown on your face."

He got through life just fine, and he frowned a lot. He was a cop. They did not teach smiling in cop school. "I don't see much to be positive about in this exact moment."

"This exact moment is about to be over and then things will get better. And you could have been out here alone for way more moments," she pointed out as she moved closer to him. She spread her slight weight out over the board, competently moving toward him. She reached out and offered him the end of the chain. "I could have chosen to stick close to the B and B. Harry could have sent me to another place to sketch. You're actually lucky."

She was annoying. Cute but annoyingly peppy. It wasn't like he was all gloom and doom, but he was absolutely allowed to see the dark lining in this particular cloud. He took the end of the chain. "Thanks."

He'd said it in a deep tone, but her smile amped up. "You're welcome. I'll go slow."

She thought he needed her to turn the winch on? "Don't. I needed something to balance against. If you turn that thing on and it goes too fast, I could break a leg or two."

She moved back to land, and Dolly came to sit beside her. Both woman and dog stared at him like he'd said something dumb. "I wasn't planning on cranking it up. But by all means, use those muscles of yours. You look like you're very strong. Again, something you should be grateful for. Not everyone could do that."

Not everyone suffered through military training and had to be ready to take down any number of threats.

He had to be able to pick up his father when he fell. Once, that would have been a mighty feat of strength, but now the man was so frail Major barely noticed his weight.

He forced himself to focus. He wasn't about to put himself in a position where he had to risk life and limb because he couldn't pull himself out. He worked, arms straining. The instinct to pull as hard as he could was discarded because, like in all things, patience would win this war.

"You're doing so well," Brynn said, and he could hear the smile in her voice. Like he was a toddler learning to walk. "That's at least an inch."

"Are you usually this peppy?" He eased his grip up the chain. She was right. He was moving, albeit very slowly. He felt his sneakers go. That was only to be expected, but damn, he'd only bought them a month ago. At least that meant he was moving.

"You say that like it's a bad thing," she replied.

It wasn't bad, necessarily. Just a little annoying.

When had he become the king grump of the world? He grunted and continued his long slog to freedom. He used to be the happy one, the smiling one. In his unit in the Army, he'd been the one who made everyone laugh, who always kept their spirits up.

He was about to be alone in the world. His father was slipping away, and no one was going to throw him a lifeline, because there wasn't one for what he had.

He banished the thoughts and tried to concentrate on the task at hand. His muscles strained but he kept moving. He would go home, take a shower, and wash Dolly off, and he might make his shift in time. *Might* because he would have to clean his vehicle. There was zero chance he was driving home in his underwear, because he was fairly certain Mrs. Dury across the street had her doorbell camera facing out so she could keep tabs on whoever came and went from his place. So the parish vehicle would need a detailing, and that would teach him never to drive it when he was off duty.

He managed to make it to the sad piece of siding. It was the safest place he'd been for hours and hours. He dragged his torso up and felt his feet come free and took a long breath.

Maybe pretty blond Brynn was right and he was lucky. Dolly was fine. He was alive. It had been pure luck that Brynn had shown up with everything he needed to get free.

"Wow. That mud was incredibly sticky."

He managed to look up, and Brynn was standing there all pretty and perfect. He probably looked . . . well, like a dumbass who'd gotten stuck in the mud for hours. "Yeah, I'm pretty dirty, but I am no longer your problem. Thank you for helping and . . ."

He had started to get to his knees when he froze.

"I don't think Harry has an extra pair of pants in the truck." Brynn's lips had kicked up in a grin.

His sweats were gone. They'd slid off while he'd pulled himself up. He was wearing nothing but his University of Houston T-shirt, his underwear, and a pair . . . nope, one sock. And naturally because he hadn't done laundry he was wearing one of the three pairs of tighty-whities he owned. The universe hadn't even left him the dignity of boxers.

A warm tongue licked the side of his face.

"Hey, we should get you off there before it slides in. Come on, Dolly. Let your dad get up. We need to get him back to his car." Brynn's voice was sweet and soothing.

"The car is a no-go because my keys were in my pants. I don't suppose they're floating." He knew better than to turn around. He forced himself to crawl up the plank Brynn had made and get to his feet.

"Oh, no." She shook her head, obviously trying not to crack another smile. "They are definitely gone."

"Then I am going to need a ride into town."

She stared at him for a moment and then a light seemed

to go off over her head. "From me. Of course." She grabbed the siding and hauled it up, then stopped. "Should I leave it here for the next guy?"

Major knew he should help her reload the siding, but he just wanted the whole thing to be over. He strode to Harry's truck and found a towel in the back. Harry was a deep believer in being prepared. "Nope. No one else would be that dumb. You leave that out here and it will be Otis's loading zone."

"Who is Otis?" She easily hefted the siding back into the bed of the truck.

"He's a gator. And he can be real lazy if you let him." Now that he was standing close to her he realized she was even prettier than she'd seemed. There was a glow about the woman that would normally call to him, but all it did now was remind him of how dark his own life seemed. She was probably one of those people who had everything together. She probably had the perfect husband or boyfriend and a great career doing something she loved.

He opened the passenger door of the truck once he was satisfied he wouldn't do too much damage. He laid the towel over the seat.

The corgi was staring at him, and he could have sworn there was an air of disapproval around the dog.

Dolly, meanwhile, was back to chasing after butterflies. "Dolly!"

The name came out gruff and way louder than he'd meant it to. Dolly stopped and went still.

Brynn immediately seemed to feel the need to make up for his grumpiness. "Come on, sweetie. Let's get you home."

Dolly jumped into the cab and then he had to deal with two dogs who were trying to sniff each other's butts in a space that was way too small for that long-held canine tradition. Dolly settled on his lap and the corgi was back to staring at Major as if he had taken something precious from him.

Brynn eased into the driver's seat and frowned briefly. "I'll be careful, Duke. Settle down, and I promise it'll be okay." She turned back to Major as she fired up the engine. "Sorry. Duke doesn't handle change well. He's a bit of a grump."

Duke huffed and moved from the passenger seat to the small second row, his indignation at being banished to the back obvious.

Dolly nearly deballed him in her haste to join the smaller dog. Major barely managed to not cup himself. He pulled his T-shirt down and did not miss how Brynn's mouth closed after her lips slightly turned up.

It was good someone found the situation amusing.

"You're going to have to give me some directions, Deputy Major. I'm afraid I don't know the town very well." She put the truck in reverse and expertly pulled it out of what could have been a tricky spot in less capable hands.

"You want to get back to the road we came in on and when we hit the highway, you'll take a right." He glanced back, and it was obvious his dog was in love. Her big body was hunkered down right next to the corgi, who looked like he was simply surviving until these strangers were gone and he could get his life back.

He was with the corgi. Though it wasn't like he had much of a life to get back to. The dogs seemed to have it better. At least someone fed them treats and gave them belly rubs.

Not that he wanted a belly rub. Any kind of rub would be nice.

"All right, let's get the rest of this rescue on the road." She eased over the rough terrain. "I'm excited to see the town. I got in a couple of days ago and I've been exploring the B and B, but I hadn't left the grounds until today."

"There's not much to it." He was going to move. Harry had the right idea. He should live in the sticks. If he lived there now then no one would be there to see him run from the truck to the front door wearing nothing but his underwear.

A horrible thought struck.

What was he planning on doing when he got to the front door? Because his keys were in the bog.

Major groaned and let his body come forward, forehead gently hitting the dashboard.

This was not his day.

chapter two

❧

Brynn hoped the hot deputy with the weird name wasn't about to flake out on her.

Major Blanchard had sat with his head down for the five minutes it had taken to get to the highway. It was obvious that the man was having some kind of unwanted revelation, but she didn't think she would be able to find the psychic powers needed to detect the route she should take. She hadn't been out of range of the B and B the few days she'd been here, so she had zero idea where to go.

"At least you picked a pretty day to get stuck in the mud." Small talk. She would make some small talk and put him at ease. It was what she did. At first she'd been tempted to tease the guy and offer to rescue him in exchange for him playing tour guide. Then she'd realized that was a little creepy and her rescue of his person shouldn't come with restrictions. "It rained so hard the last couple of days I was worried I wouldn't see the sun at all."

He sat up suddenly and turned his head her way. "Yes, it rained a lot. Hence the mud. The rain is exactly why I got in trouble today, so I should have picked a day much later in the month to jog. Or a better place to jog. Like on a treadmill.

Except lately the treadmill would likely explode or gain higher intelligence and take over the world, killing everyone, starting with me."

He was a very pessimistic deputy. And that was a shame because he was gorgeous. She wasn't sure why he kept pulling down his T-shirt. He had great legs. And honestly, those undies of his weren't any more revealing than a speedo, and she'd seen guys in plenty of those. LA was full of dudes who liked to show off their glutes.

He sighed and sat back. "Sorry. I just realized the keys to my house are back in the mud."

She hadn't thought about that. It was definitely a problem. "Do you have a spare somewhere?"

"My dad has it." He sighed again, a resigned sound. "Had it."

"He lost it?"

"Yeah. It's probably someplace crazy. He used to put his cell phone in the fridge. Once I found it in the toaster." He said it all with a deep weariness that pulled at her. "It was also over a year ago that we realized he couldn't find his key. I should have made another and left it with a friend, but time got away from me."

His father was sick. She knew what that felt like. She'd watched her mother struggle when Nana Jo had been dying. "I'm sorry about your dad."

He was quiet for a moment. "Thanks. Uhm, there's a turn coming up. Left will take you into town, and right leads to the bay. There's a good restaurant and marina there. I'm pretty sure that's where the siding came from. We need to turn left off the highway."

She did as he instructed, and she could see the beginnings of a small town up ahead. The road was shaded by huge trees covered in Spanish moss. It hung low and looked like tendrils coming off the branches. Like fingers brushing as low as they could. Like the tree wanted so badly to brush the earth below. She could already see how the colors would come together. She would have to be careful or she wouldn't capture the delicacy of the greens and browns.

She was fascinated with this place.

"I guess I'll break a window or something." He stared forward.

"Do you have a garage?" She'd noticed some of the homes had covered spots for cars and no attached garage. They seemed like older homes, though. She wondered where a guy like Major would live. Apparently not with a wife or girlfriend. Unless he didn't like them to be able to lock doors. He didn't have a ring and his watch had survived, so he probably hadn't lost a ring in the mud.

She was not thinking of Deputy Grump that way. Nope. She liked happy guys. He wasn't her type.

Did she actually have a type? She'd spent so much time working, being on sets, traveling. She hadn't really had time to have a real relationship. She'd dated off and on, usually when she was working on a show, but it wasn't like she had tons of experience. So how did she know Deputy Grump wasn't her type?

"Yeah," he replied. "But the remote is in the SUV, which I also can't get into, though there's another set at the station house. I guess we're going to have to go there."

He didn't want to go to his workplace without pants. That was clear. She could understand saving face, and she bet the guys he worked with would give him hell. "Does it have a pad and a code?"

That got him sitting up straighter. A spark of hope lit his face. "Yes. I didn't even think of that. I know the code. I can get in my garage."

Most people didn't think of opening their garage that way, but she'd played a teenaged detective who'd once had to sneak into a suspect's house to find a stolen poodle. "Excellent."

Major sighed. "But I'm pretty sure I locked the door between the garage and the house. So, that won't work."

Oh, he had so little faith. "Are you a crazy, paranoid dude who has a deadbolt on that door?"

He frowned. "No. I am a perfectly normal person who has a very fine set of locks and a security system, thank you. That door has a basic lock."

He was awfully cute when he was irritated with her. "Good, then I can break in, and you don't have to worry about your windows. All I need is something to use as a pick and a torque wrench, and Harry's tools are in the back. This truck is the gift that keeps giving."

"You can break into a house?"

There was the deputy voice. Yes, she could suddenly see him pulling over a poor unsuspecting driver who did not realize she was going twenty miles over the speed limit because she was trying to get into character for a very important scene. He had the stare thing down, too. She wished it made him less attractive.

"I can pick a simple lock," she replied. "I've worked on film sets most of my life, and I've learned a few things along the way."

"Most of your life? How old are you?"

Ah, he, like so many others, was blinded by her youthful charm. "I'm twenty-five. I've been in the business for twenty years."

Those baby blues of his widened in obvious surprise. "You've been working since you were five? What did you do at five?"

"You know how in TV shows and movies there are child characters? Well, as good as some actors are, most adults can't play five-year-olds. Oh, you'll find a ton of thirty-year-olds pretending to be high school kids, but they haven't figured out how to take those prepubescent roles yet." They would if they could. She knew some actors who thought they could play a frog better than an actual frog. "So I, as a five-year-old, was brought in for not only my talent but my authenticity. I could temper-tantrum at will and throw sass around all day long."

"You're an actress?"

He asked the question like he was truly surprised. She wasn't wearing her glam makeup or anything, but she'd thought she looked kind of cute. "You don't have to sound so shocked. I know I'm not, like, some bombshell, but not all actors are stunning."

Though most of them were. She'd been a cute kid and was attractive, but she wasn't sure she was Hollywood attractive. It was precisely why her mom was worried she wasn't making a faster transition. She'd started to gently discuss plastic surgery.

"You're gorgeous." He grimaced like he hadn't meant to say that. "I mean, you're certainly pretty enough, but you don't act the way I thought you would. Everyone's talking about the film crew coming in, and we're all pretty sure the fancy Hollywood people won't like it here. I know the mayor thinks we'll make tons of money. I was surprised when I heard the crew was going to use local restaurants for some of their catering. I thought they would bring their own."

She couldn't help but laugh. "Seriously?"

He shrugged. "We don't have a lot of kale down here."

It was good to know people were the same everywhere. People who'd rarely been out of the city would think people who lived in Papillon were rubes, and the country folk here would think anyone in the city was a snob. "I hope you've prepared, because soon you're going to have about a thousand people to feed, and please, please tell me you have enough beer in this town."

"The mayor's working with the local businesses. I've

heard they're going to be making a lot of salads and sand-wiches and soup for the lunches. But I would think they should go heavy on the salads," Major said. "I would hate to see our restaurants get hurt because they don't make the right food."

"Is the food good?"

"It's excellent, but it's Cajun food. And it's Southern food. I think someone was talking about setting up a crawfish boil, but I don't know how that will go."

"Just make sure you have a lot of food. Look, some of the actors will bring their own chefs. My mother is also my man-ager, and she'll bring a ton of protein shakes and cleanses with her, but the crew will eat anything you put in front of them. It's part of the joy of the job. Tell the restaurants to make what they love and share it with us. I used to work on this show and we filmed in Burbank ninety-nine percent of the time, but we got to go to Austin to film two episodes, and for the two weeks we were there, it was all barbecue and Tex-Mex. And if those caterers had tried to slip in a kale day, everything would have shut down."

He chuckled. "Well, that's good to know. I hope it's going to be good for the town. Take the next right and I'm the second house from the end."

She found herself on a street that looked like a postcard. Every house had a big yard and a fence around it. They all had wraparound porches and bright flowers and trees that looked like they were older than the homes. "This is a beau-tiful neighborhood."

"It's one of the older neighborhoods in Papillon," he said. "My dad bought the house ten years ago. When he had to go into assisted living, I took over the mortgage and we put it in my name. I think I'm the youngest person on the block. I'm definitely the only single guy. Pull into the driveway, please. I'm going to have to run if I want to get out of this with any dignity at all. And I'm going to ask you for one more favor. I know I've been sharp and I apologize for that."

"You were stuck in mud and lost your keys and your phone. I would still be freaking out over that. My mother would have gone under to find hers. I'm not joking. She would swim through all the mud and fight a gator for her phone." Her mom had solid priorities. "I mean, in fairness, she would do it for me or my sister, too. But probably only after she'd gotten her phone. It's phone, kids, Chardonnay. And if the phone survived and the kids didn't, well, at least she had a lot of pictures on that phone to remember them by."

She was being mean about her mom, but she got her first smile out of him and damn, but it got her heart racing.

"It's good to know she's got her priorities straight." He went quiet as she pulled into his driveway. "Could you wait while I get dressed and then drop me at the office? I know it's a lot to ask."

"Not at all. I would be happy to." She liked to help people. And she was supposed to go to the station house in a couple of days to talk to someone named Roxanne to help with her research. It would be good to get the lay of the land, so to speak.

He turned her way as she put the truck in park. "You're very kind, Brynn Pearson."

It was a better compliment than being called pretty. "Thanks, Deputy Major."

He grimaced. "I should have made up a name. It's obvious you're going to be trouble."

"Only the best kind, I promise." She turned the engine off and he seemed to brace himself.

"Tell me something. Is there an older woman staring out the front window behind us?"

She turned and, sure enough, there was a face in the bay window that dominated the front of the house across the street. And she had a phone to her ear. "Yup, and she's calling someone."

"Probably me. Somewhere in the bog, my phone is going to voice mail and she's calling to tell me my home is about to be raided by someone who already stole Harry's truck. Unless she thinks you're Seraphina and then she's calling her friends, telling them that we're having an affair."

"Seriously?"

"Oh, the grapevine moves swiftly." He did, too. He stepped out of the truck and Dolly followed, bounding over the seats and making Duke huff in protest. Major waved the woman's way. "Morning, Mrs. Dury! Everything's fine."

Brynn slipped out of the truck as the door across the street came open and a woman in a gray housedress stepped outside.

"Major Blanchard!" She wagged a finger his way. "Where are your pants?"

Major moved to the garage and lifted the pad to the door. "It's a long story."

"And who is that blonde? You should know I already called the police because that is Harrison Jefferys's truck and you can't steal things around here," the woman yelled Brynn's way.

"You can when the law is in on it," she yelled back.

Major sent her a stare that he probably used on every potential perpetrator before turning back to his own personal peeper. "She's staying out at the B and B, Mrs. Dury. Harry let her borrow the truck. There's no need to call anyone."

"Well, I did, and I also told them that you have lost your mind and are currently streaking," Mrs. Dury said with a frown.

"You are no fun at all, Mildred," a new voice said. Brynn

saw a woman standing near the driveway, a hose in her hand. She was roughly the same age as Mrs. Dury, though she was wearing jeans and a T-shirt that proclaimed she was like wine, better with age. "That young man is the best eye candy we've had in decades. Leave him be. You go on, honey. You don't need pants. It's hot anyway."

Major had gone a nice shade of pink. "Thank you, Mrs. Klein, but I'm going to go get dressed for work now."

"And I've called Sally Henshaw and told her all about the blonde," Mrs. Dury continued. "You're taking her grand-daughter out tonight. You shouldn't be playing around with some tourist who stole Harry's truck."

"I tried to steal his dog, too." Brynn picked up Duke, who had been starting to wander over to the street. "And I'll to-tally be done with Deputy Major before he needs to meet Sally's granddaughter. He might be tired, though."

Mrs. Dury gasped.

"Oh, Major, I like this one," Mrs. Klein said with a big smile. "She's got sass. You need some sass in your life."

"You can't resist, can you?" Major asked with a smile that was more like a predatory showing of teeth. "She really will call all over town."

"It sounds like she already did." A bit of guilt swelled inside. She'd had to deal with gossip all her life. She'd learned at a young age to breeze right through it, but Major seemed bothered by it. "Do you want me to go talk to her? I can explain."

"No. Absolutely not. You need to walk in that garage and break into my house and not cause more trouble."

She kind of liked the authoritative vibe but also sensed he was getting to the end of his rope.

"Yes, Sally, he's not wearing any pants. He's walking around bold as brass with that hussy," Mrs. Dury was saying.

"And she tried to steal poor Harry Jefferys's dog. What would little Luc think? Well, someone's missing a dog, because she's got one. It's a fancy one like that Queen of England has. What is poor Samantha going to think? I don't know, Sally. He might be used goods now."

Major's head dropped.

"Don't you shame him, you old biddy." Mrs. Klein had taken a couple of steps the other woman's way.

"You stay out of this," Mrs. Dury shot back. "Sally has been trying to find a nice young man for her granddaughter for years. I told her Major was a god-fearing, upstanding gentleman, but now I can see from his underwear that he's got moral issues. Those are the devil's shorts, I tell you."

That was when Mrs. Klein turned her hose on the other woman. There was a loud squealing sound and Dolly started to whine.

"I'm going to go stop a water fight between two mature women." Major said the words like he needed to hear them out loud to believe them.

At least he'd get the shower he wanted. "And I'll break into your house. I'll also remain silent if anyone else accuses me of hussiness. Promise."

Major nodded and started to cross the street.

Brynn got to work.

Two hours later Major watched as Brynn pulled out of the station house parking lot. Duke had retaken his seat next to Brynn, and the corgi gave him a death stare as she drove away.

That dog was warning him off.

Like he was going to get involved with the sarcastic actress who would only be here for a few weeks. He wasn't stupid enough to want to bask in her sunshine when he knew damn well it would go away and he'd be left with the rain again.

"So there's a bet going on," a husky voice said.

Speaking of sarcastic women. He glanced over and Roxie was walking in from the parking lot. "Hey, Roxie. What are we betting on now?"

There was always something going on at the station house. The Papillon Parish Sheriff's Department was small, and the people who worked there tight-knit. Besides the sheriff himself, there were now two deputies, two officers, and a couple of dispatchers. Someone was always on duty, but late at night it was often a one-person show, which was why Major left his police radio on most nights. If anything went wrong, he didn't want to leave his fellow officers alone.

The upshot was they acted like a family. Like a group of brothers and sisters he'd never had.

Roxie King-Guidry was dressed in her uniform, her golden-brown hair up in a neat bun. Everything about Roxie spoke of discipline.

So unlike that ball of chaos who'd just driven away. Brynn's ponytail might have started the day all neat and perfect, but by the time she'd managed to get his door open there had been tendrils of honey-colored hair around her face. He'd almost asked her if Harry had put her to work, because she'd also had paint flecks on her hands and arms, and her manicure wasn't Hollywood perfect.

He was completely fascinated by her, and that was a big problem.

"The bet is about why your cell phone got caught in a crab trap." Roxie's lips quirked up and she held up a set of familiar-looking keys. "Also, Jimmy Tremon caught a pair of sweatpants floating into the bay. I suspect these are yours."

Damn it. He should have stayed to make sure his sweats didn't resurface. He took the keys from her. "Dare I ask what's the odds-on favorite?"

"Well, I can tell you that Gene has already been in and

he thinks the rougarou is back and it either murdered you or turned you," she said with a grin. "I've got instructions on how to tell if you've become a Cajun werewolf."

Major groaned and pocketed his keys. At least Roxie wouldn't razz him too much about the truth. He opened the door, allowing her to go inside first. "I went down to the woods for a run. Dolly got stuck in the mud."

Roxie nodded sagely. "And you went in after her and also got stuck in the mud. I take it Blondie busted you free. Is that why she stole Harry's truck?"

The station house was quiet. His desk was the one closest to the door, so he moved toward it. "She's staying at the B and B."

Roxie's eyes lit up. "Was that Bria Knight?"

"No. She said her name was Brynn." He sank down to his seat. His desk was kept with the neat proficiency he'd been taught both by his parents and in the military. Not a thing out of place.

Roxie shook her head. "That might be her real name, but her stage name is Bria Knight. Come on, man. Seriously, you don't recognize her? She's been acting, like, since she was born. She was one of the kids on *Janie's World*. The sitcom about single moms trying to make it in New York City. It was huge at my place. She was also the lead mermaid's best friend in *Fins*. There was a teenage detective show, too."

"I've heard of it, but I didn't watch a lot of TV growing up." His mother had been very anti-screens. He'd played outside a lot and watched sports with his dad. At night after he finished his homework, they would play board games or read.

His father watched a lot of TV these days. They pretty much sat him in front of one, and that was a good day. Sometimes his dad thought he was in one of those shows.

"That is very intellectual of you." Roxie's head shook.

She moved to her desk, leaning on the top. Her desk was next to his. In the beginning it was hard to tell the two work spaces apart because they'd both been so bland, but now Roxie's had several framed photos of her and her husband. There was one of them with their dog and a cat, and another of both their families. "Well, I did, and Bria Knight was good. I always wondered why she didn't get a big show of her own. I tended to like her characters more than the leads. When I heard she was starring in the production coming into town, I jumped at the chance to mentor her."

"Mentor?" He wasn't sure why Brynn . . . Bria . . . whatever she called herself . . . needed mentoring from Roxie.

"Yeah, she's playing a small-town cop working on a murder investigation with her estranged dad who happens to be the sheriff." Roxie looked at him like he was missing out on something. "Sylvie came in and told us all about it. Armie's going to let the actor playing the dad shadow him, and I'm hanging with Bria."

"She's going to be here?" He'd thought that would be the last time he saw her. He'd figured he would probably catch sight of her around town, but she would be here in the station house? Hanging out and going on calls?

"Yeah. She came out early to do some research. Gavin Jacks is due here in a couple of days, too. He's playing the sheriff. They know each other because he played the guy who eventually becomes her stepfather on *Janie's World*. There were some crazy rumors that they were actually a couple during that show. She was eighteen and he was in his late forties," Roxie said, her voice going low. "But I never thought that was true because she has this amazing chemistry with the actor who played Janie's son. He ended up with another character, but I think that was a huge mistake because he was obviously meant for Bria."

"Who are you?" He wasn't sure he understood this side

of Roxie. Roxie was a tough chick, sometimes way tougher than he was.

She shrugged. "I enjoy a couple of shows that don't involve murder. Honestly, I have a hard time watching police procedurals because they're not realistic. In real life, there's way more paperwork and way less running. I mean, come on. Armie's getting tubby. He needs more people who run."

"That's why I hired younger people," a deep voice said. "It's my time to nap and let middle-age spread catch up to me." The sheriff walked in, yawning behind his hand. The man always wanted to nap now since he had two boys under the age of four at home. Though Major couldn't tell the man had let himself go even a little bit. Armie LaVigne was big and broad and as fit as any of his younger employees. He was married to the woman who served as the parish physician. Lila LaVigne was a nurse practitioner, but she was the final authority on all things medical in Papillon. "And Roxie's right about those TV shows. If they were realistic, they would show hours and hours of filling out forms tempered by the fun of getting yelled at during every single town hall."

"Hey, there's also the people we help who pay us in beignets," Roxie pointed out.

"I don't mind that," Armie admitted. He turned to Major. "Now what is this I hear about a wild-eyed blonde with a mean dog who stole not only Harry's truck, but also Major's virtue?"

Major groaned. The damn grapevine worked faster than the speed of light. "I had some problems while I was out for a run and she helped me. No virtue was lost, and she's staying at the B and B. You know how generous Harry can be. She was looking for light or something."

"Light?" Armie asked.

"I think it's a Hollywood thing." Though she seemed so

down to earth. He had to wonder what would have happened if he'd met her in a more normal way. If she'd been a woman from two towns over he'd gotten set up with, he likely would have enjoyed talking to her. Normally he would have been amused at the fact that he'd had to stop a water war between two octogenarians. When had that gotten annoying?

"It's an artist thing," Roxie countered. "She's a painter. She's good, too. Don't look at me that way. I can like art. Everyone likes art. Major has lots of paintings all over his place."

"My mom painted them." He'd walked out after showering and changing and found Brynn studying the one over his mantel. It was a painting she'd done of the trees in the backyard of their home outside of Houston. It was done from the perspective of a person lying on their back looking up at the canopy of green and the sunshine coming through it. He'd lain under those trees so many afternoons that he could close his eyes and still see them, still feel the soft grass beneath his body, still know that any moment he would be called in for supper.

He'd wanted to tell her all about that painting. The instinct had been there to share not only what he loved about it but how it also made him ache inside.

Instead he'd brusquely told her he was ready, and they'd left.

He still wondered what she'd thought about it.

"I didn't know that." Roxie's expression softened. "She was good."

"I did know." Armie leaned on Major's desk. "I remember when your dad first moved down here. He bought that house and he and Lynn had a housewarming party and your dad showed off the paintings."

He remembered the day well. It was the day he'd met

Armie LaVigne and talked about taking the job here. He'd made the decision to move to Louisiana because his father was the only family he had left. He was the only child of two only children. He'd thought he would come to this small town, find someone to settle down with, and give his dad a couple of grandkids.

He'd thought he had more time.

"She was a good artist. I'm sure she would talk about light, too." He'd seen the sketchpad sticking out of the bag in the back of the truck. Was he being obtuse because he didn't want to admit he was attracted to her? Nothing could come of it because he'd given up short-term flings a long time ago. "So, what do we have planned for this afternoon?"

"Well, first off we need to get down to the bog near the B and B because I've gotten a report of a lost item," Armie said, his lips kicking up in a grin. "Someone lost their dignity, and we've got to find it."

Major groaned again. "Who the hell told you that? I know it wasn't Brynn."

He rather thought she would keep quiet about the circumstances of how he'd come to be sans pants.

Roxie winced. "Uhm, did I mention that my husband has this new initiative about wildlife? He put up wildlife cams all over the parish."

He was going to have a heart attack. "The one that streams various outdoor spaces on the Internet?"

She gave him an apologetic smile. "Yup."

Armie gave a hearty laugh. "I can't believe your pants came off that way. I'm sorry. I was about to send someone out to help you but the pretty blonde showed and Lila forbade me from breaking up the obvious chemistry."

Landon Price looked up from his desk across the station house. He'd only been on the job for a few months, but he had the sarcasm thing down. "I managed to download the whole thing, Deputy. We've already had a couple of calls asking if you're willing to do calendars or bachelorette parties. Should I forward those to you?"

Major let his head find his desk. It was going to be a long day.

chapter three

Nine hours, another shower, and another change of clothes later, and Major still couldn't stop thinking about Brynn Pearson.

He sat on the deck at Guidry's waiting on this week's mystery date who may or may not show up if she believed the gossip about him and had the deep investment in his virtue that her grandmother believed she should have.

The deck at Guidry's was where he met most of his blind dates. It had a great view of the bay.

His mother would've loved the light here. She would be fascinated with the colors of the sunset and how they played with the water. Maybe Brynn would, too.

Yep, still thinking about her.

After the morning he'd had, it had been a blessedly slow shift at the station house. Roxie had driven him out to pick up his vehicle and they'd gone on patrol. He'd listened to her talk endlessly about some of the work Brynn had done, though she'd consistently called her Bria.

She wasn't a Bria. She was definitely a Brynn. It fit her much better. Bria was a woman who never had a hair out of place, and Brynn was adorably disheveled.

And Harry was wrong. The light wasn't best at the pier. What was the man thinking? He needed to stick to the multitudinous talents he'd been blessed with and leave art to people who knew something about it. The light out on the islands was magical. It was the obvious place to send Brynn.

Though she would need a guide. It could be dangerous to be out on the islands alone.

"Hey, Major. Can I get you a beer?" Lisa Guidry stood in front of him with a pad in her hand, despite the fact that he knew she could remember a table of ten's orders without missing a one. "Or is this your standard blind date night?"

It was sad that he had a standard for blind dates since he'd been on so many of them. "Iced tea, please."

He didn't drink on blind dates. It could lead to bad things, and he didn't need any more videos of himself haunting the Internet.

Lisa had a mass of dark hair and blue eyes. She wore her Guidry's T-shirt, jeans, and sneakers. When it got a bit hotter, she and the rest of the staff would make the switch to shorts. For now it was nice in the evenings. There was even the hint of a cool breeze coming off the bay.

"So what is this? Like number wise?" Lisa asked.

"This will make number twenty-three in the last six months." He was sure there was a bet about his love life going on somewhere in town. Probably several.

"Do you mind if I ask why you decided to become the Bayou Bachelor?"

He had to laugh at the way she put it. He wasn't handing out many roses, but then he was pretty sure some of those women would have happily taken a limo ride away from him. "Well, I turned thirty-three in December. All my friends are married with the exception of Quaid, and I'm pretty sure he's planning on dying single at his desk."

His friend Quaid was the only lawyer in town, and he showed no signs of giving in to the matchmaker's call.

"So you're looking for a wife?" Lisa asked.

"I guess." What he was truly looking for was a connection. He felt like he hadn't connected with a woman in a very long time. "I also had a talk with my father, and he made me promise I would put myself out there. Here in Papillon there aren't a lot of single women. Most of the ones I meet . . . well, it's not good to find dates from the women I end up arresting."

"Armie gave my sister a ticket and she still married him," Lisa pointed out.

"I think that's a once-in-a-lifetime thing." He sat back. "Anyway, the minute it got out that I was ready to meet women, it was like the floodgates opened. I haven't clicked with anyone yet despite the fact that they were all lovely." It was true. Mostly. There had been Inez Smith's sister who'd recently divorced and spent the entire evening talking about how she was going to murder her ex. She'd been specific enough that Major had written the plot down just in case. "So it's open season on me for every matchmaker on the bayou."

He had to have gone through most of them by now, and he wasn't sure if he was relieved or depressed at the thought. Shouldn't he have connected with one of them?

"You know, I've found that it's often when we're not looking that we find the thing we need the most," Lisa said, her expression soft. "Remy and I got together at a time when it seemed like neither of us was in a place to have a relationship. But it worked out. I know it seems like it takes forever, but sometimes you have to have a little faith. You're a very good man, and I would hate for you to settle because you think it's time."

Wasn't that exactly what he was trying to do? "I'm kind of playing the field."

She gave him a tight smile that let him know she saw through him. "You are not a player at all, Major. But you are the kind of man who might let something good pass him by because it doesn't seem perfect at the moment."

He wasn't sure he liked that characterization. "I don't need someone to be perfect."

"No, but you do want to make things perfect for the people around you. Especially your dad," Lisa pointed out. "You need to think about yourself and what you need. I think you'll find the rest of it will fall into place. I'll go get you that tea."

He watched Lisa walk away and wondered if she was right. Was he pushing too hard? Was he rushing to find a woman to settle down with before his father couldn't remember who he was?

He sat back in his chair, hearing the hum of conversations around him but not truly listening to it. He was surrounded by people he knew, but he felt alone. Twenty-two dates so far and not a real connection with any of them. Was he not giving it enough time? Or was he going through the motions so he could come out of this and say at least he'd tried?

Or maybe he was completely lying to himself and he had made a connection with someone. Just not the kind of woman he needed a connection with. Naturally the one he couldn't stop thinking about was the one who was absolutely guaranteed to leave. Brynn Pearson probably wasn't looking to settle down. She was busy with her career, a career that took her all over the world. What would she even want with a small-town deputy?

"Hi. Are you Major Blanchard?" A woman in jeans and

a button-down blouse stood in front of him. She looked to be in her early thirties with dark hair.

She would likely be very attractive if she hadn't been looking at him like he was the devil himself. He had the sudden feeling that date number twenty-three wasn't going to change his luck.

He could be someone else. He could be John Smith. Or some random tourist. He didn't have to be who this woman was looking for.

He stood and held out a hand. "Yes. I guess that makes you Samantha Henshaw."

She shook it like they were about to have a job interview and then stepped back. "Yes, I am. Sorry for the drama this whole thing has caused. My grandmother's best friend apparently got into it with a neighbor earlier today over this date that I did not set up for myself. Thank you for not arresting my grandma's best friend." She stopped, her eyes narrowing. "Or maybe I should curse you for not arresting her. She might not be able to deny reality if her bestie was in jail."

"She would get a phone call and Sally would be the first person she dialed. You would likely have spent the day driving your granny around to post her bestie's bail." He pulled out her seat and offered it to her.

She sighed and stayed right where she was. "Look, I should have called you and canceled, but I didn't actually know about this date of ours until a couple of hours ago and my grandmother wouldn't give me your phone number, so here I am. Also, congratulations on whatever debauchery happened in your life that made her warn me I shouldn't get too close too soon."

"So you're turning me down because of my lost virtue." He didn't point out that it had only been his sweatpants that had been lost. Everyone seemed to think he'd done something nasty with the gorgeous actress. Yes, she'd gone from pretty to gorgeous over the course of the day. Getting to know her a little had made her more stunning to him. If he was going to do the time, he should have at least had the pleasure of doing the crime.

She shook her head. "No, I'm turning you down because I have a girlfriend." She pointed behind her. "She's sitting in the dining room."

He turned and, sure enough, there was another woman sitting and staring at him. She actually reminded him of that corgi. Not because she looked like a corgi, but he knew that stare. That stare told him to stay away.

He was getting that stare a lot today. "Your grandmother doesn't know?"

"Oh, she knows. She's met Mandy many times, and we don't hide our relationship," Sam replied with a shake of her head. Her lips finally curved up, but the smile seemed more sad than amused. "She seems to think if she pretends it isn't true, it won't be. Or maybe she thinks you'll be so manly I'll find my way back around on the Kinsey Scale."

His heart ached for a woman he didn't know. He'd met Sally Henshaw many times, but never her granddaughter. "I'm sorry for that. It's got to be hard to deal with. I know your grandmother and I know she loves you, but she can be stubborn."

"I'm not sure she loves the real me." Sam sighed and seemed to relax. "Thanks for being so gracious. I've met a few of my grandmother's alternatives who weren't. I hope you enjoy your night."

He felt oddly relieved at the thought of being able to order a burger to go and heading home. "You, too."

She walked back to join her girlfriend, who finally flashed him a smile and nodded his way. Had she been waiting for him to yell at Sam and make a scene? Was that why Sam had called him gracious? He gave her a nod back as Lisa returned, iced tea in hand.

How hard was it on those two? The world might be easier than it was twenty years before, but there were still some who wouldn't accept them.

"One iced tea."

He shook his head. "Make it a beer, Lisa. And put their tab on mine. Someone should get a decent date out of tonight."

He glanced back and Sam's girlfriend's eyes had gone wide. "Oh, my god. Is that Taylor from *Janie's World*?"

That was when he realized Brynn was standing at the hostess station. Her eyes found his, and for a moment her whole face lit up and she started to bring her hand up. Then she seemed to catch herself. Her hand came down and so did the wattage of that smile as she simply nodded his way.

Connection. He felt it with her.

Maybe he should chuck the whole "everything has to have a perfect picket fence around it" and go with the flow for a couple of days. Or weeks.

She smiled at the hostess, and he watched as she told her she was a party of one. She gestured over to the bar as though saying she was fine there and didn't need to take up a whole table herself.

"Hey, Lisa, why don't you ask our Hollywood guest if she wouldn't mind keeping a deputy company this evening. It's okay if she wants to be alone, but if she doesn't, she can eat with me." He would be less grumpy, show her some charm. He could muster some up. Damn she was pretty.

Lisa's eyes had widened. "Did you change your mind about that beer?"

"No." It wasn't a date. It was a man having dinner and passing some time with a woman. That was all.

It couldn't be more.

* * *

Brynn liked the look of Guidry's. It wasn't elegant like the places in LA, nor did it have the forced kitsch she'd seen in some restaurants. Guidry's looked like a place that had survived and thrived over the years. After the driver had dropped her off, she'd walked past the playground where kids were scrambling over the jungle gym and laughing. She'd made her way around them to get to the building's front porch. It was wide and covered and had some rocking chairs and benches scattered about. She'd walked through the front door, and the walls on either side were covered in pictures detailing the restaurant and marina through the years, starting in black and white and ending in a picture of a pretty brunette and a big, muscular man standing in front of the Guidry's sign.

History. This building had history, being passed down from grandparents to parents and sons and daughters.

She couldn't wait to try the food.

"Oh, my god. Is that Taylor from *Janie's World*?"

She heard the question and realized her time as an anonymous tourist might be coming to an end. She glanced around but couldn't tell exactly who'd asked the question.

And then she saw him. Deputy Major was standing up on the deck outside the dining room. He'd ditched his uniform and wore slacks and a white shirt he'd tucked in. She'd thought he was kind of hot in his khakis. She'd thought he was hot even while wearing muddy underwear. The man was hot in anything, but she liked him dressed like this. He'd rolled his sleeves up, revealing strong forearms. It suddenly felt like the whole place had gotten brighter, even more interesting than before. She felt a smile cross her face and then remembered how shut down he'd been when she'd dropped him off at the station house. He hadn't acted like a man who wanted to see her again, especially so soon. She lowered the hand she'd been about to wave and gave him a nod, the simple recognition of "Yes, we're both here and I'm not going to bother you."

"Hi, welcome to Guidry's. Are you ready for a table or waiting for someone?" There was a fresh-faced young woman in a Guidry's tee and a short skirt standing at the hostess station, holding a couple of menus.

"It's just me." Her stomach growled at the smell of something heavenly coming from the kitchen.

The hostess's eyes went wide. "Oh, you're Bria Knight. I heard you were doing a movie in town. I never dreamed you would actually walk in here. I thought you would stay in New Orleans."

New Orleans was hours and hours away. "I'm staying out at the B and B. It's lovely. I heard Guidry's is the best place to eat, so I'll probably come in a lot over the next couple of weeks."

"That's so cool." The hostess wore a bright smile.

She spied a big bar in the corner. "Can I eat at the bar?"

It was always fun to talk to bartenders, and she might find other singletons like herself to chat with. She'd spent the rest of the day sketching at the dock, but it hadn't been the bayou that managed to get on her sketchpad. Nope. Every drawing had been of Deputy Major and his sweet dog. She'd shared her lunch with Duke and thought about that man all afternoon.

And she still hadn't managed to look at the scripts her mom had sent her.

"Of course," the hostess said. "But you should know you're the biggest thing to hit Papillon in . . . well, ever."

She glanced over and sure enough, several people were staring at her. She gave them a wave to let them know she wasn't unapproachable. She'd found that if she took a couple of pics and signed some things, most people left her in peace.

Of course, if her career skyrocketed the way they planned, she wouldn't be able to go to restaurants by herself. She would likely have to take a bodyguard with her wherever she went. Her mom viewed private dining rooms as a sign of power and success, but Brynn dreaded them. They were quiet and put her in the position of only being able to talk to the "right" people.

She wanted some freedom.

A pretty brunette strode up to the stand, some menus in her hand. "Hey, Ms. Knight. I'm Lisa. I run this place with my husband, Remy."

Brynn recognized the woman from the picture in the hall and prayed there wasn't a private dining room she was about to be showed to. Did Lisa Guidry want to avoid the chaos that could come with a bunch of fans making requests? Maybe she should get something to go. She was pretty sure she could get the guy with the golf cart to come back for her. He couldn't have made it too far.

Yep, her Uber driver had rolled up on a golf cart, and she'd thought it was magical.

"Hi. Your place looks amazing, and I can't wait to try the food." She didn't want to go back to her cabin. She wanted to be out, seeing this part of the world, talking to people. Real people who didn't constantly discuss back end points and who's the hottest new director.

She'd preferred the talk with the driver, who'd told her he'd actually left the golf course to pick her up because he needed some cash. He'd said someone named Herve cheated but he couldn't prove it, and now he owed the man skins of some kind. She'd briefly been worried that she was about to be brutally murdered, but then the man started talking about his grandkids, so she went along for the ride.

This place was weird. She liked it. She wanted to pretend like she was a part of it, not get shown the best room where she wouldn't be bothered. She liked being bothered.

Lisa gave her a vibrant smile. "It's so surreal to be talking to Taylor Smith-Price. I mean, I know you're not her, but you really look like her." Lisa shook her head as though realizing she had a job to do. "We're happy to have you here. The deputy asked if you would like to join him."

He had? "Major?"

Lisa nodded. "Yes. I think he sent me over because he wanted you to feel comfortable saying no if you want to. He's very thoughtful. If you don't want to sit with him, we have a small private dining room. It's pretty nice, but we don't use it often."

"I would love to sit with him." She wished her heart hadn't started pounding the way it had. "We met earlier today."

"You mean you saved his ass earlier today." Lisa started to lead her through the dining room toward what looked to be a deck. "And I mean literally, since if he'd gotten himself out, he would have been standing on the highway in his tighty-whities. I always thought he would be a boxer-brief guy. I was surprised he keeps the boys high and tight. I should tell him that those little things are not good for his sperm."

"Oh, please don't." The last thing she wanted was to put the man through more awkward conversation. "Did he tell you about it?"

Lisa waved that off. "He didn't have to. You see, my brother-in-law runs the animal services department for the parish, and he had the idea to set up wildlife cams around the area to educate people about the critters running around here. They switch around every couple of hours."

She'd seen something like that on the Internet. It was a way to engage the public. "So it was live?"

"The last part was," Lisa replied.

Brynn walked out on the gorgeous deck with its view of the bay. The Gulf of Mexico was on gorgeous display. "This is beautiful."

"Thank you. We think it's pretty spectacular." Lisa gestured to the table where Major was standing. "Hey, Major. You're lucky. This one doesn't already have a girlfriend."

Major looked adorable with a frown on his face. "You knew about Sam Henshaw and didn't say anything?"

Lisa shrugged. "I thought maybe they were looking for a sperm donor. You know me. I keep my nose out of everyone's business. Can I get you a beer or some wine, Bria?"

"She prefers Brynn," Major said, moving around to hold out a chair for her.

So he was a gentlemanly grump. "I'd love a beer. Thanks."

"Got it." Lisa nodded and walked off.

"And Lisa doesn't keep her nose out of anyone's business." Major was still frowning as he sat down. "I mean it. She's always sticking her nose right in. I'm afraid you won't find many people who keep to themselves here in Papillon. Are you still driving Harry's truck? I only ask so I can have an idea of how many people are going to call the station about the pretty blond car thief."

She winced. "Sorry. I didn't think it would be a big deal. And no. Harry had an emergency. Apparently his mother-in-law had some plumbing problems and he went out to help. I called a car service."

"We have a car service?" Major asked and then winced. "Please tell me Greg Bonham isn't still trying to make Guber happen."

She snorted. "Yes. I heard all about his plan to create a fleet of golf carts."

"That's not road legal. You are not calling him to take you back." He groaned, though it sounded like a sexy growl. "I'll drive you home, and I'll have a talk with Greg because putting twinkle lights all over a golf cart does not make it safe. So, where's your buddy this evening?"

"Duke?" She didn't have another buddy. She had acquaintances. She had coworkers. She had fans. She didn't have buddies beyond her dog. She suddenly realized how sad that was.

"Yes. I miss his royal disdain."

"Disdain?"

A brow rose over Major's eyes. "That dog does not like me. And he didn't like Dolly, either, which is a mistake on his part because she is delightful."

Brynn chuckled. "That's not what you were saying when she was wrapped around your shoulders."

"Well, we've moved on and she's delightful again. She never met a stranger, and I think she was hurt by Duke's rejection of her love."

Oh, this was an infinitely more dangerous man than the one she'd met before. Was he flirting with her? If he was, it was working, because she was ready to throw out everything she'd learned about him earlier in the day. "Duke takes his time warming up to people, but once he gets used to you, you'll find him delightful, too. He's back at the B and B. When I'm not able to take him with me, he usually stays with an assistant. In this case, he's hanging out with Shep. What has you in a good mood? Did you get to ticket a bunch of people?"

He put a hand on his chest. "I do not enjoy ticketing people, Brynn. Especially not people around here. They're mouthy and very creative in finding an excuse for not using their blinker when they turn. By the way, speaking of ticketing people, you have a lead foot. That is not going to do you well here. The boss is always on the lookout to upgrade the station house's appliances, and the money from driving offenses goes straight into his budget. He's got two small children at home now. He wants an espresso machine. He kind of needs it to keep functioning."

Ah, the joys of small-town life. "Thank you for the warning. How about I gift him one and maybe you gently look the other way?"

That jawline of his straightened, and he turned on his serious stare. "Ma'am, are you trying to bribe an officer of the law?"

That cop voice got to her. She suddenly understood why people role-played. She'd always thought it was dumb, but now she could see how Deputy Major doing a slow search of her body could be sexy. In a playful way, of course. A consenting way.

Was she thinking about hopping into bed with him?

"Brynn, I was joking." He had a sheepish expression on his face.

"And I was thinking about something I shouldn't have been thinking about." She shook it off. The man had invited her to share a table with him. He hadn't offered to play sexy games. He wouldn't. "I'm serious about the espresso machine, though. I was thinking about how I can show my gratitude to the sheriff's department for helping me research."

"Roxie mentioned you're planning on shadowing her for a couple of days."

It was part of the reason for coming in early. "Yes. I've done a lot of research, but it was all on paper. This is my first time playing a police officer. I did a couple of ride-alongs in LA, but there's a huge difference in big-city policing and small-town."

"Yes. I suspect Armie naps far more often than the LAPD chief." He relaxed back. "You can probably learn everything you need to know in about two days. This job is as much about controlling chaos as it is any kind of actual law enforcement. As you learned earlier today."

"Do you have to stop a lot of water hose attacks?"

His lips curled up. "Far more than I expected. We've got some feisty citizens around here. One of the good things about small-town policing is you get to know the people. They aren't just strangers on the street. They're your neighbors. You get to know the character of the people you're supposed to protect and serve, and they get to know you. I think it's made me far more sympathetic than I would have been had I joined a larger department."

"It sounds nice. Like you're one big family."

He nodded. "Yes, one big dysfunctional family that likes to have lots of parties. That's where the chaos usually happens."

There was a gasp and then Lisa Guidry was putting an ice-cold bottle of beer in front of Brynn. "Our parties and festivals are wonderful. There's very little chaos and a whole lot of fried deliciousness. This town knows how to throw a festival."

Major frowned up at Lisa. "You should know. Did Josie Trahan ever get her hair extension back?"

Lisa blushed. "Now, Major, you know that woman was going after my husband and I'd had a little strawberry wine."

"You'd had a lot of strawberry wine," Major countered. "And I heard Josie is back in town, so I will be watching you at the Crawfish Festival."

Lisa's nose wrinkled at the thought. "She better keep her overly manicured paws off my man or we'll have trouble. Have you had a chance to look over the menu or is Major trying to make his second date of the night go better than the first?"

She hadn't even looked at it. "I'm not picky. Bring me whatever you would order."

"And I'll take the étouffée." Major hadn't looked at the menu, either, but then, he might have it memorized.

Lisa promised to return and walked away to put in their orders.

And now something Lisa had said actually penetrated her brain. "You were on a date?"

He finally took a drink of his beer, and she realized he'd been waiting for the arrival of her beer before enjoying his own. "Nope. Do you remember Mrs. Henshaw's grand-daughter?"

"The one I ruined you for?" She was still impressed with how Major had stopped that fight before it ended in tragedy.

"Turns out she's got a girlfriend and has no interest at all in my virtue. They are having dinner behind us in the dining room. So she had a date. I did not."

"Aww, that's sweet." She wasn't showing the proper sympathy. "Are you sad about it?"

"Nah," Major replied. "It's not the first time someone's taken one look at me and walked away. Probably won't be the last."

She flashed him a frown because she was calling bullshit on that. "That's never happened."

"Oh, it did," Major insisted. "I once got set up with a friend's cousin. It was about a year ago, and we met out at the Fillin' Station. Now, before you turn your nose up, you should know they make an excellent chicken-fried steak, and it's great for people watching because the dining room is in the middle of the convenience portion of the gas station. The best seat is by the sundries aisle. Do not let them seat you by the windows. You'd think that would be a great spot because you get to watch people pump gas, but it's also by the bathrooms, and you don't want that."

"Oh, I have got to see this place." She liked how his accent was coming out now that he was relaxed. It wasn't a Cajun accent. It had a bit of Texas twang to it. "But I still don't see how a woman turns you down based on looks. You're not exactly a monster."

"I was to this woman. She walked in, realized I was sitting at the table, and ran the other way."

"Did you chase her?"

He nodded. "Yes."

"Seriously? I was joking. You chased her?"

"She was wanted for five home robberies around the parish. I think her cousin was trying to get her in trouble so he set her up on a blind date with me," Major pointed out. "Anyway, she pled out and got two years minimum security, and I spent the night filling out paperwork. Fun times. It still wasn't my worst date ever."

"Do you get set up a lot?"

"I'm a single man in a small town. I have a steady job, no debt, and I own my home."

"Ah, so you're the unicorn everyone is chasing."

"Dating is hard. It can be hard in a small town where most people pair off in high school or leave town altogether. I put it out there that I wasn't opposed to dating and suddenly everyone has a daughter or sister or friend they want me to meet. But I'm still very much single. No one has caught this unicorn yet. How about you?"

"I'm not seeing anyone right now. The last couple of years I've focused on work." She took a drag off her beer.

A long moment passed, an awkwardness setting in before Major looked at her with an earnest expression on his face. "Look, Brynn, I think we got off on the wrong foot."

"Your foot was trapped in mud, Deputy Major. I think it's okay that you were a wee bit disconcerted." It wasn't like he'd been rude. Grumpy, yes, but she was sure she would have been, too. "We can pretend like it never happened."

Major shook his head. "No, we can't. We both know someone has already taken that video apart for the most embarrassing still shots they could get and there's already a meme somewhere. But we can start over since it looks like you'll be hanging around my town for a bit. How about I pay you back for the rescue by taking you to a place where the light is so soft and perfect the world seems to hum all around you? There's an island that I'm sure my mom would have called paradise. I've got tomorrow off. I promise to be quiet so you can work if you'll convince Seraphina to make some chicken salad sandwiches and some of her cookies."

She'd known he knew something about art. She'd seen the gorgeous landscapes in his home. They weren't the kind of paintings one bought at a home décor store. Those were done with a talented hand. But he hadn't wanted to talk so she hadn't asked about them. Now she wondered who had taught him about art and light. "I think that would be wonderful."

He started to talk about the town, but she was rapidly becoming more and more fascinated with another subject.

Him.

chapter four

Brynn felt the SUV come to a slow stop, as though the driver was reluctant to end the ride.

She was reluctant, too. The evening had been lovely, and now there were stars overhead and the whole night felt soft and inviting. They'd sat on the deck at Guidry's as the sun had gone down and talked for two hours, drawing out the meal because it had been so easy to be together. There had only been a couple of times awkwardness had seeped into their bubble.

"I'm sorry about the autograph thing," she said, though she'd already apologized earlier. Three different people had come up and asked for pictures and autographs, and they'd told her how much they loved whichever show they recognized her from.

She'd found there were two types of people when it came to the fame thing. There was the type who was fascinated by it and the type who was freaked out by it. She was pretty sure Major would fall into the second category.

"I thought you handled everyone well." He turned her way, his arm resting on the steering wheel. "Do you get a lot of that?"

"I've been acting since I was a kid," she admitted. "I honestly don't remember a time when it didn't happen, so it feels normal to me. I was taught it was part of the job. It's not as bad as it could be. I'm not some huge star. Most of my work has been on TV. I don't mind usually, but I was enjoying talking to you. I hope it didn't make you uncomfortable."

"You seem pretty good at making everyone comfortable, Brynn." His lips had curled up in a smile. "I had a nice time. And I think you'll find that the people around here will get used to you very quickly. You keep being as nice and friendly as you were tonight and you'll do well. I'm sorry I misjudged you."

He'd had a day. She could forgive him. "Of course. Thanks for dinner. If you were serious about going out to the islands, I would love to. I've got the week off, and then I start actually prepping for this role. I'm going to be around the station house a lot next week."

"You know Roxie's my partner, right?"

She'd wondered how closely they were connected. She wasn't sure how the department worked, but then that was one of the things she was here to learn. It was her first time playing a cop, and she wanted to get it right. "Is that going to be weird?"

"Partners work a little different out here. I call her my partner because we tend to work shifts together, but there's no formal relationship because we're such a small department," he explained. "But you should know I'll probably be around when you are. Is this Gavin guy coming in at the same time?"

"You don't watch TV, do you?" She couldn't help but tease him. He was a gorgeous guy who was fun to talk to and seemed genuinely kind, and he didn't care at all about the Hollywood thing. Gavin would be confused at a person who didn't recognize him. It might do the man's ego good. "Gavin is kind of a legend in the TV world."

"I might recognize him if I see him, but no, I don't," he admitted. "I'm more of a sports and books guy. I know those sound like they don't go together, but they do. There are some movies I like, but I don't know many actors. It's not that I don't appreciate what you do."

"You just don't celebrity worship like the rest of the world." It was kind of refreshing. She liked that she wasn't worried Major wanted to use her as a ladder rung. It had happened more than once with men she'd dated. Even the ones who weren't actors tended to want to step into her world.

"Yeah, I don't get that. You're a person like the rest of us."

The way he said the words brought her right back to the reason for her apology. "I am. And it was weird for you, wasn't it?"

He hesitated but answered. "Okay, it was weird, but like I said, you handled it well."

"Thanks. Gavin is supposed to come in sometime this weekend. He'll shadow your sheriff." She'd known Gavin for a long time. "I should warn you—he can be a little method."

A brow rose over his eyes.

"It's an acting term. He can be intense and weird about his characters. He'll ask a lot of questions and take a lot of liberties. But he understands firmly placed boundaries. That's the key with Gavin. Once he knows where the line is, he'll respect it."

"Do you know that from experience?" Major asked.

"Oh, yes, I've worked with Gavin many times. He can be obnoxious, but you put your foot down and he's cool." She knew there had been a time when she didn't know Gavin, but she couldn't remember it. That was how long she'd worked with the man.

"What did you have to put your foot down about, Brynn?" There was a hint of cop in his tone now. She'd rapidly come to note that there were a couple of sides to the deputy. He could be quite charming, but there was a deep authoritative side that couldn't be denied.

She wasn't sure what he was getting at. "Like I said, we've worked together a lot. I played his daughter on one show. It was a sitcom that ran for a long time. I started on that show when I was five years old. And then we were on *Janie's World*. That show went on for several years. I was a teenager then. He and my mom were good friends, so the dad role sometimes went beyond the actual role he was playing. Like I said, he can sink into his role and forget that it's not real."

"Ah," Major said.

And that was when she realized what he'd really been talking about. He said he'd looked her up on the Internet. He must have gone pretty deep because those rumors finally stopped circulating a few years ago. "You read the gossip that we were dating back when I turned eighteen."

She huffed, disappointment welling. Those rumors had hurt because Gavin had never been anything but fatherly to her.

"I'm sorry. I was only asking. You talked about boundaries, and I immediately thought about what kind of boundaries a kid would have." Major reached out and put a hand over hers. "I wasn't accusing anyone of anything. I just spent time today wondering about what it must have been like to be a kid in that world."

"It wasn't so bad, and Gavin was a part of that." She hated those stupid rumors. Gavin was weird, but so was most of Hollywood. He could act like a self-absorbed douchebag, but underneath it, he was a genuine human being. "When I was young, the director would sometimes forget that I was supposed to have a certain number of dedicated school hours every day. My mom was worried I might get fired and was unsure about how to handle the situation. Gavin took care of it. He walked in and said if the production couldn't treat the child actors right, then he would quit. He was a big name so I got my school time and my break time, and my mom gained some confidence about how to protect me. I'm not saying it was perfect, but it wasn't as bad as what some kids went through. Though you should know my mom is a lot to take."

"I'm glad to hear it wasn't so bad." He frowned as a chiming sound filled the air. He slid his cell out and answered it. "Hello?" He paused. "I'll be there in ten minutes."

Well, that answered one question that had been going through her head. She wasn't going to invite him in. She unbuckled her belt. "Everything okay?"

"Yeah." He set the cell back on his console. "But I've got to go take care of something. I'll pick you up around ten tomorrow if you still want to go."

"I do." She wasn't going to let his touchy question ruin what had been a nice night. She opened the door and eased out to the ground in front of her cabin. "Duke and I will see you then, and I'll make sure we've got a nice lunch. Thanks for dinner, Major. I had a lovely time."

"Me, too." The words were pleasant, but there was a tightness to his expression that let her know he was already thinking about whatever that phone call had been about. "See you tomorrow."

She shut the door and walked to her cabin, realizing he wouldn't leave until he'd seen her go inside. She opened it with her key and wondered what had put that look on his face. She didn't know him well enough to ask, and it had seemed urgent. Probably deputy things.

The cabin was aglow with the single light she'd left on, but she realized things were wrong when Duke came running up.

"I thought I left you in your crate, buddy." Had he turned into an escape artist? She'd made sure it was secure when she'd left.

"I let him out. You know I believe animals should run free."

She managed to not let out a scream because she knew that voice. "The funny thing is I was just talking about how you need firm boundaries."

Gavin Jacks was a journeyman actor. He'd started as a leading man on a TV show back in the eighties, and he was one of those faces almost everyone recognized. He'd been set to be a film star, when he'd gotten in trouble with drugs and alcohol. It had sidetracked him for years.

Now his biggest indulgence was herbal tea and, apparently, breaking and entering.

Gavin shrugged as he sank down onto the couch. "An actor shouldn't have boundaries, Brynn. Have I taught you nothing over the years? And poor Duke was obviously in distress being in that cage. He and I understand each other. It's his nature to be free."

"Well, I hope you didn't let him out without a leash because with the wildlife around here, it's his nature to be a snack." She picked up her pup.

"Of course I didn't. We had a nice walk of the grounds with him fully leashed. You made yourself plain the last time I visited." Gavin wore loose pants and a V-neck T-shirt. He looked far younger than his fifty-four years, the outcome of several decades of clean living and a very good plastic surgeon. "So it seems you've already made contact with our hosts. Have you started the research without me? By the way, did you meet the man who owns the place? He's only got one leg. There has to be an interesting story there."

It wasn't a long story. "He lost it during his time in the military."

"Excellent," Gavin said. "It's inspirational. I like it."

"You are far too old to play him," she pointed out because if she let him go, poor Harry would find himself being asked a million questions about his life.

"Stephen isn't, and he's looking for a new project. It would be good to get the two of you back together. Besides, I'm looking to get into directing," Gavin admitted. "Television is so wearing, and I'd like to spend more time at home. I've been on the road or in a studio for ten years." He patted the couch next to him. "Imagine it. You could play the wife. If we throw in a serial killer, it might have some pizzazz."

"I don't think Harry and Seraphina had to hunt down a serial killer."

"You know every biopic is better when you embellish a bit," he said. "And I like the small-town killer vibe. We can open with a shot of how peaceful the bayou looks and then have a gator eat something and sink back into the water, revealing the horror under the surface."

"Or it could be a nice romance where the gator is just a gator and not a metaphor for the ills of American life." She felt the desperate need to point out his pretension. He was one of those types who believed a film was only art if it made a statement. And if everyone was miserable at the end.

He shuddered. "That is the bourgeoise streak in you talking. Still, romantic comedy does sell. I'll have to think about it. So when is your mother getting in? And how is it going with the locals? I've heard some strange things about this town."

"It's got its quirks." She settled down across from him. Despite the breaking-in part, it was good to see him. He'd been such a big part of her life growing up that she'd missed him over the last few months. "And Mom should be here early next week. I had Harry and Sera reserve one of the two bedroom suites in the main house for her. I made sure the Wi-Fi works. You know how Mom gets if she can't get a signal."

"Is your sister working right now?" Gavin asked.

"She's auditioning, but she hasn't booked anything since that deodorant commercial." Ally was trying, but she hadn't found her break yet.

"Then I'm sure your mom will bring her out here to work as your assistant," he said with a disapproving shake of his head. "It's only going to make her resent you. She should stay in LA and continue to audition."

"Don't be hard on Ally." She knew her sister had resented her growing up. Their mom had put so much time into Brynn's career, and Ally's hadn't taken off. Ally had been carted around to sets she didn't have a place on, and worse, left behind at times. "It's hard to think of yourself as the after-thought. She's not, but I can't convince her of that. And yes, she's coming out with Mom. She's got a job as a production assistant."

"Then I will batten down the hatches," Gavin said. "Now, who was the attractive young man who dropped you off? He's not the sheriff. I've looked him up. I think he'll make a great template for my character."

He was going to get nosy. "His name is Major."

"Oh, I love it. I do so love the odd ones." He looked her over, his eyes narrowing. "You're not dressed for work."

"I wasn't working. I went out to dinner, but there's no driving service out here yet." Driving her back and forth from the set would likely be one of her sister's duties, and wouldn't that be fun? "I met the deputy earlier in the day, and we shared a table."

He stared at her for a moment. "You were on a date."

"It wasn't a date." The last thing she needed was her mother to decide she was dating someone. She would get lectures on how important her image was and how she should carefully select all friends and possible partners to reflect the image she wanted to project.

"Who paid for dinner?" Gavin asked.

Brynn sighed. "He did, but he was only being nice."

Gavin pointed at her as though she'd made his point. "Yes, he was being nice to the woman who likely made three times his yearly salary on her last movie."

He'd insisted, and she didn't want to argue with him. The truth was it had felt a little like a date, and she'd enjoyed it. For a moment it had been nice to think of herself as nothing more than a girl who'd met a guy, and they were learning more about each other. But she wasn't about to tell Gavin that. He was a horrible gossip.

"It wasn't a date. He'd actually gotten stood up by his real date, so I was merely a fill-in," she explained. "He was there. I was there. It made sense to share a table. He knows a lot about the town, and he's partners with the deputy I'm going to shadow next week. It seemed like a good idea to get to know him. I also found out that the sheriff really wants an espresso machine."

Gavin perked up at that. "Excellent. Want to go halves? We can bring in a nice machine and a month's worth of beans."

"Sure."

Gavin could be a gossip, but he was also quite generous. He'd taught her to always leave thank-you gifts with the people who took the time to educate them about the roles they played. They would spend a couple of weeks dealing with tons of questions, and while Brynn would try to blend into the background, she was a complication they would have to deal with. "But I think there's more going on between you and this Major person. You had a look when you walked in."

He was getting way too close for comfort. And there was no reason for it. She was curious about the deputy. She wasn't thinking about trying to date him.

Although she'd thought about inviting him in. Just for a

drink. To talk more. Nothing else. "Yes, I was annoyed because someone let my dog out of his crate."

Gavin ignored her sarcasm. "No, you had a look of expectation. You looked like you were looking forward to seeing him again. I don't know that getting involved with the locals is such a good idea."

"Really? Well, you would know. How many relationships have you had with costars?"

"Many, but it's not the same. We're not the same. You are far more serious about the people you get to know. I tend to stick to partners who aren't wildly interested in getting in too deep." Gavin stood and stretched. "I'll leave you with that thought. I don't want you to get your heart broken."

That was sweet.

He wasn't finished. "After all, this film is about the father-daughter relationship. You can't use romantic heartbreak for that."

She groaned. "I'll certainly think about that."

Gavin strode to the door before turning back. "And, darling, if you want your mother to think you don't have a thing for the deputy, don't let her see your sketchpad. Your emotions are right there. Good night."

"Boundaries, Gavin." She hissed the words at him.

He simply closed the door behind him.

Duke looked up at her as if to say he agreed with Gavin. She sighed and stroked his fur. "I'm not getting in deep."

Duke huffed.

Yeah, no one seemed to believe her today.

Major walked up to the assisted living home and saw a familiar figure at the door. It was past visiting hours in the building, though Major had access like all primary family members. The building housed roughly a hundred seniors in various stages of medical need. They each had their own small apartment and shared common areas and use of the nursing staff. It was well run, and the residents seemed happy.

His father didn't hate the place when he was in his right mind.

There's nothing wrong or right about his mind. Don't make those judgments. He has a disease that breaks down his cognitive functions. He's still your dad even when he doesn't remember he's your dad.

He heard Lila LaVigne's words go through his head. He kept them in his brain so he could change the way he thought. His father wasn't crazy. *Crazy* wasn't a good word to use to describe any human being.

Juan Garcia was a nurse who managed the facility his father lived in. Major found him to be an intelligent, sympathetic man. He took the time to get to know his residents and their family members, hence his call this evening. "I know it's late, but he's having a good couple of hours, and he asked about you."

"You can call me anytime." It had been weeks since his father's memory had been clear. He would have shown up at midnight or five a.m. He would have found someone to take his shift so he could talk to his dad.

Time. It was the most precious thing in his life right now. Time with his father.

He stepped inside. At this time of night, the lobby was quiet. He moved down the hall with Juan toward his father's apartment. It was a single unit and had a security camera on the door because more than once he'd walked out thinking he needed to get to a job he hadn't held for fifteen years. Sometimes he got upset when the staff wouldn't allow him to leave. Those were the worst times.

Keeping him in the here and now was getting harder and harder.

"I was actually going to call you in the morning," Juan said. "Lila wants to run some tests. His bloodwork came back with some elevated red blood cell levels."

"Does she think the cancer is back?" His father had had a bout with prostate cancer a few years ago. It was before the dementia diagnosis.

"I think she's being careful. Don't borrow trouble, Major." Juan knocked on the door before opening it with his all-access key. "Mr. Blanchard? You have a visitor." He looked back at Major. "Stay as long as you like. I'll be out front if you need anything."

"Thank you." He stepped inside. There was a short hall and a bathroom to his right. The living room had a comfortable lounger and a sofa. The soft sound of a TV played through the room. "Dad?"

"Major." His father stood from his place on the lounger and turned. He was dressed for bed in his pajama bottoms and a white T-shirt, a robe wrapped around his thin frame. A wide smile crossed his face and he held out his arms. "I'm so glad to see you, son. You look good."

A shudder of relief went through him as he hugged his dad. Once he'd been the fragile one and this man had sheltered him. It was his turn. "You, too, Dad. I'm glad to see you."

"It's late. Is everything all right?" His dad stepped back, relaxing onto the lounger as he used the remote to put the TV on mute.

He had to take a moment or he might break down because it was so good to hear his father's voice. "Yes. I just wanted to see you."

His father's lips curved into a smile that was tinged with sadness. He gestured for Major to sit. "Juan called you and told you I was having a good day, huh?"

Major sat on the edge of the sofa. "I come see you even when you're having a bad one."

His father sighed. "Ah, but I don't remember those. Has it been hard on you?"

So hard. It was so incredibly hard to watch his father lose hold of reality. "Not at all. You're not hard to deal with."

"Somehow I don't believe you." He settled back. "But I want to know about you. Tell me what's going on in your life. I want to hear everything."

"It's pretty much the same. You know things rarely change at the station house. We hired a new guy, and he seems pretty nice." He wasn't about to tell his father he'd gotten stuck in a damn bog and needed a pretty actress to get him out.

His dad's eyes narrowed. "What happened? When you don't want to tell me something, your jaw tightens."

Major frowned. He was pretty sure he didn't do that. He didn't exactly wear his heart on his sleeve. Although . . . "Is that why Armie can always tell when I'm bluffing?"

"Absolutely. If he's played poker with you for any amount of time, he'll be able to tell. So, fess up. Something happened today. Was it bad?"

Major shrugged. "I had a date tonight and it went well. It didn't start out as a date. I was supposed to have dinner with Samantha Henshaw."

"Why? I mean Samantha's a nice young woman, but won't her girlfriend object?"

He sometimes forgot that his father had lived here for years before he wound up in assisted living. He'd been a big part of this community. "Everyone seems to know that except me and her grandmother, although that seems to be willful ignorance."

"Sally sees what she wants to see," his father said. "Samantha was a good kid. That was all that mattered. If she brings home someone who lifts her up, then good for her.

And honestly, Sally will give in eventually. She's stubborn but she won't lose her granddaughter over it. So you let Sally talk you into a blind date with an unavailable woman? And then you managed to find an available one?"

He had to smile at the thought. "I don't know how available she is. I mean she's single, but she's in town for a job and she'll leave in a couple of months."

"Then you have a couple of months to get to know if she's worth it."

"Worth it?"

His father nodded. "Worth either trying a long-distance relationship or moving. Any chance she might move here? We have some great places to work."

"Only if you want to drill oil or give swamp tours," Major said with a huff.

"Where does she live?"

"LA." Though from what he could tell her house there was more of a way station. The way she talked, she spent most of her time on the road working. She'd described herself as living out of a suitcase.

"Then you need to see if she's worth moving to LA," his father prompted.

"Slow down. We had one dinner." And he wasn't sure he could handle her world. He hadn't lied to her. She'd dealt with the fans beautifully, but it would be a lot to deal with if that happened all the time. Could she get through a meal without someone she'd never met before coming up and talking to her like they were old friends?

"Yeah, but I haven't seen you smile that way about a woman in a very long time."

"Well, it was nice to be around her." It had been the nicest night he'd had in a while. "How long did you date Mom before you knew she was the one?"

Brynn was definitely not the one. She would leave and he

couldn't, but he wasn't about to argue with his dad about that. They'd had one date, and it had been mere coincidence that it had happened at all.

"Oh, I knew right away," his father said with a smile. "She, on the other hand, took her time figuring it out. You are far more like your mom. You think too much."

"There's nothing wrong with thinking."

"There is if you completely ignore your instincts," his father countered. "Sometimes you have to go with your gut. A relationship is one of those things."

"I can't leave Papillon."

"Of course you can."

"All right. I can't leave you."

His father reached out. "Of course you can." He placed his hand over Major's. "And it's not leaving me. It's having a life, son. I'm not going to be around forever. We both have to accept that. The one thing I can't accept is that you'll give up having a life and a family because you focus too much on me. I want you to be happy."

He wasn't sure he could be without his father. "Like I said, it's far too early to know if we're even compatible. She's nice. I might spend some time with her while she's here. She's doing some research for a project she's working on, and I can help her with that."

His father sat back, getting comfortable again. He glanced over at the silent television, his lips curling up. "I like this show."

Major looked over and was shocked to see a younger version of Brynn walking through the streets of New York with another actress. "I've never seen it."

"It's amusing. I know your mother didn't like television, but it's a strain on my eyes to read too much. I find some shows comforting. This one is about family," his dad explained.

"It's not the same as ours was, but the emotions are universal. The mom reminds me of yours."

"The daughter is . . ." How did he explain that his father was actually watching the woman he'd seen earlier this evening? It was a lot to process. ". . . pretty."

His father turned to him, staring. "Major, that girl is barely sixteen. Maybe we should talk about being attracted to appropriate women."

"I meant she will be when she grows up." No one could make him feel as awkward as his father. "Which she is because I happen to know this is an old show. That actress is twenty-five now, and she's who I had dinner with. She's filming a movie in town."

A brow rose above his father's eyes. "The mayor finally got a production crew to come to Papillon?"

"Yes, and Brynn is playing a sheriff's deputy." It was surreal that she was smiling on the TV screen and he was talking about knowing her. "And she is pretty. And appropriately aged for me. And she is attracted to men."

His father's laugh filled the room. "Now I want to know everything about her. How did you meet?"

Major frowned. "Well, that's a long story."

He sat back and began his tale.

chapter five

~

Brynn sat in the tiny boat as Major navigated the dark water with an expert hand. At least she hoped he had an expert hand. She had to admit the boat made her nervous. Not that she would show it.

"It's perfectly safe, you know." He flashed her a smile as they moved along. "Well, as safe as anything is down here."

She held on to Duke. He seemed content to huddle on her lap. Dolly, on the other hand, was pretending to be the figurehead of the tiny boat. She stood at the front, her face to the wind. "I'm not used to small boats. Or water where alligators could be."

"I thought there was nothing the great Brynn Pearson couldn't handle." He winked at her. "It's good to know you're human. But you do have to get comfortable because if the movie is at all realistic, your character should spend some time on one of these. Half the damn parish requires a boat to get to."

"People live out here?" They'd only pulled off the B and B's dock a few moments before, and all the islands they'd passed had been tiny things.

"Oh, yes," he replied. "We'll pass some of the larger islands to get to Butterfly. There are some families who've lived out here for generations. There are also some fishing cabins. Most of those are pretty spartan, though my friend Rene's is very nice."

"There's an island called Butterfly? Isn't *Papillon* French for *butterfly*?"

"It is. This whole area is called Butterfly Bayou because monarchs come through here on their way to Mexico," he explained. "They cover the islands, but one in particular seems to be their favorite. They cling to every tree. It's like they replace the leaves for a couple of days."

"That sounds beautiful."

"It's early for them to be here, but in a couple of weeks you should be able to see it for yourself." He looked off to his left and held up a hand. "Hey, Dave. How you doing?"

There was a man sitting on a dock, fishing pole in hand. He nodded. "Good. Weather's nice and the fish are biting, so I can't complain."

The words were said in that Cajun accent she was starting to get used to. She'd heard Gavin practicing on Seraphina this morning as she'd snuck out of the main house with the lunch Sera had packed. She'd been determined to not allow her TV dad to meet Major. At some point that would happen, but she wanted a peaceful day with him.

"Do you make the rounds out here often?" She was curious about the man. Far more curious than she would normally be about someone who was helping her with research.

"We take turns with it, but one of us is always out here," he said as he maneuvered the boat into what seemed like a quieter part of the water. Trees rose all around her, their branches bowing back toward the surface. "They're pretty isolated, and cell phones don't always work."

It was one of the things she liked about this place. "How

did you end up down here? I assume you're not originally from here. Your accent isn't the same."

"I don't have an accent." He seemed to be in an excellent mood this morning. And a teasing one since his twang had been far more pronounced.

"I would bet anything you're from Texas." It was an accent no one could mistake. It was sharper and quicker than the molasses-coated accent of the deep south.

"Houston," he replied. "And then for a long time, North Carolina. I was stationed at Fort Bragg when I was in the military. Long story short, my mom passed away when I was in high school. About seven years later, my father married a woman who was originally from Papillon, and they decided to move here."

So they had a lot in common. Her father had died when she was young, too. His death had started all the chaos that had led her here. "Did you move here to be with your dad and stepmom?"

"I moved to be close to my dad. There wasn't anything left for me back in Houston. My father was diagnosed with early-onset dementia. His wife at the time decided she hadn't signed on for that and they divorced very quickly. I moved here to be close to him in case he needed me," he said quietly. "I lived with him for a while, but it recently got bad enough that I couldn't handle it on my own, and now he's at a facility."

"I'm sorry to hear that. My grandmother had it, too. I watched my mom try to take care of her, so I know how hard that can be." She remembered those days when her mother had to try to keep everything together. She would hear her mother crying when she thought everyone else was asleep.

There was a reason she put up with her mom, even at her most infuriating.

"He was why I left the way I did last night." Major turned the boat and then pointed. "That's where we're going. It's not inhabited, but there could be other people out here. Though I don't see any other boats."

She didn't care about the other people. She was worried she was taking Major away from something important. "Is he okay?"

"He was having a good couple of hours," Major replied. "The man who runs the facility called to let me know he'd asked about me. My dad doesn't recognize me most of the time. Well, that's not true. He recognizes me as other people. He often thinks it's a different decade."

"My grandma did, too. She thought I was my mom as a kid." Brynn could remember her mother telling her to go along with it, to be kind because her grandma had been a great mom and missed her babies.

"That must have been scary for a kid."

It had been at first, but her mom had been so calm she'd set the tone. "She was still my grandma. I think it's disturbing at any time. But last night was good? You got there in time to talk to him?"

He nodded, and she could see the peace the night before had brought him. "I did. It was the first time we've talked like that in months."

"I'm glad."

"I found out some things I didn't know before." He pulled up to the dock, and Dolly jumped out of the boat, her body nearly vibrating with excitement. The dog bounded toward land. "He's got this show he likes. It calms him down when he watches it." He stepped gracefully out of the boat, tying it to the dock before offering her a hand up. "I have you to thank for that."

She felt her heart squeeze with the emotion she always

felt when someone told her a show she'd been in helped them through hard times. "Really?"

He took her hand in his, and though the boat was unsteady, she felt safe enough to take the steps that brought her to the dock. "Really."

She set Duke down, and he looked around like he wasn't sure this was a place for dogs or people. Dolly was barking, trying to get him to come and play, but he stuck close to his momma.

She reached back into the boat for the bag that held their lunch and her art supplies. There was also a big, thick blanket Sera had told her was a necessity if they were going to spend the afternoon out here.

"I'm glad to hear that."

When he turned, she was a little too close, and for a moment they stood there, bodies almost brushing. All it would take to press their lips together would be for her to go up on her toes. He was so handsome, so masculine, and yet somehow gentle. Something about this man called to her in a way she'd never felt before.

His lips curled up as he stared down at her. "I tried to tell him I'd had dinner with Taylor. That was your character's name, right?"

She stepped back before she could make a complete fool of herself. He was far too tempting. "That was me. Taylor Smith-Price."

"He told me you were sixteen, and I should find a more mature woman," Major explained.

She wrinkled her nose. "I'm plenty mature, thank you."

"Come on. I'll take you to my favorite place." He started up the dock.

She was so flustered by this man. She followed behind him, and it was impossible not to consider that he looked as good from the back as he did the front. She was surprised he'd told his dad about her. "He didn't think you should date me?"

He glanced back at her as he moved toward the interior of the small island. "Who said anything about a date?"

Yep, definitely flustered. Why had she put it that way? Probably because she'd spent the entire night thinking about him. "A slip of the tongue. I told Gavin last night that it was just dinner. He got in yesterday evening and waited up to say hi. He was curious about who'd dropped me off. But it was dinner. Nothing more."

"Dates end in kissing, Brynn."

She followed him, Duke at her heels. "They don't always. Or are you telling me you've kissed twenty-three women in the last six months?"

She was still in awe of the amount of blind dates the man had been on. She wasn't about to talk to Gavin about it because there was definitely a rom-com in there somewhere.

"It was only twenty-two. Last night didn't count because the date didn't even start. And no. I did not kiss them all. Most of the dates ended in a hearty handshake."

"And one ended in an arrest."

"You know, I shouldn't count that one, either, since she didn't even order an appetizer," Major pointed out. "By the way, if you do go to the café at the Fillin' Station and they try to talk you into ordering the Cheese Puff Experience, don't. They make it sound all fancy but it's cheese puffs from the chip aisle. They open the bag tableside."

Such a weird place, and she was definitely ordering the cheese puffs. "So how many did you kiss?"

He stopped, his expression turning thoughtful. "A couple, but I didn't actually kiss them until we had a second date. I only went out with four of them more than once. I dated one for a couple of months. Other than that, it was mostly pleasant conversation and the agreement that we didn't fit the way we should. But I think if you and I went on a date, it would definitely end in kissing."

She didn't like how that made her heart rate tick up. The other thing she'd thought about the night before was what Gavin had said. This relationship couldn't go anywhere. She would spend her time here and then move on, and she didn't see Major fitting into her world. "How do you know that I would kiss you?"

Those way-too-full lips of his curled up at the corners. He was beautiful in a completely masculine way. "Oh, you would kiss me."

She wished that cocky look on his face didn't do something for her. "Would not."

"Now, that sounds like a challenge, Brynn."

Flirty Major was her catnip. She knew she shouldn't engage, but she couldn't help herself. She felt like she'd gone through the last couple of years on autopilot, and now she was back in a real, vibrant world. "One that doesn't matter because we're not dating. Unless this is a date. Is this a date?"

Dolly danced around her dad's legs as he considered the question. "Would you have said yes to a date?"

She didn't want to be anything but honest with him. "Yes. You know I would have said yes."

"And I also know you would let me kiss you," he said quietly before he went back to flirty. "But we're not on a date. This is my way of thanking you for saving me."

"I thought you paying for dinner was your thank-you."

He shrugged. "Let's say I'm very grateful. And just so you know, if we do date, you're going to have to be the one to kiss me."

Now, that definitely sounded like a challenge. "Oh, then we're never going to kiss, Major."

"I bet we do." He turned again and disappeared behind a large wall of green trees and bushes.

The sad thing was she wouldn't take that bet. Not even for a dollar because she got the feeling she would lose.

If they were dating. Which they were not.

She followed the well-worn trail and then Brynn stopped, all thoughts of flirting fleeing her brain because she found herself in the middle of a fantastical scene that couldn't possibly be real. She was in a circle of trees, the light flowing through the limbs and leaves like golden beams. A large dragonfly floated in and found a place to perch. It was like a scene out of a movie, like she'd walked through a mystical door and found herself in another land.

She could work here. She could think here. The world would slow down and there would be time for what she needed for once if she stayed in this place.

"Don't bring anyone else out here, Major," she whispered. "Tell everyone to keep this spot quiet. The director will want to film here, and they'll wreck it. No matter what they say about protecting the environment, they'll bring all kinds of equipment out."

"I happen to know the mayor put into the contract that they couldn't film out here. It's a preserve of sorts," Major said, his voice hushed. "You like the light?"

"It's magic and you know it." That light made the world seem softer. It drove out her insecurities and made everything seem more possible than it had been before.

"You do your thing. I'm going to be over here reading. Let me know when you're ready for lunch." He was already laying out the blanket. He lowered himself down and pulled out a book.

She'd expected him to want to talk, to treat this as more of a friendly lunch than to actually allow her to work. No one simply allowed her to work. It was why she had to carve out time to be alone. Dolly lay down next to Major, resting her head on his chest as he started to read.

He was here in case she needed him. He was here to keep her company if she wanted it.

He was here, and it was enough.

She pulled out her pad and started to sketch.

Major woke up to the sun on his face and realized it must have been at least an hour or two since he'd fallen asleep. The sun had been high in the sky before and now it was lower.

He'd read for a while and then eaten two of Sera's perfectly done chicken salad sandwiches. He'd silently handed Brynn one along with a bottle of water. She'd munched away as she'd sketched, her whole being focused on the work in front of her.

He'd managed to take both dogs for a walk, and then he'd come back and fallen asleep to the sound of her pencil moving across the paper. It had been soothing and had lulled him right into the nap he'd sworn he wouldn't take.

But when he'd fallen asleep, he hadn't had something warm and soft lying beside him.

He glanced down and sure enough, Brynn was next to him, and sometime while they'd been sleeping he'd gotten an arm under her neck and she'd curled into him, her hand resting on his chest.

Damn, it *was* a date. The best date he'd had in a long time. Maybe ever, since he already felt something for the woman next to him.

He shifted, and her eyes fluttered open.

She blinked up at him but didn't move. "Major? I must have fallen asleep. I did not start out this way. I promise."

She was so pretty, but his attraction went far beyond her

looks. There was something about this woman that calmed him. It had annoyed him that first day. He'd been the one on the verge of panic, and she'd been so calm and competent it had put him off slightly. But now he recognized how peaceful it was to be around her.

Well, except for physically. Physically it was starting to get uncomfortable, but it was far too early for that.

Was it too early to kiss her? Or for her to kiss him?

He put his hand over hers to let her know it was fine staying right where it was. "How did you start out?"

"I wanted to get this point of view, looking up at the sky through the trees, but I stayed on my side of the blanket," she explained. "I don't know how I got here."

He was pretty sure he did. Natural attraction. "You must be a snuggler. It's okay. I don't mind a good snuggle. And I used to do that when I was a kid. I would lie back and look at the sky through the trees. It was like the world changed simply because I shifted positions. I think we're on a date, Brynn."

She frowned at him, her face turning up. "What makes you think that? We've barely talked to each other."

That was true, but he'd kind of thought she'd needed some space. She'd been nervous in the boat, but the minute they'd made it to this patch of paradise, all of that had fallen away and she'd become an artist. She likely would have sat there and let a gator walk by without noticing it unless she was going to draw the sucker. But she was right that he hadn't exactly romanced her. He sought a way to turn this around because he wanted that kiss.

When he thought about it, she was using a very traditional definition of *date*. "If I'd taken you to the movies, we would have talked in the car, but then we would have simply enjoyed the movie quietly. We talked in the boat and then we enjoyed nature quietly. There was even a meal."

"We would have talked about the movie during the meal," she pointed out, but she still didn't move even an inch from him.

"You were still working. You didn't want to talk. You wanted to work."

"Did I thank you for that? Most guys would have felt like I was ignoring them."

"You were, but I don't mind. You are obviously an artist, and from what I saw today, you're a good one. You were in the zone, so I enjoyed my day off by reading a book, taking a nap, and watching you work."

She cuddled closer to him, her leg brushing his. "You are a remarkably tolerant guy, Deputy Major."

He was, but in this case, there was a reason for it. "You remind me of my mom. Not in a weird way. In an artist way. She taught high school art. She always wanted to make a living off her own work, but it never happened for her. The paintings in my house were done by her."

Now she sat up, staring down at him. "The landscapes?"

Damn, he'd lost her, but it was still nice to talk. He should have had this conversation with her the day before, but he'd been all growly and grumpy. "Yes. She worked in oils and watercolors. My dad put them up all over the house. She sold many of them, but never enough to support us."

"Most artists don't, though there are a lot more opportunities to get our work out there these days. Major, she was good. I'd like to see the rest of her work. The one I saw in your living room was beautiful. She understood composition."

"Yes, she talked a lot about composition and making sure you knew your focal point." She'd tried to teach him, but he'd been far too busy with football and science fiction. He'd been called the nerdy jock, and he'd been okay with that. But art hadn't been his thing. "How did you come to love art?"

She started to reach out, like she wanted her hand on his chest, but then pulled back.

He covered her hand with his and brought it right over his heart.

She relaxed. "I always liked to draw. Ever since I was a kid. There was a set designer on my first show who I used to hang out with because she often brought her own kids to work. She was the one who bought me my first set of paints and taught me how to use them. It's been my happy place ever since. I pretty much keep a sketchpad with me at all times. When I find the right image, something that really grabs hold of me, I use the drawing as a starting point for a painting."

"So the drawings are like taking pictures? Wouldn't most people use their phones?" Major asked. He'd been out with a couple of women who were obsessed with social media and constantly taking pictures of everything. Their food. Their clothes. Every room they happened to walk into. He was surprised because he'd checked out Brynn's socials and they were full of pictures, but he hadn't seen her take a single one. Now that he thought about it, none of the recent pictures were of her in Papillon.

"I do sometimes, but I find drawings remind me of what I felt better than pictures. There's an emotional component to it."

"What did you draw today?"

"The trees and the water. I drew the boat tied to the dock. I drew the dogs." She grinned shyly. "I drew you."

"You did?"

She nodded solemnly.

"I think we're definitely on a date, Brynn." He liked the idea that she'd found him interesting enough to put on paper. He didn't personally think there was anything all that intriguing about him, but he liked the idea that she did. And he found her endlessly fascinating. "Otherwise, it's weird that you watched me while I was sleeping."

She bit her bottom lip gently, her gaze settling on him. "Does that mean I have to kiss you?"

"Only if you want to. I can handle it if you don't." A lie. He wanted her to kiss him. He wanted her to plant those gorgeous lips right on top of his and wrap her body around him.

Her expression went serious and she shifted, getting closer to him. She stared down at him for a moment, blocking out the sun, but he didn't mind. It made a halo around her head, illuminating her eyes, and for a second, she was almost too beautiful to look at.

She reached a hand out, touching his face, letting her fingers brush over his jaw before running the pad of her thumb over his lips. He was still beneath her, allowing her to explore his skin.

Then she leaned over and brought her lips to his, a soft brushing that sparked something to life in Major, something he hadn't felt before. Her lips were warm and sweetly innocent against his, but he had the wildest impulse to take control and lose himself in her. He'd wanted women, but he'd never felt this wildfire of desire he had the instant Brynn kissed him.

He stayed still as she kissed him, allowing her to explore while his heart rate ticked up and he could feel need flood his body. It felt good. He hadn't truly wanted anything in so long. He'd been walking through his days, simply getting through each hour, and now he realized how empty that had been.

She kissed him over and over, her hands starting to graze his chest, and he wondered how long he would be able to stay still. She was driving him crazy with each touch.

Then her mouth opened and he felt the tentative brush of her tongue, and he had his answer.

His hands came up, winding around her and drawing her closer as he took over the kiss. He eased her over to take the dominant position and she went soft, clinging to him.

Then he was the one staring down at her. "This is a bad idea, but I can't seem to help myself."

"Bad idea?"

"You're going to leave me, and I'm pretty sure you're going to break my heart, Brynn. But I can't make myself care right now." Every word was proven true because he couldn't help lowering his head and kissing her again.

"You're a pessimist, Deputy Major," she whispered against his lips. "You don't know what I'll do."

But he did. She would leave and he would stay, but why did that matter now? He spent so much time worried about the future that he never enjoyed the present. He was living in the moment, and the moment right now included Brynn. "It doesn't matter. Like I said, I can't help myself."

He lowered his head down and kissed her again.

That was when Dolly decided to bark.

He looked over and both dogs were staring at them, seemingly disgruntled.

Brynn started giggling, her arms still around him.

Next time, he was getting a dog-sitter. He thought about ignoring them entirely, but then he heard the sound of a boat.

Maybe it wasn't coming here. Maybe it would power right on by them.

"Hey, Major! You here?"

Armie. He sighed and reluctantly rolled off Brynn. "It's my boss. I'm sorry. Sometimes things go wrong and I get called in on my off days."

"Brynn! Brynn! Are you out here? Baby, are you hurt? I swear to god and on every lawyer I can hire that if my baby is hurt I will make sure you never work in law enforcement again."

Brynn practically turned white. "That's my mother. Why is my mom here? She doesn't like nature."

He helped her up. He was going to bet her mom wouldn't like him, either.

chapter six

⟡

"I wish you'd had your radio on you. We could have saved a lot of trouble," Armie said as Major stepped on the dock. "Ms. Pearson doesn't like not knowing where her daughter is. I tried to explain to her that Brynn couldn't possibly be a missing person because other people knew where she was. I had Seraphina talk to her, but she wouldn't listen."

He glanced up to the dock where Brynn was currently talking to her mother. Her mom looked like a way more up-tight version of Brynn. She was wearing a power suit and what had to be five-inch heels, and he had to admit the woman made them work. She hadn't tripped on the uneven ground or wobbled when she'd strode across the island, yelling for her baby.

"I didn't bring my radio because it's my day off and I wanted to relax. I've been on call for weeks," Major pointed out.

"You're never not on call," Armie replied, his eyes narrowing. "And that is not my fault. I have to force you to take a day off. You're the man who keeps your radio on all night." Armie's lips curled up in a Cheshire Cat–like grin. "You like the actress."

He did, but he wasn't sure admitting that to one of the worst gossips in town was a smart idea. Oh, Armie wouldn't admit it, but the man liked to talk. "She helped me out yesterday, and I thought I would pay her back by showing her around Papillon."

"Yeah, we should talk about how she helped you," Armie began, his face falling.

"Hey, are you Tighty-Whitie?"

He turned and remembered that Brynn's mother hadn't come alone. She'd been accompanied by Brynn's sister, who hated everything. Everything. The young woman had complained constantly since they'd been introduced. He'd been pretty sure she wouldn't remember his name, and now he was sure. "I'm Major Blanchard."

Ally Pearson was in her early twenties, and her hair was cut in a chic bob, the tips a vibrant purple contrasting with the almost white blond. She wore a long boho-style skirt and a tiny tank top she'd tied to show off her flat stomach. She held up her phone and snapped a quick pic of him. "Nope. You're Tighty-Whitie. And if you had been smart enough to not get caught in mud, I would still be in LA. I was supposed to have another week before I got dragged to this hellhole. But no, you had to jump into quicksand with that insanely adorable dog of yours."

"It wasn't quicksand." Major was deeply confused and a little hurt. There was only one way he could think of that Ally would know he'd gotten caught in his underwear. "Brynn talked to you? Is that what she called me?"

"Brynn doesn't talk to me about anything except how I should be more like her." She made a vomiting sound. "No, that's what they're calling you on the Internet because they haven't figured out who you are yet. Although I would expect the nickname to stick. It's cooler than Major. That's a weird name, and I know a woman named Bexely."

"Yep, buddy, that's what I was about to tell you." Armie leaned in. "I'm afraid you've gone viral."

"What?" He hoped Armie wasn't saying what he thought he was saying.

"Viral, as in a viral video," Armie explained. "I told you about how the nature cams caught most of the rescue, right? Well, Roxie made Zep pull it off the website, but some eagle-eyed fans of Brynn's figured out it was her, and they managed to make a copy. It's got three million views, according to Brynn's sister."

Ally frowned at him. "I have a name. I'm not merely an extension of my sister no matter how my mom treats me. One of the things I do is run Bria Knight's social media. I found it and put it on our Insta. Bria Knight is being hailed as a hero, and you are being called Tighty-Whitie. The dog's a star, too. She's got real charisma. You should get an agent now."

His head was starting to pound. "An agent?"

Armie sighed. "She's not actually giving you bad advice. We've had a couple of reporters call, and one person who said she's a casting agent. They want to talk to you. Someone named Hyacinth. Weird accent."

Ally rolled her eyes. "That's because she's not actually from England. She's from Queens. She confuses that with being an actual queen, which she is not. Don't sign with her unless all you want to do is underwear commercials. She puts people in categories, and they never get out."

"I do not need an agent." How many people had watched the video? He was going to kill Zep.

Ally shrugged and took another picture, this one of the boat. "Are you doing my sister? I'm surprised. She doesn't usually work this fast, but I will admit you're hot in a small-town, upstanding, probably-does-it-missionary-only way."

Armie snorted but was clearly leaving it up to Major to handle the situation.

That felt like judgment. "That is none of your business. And I will not be signing with any casting agent. I have a job."

"Sure you do." Ally managed to sound like she couldn't care about anything less. "Suit yourself, but if you want to stick close to Brynn, you should understand that no man will ever be good enough for my mom with the exception of Stephen Cane."

He wished Brynn would finish up with her mother so they could get out of here. "Who is Stephen Cane?"

Those eyes rolled again, and she turned to yell her sister's way. "Brynn, your boyfriend is an idiot!"

"Apparently Stephen Cane is another actor person and he would never put Brynn at risk the way you did, and he's going to show up at some point to kick your ass," Armie whispered. "I made Roxie google him. He's one of Brynn's costars. He played a soldier on TV once. And a street fighter with mystical powers."

Why would Brynn have not mentioned she had a boyfriend? He glanced back and she looked utterly overwhelmed by her mom. Her whole body was tight, from the flat line of her mouth to the way she held her shoulders to how rigid she stood.

"She doesn't have a boyfriend," Major said. Dolly was dancing around the two women as though they would start playing at any moment. His dog didn't know how to read a room, but Duke did. He stood silently at his mom's side, looking up like he wanted to offer her comfort. "She would have told me. She wouldn't lie, and she wouldn't omit important information."

"Sounds like you learned a lot about her in, what? Two dates?" Armie asked in an annoyingly self-assured tone. "It's all over town that you dumped poor Sam Henshaw for the Hollywood actress. You should expect some harsh words from her grandmother."

He felt a growl start. "I did no such thing. Sam dumped me because . . ."

He wasn't sure she was out fully. Except she'd kissed her girlfriend in full view of Guidry's, but it was still her story to tell.

"Brynn is your second choice." A smug expression crossed Ally's face. "I like it. She's always so perfect."

She turned and jogged up the dock.

He was probably about to get in trouble with Brynn.

He shifted his attention to Armie. "I'm sorry about the chaos."

Armie shrugged. "It was a slow day. I met my guy and he started asking if there was something called Orangetheory in town. It took me forever to figure out it's some kind of gym. I told him about that Wednesday yoga group and the classes at the rec center. I don't think we speak the same language. Before these two showed up he was calling around to see if he could find something called tempeh."

"It's a vegan protein. Ask Lila. I'm sure she knows where to find it." Armie was going to have to expand his horizons. "Why didn't he handle Brynn's mom? According to Brynn, they know each other. Brynn's worked with him a lot."

"Oh, he heard the mom's voice and ran out the opposite door," Armie explained. "Just told me he would be back tomorrow, and he whispered it like he didn't want to risk her hearing him. Then he told me he hoped I lived and snuck out. I wish I'd snuck out with him. She's really loud. And creative with her threats."

"I'm sorry. I don't think Brynn had any idea her mom was coming out this early. And I don't think she knew our rescue video had gone viral."

"You okay with that? You're a pretty private guy. You know we've all been in bad spots before. There's no shame in a woman saving you."

"I have no problems with a woman saving me. I'm not some Neanderthal asshole. Roxie's saved me several times, and never once have I thought, 'You know, I wish she was a man.' Now, having my nearly naked butt out there is another story. I should have tied those sweats on tighter." Brynn's mom was pointing his way, but Major couldn't hear what she was saying. It didn't look like it was anything good. "I'm sure it will blow over quickly."

Someone would video their cat playing piano and he would be old news.

"I'm not so sure about that. Like I told you, we've already had some calls. It won't be long before you get identified," Armie replied with a sigh. "The good news is your butt looks good." Armie quickly held up his hands in a gesture of pure innocence. "That's what my wife says. She said you have nothing to be ashamed of and told me I should ask you about your glute routine. Says I'm getting soft. I don't think so. I think my butt looks good for a forty-four-year-old with three kids."

Major snorted. Armie might be well into his forties, but he would give it to the man. He hadn't gone soft anywhere but in how he dealt with the people around him. Dolly started barking. "I think I'm going to have to go save Brynn's mom from my dog."

Dolly could be a lot.

Brynn's mom huffed and then turned to the dog, and for a moment he worried he would have to save Dolly. Then the well-dressed woman leaned over and put both hands on Dolly, petting her.

Maybe she wasn't so bad.

"You sure you know what you're getting into?" Armie asked.

He had no idea, but he was pretty sure he couldn't pull away now. "Nope. But I'm going in. You should be ready to deal with an even madder momma because Brynn and I should talk, and I don't think we need an audience."

"Really?" Armie managed to put just enough whine into his tone that Major knew he understood what was about to happen.

"Yep. I like her a lot. I want to spend time with her while she's here. I'm not ready for this day of ours to be over so I'm hoping you'll do me a favor and deal with her mom if Brynn chooses to go with me." There was a time for a man to sit back and a time to take action. He'd already had his nap for the day. Brynn seemed upset and he wasn't going to let the day end this way.

Armie sighed but nodded.

And Major knew it was time to take care of Brynn.

"What were you thinking? You didn't answer your cell phone all day. What was I supposed to do?" Her mother had just stepped off the dock and the accusations were already flying. She'd come out onto the bayou in a Chanel suit, Louboutin stilettos, and enough Cartier to probably fund a whole government department in Papillon.

Brynn glanced down to where Major was talking to his boss, who'd brought her mom and sister out in one of the county boats. It was slightly bigger than Major's, but it still would have been a little scary for a woman who'd spent the last forty years of her life in cities. Not that her mother would let fear stop her. She'd stormed down that dock like she owned the place.

"Well, I didn't think your response to a couple hours of me being out of touch would be hopping on a jet to come halfway across the country a week before you're supposed to. The service out here is spotty at best. I explained that to you." She'd gathered up her sketchpad and what had been left of lunch. "I wasn't ignoring your calls. I know better than to do that."

"Don't make me sound like some overbearing stage mother." She completely ignored the fact that there was a fifty-pound overly stimulated dog barking like mad ten feet from her.

Brynn stared at her.

"Fine. I am, but there are reasons for the stereotype," her mother insisted. "I do it all to protect you and help you grow your career. You cannot grow your career if you die in the middle of a swamp with some man I don't even know."

She had no idea why her mom had chosen this moment to let her overly protective freak flag fly. While Dolly jumped around trying to get some attention, Duke settled in between Brynn and her mother, silently watching the scene play out. He never liked it when they were at odds, so Brynn tried to sound less annoyed than she actually was. "He's a deputy. He knows this place like the back of his hand. I was and am perfectly safe."

Her mom looked down the dock to where Major stood talking to the sheriff. Ally was still down there, her phone up, taking pictures of everything like it was part of her job. Which it was. "I doubt that you were safe. You can be very naive about men. I knew that man would be trouble the minute I saw his rather muscular ass."

"What?"

It was her mother's turn to stare. "You have no idea what I'm talking about, do you? I should have listened to Ally. She said you were clueless about this. Do you get no media out here? Have you not been watching your socials?"

"I pay Ally to watch my socials." She didn't need to read comments about how pretty she was, because they also inevitably came with comments about how fat she was or how she was attempting to enforce an unattainable beauty standard on the rest of the world. Ally loved dealing with that stuff. It never seemed to bother her, even on her own socials.

Her mom sighed. "I should have known you wouldn't even be looking when something fabulous happened. You went viral, darling. We need to jump on this now. I've got all the morning shows fighting over who gets to talk to you first."

Brynn was so confused. "Why would I go . . ." It hit her forcibly. Major had told her there was a camera out in those woods. A nature cam that caught the whole thing. But from what he'd said it was something the Papillon Parish Animal Services Department did to get kids interested in nature, and it almost never caught anything interesting. "How did it get out? I can't imagine there are a bunch of eyes on that website."

Her mother rubbed a hand over Brynn's cheek, a familiar gesture of her affection. "Well, there are now, and this tiny town should thank you. You're going to put it on the map."

She wasn't sure they wanted to be on any map her mother would consider worthy of her time. "Okay, so let me get this straight. Someone found the video footage of me helping Major out of the mud, it's gone viral, and you really came here because you want me to go on a bunch of news shows to get publicity out of it."

Her mother frowned. "Well, I was also deeply worried about you. If they'd told me there was quicksand out here, I would never have allowed you to come alone. I would have sent a bodyguard with you."

"A bodyguard to protect me from mud?"

"Or a highly rated nature guide," her mom argued. "The point is this place is dangerous, and you shouldn't be out here all by yourself. I know you're trying to get into the role, but your safety comes first. You know rural people have odd ways."

Her mom was going to be such a hit in this town. "And

city folk get vampire facials. Mom, it's a nice small town. It's not some horror show where they're going to sacrifice me to keep their crops going."

Her mother's expression changed. Well, as much as it ever changed, because she was serious about frown lines.

Brynn rolled her eyes. "No, we're not making that movie. It's already been done. *Wicker Man.*"

"Never mind. The point is we're here now and you're safe." She glanced around. "What is this place and why are you here? The sheriff person said something about butterflies."

"It's what they call the island. I was out here relaxing."

"You were out here sketching. Of course. I can see the appeal. If I looked through those sketches, how many would be of that man? I don't blame you, Brynn. Like I said, I see the appeal. He has a very nice body."

Apparently a whole lot of people had seen the appeal. The thought made her gut knot. "How bad is it?"

"Oh, it's quite good. Those shorts of his don't hide much. Do you think Ally could get a couple of pictures of him out of his shirt for your website? And also, could we get him to smile? He's so frowny in the video."

"He thought he was going to die."

"So he's very dramatic. Well, that's disappointing. I thought he would be stoic given his living circumstances and his job. I don't know that a police officer should have a dramatic streak."

"He could have actually died. There are snakes and stuff in the water. Look, none of this matters. I'm not going on a talk show. Major isn't going to like the attention."

"Then he shouldn't be escorting you around." Her mom said the words gently, as though this was where she'd been leading her to all along. "Attention is part of who you are. It's part of your career. I did come out here because I think you should use this. It's excellent publicity. You look good on that video. You don't look like some pampered Hollywood princess. You look calm and cool and competent. You look like you."

It was something they talked about all the time. Brynn hated the stereotype she often faced. She was nothing more than a pretty face with no real talent, that she was richer than she truly was, that she didn't work for any of it. She was blond, so many people thought she didn't have a brain in her head. When she did pressers, her male costars got asked thoughtful questions about what the film had to say or how their characters changed them. She was asked about her costumes and if she was in a romance with the male costar. Even when said male costar was the closest thing to a father she'd ever had. "Can I think about it?"

"You know if you want to change the narrative, you have to be willing to do what it takes," her mother said sagely. "And I don't understand why the major wouldn't want some publicity. He could get something out of it."

"It's not *the major*. It's Major. It's his name."

Her mom nodded like she'd made an important point. "And the sheriff's name is Armie. I'm sensing a theme here. Does everyone have military names? I've heard the rurals can be very patriotic."

"The sheriff's name is Armand. It's a Cajun name. Armie is his nickname. And I don't think Major's going to be happy his nearly bare backside is all over the Internet."

"All right. That's not ideal, but we can work with it," her mom allowed. "You're the important one here. You know, when you think about it, you really saved the dog. Do you think he would let the dog be in the spot?"

"Mom, I just found out that Brynn was on a date with Tighty-Whitie last night, but only because his actual date turned him down." Ally strode up, a smug look on her face. And a familiar skirt on her body.

Brynn gasped at her sister's entitlement. Especially since she had only bought that skirt last week and hadn't even worn it yet. "Hey, that's mine."

Ally twirled around. "Looks better on me. Can you get TW to pose with you? I want to do a whole post on how you're getting comfy in the sticks with the man you saved from certain death by quicksand."

"It wasn't quicksand, and don't call him that." She shouldn't have left her sister anywhere close to Major. Ally was known for being able to offend even the most laid-back of people. "You already did, didn't you?"

Ally shrugged. "It's better than his real name. Oh, and you should know there are already some reporters coming out here because the rumors about you and Gavin are starting up again. You should have known that would happen when you agreed to do a movie with him."

"I'm playing his daughter," she said between clenched teeth. She could feel herself flushing with the old embarrassment. The rumors about her and the man who'd been like a father to her could always bring her low.

Would Major hear the rumors? Would he believe them?

"That only makes it more interesting to the tabloids." Her mother sighed, a long-suffering sound. "Darling, you know everyone loves a good scandal."

"There is no scandal. He's always been kind to me, nothing more," Brynn insisted. She felt tears pulse behind her eyes and her fists were clenched at her sides. All the relaxation of the day was gone in a rush of anxiety.

"Well, of course he has." Her mom's voice had gone soothing. "Darling, I'm not saying Gavin ever made a move on you. But no one wants to hear that. It's an age-old story.

Beautiful young woman and an aging-somewhat-gracefully old man."

"He's only a year older than you," Brynn pointed out.

"Is he? He seems older." Her mom smoothed back her hair. "Don't worry about it. I'll bring Stephen out. He's dying to see you. Between letting the photogs take a couple of pics of you with him and doing the morning shows with the dog, everyone will forget those nasty rumors."

"She's doing the morning show with the dog?" Ally asked.

"Well, that Tighty . . ." Her mom seemed to change her mind when she heard the growl that came from Brynn. ". . . Mr. Major Deputy person doesn't seem to want to go on television for some reason. Perhaps he's got some secrets he needs to hide. So we're going to focus the whole story on saving this beautiful, crazed, poorly trained animal." Her mother huffed and turned her attention to Dolly. Of course, the minute she actually looked at the pup, she melted. "Oh, you're prettier than he is. And you were a smart thing, weren't you? You barely got wet and he lost his pants."

Her mom had never met a dog she didn't love. Her mother would turn up her nose at a person not wearing the right clothes for dinner, but a mangy dog covered in fleas was something to save.

It was another reason she put up with her mom. She was complex. She was human.

"I'll ask Major if he's okay with us hijacking his dog." She wasn't sure she wanted to do the morning shows, but she also knew if she didn't, they might show up here in town to track her down. If they tracked her down, they might find Major, and she didn't want that for him. The press could be invasive when they wanted to be, and fans could be less than pleasant. Sometimes they forgot the person they claimed to love was an actual human being. Sometimes they were terribly cruel. They could make life very uncomfortable for a private person.

Was she being selfish trying to get close to him? Would she bring him trouble? More trouble than she was worth.

She brushed a frustrated tear off her cheek. If the press was around, she couldn't show a moment's weakness.

She wished they were back on that blanket. The day had been so peaceful. She'd felt . . . free. She'd known she wasn't really free. No one was, but for those hours she'd been with him, she'd felt all of her burdens lift. She'd been able to concentrate on what felt important to her.

"Well, we should go and settle in to the hotel." Her mother reached out and picked up Duke, cradling him to her chest like she had so many times before. "Come along, dear. That sheriff person's boat will hold us all. When we get back to dry land, we'll need to send someone out to get the essentials."

There were a couple of problems with her mom coming out early. "Production assistants aren't here yet, Mom."

Her mother turned to Ally. "Oh, but one is."

Ally groaned. "Naturally. I get to run around this place looking for decent coffee."

"This place has excellent coffee. There's a grocery store close to the town square. You can't miss it. It's the one with the alligator statue in front of it in honor of our town mascot." Major was walking down the dock, a determined look on his face. When he concentrated his jaw went straight.

She couldn't help but remember how his whole face had softened when she'd kissed him. He'd relaxed and let her explore right up until the moment he'd taken over.

That had been a revelation. Her whole body had felt electric, and she'd realized that this was what it meant to deeply want a man. She'd thought she'd felt desire before, but it had been nothing like the need that had flooded her system when Major had flipped her over onto her back and pressed her into the blanket. In that moment, she would have gone anywhere he led. She wouldn't have cared if he'd stripped her down and taken her right there on the ground.

He was a dangerous man. Dangerous to her goals and her heart. He'd talked about how she could break his heart, but she thought he could do the same to hers. The right play would be to walk away now. It would be best for both of them. She could thank him for the lovely day and then avoid being alone with him again because she wouldn't be able to trust herself.

He held a hand out. "Brynn, come with me. We need to talk."

"Uhm, hello, I flew for hours to get here. Brynn will come with me," her mother said. "If you are so inclined, you may join us at our hotel later this evening. I would like to talk to you about your dog. I think she could be a star."

Her mom had given him her brightest smile, the one she used on producers and directors.

Major kept his hand out, and she realized he was allowing her to make the choice. The one she knew she had to make and had just had a whole inner monologue about.

She didn't even hesitate. She threw that inner monologue away. It needed a rewrite. She put her hand in his and felt warmth flood her system, her instincts telling her this was the only place for her to be. "Take care of Duke for me. I'll be back later."

"Brynn!" her mother shouted.

She ran with Major down the dock, Dolly barking and racing beside them as though this was the best day ever. The dog bounded onto the boat and took her place at the front, eager for the next adventure.

When Brynn got in the boat this time, she wasn't afraid.

"Seriously?" The sheriff was frowning at Major from the dock. "You're leaving me with them?"

Ally was still taking pictures, but her mother was making her way down the planking, Duke settled into her Louis Vuitton bag.

Major flashed a grin. "Do you remember when you left me to deal with the entire bachelorette party after they found out the groom was sleeping with the bride's sister?"

Armie held a hand up. "Peace, brother. Now we're even."

"Sheriff! I demand you arrest that man." Her mother's glare promised retribution somewhere down the line if her will wasn't exerted. "He is stealing my daughter."

Her mom should have been the actress. She was very dramatic, and she could sell a scene when she wanted to. "I'll see you soon, Mom. I promise."

But as Major started to pull away from the dock, she kind of wished they could float away forever.

chapter seven

Major maneuvered the boat away from the island.

"Aren't you going the wrong way?" Brynn sat on the seat across from him, watching the water. "This isn't the way we came in."

"If I go that way, I assure you we'll be able to hear your momma cursing my name the whole ride. The point was to get away, not gain a soundtrack," he grumbled.

She turned in her seat and then those gorgeous eyes were on him, her lips curled down in the cutest frown. "You're going to be grumpy again." She sighed. "Not that I can blame you. My mom can be a lot, and we're in a situation neither of us planned to be in. I need to talk to you about that."

"Armie mentioned it. Apparently we've gone viral, and I have a new nickname. That will teach me to skip laundry day. I usually wear boxers. I've come to realize boxers are absolutely the more respectable of the underwears," Major replied. "And I'm not grumpy. Your sister irritated me, and it's obvious your mom is not a big fan of mine. Who is Stephen?"

How much had Ally managed to spill in the short time

she'd talked to Major? "He's a friend. We grew up in the business together."

He nodded. "She tried to tell me he was your boyfriend, but I knew he wasn't. You wouldn't have kissed me if you have a boyfriend."

"I don't have a boyfriend, though the press will try to twist any relationship I do have into something serious, and that's what we should talk about."

This was why he'd decided to sweep her away from her mom. They needed to talk and he didn't think it was a good idea to wait. He'd seen the worried expression on her face, and he rather thought the anxiety wasn't for her. He'd known her mom had told her something that made her rethink what had happened only moments before. Deep down he knew he should rethink it, too, but he didn't want to. He wanted to kiss her again, wanted to explore this thing they had for as long as they could. "I suppose we should have expected it would get out. I thought we might escape unscathed because who watches that feed? Who spends their time watching a bunch of birds or deer or gators do what they do?"

"Habitat streaming is a big thing right now," she replied. "And someone is always watching."

"Out here they usually aren't." Had she been reminded of how she always had eyes on her? They hadn't talked much about how she felt about that aspect of her career. It had to be the worst part. He was sure some people thrived on the attention, but he didn't think Brynn was one of them. "I know it seems like everyone is up in everyone else's business, but it's usually well-meaning."

"You think you understand gossip, but you don't until the whole world is talking about you. People you don't know. People you'll never meet. People who think they know exactly who you are." She turned back to the water. "I'm sorry. My mom told me that the rumors are back about me and

Gavin. It hurts because he's like a weird boho dad to me. It upsets me when I'm accused of sleeping with him."

It would upset him, too. "I'm sorry about that. Is it because you're working on a movie together?"

"Yes, but I'm sure it's come out now because we both came in early to prep," she said. "We're staying in a romantic B and B close together, and my mom and sister weren't here with me. So someone put two and two together, and I'm in a gross relationship with my TV dad. He's almost thirty years older than me. I know that works for some people, but he really is a father figure."

"You know there's a simple solution to this problem."

"Getting out of acting entirely? Don't think I haven't thought about it," she said, almost too quietly to hear over the hum of the motor.

"That wasn't what I meant." She'd worked hard for her career, and she'd started so young. She seemed to have escaped all the pitfalls of child stardom. From what he could tell, Brynn was confident and steady and well adjusted. "I meant maybe it'll quiet those rumors down if we see each other."

She was silent for a moment. "I should have known that would be your solution. You're very much a gentleman, Deputy Major." She glanced around. "Where are we going? Are we just drifting?"

"There's a fishing cabin up ahead." He pointed toward the island they were heading to. "A friend of mine owns it, and I happen to know he's not using it this weekend. He lets me hang out here when I want to. I thought since it's getting late, you might be hungry again."

He thought they needed to talk before she started making decisions without him. If her mom had her way, she likely wouldn't even show up at the station house to shadow Roxie. She might go back to LA and not return until filming started.

"I could eat. Are you going to fish for our supper?"

"I won't have to. This particular cabin is owned by my billionaire friend. He doesn't do a ton of fishing. It's more a place for him and his wife to get away when they need to. He keeps it well stocked."

"Billionaire friend?"

"Doesn't everyone have one of those? His name is Rene, and we've been playing poker together for years." He started for the dock as Dolly's tail thumped. "He probably has some beer in there, too. You look like you could use one. I know I could."

She stared at him, her hands in her lap as he cut the motor. "I don't think this is going to work."

"The beer? It's probably pretty good beer. Like I said, he's a billionaire."

She frowned his way. "That's not what I meant."

"I know what you meant, but I think we should talk about it." He stood and moved to tie the boat off before stepping onto the dock. Dolly was already halfway up to the cabin. Rene and Sylvie had fixed the old place up since they got married and had their daughter. It was a nice place to bring Brynn. A place where she would be comfortable.

Though she'd seemed awfully comfortable anywhere they'd been. For a city girl, she took all the crazy country stuff in stride. It had been her mom who'd shut her down. Or rather the news her mom had brought.

She allowed him to help her onto the dock. "Yes, we should, because I don't think you understand what's happened."

"The world saw me in my shorts getting saved by a gorgeous woman. And they now know that my dog is willing to leave me behind for a couple of treats." He pulled her close, bringing their bodies together. He stared down at her lovely face. "I wish it had stayed private, but it didn't. I'm not ashamed you saved me. You know that, right? I'm very grateful you were there."

"It's more than that." Despite the pessimism in her tone, her body had relaxed, her hands finding his waist in a natural way. Like they'd been getting close for years instead of only sharing a few kisses. "You don't know how crazy things can get."

"Then tell me," he said, his head dipping low. "Tell me, and maybe this time I can save you."

She groaned when his lips brushed hers, but she didn't make a single move to get away. "You're not taking this seriously."

"I assure you, I'm taking you very seriously." He cupped the nape of her neck and deepened the kiss, allowing their mouths to play for a moment before stepping back because they did have things to talk about. "Come on, Brynn. Steal a billionaire's beer with me and we'll see if he's got some canned chili for us."

Her nose wrinkled but she was grinning again. "Shouldn't he have caviar or something?"

He took her hand and started to lead her across the yard. There was a walkway made of natural stone that led up to the pretty cabin Rene's grandfather had built seventy years before. "Rene's a laid-back rich guy. There's a reason he's stayed here in Papillon when he could live anywhere he wants."

"All the rich people I know are obsessed with the business." She studied the cabin as he retrieved the key from the hiding place in one of the rocker's cushions. There were three rockers now—two full-sized ones, and a tiny rocker Major had given Sylvie as a baby gift. His father had loved woodworking, and Major found comfort in it. He'd had Harry help him in Harry's shop.

"I think that is a universal thing." He opened the door

and whistled because Dolly had gone completely rogue. She was running circles around the cabin, zoomies taking over. "All the cops I know are obsessed with cop stuff." He followed her inside. Dolly would run off some of her energy and then come barking at the door when she wanted to be let in. "Now, why don't you tell me what you're worried about? Because I get the feeling you are rethinking the idea of giving me a second date. I should warn you. I'll be let down. I was counting on it after the Sam Henshaw debacle. I need you to lift my profile in the parish or I might end up alone the rest of my life."

"You were easier to deal with when you were grumpy," she said, perching on the comfortable sofa.

He moved to the fridge and sure enough, Rene had it stocked. He pulled out two longnecks and popped the tops. "Talk to me, Brynn. Tell me why you went from happy to on the edge. It can't be about that video going viral."

She took the beer and took a long swig. "Yes, it can. You don't understand what it means."

"Are you sure this isn't about your mom? Were you upset she found us together?" It was the explanation he was most afraid of.

"I don't care that she found us together. Despite what she thinks, she is not in charge of my romantic relationships. I date who I want to date."

That's what he wanted to hear. "Good, then we can get back to it. Your mother doesn't intimidate me."

"She should. All of this should intimidate you."

"Then how should we handle it? I overheard your mom saying something about doing an interview. I can handle that. We give them what they want, and two minutes after something else will happen and they'll forget all about us," he said. "What would you do if you weren't worried about me? What if it had only been Dolly you'd saved?"

"I would likely do some talk shows and talk about keeping your pets safe and adopting animals."

"Then let's do it, and you can talk about the dangers of allowing men to run wild and off their leashes." He thought it was kind of funny. He'd been embarrassed, but it wasn't like he'd done anything wrong. He'd panicked and tried to save his dog.

He'd watched Dolly go down and thought, *Absolutely not.* He couldn't save his dad, but he could save her. He couldn't let one more thing he loved go under without trying everything.

She stared at him for a moment. "I don't know. Maybe. But then I also think that I could be getting you into something you won't like and all for what . . . a couple of weeks of seeing each other? I'm very attracted to you, Major. I haven't been so attracted to a man in forever. But my job doesn't allow for a lot of relationship time. There's a reason actors' relationships don't tend to last. We're always off somewhere working. People on the outside make it look glamorous, but it's a hard industry. Unless you're working on a long-running TV show, you're most likely on a set for six to eight weeks and then it's off to another one, if you're lucky. I've got a couple of weeks off after this movie is done, but only because I haven't booked a gig yet."

"Brynn, if you're afraid you're going to hurt me, then you should know that I'm a big boy. I can handle it. If it's not worth it because we both know this isn't a forever thing, then I can take you home right now and we'll remain friendly. But I think I might be willing to spend a couple of weeks with you even knowing you'll leave."

He wanted to get to know her. Some deep instinct told him this could be an important relationship. Even if it wasn't a permanent one. "The decision is yours. We don't have to go fast. We can just hang out when you have the time."

"Why do you have to be so damn perfect, Deputy Major? Be like other men. Be an asshole. Be selfish."

"Oh, I assure you I'm not perfect." If she got to know him, that would be clear. "I can be stubborn and shut down. I can be needy. My father is very sick, and I think I might be looking at you like some respite from worrying every second of the day."

He shouldn't be so honest with her, but it felt like he could be. Maybe it was precisely because she would be leaving that he could open up. He had friends and he knew they would listen, but the words wouldn't come out. He was surrounded by people who would help, but he couldn't ask. He knew damn well he could go have dinner with Armie and Lila or Roxie and Zep for the holidays, but they weren't his family. They weren't his. He would always be secondary, that friend they invited so he wouldn't have to be alone.

The women he dated weren't his either. She was the only one who'd made him feel some modicum of peace, and he was suddenly a little desperate to hold on to it. It didn't make a bit of sense. He knew he would get hurt. He should look for someone who would stick around, someone he could try to build something with, but he couldn't force himself to think logically around her.

He wanted her, and if heartache was the price, he would pay it.

Her whole expression had softened, and she was suddenly closing the distance between them, putting her hands on his shoulders. "I'm so sorry about your dad. I'm here if you want to talk about it. But I'm also here if you don't. If you want to, I wouldn't mind if you kissed me and touched me and we forgot about everything else for a couple of hours."

He didn't need her to say it again. He'd let her take control the first time. Now he meant to show her how well he could take care of her.

For once in his life, he was going to let go and live in the moment. He was going to enjoy something without knowing if it would last forever. Not everyone got what his parents had.

And that hadn't been forever, either. He was starting to think there was no such thing.

The woman in his arms was real, and she was here for now. He wouldn't make the mistake of missing out on this chance.

He kissed her, his mouth covering hers, his body warming up as she went soft for him.

He thrust his hands into her hair, loving the silky feel of it. Brynn moved with him, her palms smoothing down his back to his waist, where she pulled his shirt free and laid warm hands on his skin.

He deepened the kiss, sliding his tongue along hers.

He wasn't going to push her. Despite the fact that they were on a timeline, she was already important to him, and he didn't want some one-night stand.

She'd said she wanted to forget for a little while. He could absolutely give her that. He could take care of her, and then they would take the time to figure out how far they wanted to go.

He broke off the kiss and pulled her onto his lap, wrapping one arm around her waist and bringing her close. "What do you want from me, Brynn? I want to hear you say it. Do you want a few kisses? Or do you want me to touch you? I promise nothing more than my hands on you tonight."

Her head fell back against his shoulder. "Please, Major."

His heart rate ticked up and he held her close, ready to show her some of what he could offer her.

Brynn let all of her worries fly away. Major was an adult with a good head on his shoulders, and he knew what would happen. She would have to leave, have to eventually take the next job that would keep her family afloat and that would take her away from this magical place she was starting to love.

But did it have to be forever?

She let that question float out of her head, too. She was sitting on Major's lap, hugged tight against his body. One of those big hands of his was flat on her torso just under her breasts, and she had to force herself to breathe.

"How long has it been, baby?" Major asked, his breath warm against her ear. His voice had deepened, taking on a sexy growling quality that did something to her.

"I haven't had a boyfriend in over a year." She'd dated another actor for a while. He'd been a nice guy, but time apart had ensured they couldn't work.

It was precisely why she and Stephen had an agreement to attend red-carpet events together when they weren't in a relationship.

How would Major look in a tuxedo? How proud would she be to have this gorgeous man on her arm, escorting her? She would feel safe for once.

She definitely felt safe now. There was something warm and infinitely calming about being around the man. Even when he was grumpy.

"I haven't had a sexual partner in two. My dating life isn't as fun as it sounds," he admitted with a self-deprecating chuckle. "And honestly, I haven't felt the need to get this close to anyone in a long time. You're the most gorgeous woman I've ever seen, Brynn, but you need to know that my attraction goes deeper than your looks."

Sometimes she felt like her whole world revolved around her looks. Every piece of her body was taken apart and ana-lyzed by casting directors and reporters and people on the damn Internet. She rarely had the chance to simply enjoy what it meant to be young and healthy and a woman. Some-times she felt like those eyes on her never blinked. Not even when she was alone, but somehow it felt different with Ma-jor. "You're not bad yourself, Deputy."

He kissed her neck, one hand moving up to cup her breast. "I appreciate that, but I promise my good looks don't make me lazy. And I'm now remembering everything I miss about sex."

So was she. Except she wasn't sure she'd ever connected to a man the way she did with this one. She'd never had that brilliant combination of attraction and like. She liked Major, liked how he'd treated her and how he'd taken charge of a situation she'd felt paralyzed in.

Desire flooded her system. This was exactly what she needed. She'd needed this whole day with him, needed that peaceful time when they'd simply existed side by side, and then she needed this moment when they could come together. Her mom's arrival had dragged all of her worries and cares back to the surface. If she'd done what she usually did, she would be back at the B and B with her mom and sister. Ma-jor had identified what she needed and been strong enough to offer it to her.

She was quickly coming to a point where she had to make a big decision, one she wasn't sure she could make. She could hide from it for a few weeks, shelter here with him. She could lose herself in his kisses and the way his hands felt on her body.

His hand slipped under the waistband of her jeans, and she had to force herself to breathe. She could feel his lips running along the curve of her neck, the gentle squeeze of his palm as he explored her breasts. She suddenly wished there wasn't the material of her shirt and bra between them. She wanted to feel how warm his hand was, wanted to be skin to skin with him. Her nipples grew taut and wanting under his caress. He bit the shell of her ear gently, with enough of a nip to get her panting.

Beyond that she could feel the tight line of his erection under her backside. He wasn't lying. He wanted her and if he pushed her the slightest bit, he could have her on her back, welcoming him inside.

But here he was, offering her pleasure and requiring nothing in return.

"Tell me if I go too far," he whispered.

She was worried he wouldn't go far enough. "Just touch me."

It was all she could think about right now, how close he was to the core of her. His fingers skimmed her sex and she found herself pressing up against him, feeling free and sexy for the first time in forever. She wasn't Bria Knight, actress. She was simply Brynn and he was Major, and they could be together for a moment.

Again and again Major slid his finger over her, pushing her higher and higher. In those moments she couldn't think of anything but how she felt. His other hand tightened on her breast, finding her nipple through the material and squeezing enough to send the sensation straight to her core. Brynn pressed against him, trying to draw out the orgasm exploding through her.

She was still shaking as he withdrew his hand, her whole body going languid.

"Better, baby?"

She'd always hated it when a man called her *baby*, but somehow it felt right coming from Major. Like she hadn't liked it because deep down she'd known she wasn't that man's baby. Like she'd been waiting to hear it from the right man.

She was getting in way too deep, way too fast, and she couldn't make herself care.

"Much better." She could breathe again, and that awful

veil of anxiety she'd felt when she'd realized her mom was here was gone.

Couldn't Major use some of that relief, too?

She shifted off his lap, looking up at him. His normally restrained hair was messy, probably because she'd let her hand drift back to play with it while he'd been touching her. She'd run her fingers through it, loving the connection they'd found. His hair was dark, contrasting with the blue of his eyes. He really was swoon-worthy. "Can I do the same for you?"

He winced. "Don't have to. In fact, I'm going to hope Rene still keeps some spare clothes here or it's going to be another weird trip back to town for me." He leaned over and kissed her. "You were so hot I went off like a rocket."

There was a bark at the door.

Major stood, letting Dolly in. He reached down to run a hand over the dog's head. "You keep her company while I get cleaned up, and then we'll see about dinner, and maybe she'll show us what she worked on today."

She had her work because Major had thought to bring it along.

"I can do that, and you take your time." He'd taken care of her. The least she could do was to warm up the man's dinner. She could heat up a can of chili. It might be the extent of her kitchen skills, but as long as there was heat, she should be able to manage it. "I'll make us supper."

He moved in close and brushed his lips against hers with a sigh. "I would love that. I'll start a fire. It can get chilly this time of year. I'll be right back."

Her whole body hummed with pleasure, and it was about more than the orgasm he'd given her. There was a sweet domesticity to the idea of making something for them to eat, of sitting with him and talking about the day.

And then maybe they could kiss again. Maybe this time she could be the one touching him.

There was a buzzing sound, and she realized it was a sound she hadn't heard all day. The sound of a text coming through on her phone. She glanced over at where she'd placed her tote bag. It buzzed again. And again. And again.

"I thought we didn't get cell service out here." She stared at the bag.

"Rene paid to have a receiver installed. It covers the cabin and a couple of the other inhabited islands. He didn't like the thought of being out here with his wife and daughter and not having a way to contact someone during an emergency," Major said. From the distance of his voice, she thought he was somewhere in the back of the cabin.

Lucky her. The billionaire had made it easy for her mom to find her. She should turn off her locator service. And then her mom would call the sheriff again.

When would her mom realize she was an adult and had been for a long time? Brynn pulled her cell out of the tote bag and glanced down. Sure enough, there were twenty-four unread messages. She should have answered that call early this morning. Though she likely couldn't have stopped her mom from coming, she would have at least had a heads-up. She could have warned Seraphina.

She started going through the texts, each one more dramatic than the next.

"Hey, how long can we hide out here?" Her mom would be waiting for her, planning the lecture of a lifetime.

"A little while if you like," he replied. "But I have to be at work in the morning. Why? You want to run away from your momma?"

Put like that she sounded like a wayward teen. "Just not looking forward to the conversation we're going to have to have. I need to stand my ground, but I haven't done that a lot with her. It's funny because I'm actually pretty good at it everywhere else in my life."

"She's your mom." Major stepped back into the main room. He'd changed into a pair of sweats that fit him like a glove, showing off some very muscular legs. She'd seen those gorgeous gams of his, but somehow it was different since they'd begun a physical relationship. "Moms are hard to deny even when they're overbearing." He grimaced. "Sorry. I shouldn't judge."

Oh, he should. "She's completely overbearing. She still thinks I'm a child who needs every moment of my life managed so I don't screw things up." She took a deep breath. The last message had been sent fifteen minutes before. Her mom must have gotten back to Papillon quickly. It asked her to please come back to the B and B when she was done with her date, and she was sorry she'd interrupted. And she loved her very much. Yup. Sometimes she wished her mom was the monster people made her out to be. "She's spent most of my life looking out for me. It's hard for her to let go. It doesn't help that she's also my manager."

"Have you thought about getting a new one?"

A laugh huffed from Brynn's mouth. "Only four times a day since I was six years old." She slid the phone back into her bag. She moved around the comfy sofa toward what looked like the kitchen. "But she's done a good job, and she's avoided the pitfalls of the celebrity momager."

"What would those be?" Major asked, slipping his sneakers back on.

"Little things like using every dime her kid makes to buy things for herself. I watched that happen a lot. My mom only took ten percent of everything I made."

A brow rose over Major's eyes. "That sounds like a lot. Is that why you work so hard?"

So many people misunderstood her mom. "My mom took the other ninety percent I brought home and put it in the bank for me. The only thing she bought with my money was a halfway decent condo, and even that was in my name. She paid for everything else from her ten percent. She paid for my food and Ally's school, all from what she had after my father died and what she made managing me and later on a couple of other actors. It always bugged me because we had to live in Hollywood while all my costars were in Beverly Hills or Malibu with big houses and every kind of luxury you could imagine. I didn't even have a game console until Gavin bought me and Ally one for Christmas when I was thirteen. He also bought me my first iPad. Mom wouldn't because we didn't have the money. But we did have the money."

"No, *you* had the money, and I respect her for that," Major said with that slow drawl of his. "I suspect it would have been easy for her to take more."

"Oh, yeah. She had control of all the money. She could have done whatever she wanted with it. Child actors are often preyed on by their parents. A lot of people thought she was insane to stick to ten percent. I often heard her talking to my fellow child actors' parents. My friend Stephen's dad bought a house in Malibu, cars, clothes, jewelry. Stephen had to emancipate himself at seventeen to keep anything at all. When I was eighteen and I could, I bought us a nice place in Calabasas." Her mom had cried. It had taken Brynn ten minutes to realize her mom didn't understand that she'd bought it for all of them to live in. Her mom had thought she was moving out and leaving her and Ally behind. "I'm hard on her, too. Sometimes we don't realize the sacrifices our parents make until we're adults."

"So your sister is an actress, too?" Major seemed very curious this evening. "You mentioned something about her doing some commercials."

Brynn opened the pantry door, and Major crowded in behind her. Warmth flooded her system as she felt him kiss the back of her neck. Maybe the night wasn't over physically.

"She's trying. She's done some modeling, but it was all catalog. She could make a good living off that, but it's not what she wants."

He shifted her hair to the side and ran kisses along her shoulder. "What does she want?"

"Five Oscars, a rapper boyfriend, and a makeup empire. Oh, and a reality show based around her life. Basically, she wants to be a Kardashian." It wasn't fair to make fun of her sister, but Ally wanted it all, and she wouldn't accept anything less. She'd turned down decent jobs in the hopes of getting something better.

"What do you want, Brynn?" The question was whispered softly against her ear.

Wasn't that the question? It was something she'd started to ponder more and more lately. There was one easy answer, though. "Right now, I'm pretty sure I want you."

His arm wound around her waist. "Now, that is a coincidence because I was thinking the same thing. I told myself I wouldn't let this go any further tonight."

She turned, putting her back against the wall. He was about half a foot taller than she was. She had to tilt her chin up to look at him. "I think you can let it go a little further. Maybe a lot."

"Don't tempt me, baby." But his head was lowering, eyes closing as he moved in.

That was the moment his cell rang.

She wished they'd stayed out of the reach of technology.

Major pulled the phone from his pocket and his eyes went tight when he looked at the screen.

And she knew their nice day was over.

chapter eight

❧

Major pulled into the parking lot and thought about what a mistake it was to bring Brynn along. He should have insisted on dropping her off at the B and B, but Juan had said it was something of an emergency, and taking her to the other side of town would have cost him half an hour.

He'd already taken far too much time because he'd been out on the islands instead of at his place or the station house where he should have been. He'd wanted a day where he didn't have to worry. Well, he'd been reminded vividly that his worries didn't care if he needed a day off.

He also hadn't managed to drop Dolly off at his place, but it was a nice night. She could stay in the car or he could put her on a leash and leave her with one of the nurses. Dolly was a hit with the residents of the assisted living home.

He wasn't so sure it would be as easy to deal with Brynn.

"Did they say what was happening?" It was the first question she'd asked since they'd argued about him taking her home. She'd been the one to point out the fact that the B and B was in the opposite direction of the residential home when he'd explained where he had to go. Apparently she'd been learning the layout of the town.

She'd given him space when he'd gone quiet. She hadn't pushed him on anything except going with him.

"All I got was that my dad was upset by an incident that happened." There was cell service out at Rene's, but it was spotty, and he'd gotten about half of what Juan had said. He'd called as soon as he'd gotten back to the marina, but it had gone straight to voice mail, which worried the hell out of him.

As did the sight of another SUV. As he turned into the parking lot, he caught sight of a familiar vehicle. It was identical to the one he drove. The parish had been called out? How bad was it? He hadn't heard anything about the sheriff's department being brought in.

"Is he hurt?" Brynn asked.

"I don't know." He pulled into the spot beside the parish SUV. He was almost certain it was Roxie's. She was working the second shift through the weekend. "He's not violent, but he forgets he's not twenty years old."

He sometimes tried to do things his frail body couldn't handle anymore. He'd broken his wrist once trying to show another resident he could do a handstand. Because he'd thought he was in gym class at his old high school.

Major's gut twisted. What had gone wrong now? Would this be the incident that his dad didn't come back from? Was last night the last time he would see the father he knew?

It was a constant worry. And a constant guilt. He could have been here sooner if he hadn't been running around on the islands. His father needed him, and he'd been trying to get into a Hollywood star's panties.

Damn it. That was cheapening it, but his mind kept going there.

"I'll keep Dolly with me," Brynn offered. "I can walk her around the parking lot so she's not in the way. Unless you'd like me to come with you. I would love to help. Or just be around for you."

She would distract him. He would worry about her rather than his father, and his dad had no one but him. He turned to her, and she was so pretty it made his heart clench. "I don't know what I'm going into. Please take care of Dolly. I'll get you home as soon as possible. I'm sorry."

She shook her head. "Don't be. I'm fine here. We all have family. I'll be close if you need me."

He forced himself to slip out of the SUV without doing what he wanted to do. He wanted to kiss her and pretend like she really was here for him. It wasn't that he doubted her goodwill. Brynn seemed to be a genuinely kind person, but he wasn't sure she was ready for the kind of chaos Major had gotten used to.

He strode toward the front of the building and sure enough, there was Roxie. The lobby was lit up, and through the sliding glass doors he could see Roxie standing there, hands on her hips and her head nodding. Juan was there, his jaw clenched and hands in his pockets. There was a man he didn't recognize. He had a bag strapped across his chest and a camera in his hand.

His father wasn't in the room. At least no ambulance had been called. That meant any injuries would be minor. His mind was whirling with the possibilities as he started up the path to the entryway.

"Well, well, look who showed up. I didn't think this plan would work."

A flash went off from his left side, and for a moment Major was blinded by it.

He stopped, and his vision started to come back. "What the hell?"

"I'm Jeannie Carbo from *Entertain America*," a no-nonsense voice said, and he realized there was a woman standing in front of the big oleander bushes that decorated the path leading to the lobby of the building.

Had she been standing in the bushes? She wasn't alone. A man was with her, and he seemed to have put his big camera on video function. He turned the lens to catch the woman.

She smiled at the camera, a big bright expression that didn't come close to reaching her eyes. "I'm here with the small-town deputy who's taken the Internet by storm. His name is Major Blanchard, but America affectionately knows him as Tighty-Whitie. Deputy, how does it feel to be an instant celebrity?"

What the hell was going on? "I don't know what you're talking about. I have to go check on my father."

He turned, still a bit shocked. What were these people doing here?

He heard footsteps behind him, the *clop clop* of heels against the concrete.

"Are you dating Bria Knight? Was she out there with you for a reason, and do you know if she's stopped seeing her costar, Gavin Jacks?" The woman was following him, and her friend seemed to have turned on a flashlight, because there was a bright beam lighting the path now.

Who the hell was . . . Brynn . . . she was asking about Brynn. He remembered what she'd said about those rumors. They hurt her. "She's not seeing Gavin. She was never seeing him. He's like her dad."

He heard the whooshing sound of the doors coming open ahead.

"Hey, who are you?" Roxie strode out. She was dressed for work and had the frown on she usually reserved for the most obnoxious of calls. "This is a private residence, and you are trespassing."

"It's a hospital. I'm completely within my rights to be here," Jeannie replied. "And I find it very interesting that Bria's new guy doesn't seem to know her history with the old one. Is Gavin here in Pappadeaux?"

He didn't bother to correct the woman. If she couldn't be polite enough to learn the name of the town she'd invaded, that was her trouble. "Ma'am, this is not a public hospital. This is very much a private business, and if you do not leave in the next five minutes, the deputy will arrest you."

"Did you get that on camera?" Jeannie asked her partner. "I want everyone to know that Bria Knight is now dating an aggressive cop. That should affect her career."

"I'm not trying to affect anything." Frustration was starting to swirl with the worry and guilt. A toxic combination. "I'm trying to explain the law to you since you don't seem to understand it."

That smile of hers turned a bit predatory. "Look, you can make this easy on yourself or hard. I don't care as long as I get my story."

"You know, you're like a cartoon villain," Roxie said with a shake of her head. "At least the one in there is trying to convince me he's doing it to help his family."

Jeannie rolled her eyes. "Like he has a family. Look, officer, I don't know if you get the Internet here in Podunk, Louisiana, but this guy is now a huge celebrity. That video of him getting rescued and losing his pants has twenty-two million views and climbing. Everyone wants to know his story. I'm going to be the first to tell it."

He didn't even want to think about the ramifications of that. He just wanted to get to his father. He turned to Roxie. "Where is my dad?"

"The better question is, where is Bria?" Jeannie didn't seem willing to let go. "We asked around and it seems like she might have been with you. Are you aware that her mother is in town? Is Diane Pearson trying to warn you away from her daughter? Did you and Bria fake that video to get attention?"

"I don't want the attention I have," he argued. He couldn't

imagine why anyone would want this. "I only want to see my father."

"Has he met Bria yet? He told me you two were dating," a new voice said. The doors had come open again and the man who'd been standing in the lobby was in handcuffs being led down the walkway by Landon Price, the officer they'd hired a couple of months back. The man was in a dark tracksuit, his longish hair tied back. "Deputy Blanchard, I'm a freelancer and if you'll give me an exclusive, I'll cut you in on the sale. Jeannie here works for a network. She won't give you anything."

"Except excellent exposure, you bottom-feeder," Jeannie argued. "If you were halfway decent you wouldn't have to freelance."

"Keep it moving, buddy," Landon said, gently pressing the man along. He nodded at Major. "Your dad is fine. He had a scare because this asshole snuck into his room. He got in the back when Juan went to take some trash out."

"I'm sorry. I propped the door open." Juan had followed them, a worried look on his face. "I didn't have my keys."

And why should he? Major bet in all the years Juan had run this place no one had tried to sneak in the back. "It's okay. I think this might be my fault."

He'd probably brought this down on Juan and his dad since they'd been looking for him and Brynn. When they couldn't find what they wanted, they'd gone after his father.

"It is one hundred percent not your fault, Major. You're not the one causing trouble." Roxie turned to the journalists who were following him. "You have two minutes to get out of here before I take you to the station with your friend. You've been warned and now you're trespassing."

"We are not friends," Jeannie complained. "He's a washed-up loser."

"I'm a washed-up loser who got an exclusive from the

dad," the reporter crowed. "I've got it all on camera. The old man might be crazy, but he told me all about his son and Bria. They've been dating."

He'd filmed his father? His vulnerable dad, who'd always protected his privacy? Rage filled Major and he actually saw himself punching this guy. He saw his fist hitting the reporter's face and going right through it.

Roxie stepped in front of him. "Landon, get him in the car. Let him know how close he is to having a former Army Ranger go berserk on him."

"Hey, I said I would share some of the money," the man reiterated.

Landon shoved him along. "You'll need the money to make bail. Although it is the weekend. The judge tends to go fishing on the weekends. I guess you'll be staying with us until Monday. Welcome to Papillon."

That seemed to work some magic on the other reporters.

"Look, we don't want trouble," Jeannie said. "We just wanted to give Tigh . . . the deputy a chance to tell his side of the story. I assure you we won't be the last journalists interested in him. And I would watch out for the mom if I were you. Everyone in the industry knows she'll do anything to move Bria's career forward. If that means running over her new boyfriend, she'll do it. I would bet she's the one who came up with the idea to do the viral video." She held her hands up as Roxie approached. "I'm going. My car is parked across the street. I promise, we're going. It's obvious this guy isn't going to give me anything."

She started moving away from the parking lot where Brynn was probably walking Dolly. At least he didn't have to worry he was sending her Brynn's way.

How did she handle this? How many more of these people would he have to deal with?

You think you understand gossip, but you don't until the

whole world is talking about you. People you don't know. People you'll never meet. People who think they know exactly who you are.

This was what Brynn had been talking about. This was what had put that anxiety in her eyes. Anxiety that had only drifted away when he'd kissed her and taken her mind off her troubles.

Well, trouble had found them again and he was pretty sure he couldn't make this go away by holding her.

"I'm sorry, Major." Roxie's eyes were on the reporters as they made their way across the road. "I can't arrest them. They didn't try to get inside."

"No, they hid in the bushes and waited for me." His mind started in on worst-case scenarios. "Are they at my house?"

"I haven't heard anything, and you know your neighbors like to call us. They might not have figured out where you live." Roxie sighed. "Although I have no idea how they found out where your father is. I'm at a loss. I don't get why they think you're dating some Hollywood star. The video's cute and all, but I don't get why they think you two are together now . . . Oh."

"What?" Roxie was staring at him like she'd figured something out.

Her lips curled up in a wry smile. "You put on your blank face. You are seeing her. That's some fast work."

He shook his head. "We had dinner last night, and I was with her this afternoon."

"I know. I thought you were just showing her around. It's what we're supposed to be doing."

"It's what you're supposed to be doing. You're the one she's supposed to shadow. I should have stayed away." He turned to Juan. "Where is my dad?"

Juan's brow wrinkled with the obvious strain the night had brought. "I'm sorry, Major. He's asleep. We had to give him something to calm him down. I'm afraid that reporter spun him up. I didn't realize anything was happening until one of the nurses heard them yelling. I can't tell you how upset I am that this happened. I'm calling a meeting tomorrow to look over our security system. The guard had left his post because Mrs. Adams had locked herself out of her apartment."

"I'll help you. This isn't your fault. You're a small operation. You couldn't have known there were aggressive reporters coming." But Brynn had warned him. She'd told him it could get bad and all he'd seen was blond hair and a gorgeous face. All he'd thought about was how nice it was to be around her.

While his father was being abused.

"Can I at least see him? I want to look in and make sure he's alright."

Juan nodded. "Of course. And I'm locking everything down."

"I'll help you," Roxie promised. "Landon and I can do a perimeter sweep to make sure we don't have others hanging around. Our trespassing friend can sit in the back of the car for a little while and think about his life choices."

Major walked in to check on his dad, all those toxic emotions still whirling inside.

Brynn watched the road ahead as Major turned toward the B and B. She could see the warm lights in the distance and wondered if her mom and sister were already cozy in their rooms. She wanted to invite Major in, to get him to open up and talk to her. She still didn't understand what had happened.

She'd walked Dolly around a bit and then Major had shown up and told her they could go. He'd explained his father was sleeping and physically fine and then he'd gone silent.

No more affection or sweet words. No ease between them.

"Is everything all right? You said your dad was fine, but it's easy to see you're still upset." She wanted to give him space, but the tension between them was killing her.

"Because I'm pretty sure it's not over."

"What's not over? Please tell me what happened because I think maybe this has something to do with me. Are you feeling bad because we were out of touch for so long? Or did it have something to do with the man in the police car?"

She'd taken Dolly to the green space attached to the building. It was obviously a place where the residents of the home gathered to enjoy the outdoors. She'd walked the dog around for a bit and when she'd come back to the car, she'd seen the police SUV driving away and had gotten a glimpse of someone in the back seat. The woman deputy had been driving. Roxanne. She was the one Brynn was supposed to start shadowing on Monday. She hadn't noticed Brynn, nor had her male partner, but the man in the back put a hand on the window and shouted something she hadn't been able to hear.

"He was a reporter," Major explained.

The words hit her like a kick to the gut. "What did he want with your . . ." She stopped because that was a ridiculous question to ask. The answer was clear. "He was looking for you and me."

"He was." Major kept his eyes on the road, the lights of the B and B coming closer. "When he couldn't figure out where we were, he went looking for my father. Apparently my dad gave an interview and then they got into an argument. The staff had to sedate my dad to get him to calm down."

"Major, I am so sorry." She'd known something like this could happen. This was what she'd worried about since her mom had told her how crazy popular the video had gotten.

"He wasn't the only one. He was simply the one who actually got inside. Some woman was literally hiding in the bushes. She had a lot to say to me." His voice was low, anger in every word.

"A woman?"

"A reporter. Jean or Jeannie. I don't remember. What I remember was her threatening me if I don't give her what she wants. She wants an interview, of course. If I don't give her one, she says she'll have to assume that you and I faked the video so we could get attention."

Her stomach turned. She'd been hungry moments before, ready to beg Seraphina for a couple of sandwiches, but all thoughts of food were gone. Unfortunately, she knew exactly who Major was talking about. "She's with a tabloid show called *Entertain America*. She's pretty awful."

"She asked if I knew about your affair with Gavin Jacks."

Tears threatened. This was happening faster than she'd believed possible. "Of course she did."

"I told her you'd never had an affair with him." His tone softened as though he'd realized she was getting emotional, too. "I set that record straight."

"You shouldn't have talked to her. You can't win. Just tell her no comment or walk away. Don't give her anything to work with." If she'd known what was waiting for him, she would have gone with him. "If you see her again, don't say anything. I'll handle her."

He didn't understand how the tabloids worked. He probably thought they were like actual journalists who cared about the truth. Truth didn't matter to a person like Jeannie Carbo. All that mattered was ratings, and more salacious stories brought in ratings.

Major pulled into the small parking lot and put the car in park, slamming a hand on the steering wheel. "You shouldn't have to. She should leave you alone."

At least his rage didn't seem to be pointed at her. She took a deep breath, trying to banish the emotion that threatened to overwhelm her. She'd wanted a few weeks with him, but it looked like he might need to end things now. "I wish she would, but it's part of my job. It's the part I like the least. I'm so sorry they upset your dad. I'm sorry they upset you. I'll handle it. I'll do a couple of interviews and make it go away."

He went silent for a moment, his head down, and when it came up there was a weariness in his eyes. "I don't know if that will work. I think those sharks scented blood in the water."

She hated the fact that his imagery was so grim. And accurate. "They'll find something else to amuse them. I promise. I'll talk to all of them. I'll give so many interviews they'll be bored with me."

"And then they'll think we really did it to get attention," he concluded.

"No, they'll think I did it to get attention because we won't be seen together anymore." She'd known earlier in the day that it would likely come to this. The minute her mom had shown up she'd known deep down her time with him was almost done. "Once they get some pictures of me and Gavin around town, they'll forget about you. I promise."

His jaw tightened. "You don't have to do that."

"Do what? Work with the man I'm being paid to work with? Hang out with the guy who's been my father figure most of my life? I can't stop living because people choose to misunderstand. I can't stop caring about someone when the press pushes a more interesting narrative." How had it all gone to hell so fast? Her mother had warned her, but the idea of not seeing him again made her heart ache.

Couldn't she have one thing for herself? One thing that was just for her, that she didn't have to share with the world?

She still wanted these days with Major. She wanted them more than she'd wanted any role.

"They're going to say it no matter what you do, huh?" Major asked.

"Now that the spotlight is back on me, yes." She was in for a couple of nasty weeks. She would have to turn off the comments on her social media for a while. And not watch live TV. And not look on the Internet. She turned in her seat. "But the heat will be off you and your dad. That doesn't mean we can't see each other. There have to be lots of places for us to be alone together. I can't stand the thought of not being . . . friends."

She was pretty sure she wanted to be more, but she also couldn't put it out there. She felt vulnerable in a way she hadn't in a long time. She had a pretty thick skin. She had to, but she suddenly understood how hard his rejection would hit her.

"I'm sorry, Brynn. I don't think that's a good idea."

Yes. There it was. There was the pain that shouldn't be so strong since she hadn't known him long. There was the rush of sorrow she'd hoped wouldn't come. She felt herself flush and those tears were back. He didn't want to see her. She was too much trouble. Most of the men she'd dated would have jumped at the chance to get some attention from the press, but then they had all been actors.

No normal guy would want to go through what she had to go through.

She nodded, determined to get through this with her dignity intact. As much as it could be. She'd been intimate with this man and while she understood, the rejection still hurt. "Okay. Well, I'll do those interviews and keep you out of it. I'll also keep my distance. Maybe Roxie can work different hours than you."

"Brynn, I . . ."

She didn't want to hear all of his *it's not you, it's me*, when it was clearly her. She popped the seatbelt off and opened the door, sliding to the ground below. "Thanks for showing me around."

She grabbed her bag and shut the door. The path to her cabin was illuminated with garden lights.

She heard a door slam and then Major was behind her, his hand on her arm, twirling her around. He pulled her close, those big arms wrapping around her.

"I don't want to leave you, but I have to take care of him. I'm sorry, baby. He's the only family I have left in this whole world, and I can't fail him. I can't."

The tears started to fall because she'd only been thinking of herself and not what he needed, what he was feeling. His father was dying, and she'd thrown more chaos his way. She hadn't meant to, but she had. He wasn't rejecting her. He was choosing his father. The way she would choose her mom or sister.

She held on to him, letting her head rest on his broad shoulder, and she wished that she was a different person. She wished she was simply an artist who'd met a deputy because then she might have been able to hold his hand through this. She might have been a strength for him instead of a weakness.

She stepped back because if she didn't now, she might not let him go. And he needed her to let him go.

She looked up into those blue eyes of his. "I understand. But if you ever change your mind, you call me and I'll be there for you. Take care of yourself, Deputy Major."

He leaned over and kissed her forehead. "You take care of yourself, Brynn Pearson. It was . . . well, it was good to get to know you."

She turned and strode down the path as quickly as she could. She needed to get inside her cabin, have a good cry, and then clean herself up so she could talk to her mom about what they should do. She could start to make this whole thing right for Major.

She got to the cabin and slid the keycard in as the tears began to fall.

"It won't go well," her mother was saying. "You should have called me the minute you realized she was getting involved with that man."

"She's an adult, Diane." Gavin stood in the living room, pointing at her mother, who was on the couch with Duke on her lap and a martini in one hand. "You have to let her make her own choices and have her own life or you are going to lose her."

She should have known they would be here. They had their own rooms, but they wouldn't think twice about taking over hers.

"I'm not a monster," her mother insisted. "She's not threatening to leave."

"I wasn't talking about her leaving you," Gavin replied. "I was talking about her losing herself, the core of who she is. This industry is going to kill a piece of her soul if you don't watch it. She's not like us."

"Don't be so overly drama—" Her mom looked up and went a little pale. "Brynn?"

"I'm not seeing him anymore."

Her mom stood and put down her drink. "Oh, sweetie, I'm sorry. Come here, honey."

Brynn took a step back. "Isn't this exactly what you wanted? Isn't this why you flew all the way out here?"

"This is exactly what I didn't want," her mom said with a sigh. She moved in and brushed back Brynn's hair. "That look on your face is what I was trying to avoid. I didn't want you to get your heart broken. What happened?"

She fell into her mom's arms. No matter what had happened along the way, her mom had been there. She was tough but she'd had to be.

And Gavin was there, too. He put a hand on her back, patting her the way he would when she'd skinned her knee on set or taken a fall. "Tell us what happened, sweetheart. We can find a way through this."

She cried and told them her story.

chapter nine

Two days later Major watched the screen in the conference room at the station house.

"I was happy to help the deputy," Brynn was saying. She smiled at the camera, sitting on the big patio of the B and B. Morning light shone down on her, making her hair even more golden. She practically had a damn halo, and someone had gotten her makeup perfect. She was gorgeous, and yet he thought he could see the strain. Her smile was bright but not vibrant. "Apparently things can get sticky down here on the bayou, but I've learned that the people are always willing to help."

"There you are." Roxie poked her head in. "I was looking for you. Hey, is that Brynn?"

He turned. "Yeah, it's her third interview in the last couple of days. I saw she did one from the shelter."

He'd watched them all. In every one, she'd talked about how much she loved the town and how she felt so welcome here. In the one she'd done from Papillon's shelter, she'd been surrounded by dogs and cats, and a pet rabbit who'd been surrendered.

"We nearly cleared out the shelter in one day." Roxie

walked in, letting the door close behind her. "She's been busy. We were supposed to have breakfast this morning, but she canceled because she had to do this show. She's recording a podcast this afternoon, so she's not going to get much time in today. I don't know why she came out early if she was going to do nothing but press. I'm staying far away from that part."

"It's not her choice." He hated the fact that she was doing all of this for him.

He also hated the fact that he'd thought of nothing but her for days. He couldn't get those tears in her eyes out of his head.

I can't stand the thought of not being friends.

They'd gotten to be more than friends. In a short time, she'd become important to him. It had taken everything he had to not go out to the B and B to check in on her. He'd texted her when he'd watched the first interview. Nothing more than a simple thank-you and request to know if she was okay.

She'd sent back a heart emoji and nothing more.

She was respecting his decision.

The trouble was Major wasn't sure he wanted her to.

"What do you mean it's not her choice?" Roxie settled into a conference room chair, the interview playing on behind her head.

Brynn smiled and waved at the camera, and then the host ended the segment by playing the video again. He groaned and reached for the remote.

"Don't." Armie walked in, a stack of files in his hands. "This is my favorite part."

"Which one? When the dog abandons him or when his pants do?" Roxie asked.

"When he stares at Brynn like she's the last ice cream cone in the world." Armie took the seat at the head of the table.

"I do not." He looked back at the screen as Dolly eagerly ran to Brynn and she gave her a treat, her hand petting the dog's head.

And there it was. He was staring at her like she was a golden goddess.

Armie snorted as he settled in. "Sure you do."

When she looked up, his expression went back to grumpy. Even then he'd known how gorgeous she was.

There was a knock on the door.

"Come on in," Armie called out.

The door opened and Gavin Jacks shouldered his way in, a bag in his hand and a tray of coffees in the other. They were from the café across the street, but the bag in his hand was from the B and B. "Sorry I'm late. I stopped by to get you all some coffee. And I brought you some pastries. My gracious hostess made far too many for a group who is always watching their carb intake. Not me, of course. I was blessed with a naturally high metabolism. Between good genetics and a strong workout ethic, I can eat what I like and maintain my film bod. Not superhero body, of course. I would have to cut out carbs for that, but I'm not in that particular club."

"You're basically playing a version of Armie," Roxie replied. "Eat all the carbs you like. He's got a dad bod."

"Of course I do. I'm a dad. I've got three kids." Armie was frowning Roxie's way. "What else would I have?"

It was obvious Armie wasn't up on the current lingo. Major chuckled. "It means you've let yourself go a little. Gotten a bit paunchy around the middle. Which you absolutely haven't, boss."

Roxie snorted and rolled her eyes. "I was joking. The man won't let any of us rest. He puts us through physicals every year. Won't take his wife's opinion that we're all perfectly fit."

Armie shrugged. "Can't have you all getting soft."

"I'd love to know what kind of routine you put them all through." Gavin started passing out the coffees. "I'm sure Brynn will want to go through some training, too. Physicality is very important to our process. You should know that I've already gone through SWAT training, FBI training, and I spent a day at BUD/S."

"You trained with the Navy SEALs?" Roxie asked.

Gavin gave her a grin that likely melted the hearts of women everywhere. He was one charming man. "Absolutely. For a day. And then I washed out. There's a reason I'm an actor."

"Well, Armie's yearly fitness tests remind me of being back in grade school. You remember that day every year in PE when they made you do sit-ups and climb up a rope," Roxie grumbled, taking the coffee with a nod. "It sucked then. Sucks now."

"It's not that bad." Major kind of liked fitness test days. Sure, there was a lot of ribbing and joking around and Armie was serious about everyone being able to run a five-minute mile, but there were fun times, too. They usually ended with everyone getting a beer and hanging out.

"Says the man who runs every day," Roxie returned. "I don't have to anymore. I caught my man. Literally. Like I put him in the back of my SUV in handcuffs. I can let myself go. Or I could if Armie didn't insist on his staff being in peak physical condition. Oooh, are those Seraphina's muffins?"

Gavin passed her one. "Absolutely, and they are delicious. But try getting a Hollywood actress to eat one. When I left, our hostess was making egg-white omelets for Brynn and Diane, and the brat princess was doing her usual sleep-in. Ally rarely eats until the afternoon."

Brynn probably had to be up at the crack of dawn.

In every single interview she'd been asked about him,

and all she would say was that he was a deputy and a nice man, and no they weren't seeing each other.

Over and over she'd been asked the same questions, and she'd handled them all with that smile that wasn't as sunny as it usually was.

"How is she doing?"

The question came out of his mouth before he could think to keep it inside.

Gavin turned his way, a brow cocking over piercing blue eyes. "She's fine. Why would you want to know?"

"I like Brynn. She's a nice lady," he replied.

Gavin pulled out a chair and set his own coffee on the table. "She's been busy doing press surrounding the incident where she saved your ass. It's been hard on her because she's also prepping for a role. She's sat down with every reporter who wanted an interview. It's been exhausting for her."

The thought made his heart constrict. He hoped her mom and sister were taking care of her, but he worried they might push her to take advantage of the attention. Who was hugging her and making sure she got some rest? "I'm sorry to hear that."

"She's doing it for you, you know." Gavin had been in the station house all weekend, following Armie around. He generally came off as intelligent and amiable. He smiled a lot. Now his eyes were lasers piercing through Major. "She's insisted on taking care of anyone who might want to talk to you. She even talked to *Entertain America*. The interview should run tonight."

"How much longer does she have to do this?" Major asked, heartsick at the thought of Brynn putting herself out there for him.

Gavin shrugged. "I think she's through the worst of it, and earlier today I saw that there was a TikTok of Angelina

Jolie's cat playing the piano, so they'll lose interest very quickly. We should be able to spend the next week the way we'd planned. With the exception of having to deal with Diane. She'll want to have a say in every minute of Brynn's schedule and we were hoping to mostly just hang out. That could have been avoided, and I blame you. If you hadn't gotten stuck in the mud, Diane would still be in LA. You need to find a new place to work out. Might I offer Miss Tilly's gym?"

"Tilly Highwater has a gym?" Armie asked.

Roxie chuckled. "Her granddaughter bought her a set of free weights for Christmas, and now she's offering memberships to her gym. It's in her garage. She also has an old TV and VCR in there and runs 1980s Jane Fonda videos. But you should know Gene is planning on protesting her over Jane Fonda's Vietnam War stance."

"I don't think that's legal," Armie said with a frown. "Doesn't she need a permit?"

"Her rates are very reasonable." Gavin pulled out his notepad and a pen. "And she claims she can help me work on my traps. I'm not sure if she's talking about my shoulders or if she's worried about the level of what she called *critters* out at the B and B. Apparently I need to be on the lookout for possums."

Well, at least Gavin seemed to be getting a full dose of Papillon fun. Sometimes Major thought half his job was making sure no one got killed by kookiness. "I'll check into it, boss."

There was another brisk knock and Landon stood at the door. "Hey, we've got a delivery I could use some help with."

Roxie stood up. "That should be the office supplies. I'll help unload."

Armie followed her. "I will, too. We'll get this meeting started in twenty, Gavin." Armie gestured around the room.

"This is what small-town sheriffs do. A little bit of everything. I'm sure the chief of LAPD doesn't unload his own office supplies."

Whoa. He was about to be left alone with Gavin, and that didn't seem like a great idea. The man had avoided him for the most part. "Hey, the sheriff shouldn't have to do that. I'll help them."

Armie shook his head. "Nah, I want to make sure the state paperwork we requested came in. You sit and talk to our guest. Tell him about that time you had to convince a resident there weren't big cats hanging around in the trees. She didn't believe him because he hadn't been in Louisiana long enough to know whether or not we have lions."

Damn. The door closed behind them, and he was left with the man who seemed to be a dad to the woman he'd recently broken up with.

Could he call it that if they'd never really been together? It felt like it. He felt her loss far more than the woman he'd dated for months two years before.

"So someone thought there were lions in Louisiana?" Gavin asked, a brow raised.

"It was tigers, actually. It's a long story."

Gavin gestured around the empty room. "We seem to have time."

If only he'd been quicker to offer help. He was off his game because he'd spent much of the previous night at the assisted living home helping with his father and going over the new security system with the staff. "She'd watched *Tiger King* and then there were rumors about a rougarou. That's a—"

"Cajun werewolf," Gavin interjected. "Yes, there are still rumors. I spent some time at the VFW. They have plans in place to protect the town."

He would have to look into that. The last thing he needed was a group of armed veterans roaming the bayou at night.

"It's a legend around here. A while back there were rumors that we had one skulking around. Turned out to be overly ambitious teens."

An awkward silence spread between them, making Major antsy.

"I guess it wasn't so long a story," said Major.

The silence with Brynn had been peaceful. He hadn't felt the need to keep up conversation. They were able to exist in the same space in a harmony he enjoyed.

"Is she really okay?" He shouldn't have asked again, but now that they were alone, he might get more of an explanation.

Gavin sighed. "If you care about her, why not ask her yourself?"

He didn't have to explain anything. He could walk out and get some work done. Yet he felt the need to make someone close to Brynn understand. "My father is sick."

"Yes, she explained that. I understand you need to protect your father. It's probably for the best." Gavin leaned forward. "She's going to pick a new project and she'll go straight from here to there, and you won't see her again because that's how the next decade or so of her life is going to be. Always on a set."

"I don't understand that. I thought movie stars lived luxurious lives. Shouldn't she get time off?" He'd thought about it the night before, wondered if he'd been hasty. Brynn started filming soon, and then maybe she could take a couple of weeks off. He had some vacation time coming. He couldn't leave town, but they might be able to spend some time together.

He'd been questioning the decision to keep her at arm's length from the moment he'd made it. He'd had to force himself to get back in his SUV that night. He'd wanted to run after her and apologize, to tell her he hadn't meant it. He'd thought about calling her every minute of the day.

146   *Lexi Blake*

And then he would be reminded that his father was still fragile and couldn't handle the fallout if the press showed up again.

"She could take time off, but if she wants a career as an adult, she pretty much needs to work constantly," Gavin explained. "Brynn isn't what I would call a star. She's a working actress. She's in this time period nearly every actor goes through when he or she figures out if they've got what it takes to last in this business."

"And they do that by working all the time?"

"Every now and then you get someone who hits immediately, but most overnight success stories are built on years and years of grinding work," Gavin explained. "Brynn needs to take as many good roles as she can because it's a bit like the lottery. A script can be excellent. The director can be good. Then somewhere along the way the movie goes to hell because the producer decides to stick their noses in. Or it simply doesn't connect the way you hoped. She's looking for the movie that catapults her out of the mid-range she finds herself in."

"And if she finds that movie, then she gets to take it easier?"

Gavin chuckled, though it wasn't an amused sound. "Heavens no. Then she makes as much money as she can and tries to survive the next culling."

"Culling?" Major didn't like the sound of that.

"It's a hard business, Deputy. There's always a transition as an actor ages. The roles get harder to come by, and when most people are hitting their stride in their career, being held up as masters of their crafts, actors are often done. Actresses, especially, are told they're too old to play roles that are literally written for women their age. Hollywood is littered with stories of actors in their fifties and sixties partnered with actresses in their twenties. It leaves little room for more mature, experienced actresses. The good roles will be fought over by the few who are still in favor, and the rest will end up working for scraps or not working at all."

"It sounds like you don't like your business very much."

Gavin sat back. "The business, absolutely not. Acting. Filmmaking. Telling stories. Those are wonderful things. Those things fill my soul, and I was born to do what I do. I can't think of anything else I would want, and so going through all of that, playing the game, is as necessary to me as breathing."

"And this is what Brynn wants?" The thought made him wonder if he was missing something. He'd never wanted anything enough to go through hell to achieve it. He'd gone into the military because it seemed like the best way to pay for college. After, he'd gotten his degree in criminal justice, and then his father had gotten sick. He liked his job, but he wasn't sure he would suffer for it the way Brynn was.

"So she's been told," Gavin replied.

"What is that supposed to mean?"

"It means she's been working since she was a child. Don't get me wrong. Diane had her reasons, and I respect what she did to save her girls and herself. She and I have our differences, but she's a good mother and a good manager. I merely worry that acting has become a habit for Brynn when her passion is something else."

"Her art."

Gavin stared at him for a moment. "She's showed you her art?"

"Yes. We talked about it. My mom was an art teacher, so I know about the subject."

"No wonder you made an impression." Gavin looked like he'd just figured something out. "She rarely finds anyone who's interested in her art. Her mother views it as a distraction. Her sister views it, and everything that isn't about her, as an annoyance. Did you realize she's drawn you several times?"

He shrugged. "She draws everything. She told me it's part of her process. She draws a bunch of things and then figures out what she wants to paint. She paints from the drawing."

He'd caught sight of her easel when he'd picked her up. She had several canvases waiting to be used.

He wondered how she looked while she was painting. He would love to watch her. They could spend weekends like that, with her painting and him taking care of their lives so she didn't miss the light.

"Yes, I believe that's what she does. I know she thought she would get to spend more time on her work while she was here. I'm afraid real life came into play."

"Again, I'm sorry about that. I wish that footage hadn't gotten out."

"I think it's good that it did. It's better to nip it in the bud, so to speak. All that would have come of it is heartache, and she doesn't need more of that. It sounds like you don't need it either, Deputy."

He was starting to wonder about that, to wonder if it might be better to have an aching heart than an empty one.

The door opened, and Armie was coming through. "Hey, I got a call from the clinic."

Major got to his feet. Lila LaVigne's practice was an easy ten-minute walk from the station house. "Is it my dad? His appointment wasn't supposed to be until Thursday."

"No. I think it might be Brynn," Armie said. "Lila told me they're bringing in someone from the B and B. One of the guests. We got an emergency call from out there. It must be about the same incident."

He didn't walk. He started to run for the clinic.

* * *

"You doing okay?" Harry asked as he took the turn that would take them into town. "Let me know if I'm going too fast."

Brynn winced as she shifted. Pain flared through her, but it wasn't scream-worthy. More like a hearty groan. She held it in because the last thing she needed was anyone panicking. "As okay as I can be given the fact that I'm a klutz."

"You're not a klutz. You're quite graceful. And I don't know that we're going fast enough." Her mother reminded her that she wasn't alone in the truck. After she'd tripped over the cables of the equipment she'd used for this morning's interview, Brynn had taken a header straight into the pool, twisting her ankle in the process. She might have gotten out of this trip to the ER if she hadn't hit her head when she'd fallen getting out of the pool. That had been Duke's fault. He'd been frantic and had gotten under her feet as she'd been exiting the pool while still wearing the Louboutins she always wore for interviews. Well, the ones she used to wear, since she'd broken the heel. When she'd tripped over the dog, she'd gone down again, this time without the aid of falling into water. She'd hit her head on the guide rail that led down into the pool.

She'd stared up at the sky for a moment while Duke had wailed. She wondered where she'd gone wrong in life. She was wet, cold, possibly concussed, and she'd lain there and thought about how to get the blue of that sky right, how to make the clouds look like the marshmallow dream she saw. It was so stunning, the contrasts. The blue sky and white clouds with golden sunshine filtering through both.

Then her mom had walked out, and everything had sped up again.

It had been a catastrophe.

"I don't want to do anything that could make Brynn sick,"

Harry explained. "If she's got a concussion, she could be nauseous."

"I'm fine. I'm actually a little hungry." They kept going on about a concussion, but she was sure she didn't have one. "I'm sorry about the trouble. And my mom's wrong. I can be very clumsy."

"You've had a rough couple of days, and I don't think you've been sleeping enough," her mom continued. "I'm glad the camera was off. Thank you, Mr. Jefferys, for riding in to the rescue."

"It's Harry, and it was my pleasure," he reassured her. "And I promise there's no security camera on the swimming pool. We learned that lesson after we hosted a group of new-lyweds. No one needs to see that."

She could only imagine. "I'm feeling better."

"I'm not." Her mom leaned forward. "I won't feel better until I'm sure you don't have a concussion. And we need to figure out if you broke your ankle. If you did . . ."

Then the film would be done for her. They would find someone else, and she would have to move on and hope she didn't lose more work. "It's not broken. I can move it. It's probably a sprain."

"That can be just as bad," her mom muttered. "You can't play the role if you can't move properly."

The role was a physical one. She'd been training to en-sure she could reasonably play a fit deputy. Her mom was right. If she couldn't do it, they would dump her. Insurance would pay her salary, but she would be out the opportunity, and it would get around that she wasn't available. She would likely lose out on the offers she had on the table.

Her life felt so precarious. She was always aware that her career could be over in the blink of an eye.

"I'm going to talk to your sister," her mother was saying. "She's the one who set the system up. She should have organized those cables better. And she shouldn't have put them anywhere near that pool."

"Don't blame Ally. She's doing the best she can." Her sister was the only one who actually knew how to set that stuff up. Normally she would go into a studio to record interviews, but the nearest one was in New Orleans, and she still didn't have a car. The idea of driving in via golf cart hadn't appealed.

The truth of the matter was she didn't particularly want to go into a studio. It was nicer to stay in Papillon. When she wasn't doing press, she'd joined Gavin in one of his classic on-set adventures. That was what he called exploring their environs. When she was a kid and filming in Europe, her mom had been nervous about taking them anywhere that wasn't pure tourist stuff. Gavin had been the one to scoop them all up and go *adventuring*, as he called it. There was something about Gavin Jacks that people responded to. He didn't come off like some pretentious Hollywood elite even when he was eating tofu or practicing yoga. People naturally liked him, and that meant they were willing to share their stories with him. When they were working together, Gavin would take Brynn, Ally, and her mom with him.

She'd enjoyed hanging out with him at the bar, playing pool and dancing with some of the locals. She apparently was now a member of a gym here in Papillon as well. And she was attending what had been called an all-new vision of *Cat on a Hot Tin Roof* with a cast made up entirely of actual cats.

She kind of loved this place.

"Ally needs to think about you. She cut corners because she's too busy doing her own social media to think about her sister," her mom said with a huff. "She doesn't have a job if you don't have a job."

And that was truly the problem between her and her sister. Ally never got to forget that Brynn was the breadwinner.

Her mom constantly reminded her that all things flowed from Brynn.

Of course her sister resented her, but it wasn't like she'd tangled the cords so Brynn would fall. And she'd only laughed a little. She'd been the one to call 911, only to have Harry tell her it would be far faster to drive to the clinic themselves.

Ally had been left behind to pick up the mess. Like usual.

Brynn sighed because she wasn't sure how to heal that breach between them. Most of the time Ally was great. She could count on her sister, but there was something fragile about their relationship. Like a thread that had been pulled too taut and could break at any moment.

"She's had to do a lot of tech work over the last couple of days," Brynn pointed out. "Don't make it worse than it needs to be."

"You sound exactly like Gavin. Has he been filling your head with all of his hippie nonsense?"

Brynn bit back a groan. "Gavin isn't a hippie, Mom, and you know it. He just doesn't think you need to be so hard on Ally, and I agree."

"Well, when you're a parent, I suppose you can handle things as you see fit," her mom bit out.

"You aren't treating her like a parent. You're acting like you're her employer," Brynn pointed out.

"Because I am," her mom shot back.

Her mother could be so touchy. She and Gavin had been arguing every single day, and it wasn't really Gavin's fault. Her mom snapped at him and he snapped back.

"That's the clinic up ahead." Harry completely ignored their argument like the gentleman he was. "And it looks like something's going on with the sheriff's office. I wonder what's happening. I hope everyone's all right."

She turned and saw what Harry was talking about. Major was sprinting up the street. He was in his uniform, and she had to admit the man made khakis work. Gavin was follow-ing behind him, though at a slower pace.

Harry passed him and pulled into the clinic's circular drive.

"Are you sure this is the only medical care we can get here?" her mom asked. "I would prefer an actual hospital."

"The closest one is in Houma, and it's an hour away." Harry put the truck in park. "Lila's excellent, and she's got everything Brynn will need. She can do X-rays and a CT scan. Her brother is a neurosurgeon in Dallas. She makes him read her CTs for free."

"I'm sure it's fine. Thank you for the ride, Harry." She prayed her ankle wasn't as bad as her mom was making it out to be.

"From what I understand, this woman isn't even a real doctor." Her mom wasn't as enamored of this small town as Brynn was.

"She's a nurse practitioner." She hoped this wasn't going to be one of those times her mom went all LA diva on every-one. There was a reason her mom was often misunderstood. It was because sometimes, she was terrible.

Where was Major going? Was there some kind of emer-gency? She opened the door to the truck as the glass entrance to the clinic whooshed open and a woman in scrubs walked out. She was a petite woman with an unmistakable air of com-petence about her.

"Good morning, Ms. Pearson. I'm Mabel," she explained. "I'm Lila's nurse, and I'll be doing your intake today."

"The nurse has a nurse?"

Yes, her mother was clearly going to be obnoxious. "Thanks, Mabel. It's my ankle. I twisted it while I was going into the pool. Sorry I'm still wet, but my mom wouldn't let me change first."

That was why she was sitting in Harry's truck wrapped in her wet clothes and a towel, looking like a half-drowned rat. Her hair was plastered to her head, and it was about to get crazy frizzy as it dried.

"She's likely sprained her ankle." Her mom stepped out of the truck. "And she has a possible concussion. She struck her head, and I want you to check her for dry drowning."

"Dry drowning?" Brynn asked. Sometimes she thought her mom was on the Internet far too much.

"You would know what I'm talking about if you had read the scripts I sent you," her mom complained. "It can happen."

"Very, very rarely." Mabel walked back and grabbed a wheelchair, unlocking the wheels and pushing it along. "And usually only to children. Ms. Pearson, did you inhale water?"

"No. I did not. I fell in the pool. I held my breath when I went in and swam to the shallow end. I hit my head when I was coming out. I didn't go back into the water. At no point did I have water in my lungs." Brynn started to ease out of her seat. Maybe she could get a glimpse of Major and figure out why he was running so hard.

What if he was going into something dangerous?

"Brynn!"

Then there he was. Major ran up to her as she hopped on one leg, not wanting to put weight on it until the doctor told her it was all right.

"What the hell happened?" Major looked her over, his hands on her shoulders. "Was it the reporters? Did they come out to the B and B?"

Did he think reporters routinely attacked her? "No. I was doing an interview for one of the morning shows and tripped over the cables and it was a whole thing. I'm fine, but my mom is insisting I get checked out. I twisted my ankle."

She'd barely gotten the words out before Major leaned over, hooked his arm under her knees, and hauled her up against his chest.

"Mabel, where's Lila?" Major asked.

"Young man, unhand my daughter." Her mom had her hands on her hips, a gleam of pure outrage in her eyes. "Put her down right now. She needs medical attention, not some ridiculous romantic gesture."

"Lila's inside getting exam room two prepped," Mabel said. "She should be ready by now. Be careful with our patient."

"Hey, shouldn't you tell him to put her down?" her mom argued. "It's dangerous."

Mabel shrugged. "Major's strong enough to carry her without falling, and I for one do enjoy a nice romantic gesture."

She heard her mom saying something, but Major whisked her through the doors and into the neat, clean clinic. She wrapped her arms around his shoulders for balance as he moved swiftly from the lobby to a corridor. "What are you doing here?"

"Someone dialed 911 and Armie overheard our dispatcher taking the call."

"My sister called. Harry thought it would be easier to come into town than to wait for an ambulance. It's not serious."

"Lila can make that decision." He didn't look down at her, merely kept walking. "Why are you wet? Did someone push you into the pool?"

His jaw was so tight, each word grinding out of his mouth like he could barely speak.

She reached up and cupped his cheek. "I'm fine. No one tried to hurt me. It was all an accident. I told you. I tripped and went into the pool, and then when I got out Duke tripped me up again and I hit my head on the guard rail. I did not lose consciousness. The only reason I stayed down so long was the sky was pretty."

He stopped, staring down at her, and then a smile crossed his face. "The sky was pretty?"

She nodded. "Puffy white clouds and a perfect blue, with

gold shining through. I wanted to take a couple of pictures because I can't draw those colors. But no one would let me."

"Because you might have a concussion." That smile on his face nearly melted her, and then it faded. "I heard some-one from the B and B was hurt, and I guess I panicked."

Because he was used to losing people he cared about. Because he'd lost his mom, and now his dad was dying.

"It's okay, and so am I," she reassured him. "I twisted my ankle. It's not a big deal."

"Is that my patient?" A woman in a white coat stood in the doorway. She was lovely, with dark hair and eyes that sparkled with amusement as she looked them over.

"Lila, this is Brynn Pearson." Major moved into the exam room when Lila allowed him by. He settled her on the table.

"Yes, I recognize her, though I know her by another name." Lila LaVigne pulled a stethoscope out of her jacket. "You know, normally we would use a wheelchair to bring you in. The handsome young man carrying you in is an upcharge."

She already liked the nurse practitioner. She appreciated a dry sense of humor. "I'm sure my insurance will love that."

"I was faster than Mabel." Major had the faintest blush to his cheeks.

Lila chuckled as she placed the stethoscope in her ears. "I bet you were. All right, then. Go to the waiting room. It's too tight in here for all of us, and from what my husband has told me, if I let you back here, the mom is going to want to come, too."

"Please, no." She didn't want her mom questioning every-thing the woman did. Her mother would be insufferable.

"I'll go and wait in the lobby." He gave her a half smile. "I'm glad you're okay. Seem to be okay." He frowned again and turned Lila's way. "She needs a CT scan, and you should call your brother. He needs to clear her before you let her leave. She hit her head."

Lila was already placing the chest piece against Brynn's heart. "Thanks for the mansplain, Deputy. I think I have it from here."

Major huffed. "I wasn't . . . I'll be outside."

Major hustled out the door.

"I don't think he was trying to be rude." Brynn watched the door close and wondered what it all meant. He'd come running at the thought of her being hurt. He hadn't let anyone touch her.

"No, he was being a bossy cop. Believe me, I know how to handle that specific type of man. They can be incredibly overprotective about women they care about. Sometimes it's nice. Sometimes it's a bit suffocating. Take a deep breath for me."

He'd come running when he'd thought she was in danger. That had to mean he'd been thinking about her as much as she'd been thinking of him. It had to.

"And another," Lila said.

Brynn did as asked and wondered if maybe the day wasn't going better than she'd imagined.

chapter ten

Major stepped out into the lobby and was immediately accosted by Diane Pearson.

"Where is my daughter? What did you do with her?" Diane was a tall woman, but even in heels he still had a couple of inches on her. She got into his space, and he had to take a step back.

"She's in the exam room with the nurse," he replied. "She's being taken care of, and Lila asked us all to wait out here."

"Well, I don't have to do that. She's my daughter." Diane stepped around him.

"She's your adult daughter who will be mortified if you walk in there like she's three," a familiar voice said.

Gavin Jacks had taken a seat and made himself comfortable.

"Mr. Jacks, can I get you anything?" Mabel was staring at the man like she'd never seen one before. Which was weird since she was closing in on sixty and had been married for almost forty years. "We've got coffee and tea and bottled water."

Gavin's countenance changed from slightly annoyed to

sunny in a heartbeat. "Dear woman, thank you for thinking of me. I would love some tea. Something herbal, if you have it. I find tea so soothing, don't you?"

Diane's frown deepened. "Are you a waitress or a nurse?"

Mabel didn't look back. "I'm such a fan, Mr. Jacks. I've watched you for years. All of your shows bring so much joy."

"Does Dale know?" Major couldn't help but ask because he was with Diane on this one. Mabel was a perfectly reasonable woman, a practical woman who didn't swoon at the sight of a man.

Mabel waved that off. "Of course he does. Gavin Jacks is my hall pass. I'll go see what we have."

Gavin stood and took Mabel's hand between both of his, charm pouring off him. "I'm honored. Why don't you show me where the break room is and I'll make us all some tea? Perhaps you could check on our Brynn and bring us some news. It might ease her mother's mind."

Mabel beamed up at him. "Of course. Come with me and I'll show you where it is." She started down the hall. "And don't worry about your girl. She's in excellent hands."

Gavin stopped in front of Diane, his voice going low. "Careful, darling. I can almost see an expression on your face. Wouldn't want your dermatologist to hear about that."

Diane practically growled his way. "Stay out of my relationship with my daughter."

"I'm trying to ensure you keep a relationship with your daughters. Emphasis on the multiple. Think about that." When he looked Major's way, the amiable smile was back on his face. "Excellent work, Deputy. The wheelchair would have been far too slow. And congratulations on your speed. It's easy to see why you looked so fit in your too-tight underwear. I'm going to gift you with some boxers."

He turned and walked after Mabel.

"I have boxers," Major said under his breath. "It was laundry day."

"Don't mind him. He's cranky." Diane turned back to the hall that led to the exam rooms, and for a moment Major was worried she would make a run for it. "Did Brynn seem all right? Is this Lila person competent?"

"She's great. Lila's smart, and she takes good care of every person who walks through those doors."

"My daughter didn't walk, though, did she?" A brow arched over her eyes.

"She's in good hands."

Diane turned his way. "All right, I'll accept that. But she's not in your hands, is she? You dumped her."

"I didn't dump her. I can't see anyone right now. I've got too much going on in my personal life."

A sigh came from the woman, a weary sound. "Yes, she mentioned your father is sick. I dealt with something very similar. I'm sorry to hear it's happening to you."

The compassion in her voice moved him because it wasn't expected. He'd thought he would have to fight to keep her in the lobby, but she seemed resigned. She seemed almost tired. Human. For the first time, she seemed less like a perfectly made-up warrior queen and more like a mom who genuinely loved her daughter.

Diane moved to the row of chairs along the far side of the waiting room. She would be able to watch the hallway for anyone coming from the exam rooms.

He joined her, sitting a couple of seats away. "He has early-onset dementia. He was diagnosed right about the same time we found the tumor. We cleared up the cancer, but the dementia has only gotten worse."

"Yes, it doesn't get better." Diane's eyes stayed on the hall. "I know how hard that is, Deputy."

"Brynn mentioned you lost your own mother to it." He was curious. He knew he'd been the one to break things off with Brynn, but he still thought about her, still wanted to know how her life worked and what her family was like. That desire to feel close to her made him willing to open up a bit.

"Oh, technically we lost her to a fall she took," Diane said quietly. "It's an odd thing. Her death certificate calls her death an accident, but she was gone long before. I sometimes wonder if that's why we don't do as much research on dementia as we do other diseases. It takes the soul and leaves the body behind."

His gut clenched because it wasn't like he hadn't thought the same thing before. Hearing it verbalized felt harsh but true. "I have to take care of him. I can't have reporters showing up at his home."

"I think it was a good decision on your part." Diane straightened up, obviously shoving her way through the emotions she'd been feeling. "Any relationship you could have with Brynn would be short and probably painful. Even if I thought you could handle a short-term physical relationship—which I do not—Brynn couldn't be with a man like you."

"A man like me?"

"I'm afraid you're my daughter's catnip, and not in a sexual way. Like I said, I have no issues with Brynn having a mutually satisfying affair, but she can't have one with you. You're the upstanding Captain America type with no real hint of bad boy inside, despite your choice of underwear."

He wasn't sure he liked the sound of that. "I'm not Dudley Do-Right."

She chuckled, rolling her eyes. "Oh, yes, you are. Let's see. You went into the military right after high school. You served honorably, even earning a medal for gallantry in battle. When you got out, you went to college and did what only a small percentage of police officers do. Most get an associate's certificate, but you got a bachelor's degree. Tell me. Why not go into a more lucrative profession?"

"I thought about going to law school, but honestly, I wasn't particularly passionate about it, and then my father was sick and I moved here. The best job I could get was with the sheriff's department, and I enjoy it."

"So you gave everything up to help your father."

"That just makes me a good son, not a saint."

"No, visiting your father would make you good. Changing your whole life for him makes you a saint. And that is why I think it's best you stick to your plan and stay away from her. Save her the heartache. Brynn is a very emotional person. She's also worked hard for her career. Do you understand how precarious her position is?"

"Gavin mentioned how she's got to take as much work as she can right now."

"Exactly. The man is obnoxious, but he knows what he's talking about. The last thing Brynn needs is distractions. Like I said, if I thought this was all about sex, I wouldn't mind. The girl needs some stress relief, but she's already emotional about you, and from what I saw a few moments ago, you're the same with her."

"I was worried."

"Yes, you became an Olympic sprinter because you heard a woman you barely dated might be injured in some way," Diane returned. She shifted so she could look him in the eyes. "Deputy, you made the right decision the first time. You made a mature and a kind decision to not involve yourself in what could be a very painful relationship for my daughter."

"You don't think she could handle a long-distance relationship?"

"I don't think you understand how that relationship would

have to work. I think she might decide to throw away what could be a stellar career for a small-town deputy. Do you see yourself in her world? Because if you couldn't handle that small kerfuffle, then I have no idea how you would function given what Brynn has to go through every day."

Brynn had told him it wasn't usually so bad. But then maybe Brynn hadn't wanted to scare him off. "I don't want to hurt her career, but I have to wonder if anyone worries about Brynn."

"I worry about Brynn all the time."

"I think you worry about Bria."

She flushed, her shoulders going straight. "I assure you I think of my daughter every second of the day, and I don't need someone who has no idea what we've gone through to tell me how to handle myself."

"I'm sorry. I was only trying to look out for Brynn."

"Well, that's my job, Deputy, and yours is to look out for your father. I thank you for coming in to see how she's doing. I'll take it from here. I've been taking care of her for a long time. I'll be doing it long after we've left this town. You don't have to wait around. It will only be painful for her, because nothing has changed."

He wanted to argue with her, but now that he knew Brynn wasn't having some kind of heart attack and hadn't been assaulted, he was starting to calm down, and all the things that came between them were right back at the front of his mind.

Then they were in front of his eyes as the doors to the clinic came open and a man walked through carrying a camera.

He recognized the photographer. It was easy. The man had spent all weekend at the station house since the judge had been out of contact and no bail could be set. Mickey Gunn strode into the clinic wearing the same clothes he'd left the station house in.

"Deputy, I'm surprised to find you here. Were you with Bria Knight when her sister called 911?" Mickey had his camera up.

Diane stood, blocking the photographer. "Deputy Blanchard was already here when we brought Bria in. He was helping out one of this town's citizens. How did you hear about Bria's accident? It's nothing more than a slight sprain. She tripped and fell. We brought her in out of an abundance of caution. Nothing more."

He had to give it to her. Diane knew how to handle the press. She was giving him a way out.

"Mickey." Gavin walked back in, two cups of tea in his hands. "Good of you to join us. Have you been listening to the police radio again?"

Gavin held the tea out to Diane. She stared at it pointedly.

Gavin rolled his eyes. "It's chamomile. And I didn't even poison it."

She huffed but took the mug. "Like you could kill me."

Mickey chuckled. "Well, it looks like things are normal here. And yes, you know I always like to listen in. It's how I get the jump on everyone else. I'm the last one standing, by the way. Jeannie and her crew went back to LA. She thinks the story is over since you've had your girl go on every talk show that will have her. I like the 'nothing to see here' vibe she's putting out."

"Did you like the 'sitting your ass in jail' vibe of this weekend?" He really didn't like this guy. Armie had kept him in the field the day he'd worked, and now Major realized why. Armie hadn't wanted him to listen to this guy talk and potentially lose his cool over what came out of the tabloid journalist's mouth.

Diane chuckled and moved in front of him, putting a hand on Mickey's arm and basically looking like she was the hostess at some cocktail party. "Don't mind our deputy friend, dear. And you know why our Bria is doing publicity. She loves to talk about the issues closest to her heart. She's such a softie. Especially when it comes to animals. I suspect she might not have even noticed someone was in trouble if it hadn't been for that precious dog."

Why were they talking to this guy? Pretending he wasn't some massive problem? Diane was treating him like an old friend.

"Why don't you leave Brynn alone?" Major didn't understand why they were talking to this jerk.

Diane turned to him, a humorless smile on her face. "It was good to talk to you, Deputy, but I'm sure you need to get back to your job. Didn't you say you were busy and couldn't handle any extra attention right now?"

The last bit was said under her breath, a reminder that he was walking a fine line.

Was she trying to help him? He didn't understand this world he'd been inadvertently brought into, and he had a million questions.

He wanted to stay but everything Diane had said came flooding back. Brynn had a career she'd worked hard for, and he could screw that up for her. They couldn't have more than a couple of weeks. Was it worth the inevitable heartache? For them both?

"You're right. I do need to get back to the station house." He tipped his head. "I'm glad it wasn't serious. Tell Brynn I wish her well, but I had to get back to work."

"Will do," Gavin said. "And let the sheriff know I'll be back later this afternoon. I need to stay and make sure the ladies don't need anything."

"We don't," Diane said, sitting back down.

"You might," Gavin countered.

Major walked away as they began arguing—something they seemed to do a lot. His gut in a knot, he stepped out as a golf cart turned into the circular drive.

Major stopped staring at the absolutely-not-street-legal vehicle and felt his teeth grind. "Greg, I thought the sheriff talked to you about not doing this anymore."

Greg's eyes widened and he paled slightly. "Nah. Sheriff just told me not to use the highway."

A blond wisp of a young woman stepped out of the back of the cart. "He didn't use the highway at all. He did manage to get this thing over some crazy terrain, and he avoided an alligator."

"It was Otis. I told you there was nothing to worry about," Greg insisted. "And I got you here right quick. Like I said I would."

Ally Pearson handed him a twenty with a regal nod. "That you did. You drive that sucker better than any New York cabbie and with far less care for anything resembling caution. I like it. I've got a good dose of adrenaline going. I'm going to be here for a while, and then I'll probably need a drink. Pick me back up in an hour and I'll pay you a hundred for the night."

Greg's eyes lit up.

Major had to put a stop to this immediately. "No. Absolutely not. This is not a legal business. He doesn't have a commercial license. And he's definitely not driving you around at night in a golf cart."

"I don't see why not. He's got lights and everything," Ally replied.

"I'll be back. Papa needs new shoes." Greg sped away.

Well, he went as fast as the golf cart allowed. Major could probably have chased him down, but it wasn't like he didn't know where the guy lived. This was how it went in Papillon. "The service Greg is providing isn't legal."

Ally shrugged. "It's easy to see you don't support entre-preneurism. Personally, I think Guber is a brilliant idea. I told him he should begin a Kickstarter campaign and raise money for a whole fleet."

The idea made him shake in his boots. "Tell me you didn't."

A ghost of a smile crossed Ally's face. She looked a lot like her sister, only even more slender. "Maybe I did. Maybe I'm joking. Either way, I think it's fun to make you sweat a little after what you did to my sister. Way to break a girl's heart, TW."

He was never living that down. "I didn't mean to."

Ally settled her bag over her shoulder. It was an expensive-looking thing. "Men never do. Tell me something—did my mom get to you? She likes to have talks with the boys . . . I guess I should call them men now . . . Brynn dates."

He could see where Diane might be a meddling momma, but in this case, she hadn't affected his decision. "It had nothing to do with your mom. It was a personal reason."

A perfectly arched brow rose over her eyes. "And you're here today by coincidence?"

"I heard something happened to Brynn and I wanted to check in on her." He didn't mention that he would likely need a shower because he'd sprinted here.

His heart had constricted at the thought of Brynn being hurt. All he'd been able to think about was how anything could have happened to her. His mind had played out all the worst possibilities as he'd made his way here, every one of them ending with her being gone.

He wasn't a very optimistic person when it came to this.

"She's already done? I knew she wasn't that hurt. Faker." Ally crossed her arms over her chest, her perfectly straight hair swinging.

"No, she's still in the exam room."

"So you came to see how she is but you're leaving before

you find out?" Ally was staring at him again, her attention laser focused as though she was studying him.

"Your mom might have mentioned it would be better if I didn't stir things up again," he explained. "And then a reporter showed up."

Ally snapped her fingers. "I knew it. My mom is good at manipulating people. I would bet she gave you the whole 'Brynn is a brilliant actress, and her career is worth more than any relationship' speech."

He'd said Diane had nothing to do with his decision, and she hadn't originally. That had been all about protecting his father. But maybe she had run him out today. Though mostly she'd reminded him of all the reasons he shouldn't have come here in the first place. "She might have mentioned that Brynn doesn't have time for a relationship and that she's worked hard to get where she is. It would be bad to derail her. I don't know what that feels like. I've never desperately wanted something."

"You didn't know what you wanted to be when you grew up?" Ally sounded surprised.

He thought about what his father would say to him every time he worried that he didn't have the same surety about his future others seemed to have. His father had figured out early on what he was good at. Major liked his job, but he'd never felt that deep passion others seemed to find. "I just wanted to be happy."

"Brynn started acting when she was five. It's all she knows. Do you know the one thing no one asked her at that age?" Ally didn't wait for a reply. "What she wanted. What would make her happy. My mom is so invested in Brynn's future that she never thought to ask what Brynn wanted, and over the years Brynn forgot to ask herself the question, so don't think she's smarter than you, TW."

What was Ally talking about? "Brynn loves acting."

"Has she told you that?"

Had she? Not in so many words. What she'd talked about was art. She'd talked about how much she loved being on set because she enjoyed meeting new people and learning things from them. She'd talked about the dark side of the industry as much as she'd talked about the good parts. "Why else would she work so hard?"

"Because she doesn't know another world. Because she grew up in this world, surrounded by people who want what she has. Including me."

"I don't think anyone wants all the scrutiny. Your mom is in there pretending like that jerk is some kind of friend of hers."

"Mickey? I heard he was the last one standing." Ally glanced in before turning back Major's way. "He's pond scum, but he has connections. And don't think my mom doesn't calculate her every move when it comes to him. No one loves that part, but some of us handle it better than others. I would handle the attention far better than Brynn because I don't have the same level of human emotion that my sister has. I'm an actress. All my emotion is for the stage or screen or wherever I happen to be working. My career is everything to me. It's my heart and soul. It's the only child I ever want, the only spouse I'll ever have. That's what it takes. There are very few real movie stars who have happy families because a Hollywood star belongs to the world. Brynn will be miserable, but I can't convince anyone of that. Including Brynn. I thought you might be the one to do it."

"I can't tell her what to do. It wouldn't be right." No matter how much he wanted to. "Brynn is smart, and she knows what she wants."

Ally shook her head. "So hot, and you haven't listened to a word I said. It's okay. I'd try to seduce you myself because I could enjoy all that hotness and not get involved.

See my prior comments on emotions. But it wouldn't work, would it? What do you say I skip my Guber ride and you take me out?"

"Absolutely not."

"But I would give you what you want, and you wouldn't have to worry about hurting me. You wouldn't have to worry about reporters showing up. I'm a very good time."

He backed up, the thought repulsive to him. "No. I'm not looking for a good time."

Ally relaxed. "Yeah, that's what I thought. Good for you. Not many men pass that particular test. You're different, TW. So is Brynn. I hope my sister sees it before it's too late."

She turned and walked into the clinic.

He stared inside as Ally walked up and her mother frowned her way. Gavin was talking to the reporter like they were old friends.

He didn't understand any of it.

He turned because it was time to get back to the world he did understand. Diane was right. There was no place for him here.

He started walking back down the street, passing the café and making it to the park where kids were playing. It was the place where Wednesday morning yoga happened. It was a place where he could breathe.

He stopped for a moment and looked up at the sky.

Brynn was right. Those colors were spectacular, and she would miss it. How long would it be before these specific colors graced the sky again? There was a golden haze coming through the blue and white.

Maybe there was one thing he could give her.

Major didn't care that he probably looked like a weirdo. Hell, weirdo was a good description for most of this town. He walked out on the green grass and laid down on his back, his cell in hand. The sun felt good on his face.

He took pictures, playing around with the capabilities of the camera to catch those colors for her.

A shadow fell over him, and suddenly, instead of a brilliant sky, all he could see was Zep Guidry's face staring down at him.

"Hey, you okay?" Zep looked concerned.

Major pulled back his phone. "I'm fine. I'm taking some pictures for a friend."

Zep straightened up. "Oh, good. Then you weren't attacked by a group of raccoons who've formed a small army. Not that they have. That's only a rumor. I hope. By the way, if you see anything weird, let me know."

And that was life in Papillon in a nutshell.

Brynn would think that was funny.

Not that he would tell her the town's animal expert was worried about armed raccoons. But he would send her the pictures of the sky.

It was the least he could do.

"She doesn't need an MRI." The nurse practitioner had lost her smile. Lots of people did when dealing with her mother. They stood in the lobby of the clinic, having finished with Lila LaVigne's very thorough scan. "I gave her a CT scan and had one of Dallas's best neurosurgeons read it."

"But he's not here," her mother argued. "You don't have one on staff, one who could examine her himself."

"No, oddly enough in a town of less than five hundred we don't have a neurologist on staff," Lila said with a sigh.

"I'm fine, Mom." Brynn felt a small wave of embarrassment rush over her. It was the same feeling she had any time her mom treated her like she was five and if she broke, the world would break with her. "I don't have any kind of a concussion and my ankle is much better. All I need is some over-the-counter analgesics and ice. We don't even have to call the production company, because I'm fine."

"She's got some minor swelling but there's no fracture. I wouldn't even call it a sprain," Lila assured them all. "She's got her full weight on it. If it hurts, I'd advise her to ice it. Otherwise, she's fine. If you need a second opinion, Houma is that way." Lila pointed to the west. "I'll send you my bill."

Lila turned and started to walk away.

"Thank you."

Lila turned back, and her expression warmed. "You're welcome, Brynn. And if you have any questions or concerns, feel free to call me. But don't give my card to anyone else, please."

She didn't want her mom to call at all hours. "Understood."

"And if you're going to the station house, maybe you should spend the afternoon listening. Take it easy. Tomorrow is soon enough for a ride-along. I know it seems quiet out here, but sometimes things get crazy. Give it a day before you test that ankle out again," Lila said before heading back down the hall.

Brynn looked around the small waiting room, wondering where Major had gotten to. The only people left were her mom and Ally. Had Major taken Gavin back to the station house? She was surprised Gavin had left. He usually hung around during times of crisis. Gavin tended to show up whenever he was needed. Sometimes it was like the man had psychic abilities when it came to her family.

"Why would you go to the station house?" Her mother had crossed her arms over her chest. "You've had a day. You need to be resting."

"I came out here early so I could do some research. I can't do that if I'm lying around the B and B." The truth was she hadn't really thought about going in. She'd rather dreaded it because it meant she would be around Major, and he would behave in one of two ways. He would be courteous and ignore her as much as possible. That would hurt, but what might hurt more was him being his normal nice-guy self and reminding her how much she missed him.

Now it seemed like a perfectly reasonable thing to do since all her interviews were over. They were out of crisis mode, and her mom would go right back to trying to get her to decide on a new project. This morning, her mother had announced that she'd gotten two new scripts from the agency and Brynn could tape her initial auditions right there at the B and B.

So getting her heart broken seemed like the better bet.

Her mom huffed and looked over the paperwork Mabel had handed her before Lila had walked her out. "I don't understand why. Don't you think the screenwriters know what they're doing? I will never forgive Gavin for putting these thoughts in your head. You don't need to research. The writers have already done it all for you."

Ally snorted. "Yeah, because no screenwriter was ever lazy about research."

"Not everything needs to be realistic," her mom shot back. "After all, we're selling fantasy. I assure you there are no hookers working Hollywood who look like Julia Roberts, and yet everyone loved *Pretty Woman*. Also, does anyone actually believe most of those sitcom men could get wives like that? Of course not."

"Did you read this script, Mom?" She glanced around again, trying to figure out if Major was perhaps getting a snack or something. "It's not a fantasy. It's a gritty drama about a father and daughter trying to solve a mystery. Their whole lives revolve around their jobs. I'd like to get it right."

"Yes, and you and Gavin were cast in the roles. How many—" Her mom seemed to rethink. "All right, the deputy aside, how many police officers look like Gavin? Again, we're selling the fantasy that a man with that face would be stuck in a small town. Well, the sheriff is very attractive, too. It's odd. It's almost like they didn't know how attractive they were so they didn't realize they could get better jobs. It's a shame."

"You know it takes more than a pretty face to act," Ally tried to point out.

Her mom shrugged. "Of course, darling. You're extremely talented. And so is Brynn. We should get back to the B and B. I'll call our driver to come get us. I wish he'd stayed around, but he said something about having to pick up a child."

"Luc has school." Her mom wasn't great about getting to know people who weren't directly involved in the industry. She genuinely preferred dogs. She already knew Harry's German shepherd's habits but had no idea how old his children were. "And he's not our driver. Taking us here was a favor."

"Ooooh, I'll call Greg. I think we can keep him on retainer for pretty cheap," Ally offered.

"I'm not riding in something called a Guber," her mom said between clenched teeth, as though they'd already had this argument.

She'd taken Greg's golf cart already. He needed to put better shocks on that cart if he wanted to drive it over rough terrain.

"Well, I'm going to walk to the station house. If I can't get some time with Roxanne, I'll hang around and figure out how things work. I don't think it's far from here." She knew it was close to the town square. "Where's Major? I can walk with him."

Her mom's expression shuttered. "He's not here. He went back to work."

He'd seemed so concerned about her. She couldn't help

but feel disappointed that he'd walked away without finding out how she was. "Did he take Gavin with him?"

"Gavin is distracting that awful reporter so you don't have to deal with him." Her mom pulled out her cell. "I'll tell him to draw it out since we need to find a ride."

No wonder her deputy had gone. She'd thought all the reporters had left town when she'd started granting interviews. She'd done a sit-down with *Entertain America* to get rid of their crew, but she hadn't seen the freelancer around town. She'd hoped he'd left. "Tell me you didn't let him harass Major."

"Of course I didn't. I know you care for the young man. I was also worried that if Mickey kept his mouth going, your deputy might have shut it for him," her mom replied. "I don't think Mickey understands that no one out here cares his brother is a lawyer."

"I'm all for TW pounding on the guy," Ally added. "I mean, what does he have to lose? Mickey can sue all he likes and he's not getting anything out of the deputy but a couple of pairs of briefs."

Her sister could be so obnoxious. "He's not some broke guy. He owns his own house and has a good job. Stop calling him that. He has a name, and he deserves your respect."

"Probably." Ally held up her phone and snapped a quick pic. "After all, he totally turned me down when I offered him no-strings-attached sex."

"You did what?" Had she meant to screech that question?

Ally held the camera up again. "Could you smile? I can't Photoshop that expression off your face."

Her mom glanced down at the screen. "You can't use that one. It's horrible. Take another."

"Stop." She wasn't going to do some social media campaign right now. They had other things to talk about. "Did you hit on Major?"

Ally didn't look up from her phone. "Of course I did."

Her mom put a hand on Ally's shoulder. "That was a good plan. Turned you down flat, huh? I rather thought that would be his answer. Did he look scared?"

Ally chuckled even as she was typing on her phone. "Terrified. The man has no idea how to handle someone like me. He's one hundred percent into Brynn and isn't about to use her family to get to her. I almost think he views us as a minus instead of a plus."

"Yeah, I'm thinking the same thing right now," Brynn complained. "How could you?"

Ally slid her phone into the LV crossbody she'd bought a couple of weeks back. She'd claimed it was the bag of the season. "I always test your boyfriends. Not that I would actually sleep with any of them, but I test them. If they say yes, I explain the way of the world to them, complete with the recording I made of our conversation, and then they go away and can't hurt you again. I have the one with Major. You can practically hear his revulsion. It was a little offensive."

Brynn stared at her sister for a moment, not sure whether to be horrified or sort of grateful. It was awful, but it was also the way Ally showed she cared. By offering to sleep with her boyfriends.

"Honey, you know she worries about you," her mother replied in a soothing tone. "But while the deputy passed the sleep-with-Ally test, he still isn't right for you. I truly did have to hustle him away from Mickey. There's a level of political savvy required to work in this business. We can't have a man attached to you who punches reporters. I know you think I was looking out for you, but I was also looking out for him. He would be miserable in our lifestyle."

"Yeah, well, maybe I'm miserable, too." She turned and walked out. Gently. It wasn't really a hobble.

Her mother hurried behind her. "You do not mean that. You're sad, and I understand. He's a lovely man and he seems to be nice, but he doesn't fit in our world."

There was no arguing with her mother. Not about something like this. She wouldn't waste her breath.

The truth of the matter was she didn't want Major to have to deal with that part of her world, either. She'd spent days doing the worst part of the job, and she was tired. She wanted to be alone for a while and decompress, but they started principal photography in a couple of weeks, and the pressure would be on.

On? It was already building.

"Brynn, I'm not trying to be mean."

"And yet you manage beautifully." She continued down the road. Up ahead there was a park. It was pretty and green. She'd eaten lunch out here a few days before, watching the squirrels and enjoying the sunny day. She'd pretended she lived here, tried to put herself in this place and in the mindset of her character.

Except she hadn't thought about the script. She'd thought about what it would be like to do what she wanted. To paint and read and build something without all the expectations that came with being Bria Knight.

She'd thought about how cool it was that almost everyone here called her Brynn.

She'd daydreamed about what it would mean to be Major Blanchard's girlfriend.

"I know you're going through some fatigue right now. You've been working constantly for months, and you've got the press junket for the comedy coming up." Her mom kept a steady pace beside her. "It's a lot, and it's normal to feel emotional. Many people your age seem to have a quarter-life crisis, but you can't afford it, honey."

Brynn stopped. "I'm not emotional. I'm tired. I've been working this way for most of my life. Don't try to tell me I'm in some childhood-to-work transition. I went through that at five."

"Are you saying you're going through some sort of child-hood regression? Should we call a therapist? Gavin has one on speed dial. You know he's very sensitive."

He was definitely more sensitive than her mother. Gavin would have realized she needed some alone time. Gavin had likely been the one to come up with the plan to waylay the reporter so she could get away. Her mom would have told her to smile and give the man what he wanted.

She knew deep down that wasn't fair. Her mom didn't throw her to the wolves or anything, but it didn't matter in that moment.

She wasn't even sure where she was going. She could go to the station house and try to avoid Major. She could wait for a ride to take her back to the B and B, where she would have to listen to her mother make phone call after phone call checking on her other clients and negotiating deals most peo-ple would die for while Ally practiced for her auditions and made bratty remarks.

She could sit here for a while.

"I'm sorry, sweetie." Her mom didn't seem to be reading the room. Or the park. She simply followed her as she started for an empty bench near the gazebo. "I know you're tired and I've been pushing you. I promise, when you get through the next couple of projects, I'll make sure we all go to Hawaii or something."

Brynn turned on her mom, and there must have been something about the look on her face, because her mother actually took a step back.

"Or you can go wherever you like all by yourself as long as it's safe." Her mom gave her what Brynn had come to think of as her manager smile. It was upbeat and sympathetic and promised the world as long as every single thing went exactly right. "You can paint and play the artist for a week. Or two."

Brynn ignored her and made her way to the bench. She needed to think about what she wanted to do. "Go away, Mom. I want to be alone."

The smile left her mom's face. "You're never alone, sweetie. I'll sit on that bench over there, but I can't leave you out here without a ride. Gavin won't be able to keep Mickey occupied forever, and I don't want him to catch you alone. I don't trust him. I'll be quiet. I'll do email. You know I'm here so you can do your thinking thing."

"Hey, should you be walking around? Are you okay?" a familiar voice asked.

She turned and Major was standing there dressed in his khaki uniform and looking good enough to eat. He wasn't alone. There was a man with a big net by his side. He had on a set of utility overalls that did nothing to lessen the fact that he was also a gorgeous man. Still, he had nothing on Major. "I'm fine. I was coming out here to sit for a while. I thought I could catch that sky."

"I'm afraid it's changed. Storm's coming in." Major gestured to where the gray clouds had started to overtake the sky she'd seen earlier.

Wasn't that the way her life worked? She saw something she wanted to hold on to and it slipped through her fingers because she was chasing someone else's dream.

Had she just thought that?

"Hey, it's okay." Major held out a hand as thunder rumbled. "Come here." He led her up the steps to the cover of the gazebo. "It's only light rain. I checked the weather while I was helping Zep track down our trash panda army."

The man named Zep didn't seem to be worried about the

oncoming rain. He gave Major a thumbs-up. "Thanks for that. I'll let you know if the rabies tests come back positive."

"What?" She turned his way.

He shook his head. "I didn't get bitten, though it was a close thing. And I took some pictures. Did you get my texts?"

"Deputy? My daughter is very irritated with me and obviously needs some space." Her mom had her handbag over her head, making it clear that her hair was more important than any designer bag. She stood outside the safety of the gazebo, a clear sign that she truly understood how upset Brynn was. Her mom always knew when it was time to give her space. "But I can't leave until I know someone will bring her home. I don't think she should get into that golf cart Ally loves."

"No one should," Major replied. "Seriously, it's not legal. Anyway, I'll make sure she gets home."

It was all her mom needed to hear. She ran back toward the clinic as fast as those Chanel pumps would take her, probably to try to protect her precious hair from the rain.

It was good to know she hated wet hair more than Major. It was also nice to see that her mother—no matter how overbearing she could be—respected her enough to give her space when she clearly needed it.

He'd texted her?

She pulled her phone from her pocket and sure enough, there they were. Pictures of the sky. He had to have taken them while he was lying on his back, camera facing up toward the sun.

"I hope they help," he said, taking a seat.

She sat down across from him, looking down at the pictures. He'd taken them because she couldn't. He'd thought about what she'd missed and made sure she had an alternative. "They're beautiful."

"I'm glad, because taking those pictures resulted in me having to help Zep round up raccoons. They had colonized the trash bin behind the convenience store." Major sat back. "I'm pretty sure they're responsible for several theft incidents that have been reported lately. All snack foods. They like snack foods."

For the first time in days, she felt a real smile cross her face. She put the phone away. It could wait. "Tell me all about it."

She sat back and listened as the rain fell softly around them.

chapter eleven

"Okay, so according to Zep we have a real raccoon problem on our hands." The sheriff stood in the middle of the main room of the station house, his fists on his hips as he stared out at his employees. He looked like a man going to war.

With raccoons.

Brynn looked up from the desk she'd been assigned to. It was a bank of two desks facing each other. Gavin sat on the other side when he wasn't out with the sheriff. They'd fallen into a pattern for the last week. They shadowed the officer they'd been paired with, working the same hours, though their version of work was mostly hanging out, asking questions, and getting out of the way when they needed to.

It had been a peaceful week. She liked Roxie a lot, and she'd spent some time with the deputy and her handsome, funny husband, Zep, who turned out to be Seraphina's younger brother. She'd been invited to dinner, where the couple had grilled steaks and told her stories about living in their quirky town.

She and Gavin had also been invited to the LaVigne house. It was busy and happy and chaotic.

But she hadn't had more than a glimpse of Major since

that rainy day in the park. She'd seen a schedule and knew he usually worked the same shifts as Roxie, but she'd been told he'd changed with Landon Price. Roxie had mentioned something about spending time with his dad.

She rather thought he'd changed his schedule so he wouldn't be around her.

"Isn't that Zep's problem?" Landon asked. "He's in charge of animal services."

Roxie looked up from the paperwork she'd been doing. Paperwork, Brynn had learned, was a whole lot of her job. The screenwriters got that wrong. "Yes, he's in charge all by himself with no staff except a couple of high school volunteers who really just want to pet dogs and cats. We can't send them out to fight a war."

Landon's eyes rolled. "War?"

"Well, someone taught one of those raccoons how to open the doors to the crates Zep had them in." Roxie put her pen down and sat back. "We were scheduled to release the little suckers on protected land two days ago but Brian got out, and we're pretty sure he was the one who sprung the other three. I think they waited until Zep came in and snuck out the back. He likes to leave that back door open. Says there's a nice breeze in the morning."

"Brian?" Gavin was paying attention now, a grin on his face like he knew this was going to be good.

"It's what Leonard Denmore named him," Armie explained. "He found Brian in his backyard. He was a baby abandoned by his mother, probably because she died. Leonard took him in and fed him and got way too invested."

"People keep raccoons as pets?" Gavin asked, obviously fascinated. Gavin loved any quirkiness. He called it the ultimate expression of humanity.

"As babies, raccoons are adorable and quite affectionate, and then they hit mating age and become feral demons who love to throw their own feces around," Roxie replied. "Leonard's landlord had Brian removed before he could chew up all the wiring in the house and now Leonard has two very nice cats who don't toss food at visitors. Zep relocated Brian to a more appropriate habitat, but he's pretty sure Brian found his way back to town and brought along his new gang. They've hit at least three different streets on garbage day. It was not pretty."

"Trash collection is early here." Armie leaned on one of the free desks. "Most people put their cans out the night before, and that's when the critters go to work. We always have problems, but I've got to admit Brian has taken it to a whole other level. It's like *The Purge* but with garbage."

Landon frowned. "I still don't see how this falls under our department. Maybe Zep should call sanitation."

Rachelle Martin was one of two dispatchers. She wore a wrap dress and sensible shoes. She was probably in her mid-twenties, but she dressed like she was trapped in her fifties. "It's our problem because I'm getting calls every single day, Landon Price. You don't even live in town, so you don't know how bad it is. Hallie Rayburn is in a state of terror. She'd just tossed out her new baby's trash. Do you know what a group of raccoons can do with a bunch of diapers? It is horrifying. You have to catch them. They are menaces."

Landon seemed to have lost his arrogance and simply nodded. "Will do. So how do we police what are essentially large and apparently organized rodents?"

"One of you on night shift, go out with Zep tonight," Armie ordered. "He's got a plan to catch them in the act, so to speak. Luckily we're pretty sure they aren't rabid, but I would wear gloves. And maybe goggles. They're good at throwing stuff."

"Major's on night shift this week," Landon pointed out.

Armie's face went grim. "I think we're going to need to cover for him for a couple of days."

Roxie was sitting up straight again. "He has an appointment with his dad's doctors. He told me he would be done long before he had to come in." Her face went tight. "He's going to need the night off, isn't he?"

Armie nodded. "You know I can't talk about things my wife might know. Or that I might have overheard. But I think we should be ready to take care of his shifts for a couple of days."

"I'll do it," Roxie volunteered. "I'll go home and feed the pets and come back and work his shift."

"We'll split it," Landon offered. "One of us can stay an extra couple of hours and one comes in early. We can handle it for however long Major needs."

Brynn's heart threatened to constrict. What was Major going through? She couldn't ask because Armie couldn't answer. It was obvious he knew something about Major's father he wasn't supposed to know.

Brynn stood. She needed some air. It had been a week since she'd done anything more than wave hi to Major when she saw him, and she couldn't shake the feeling that she was missing something good.

She pushed through the station house's doors and out to the front, where there was a green yard and a big oak tree. There was a bench where she'd seen some of the local kids sit and eat ice cream they got from the truck that wound its way across the town.

She missed him. She hadn't known the man for long and she missed him like they'd been together forever.

"Hey, you okay?" Gavin sat down beside her.

She stared out across the lawn. The park wasn't far, and she could smell the heavenly scent of fried chicken coming from the diner. "I've gotten to like this place."

"Me, too. Are you upset that we start work next week? Or are you worried about him?"

She thought about the question for a moment. "Can I be both?"

"Of course you can." Gavin slung an arm around the back of the bench. "His father is sick, right? I heard him talking on the phone to a nurse."

"He has early-onset dementia," she replied. "He's on a new protocol, and according to Major, it seemed to be helping him a lot. I suspect he's getting bad news today. I wish I could be there for him."

"It sounds like he's got a lot of friends."

"But no one who's going to hold him."

Gavin was quiet for a moment as though thinking about what he should say next. "Your mother is wrong about this, isn't she? You truly care for the man."

She was starting to think she might be in love with him and that the situation was utterly hopeless. "I do."

"Your mom thinks once you get to work, you'll forget about him. You'll get all into character and forget you're crazy about the deputy."

She snorted at the thought. "My mom thinks I'm a way better actress than I am. I know you tried to teach me all the Stella Adler and Stanislavski stuff, but it never took. I'm not the actress who stays in character and you know it."

"Yes, I think that's more Ally's style," he mused. "She's actually quite good. I wish your mother would see how hungry she is."

"She's getting Ally auditions."

"All the wrong ones," Gavin countered. "She's trying to push Ally as some bright, innocent ingenue. She should be looking at indie projects with teeth. Quirky characters. Her insistence that Ally should play likable characters is wrong. She should play to type."

Well, at least Gavin was honest. "Mom is doing what she thinks is best."

"Is that what you're doing?"

"What does that mean?" Brynn asked.

"It means I've watched you for the last couple of years and you're not happy, honey." He turned her way, giving her what she liked to think of as his dad look. It was the earnest expression he got on his face whenever he wanted her to talk about something she didn't want to talk about.

He'd had that expression on his face when she'd been seventeen and scared of a director who told her he couldn't wait until she was legal. The director had a countdown to her eighteenth birthday put up on the set. As a joke, of course. It had been creepy and she'd been deeply uncomfortable.

Gavin had been the one to take care of the problem. She wasn't sure he could take care of the problem now, though, since she wasn't truly sure what the problem was.

"I have a life most people dream about," she began.

"That's because most people don't understand what it entails," Gavin replied. "They see you and think you have all the money in the world and not a single care. Of course, that's not true. You're human. You have problems. But I worry you've been in this lifestyle so long that you don't know what you want anymore, and meeting that man was a turning point for you."

"I think meeting Major has definitely made me wonder if I'm missing something. We have a connection I haven't felt before. Being in this town has made me consider slowing down." Back in LA, it felt like every moment of the day was scheduled. When she was on set, every minute absolutely was scheduled. It had been years since she'd had more than a handful of days off, much less time to sit and think without worrying about what was coming next. "Since the press left, it's been nice. People here mostly treat me like anyone else. It's a refreshing change."

Even her mom had calmed down after she'd agreed to pick

a script. She was waiting on the contracts and was due to be on set outside of Atlanta for a romantic comedy a few days after she wrapped this film. She was playing the best friend, and it looked like a fun role.

So why wasn't she looking forward to it?

She only had a few more weeks here, and starting Monday, every one of them would be spent working. No more sitting on the dock watching the water. No more early mornings hanging out with Seraphina in the kitchen. No more walking Duke around the town square and grabbing an iced tea before joining the Wednesday morning yoga class.

"You seem to fit in well around here," Gavin remarked.

"So do you," she pointed out. "I've heard they asked you to lead the yoga class this Wednesday."

A grin crossed his face. "The yoga ladies are lovely. I'm excited to help lead them through one of my routines. I like this place enormously, but I'll also leave it because I know where I belong."

"In LA?"

"On the road," he corrected. "I belong on set, in a theater, or on a soundstage. It's what I've always wanted, and despite the drawbacks, it's still what I want. I've come to understand that I won't ever be Laurence Olivier or Marlon Brando. I'll always be viewed as a journeyman actor, but the work is good. The work fills my soul. I have to ask you a hard question and you don't have to answer me now."

She knew exactly what he was going to ask. "I don't know. I don't think it fills mine. I worry you're right. I've been in it for so long that it would be weird to be out of the business. It's all I know."

"Then maybe it's time to learn something new," he said quietly. "Have you thought about the fact that you worked during the time in your life when you should have been exploring the world and figuring out what you want? When other kids were being kids, you were earning a living. Maybe it's time for you to be a dumb kid for a while."

She didn't see how that could happen. "I've already agreed to a new project, and I think Mom's got a few ideas for the one after that. She wants me to do at least four projects this year. You have to strike while the iron's hot, you know."

"Yes, I've heard that expression myself." He sat back. "But what I'm hearing is what your mother wants. Not what you want. I'm worried that you've been listening to her for so long, you don't know how to listen to yourself. I don't think you ever learned how to."

She didn't like the sound of that. "I'm not a doormat, Gavin."

"I didn't say you were. You've always been able to stand up for yourself. Even when you were a kid."

"Well, I had a couple of good role models."

"It helps that you worked with the same people for long periods of time. You know, I was the one who convinced your mother to let you do *Janie's World.*"

That was something she hadn't heard. "Why wouldn't she have wanted me to do a TV show?"

"Because you'd recently come off a long-running show where you weren't the lead, and obviously you weren't going to be the lead in *Janie's World*, either. I convinced her to let you do the pilot by telling her it probably wouldn't get picked up. I lied. It's the only time I've ever lied to your mom."

"Why would you do that?"

He sighed. "For selfish reasons. And unselfish ones. The selfish reason was I viewed you as a daughter. We spent six years playing father and daughter, and we spent a lot of our off time together as well because your mother and I were friendly. I enjoyed being part of your family since I had none of my own."

She'd always known that was why he would show up

around dinnertime with the excuse that he wanted to talk some point of business with her mom and would stay to help clean up and have a glass of wine. Gavin's parents had cut him loose as a teen, and he hadn't heard from them except when they asked for money. He'd never married and didn't seem to want to. But he'd still wanted a family. He'd still wanted people he belonged with. "And the unselfish reason?"

He seemed to think about what to say for a moment. "You were fourteen and I thought you needed a stable environment where you could make the money you needed to make without the pressure of having a whole show on your shoulders. Your mom wanted to try to make you a teenage sitcom princess, but I've known how hard that was on some of those girls. I thought *Janie's World* was a better fit. Your character was in every episode, but the pressure wasn't on you to carry the show. I knew it would get picked up and I suspected it would have a long run. I didn't want you constantly auditioning and making pilots and getting disappointed. I wanted you to be able to finish school and have as normal a childhood as you could."

It struck her suddenly how much of an impact he'd had on her upbringing. "Did I ever thank you for that?"

His arm came around her shoulders and his head leaned against hers. "You don't have to. I know your mom and I fight a lot, but you and your mom and Ally have been the closest thing I have to a family, and I'm a better man for it."

"Yes, I think you're the brother Mom never thought she would have." They bickered like siblings and then leaned on each other when they needed to.

"I suppose that's one way to describe us." He hugged her tight. "In the spirit of me thinking of you as a daughter, I wanted to talk to you about taking some time off. I know you're worried about what your mother will think and that it's going to set your career back, but I promise if you decide this is what you want, I'll make sure you get back on track with your career."

"You can't promise that."

"I can," he said with a level of surety. "I've got good connections, and I'll make it work. Brynn, I've got some friends in the art world, and one of them teaches at the Sorbonne in Paris. I sent him an informal portfolio, and he thinks he can get you into a summer program that could lead to being admitted on a full-time basis."

"You did what?" She couldn't have heard him right.

He backed off. "I took pictures of your best work, some of the paintings you gave me. I sent them to my friend. Do you remember when I played Van Gogh's drinking buddy in the biopic? I spent some time with a man named Jean Paul Goden. He's a professor of art."

She wasn't sure how she felt, apart from being shocked. She painted for herself. It was a hobby. It was how she relaxed. She was an actress.

Did she have to be?

"He liked it?"

"He loved it," Gavin said, the words coming out quickly. "I can let you see the email he sent. He was surprised when I told him how young you are. He thought they were done by a much more mature and experienced artist. He wants you to come to the eight-week emerging artists program he sponsors in France. I'll get you an apartment in Paris and I'll make arrangements for Duke to be taken care of. If you decide to pursue the full Sorbonne enrollment, I'll deal with getting Duke out there to you. It's a lot of red tape, but it can be done."

Her head flooded with possibilities. The idea of being in Paris was almost too much to deal with. Working on painting with no pressure or expectations, just the opportunity to figure out if she could make that life work. She hadn't imagined when he'd sat down that this was what he wanted to talk to her about. "I thought you were going to tell me if I wanted Major, I should put him first. I thought you were going to tell me I should think about staying here."

He shook his head, looking her right in the eyes. "I would never give you that advice. Listen to me, my darling girl, and listen well. Don't ever dim your light for a man. Never. You are smart and talented, and you can have any life you want. If the man is right for you, if he loves you, he'll support you and not drag you down. I am not saying you should make selfish choices. That's not who you are, but at some point in time you must choose yourself, you must understand you've done what you can and choose the life you want, the one that you can look back on and be content. You have to live for yourself, and I believe now is your time."

There was only one problem with that scenario. "I can't. I've got another film."

"You haven't signed the contract yet," Gavin pointed out.

"But Mom already told my agent I would do it."

"And they can find someone else. This happens all the time."

"But what if I can't make it work?" That question was what made her hesitate. "What if I need to come back? They'll remember I dropped them."

"It happens all the time, Brynn. If you need to come back, I'll make sure you have work."

She stared out at the park across the street. In the distance, she could hear the sound of the ice cream truck starting to round the corner. "I'm not sure if I should hug you or be mad at you."

"I would prefer a hug, but I understand. I should have asked if I could share your work with my friend."

She shook her head. "No, I gave those paintings to you. They're yours. They're meant to be shown and shared. I just didn't think you actually would."

"You didn't think I would put them up and show them off?"

"I guess I thought you would when you knew I was coming over."

"You don't think you're good."

"I think I like my work. I hadn't considered that someone else might," she allowed. "I think there's a part of me that's always been scared to even consider that I could make art my career. I'm not mad at you for trying to help me. I'm scared of making the wrong decision."

"There is no wrong decision here, Brynn. That's what you need to come to terms with. There is only the choice to explore something that could make you happy. Your path has been set for a very long time, and you didn't get to choose."

"She didn't make me work. I offered."

"You were too young to make the choice. Like I've said before, I understand why your mother did it. She was drowning in debt and her mother was sick. But the family doesn't need you to work now. They can take care of themselves. I will help Ally the same way I did you, even though she's annoying and obnoxious. I think I find her annoying because I see so much of myself in her." He reached out and tucked a stray lock of hair behind her ear, an affectionate gesture he'd performed a hundred times before. "And I adore you because I see the me I wish I was. If that makes sense."

It didn't make sense, because Gavin was a good guy, but she simply leaned against him and rested her head on his shoulder. "Thank you. You've been so good to me. To all of us."

He sighed and settled in, an arm around her shoulders. "Like I said, you're my family. I would do pretty much anything for you. Take some time before you sign that contract. Think about what you want."

She wanted Major to be okay. She wanted these choices to be easy.

The ice cream truck pulled into a spot across the park.

One choice was easy. "How about a raspberry Popsicle?"

He chuckled and stood. "Now, that I can do. Come on. Everything is going to be all right."

"Until I tell my mother I'm quitting acting and running off to France to study art," she pointed out.

Gavin paled. "Yes, I think that might cause her concern. Maybe we don't mention it until you're actually in France. And maybe we don't mention my part in it."

"Scaredy cat." Though he was probably right.

She thought she saw something out of the corner of her eye. Something moving in the trees to her left. When she turned there was nothing there. It had probably been the wind. Or kids swarming the ice cream truck.

She shook her head and started across the park.

Maybe she would get an ice cream sandwich instead.

It was nice to have choices.

Major breathed deep for the first time since Lila had called and told him they needed to meet. He had to admit that he'd thought the worst when she'd told him she wouldn't talk to him over the phone, that this meeting had to be in person.

"I have cancer?" His father was beside him. He'd been fairly lucid up until this point, though he'd spent most of his time reading a book. They were in his father's apartment, sitting in the living room, and his dad had ignored Lila LaVigne and Juan for the most part. He'd been far more interested in telling Major about the book on World War II battles he was reading than anything else.

But Lila's latest pronouncement seemed to have gotten his attention.

Lila sat on the couch next to Juan, a folder on her lap. "No, Mr. Blanchard. The tumor on your kidney was benign. That's the good news."

Major felt every muscle in his body go tight. Something about the way she'd said the words made him think there was another shoe waiting to drop. "Is there bad news?"

His father set down his book and leaned forward. He put a hand to his head. "Where is Doc Hamet? Shouldn't he be here? Or Dr. Cline? She's my oncologist. I'm afraid I don't remember who you are. You look familiar. I'm sorry. I know I should know you and I know Doc hasn't been around for a while. I need my memory jogged."

Juan glanced down at his watch. "This is usually the time his brain is the least foggy."

If Lila was offended, she didn't show it at all. She simply gave his dad a sympathetic look. "It's all right, Mr. Blanchard. I'm Lila LaVigne. I took over for Doc Hamet when he retired a few years ago. Dr. Cline is in New Orleans. She's who I've been consulting with so she's up to date on all the tests. If you would feel more comfortable talking to Dr. Hamet, I can arrange for him to speak with you."

"I thought he spent all his time fishing," Juan interjected.

"He'll come out for an old friend," Lila replied. "He can explain the test results if you like."

Major didn't want to wait. "Dad, she's good. We should listen to her."

"Well, I'm certainly happy to find out I don't have cancer." He frowned and looked Major's way. "Did we think I did?"

"We were worried about it," Major admitted. He'd spent a lot of time with his father in the last week, and Juan was right. He was usually at his best around this time of day.

"Your test results from a few weeks ago made me take a closer look, but I'm happy to say you're still in remission," Lila explained.

"Remission." His father seemed to ponder the idea. "I seem to remember something about cancer. Did I have it before?"

"Yes, Dad." He almost wished they had done this in Lila's

office without his father present. It was hard enough to deal with these conversations without having to explain it to his dad.

He hated that he thought those things, hated that it crept into his mind that his father was a burden. Over the course of the last week, he'd seemed to be getting better. He'd been placed on some new drugs, and Major had hope for the first time in forever. He loved the man. He couldn't stand the thought that he might be gone one day.

"You had cancer several years ago, but you got excellent care and it's gone, at least for now," Juan explained. "We have to be vigilant about it. Lila is your primary care provider. She's excellent and knows your case very well."

His father nodded, and his tone went low. "She seems nice. And pretty. Is she single? I have a son who can't seem to find a proper girlfriend."

"She's married to my boss, Dad."

His dad gave Lila a smile. "Are you happily married? Major is a catch."

Lila chuckled. "Of course he is, but alas, I have already caught my sheriff."

He was going to ignore this line of conversation. "You said this was the good news. I'd like to hear the bad."

Lila's smile faded, and she became somber. "The medications we've been using to treat his dementia are having a bad effect on his liver and kidneys. It's why the bloodwork came back the way it did."

"Wait. Now I have dementia, too?" His dad sent Lila a frown. "Young lady, you are not much of a doctor. First it's cancer, and now dementia. I assure you that didn't happen when Doc Hamet was around. Everyone stayed very healthy because he was rarely in his office so no one got tests. You should learn by his example."

"I'm not a doctor at all. I'm a nurse practitioner," Lila

replied. "And you still have a good sense of humor, Mr. Blanchard."

His dad winked her way. "Life is pretty funny, isn't it? I know about the dementia. At least I do most of the time. The medications you've had me on are new, aren't they?"

"Yes," Lila replied. "They are part of a study going on right now. And the fact that you remember that makes me think the regimen was working."

"He's had several long periods of lucidity," Juan agreed.

"I was with him for almost seven hours the other night and he was right in the moment with me." Major had so much hope when it came to the new study. "Does he have to stop now?"

"This is a blind study. I don't know for certain if he's had the actual drug or the placebo," Lila began.

"I'm certain he's gotten the drugs," Juan said. "I've worked with patients like Nelson for a long time. They don't get better without medical intervention."

"I tend to agree, but I also worry that if he stays in the study, these labs are going to get worse." Lila put a hand on her folder.

"But the drug therapy we used before didn't work." His father hadn't responded well to the more established meds.

"Which is why I got him in the study." Lila folded her hands on her lap. "My brother believes in these drugs, and the effect should be cumulative."

"So the longer he's on the drugs, the more lucid he'll be," Juan pointed out.

"And the longer he's on the drugs, the more damage they'll do to his liver and kidneys." Major didn't want to think about how close they'd come to finding something to help his dad. It would make him bitter and resentful. "We have to find another way."

"There is no other way. Our only real choice is to go back

to the original medications and therapies." Lila looked at his father. "I can pull you from the program starting tomorrow."

"Why would you do that?" his father asked.

"Because the medications are harming your liver and kidneys." Maybe his father wasn't listening as well as he'd seemed
to be. Major prayed he wasn't going into another bad period.

"And dementia is killing my brain," his father said quietly before turning back to Lila. "Ma'am, do you keep some
patients on medications that harm them because they are in
pain?"

Lila nodded. "Of course we do."

"All the time," Juan agreed. "It's palliative care. We keep
dying patients on pain medications. We don't want the time
they have left to be spent in pain."

"And I don't want the time I have left to be spent somewhere else," his father said with a sigh.

"You aren't dying." His father wasn't thinking. He was
otherwise healthy now that they'd gotten through the cancer
scare.

"Am I not?" his father asked.

Lila stood. "I think Juan and I are going to let you two
talk about this. Look, the damage isn't something that will
kill him tomorrow or even next week or month. We don't
have to make this decision today."

"The decision is made." Major didn't understand why there
was a decision at all. His father was taking medication that
could lead to his death. He needed to stop. "I have my father's medical power of attorney."

"Which I gave to him when I needed him to make decisions for me." There was no anger in his father's voice. "I
think you're right, Lila. I remember you now. I'm sorry. It
comes and goes. Please forgive me. You've been wonderful
these past few years."

"No apologies necessary," she replied, straightening her skirt. "I'm glad you've had some better days recently. I'm sorry it's costing your body."

He reached out and squeezed her hand. "It has been a blessing."

Lila nodded and she and Juan walked out.

"It's a shame that woman is married. She could have been good for you," his dad said, shaking his head. "And she's got a good job. Don't discount that. The sheriff doesn't even have to pay a copay probably. All that health care right in his own home."

"Dad, this is serious."

"I understand, but so is finding you a wife." His father eased out of the lounger. "I'm going to make some hot chocolate for us. Tell me, did you go for a second date with the actress?" His dad stopped and turned, a frown on his face. "Was there a reporter?"

Major followed him into the kitchen, frustration welling. "Yes, and he upset you."

"I was not having a good day. I've felt better the last week or so, but I still have crazy moments. I sort of remember him. He kept asking about how long you'd known her and if you were trying to make a buck off her. I said my son didn't need to make a buck off a woman. He has his own bucks, and they might not be as multitudinous as the young woman's in question but they're still respectable for a civil servant. That was not a nice man. You should tell your girl to stay away from him."

It was good that his father remembered, but there were some things he seemed to intentionally forget. "Okay, first of all, she's not my girl. We decided to save each other the heartache and keep our distance."

"Well, that doesn't sound like a good idea. It sounds a bit

on the cowardly side, Major. I didn't raise you to run away in the face of a challenge."

"It's not a challenge," Major countered. "It's pure logic. She's here for six more weeks and then she'll be gone and she won't come back. Now we need to talk about the meds."

"Why can't she come back?"

Major sighed. They had other things to talk about. "Because of her work. She works a lot, and she's always on the road. Dad, I need you to focus."

"Well, you always wanted to see the world. Maybe you should go with her. And I'm perfectly focused. I'm just not focused on what you want me to be focused on. I think you're the one with the focus problems." His dad reached up and grabbed the tea kettle.

"No. I'm focused on the right things." He didn't want hot chocolate. He wanted his father to be okay, and it looked like that wasn't going to happen. "You can't keep taking the medication. It's hurting you."

"And so is dementia." He maneuvered his way around the child locks on the stove after filling the kettle with water. They'd put those in about a year ago when he'd burned himself. "It's killing my soul, son. These hours I've had since Lila put me on the new medication have been my salvation. I would rather go out early with my mind somewhat clear than live another ten or twenty years in the prison of my own brain."

On one level, he understood what his father was saying, but all he heard was the fact that his father was choosing to leave him. "You're not thinking straight. I have to make this decision for you."

"Do you honestly want me to live in pain? To be afraid every moment of the day because I can barely remember where I am?" His dad took a long breath. "We need to take some time. Both you and I. Yes, I gave you the power to make this decision for me, son, but I did that because I trust you—not to make the right decision for you, but to make the right decision for me. In this case, I think it's the right choice for us both. Now, let's have some hot chocolate. These good moments of mine only last so long, and I want to hear about why you aren't seeing Brynn. I remember how much you smiled when you talked about her."

"Dad, we need to talk about this now."

"What is there to talk about?" He put a generous amount of cocoa powder in two mugs. "You've stated plainly that you'll make the decision. I'm asking you not to make it for the next week. You heard what she said. My liver's not going out in a week. I'd like a week before you choose. Can you give me that?"

He didn't want to wait. He wanted the decision to be made so he could move on to whatever awful thing would happen next. "How am I supposed to let you stay on drugs that will kill you?"

"I'll die one way or another," his dad replied, as though they were talking about the weather. "I'd like to do it on my terms. In some ways, I'm happy we have this choice. Now, do you want marshmallows or no marshmallows? I seem to have the little ones."

He stared for a moment, his father's nonchalance making him shake his head. "Marshmallows. I have to go to work soon."

His father considered him for a moment, his eyes on Major as his hands expertly doled out the mini marshmallows. "Are you in the head space to work? You've had a shock."

He didn't want to go to work. He wanted to go somewhere in the woods and scream out his frustration. "No, I'm not, but what else am I going to do? I'm on the schedule."

One shoulder shrugged. "How often do you help out your coworkers?"

"Dad," he began. He knew what his father was getting at. He'd often taken extra shifts when his coworkers needed help. But he was perfectly capable of shoving this pain and anxiety down and moving on. It was what he did. He plowed through life because what else was he supposed to do?

"You get to have needs, too, Major. You get to have bad days. You get to ask for help. If you never ask for help, you never give the people who love you the opportunity to show you how they feel. I grew up with a father who told me I needed to never show a single emotion if I wanted to be a man. Never show weakness. Your mom taught me a different way to live, and I hope I showed you the same. A kinder way to live."

Emotion choked him up at the thought of his mother teaching his father he could be human. "You're always kind. I try to be."

"You are to everyone else. Now it's time to be kind to yourself. Call in and stay here with me until I fall asleep. I want every moment I can have with you."

The kettle started to whistle.

"Time is all we have," his father said, using a potholder to pull the kettle off. "That's what I've found. Time is currency we use to pay for the most special thing of all."

"And what's that?"

"Memories. We are made of them. That's all a life truly is in the end. The memories we make, the ones we leave behind." He stirred one mug and then the other. "I wouldn't give up a single memory with your mother. Even the sad ones. They're mine. I'll hoard them for the gold they are."

His heart felt too big for his chest. How could he take those memories from his dad?

How could he let go? Because that was what his father was asking him to do.

He took the mug and sat down at the kitchen table. "I'll give them a call."

At least for tonight, he could give his father what he wanted. And when the time came, maybe he could find a way to get what he needed. His father was right about one thing. Memories were all a man had. It might be time to make a few.

chapter twelve

"Where's your mom tonight?" Seraphina poured out a glass of rosé as she asked the question.

When Brynn had returned from her shift at the station house, she'd found Sera and a couple of friends out on the back patio by the pool. They had bottles of wine and a big charcuterie board, and they'd invited her to join them.

"I thought I saw her going up to her room. She had your dog with her. Cute thing." Hallie Rayburn was a pretty blonde. She had her hair up in a ponytail this evening and wore jeans and a bright pink sweater. "She was on the phone and didn't notice me, which is good because when she does, she tells me that I could be a catalog model but only if I stopped eating muffins. In her defense every time she sees me, I do have a muffin in my mouth. It's uncanny."

She might need something stronger than the rosé. At least she didn't have to worry about Duke being stuck in his crate. "I'm so sorry. She can be awful sometimes."

Hallie shrugged and reached for the brie and crackers. "She also offered to get me an agent if I wanted one. I don't, though. It seems like a lot of work."

"She just sees that you're gorgeous and she could make

money off you," Sylvie Darois offered before looking Brynn's way. "Sorry. No offense. Your mom seems pretty nice despite all the Hollywood stuff. She spends a lot of time on her phone."

Her mom was married to her phone. "I'll talk to her about putting things in a more polite fashion. I want to say the business made her this way, but I think she was born like this. My mom believes tact is something that costs people time when they should get to the heart of the matter."

"She can be very helpful. She helped me with a problem I was having with Ella. I couldn't get that child to burp to save my life. She was crying up a storm due to gas, and your mom came in and turned her over and gave her a gentle push and now I can get her to burp on cue. Then she turned around, walked back out, and didn't say a word." Sera held her glass up in a toast. "So here's to your kind but not nice mom. I've come to learn I'll take kind over nice any day of the week."

"I think we're both kind and nice," Hallie said. "We can be both, right?"

"As long as we know the difference." Sylvie was the mayor of the town. She also had a daughter. Apparently this was a new-mom night out. Or in, for Seraphina. "Too many people mistake politeness for kindness."

"Well, my mom could stand to learn a few manners." She wondered where Major was. Probably with his father. She'd heard Armie talking to him and promising him that he could take as much time as he needed. Something had happened to Major's father and the gossip hadn't seemed to have gotten around yet. She thought about asking Seraphina since she seemed to know everything that went on in the town, but it seemed rude. It was obvious Major didn't want to share his troubles with her.

She wanted to share hers with him, wanted to talk to him about the offer Gavin had put on the table today.

"I like her," Sylvie admitted. "She's forthright and honest, and she has some killer shoes. I wore the new Chanel suit I bought when Rene and I went to Dallas last month and we had the best discussion, Diane and I. She knows a lot about fashion."

"Well, I like her boyfriend," Hallie said with a sigh. "I can't believe Gavin Jacks is staying here in our town. He walked into the café the other day and all the women nearly fainted. You should have seen Dixie tripping over her sneakers to get that man a latte. I didn't know she knew how to make a latte. When I asked her for one she pointed to the cream and sugar and told me to make it myself. I guess you need a chiseled jawline to get Dixie's attention."

"He has that," Seraphina agreed. "And he's a nice man. He's very easy to talk to. He likes tofu too much for my tastes, but otherwise he's a doll. He even helped Harry in his shop the other day. Says he had to learn woodworking for a role. He knows so much."

"He knows just enough to be dangerous," Brynn pointed out. "We tend to learn a lot on sets. I know how to sew on buttons and I can hem like a pro, but I'm not a seamstress. And they're not boyfriend and girlfriend. They've been friends for a long time. They help each other out."

"I think that's great. But they're totally doing it," Sera said with a wave of her hand.

Sylvie nodded. "Oh, yeah. I would bet those two go at it hard."

Brynn had to laugh at the thought. "Not even once. They annoy each other. They fight way too much to ever even consider falling into bed."

"Fighting is how Johnny and I usually rev our engines, if you know what I mean," Hallie admitted. "You know we have two kids, so most of the time our wild date nights involve sucking down a couple of hurricanes at Guidry's before we go home and fall asleep watching Netflix. But when he annoys me, he gets this look on his face and I can either smash a pie in it or my . . ."

"Hallie," Sera said, her eyes wide.

Hallie blushed. "I was going to say my lips. Like kissing him. You have a dirty brain, Seraphina. Named after an angel and your mind goes there."

Sylvie laughed. "Mine, too. Because it can be a heavenly experience."

One her mom and Gavin definitely weren't having, but it was nice the rumors weren't about her for once. It wasn't like she hadn't wished her mom and Gavin would get together. When she was a kid, it had been all she wanted, and watching Gavin on the red carpet with gorgeous actresses had made her sad.

Seraphina turned Brynn's way, her laser-like gaze focusing in. "Speaking of attractive men, how are things going with the deputy? I've heard he's avoiding you."

Well, at least the rumors were right for once. "And that should tell you how it's going."

Seraphina sat back, glass in hand. "He's been through a lot, but everyone was talking about how you could make him smile."

"I think he doesn't see the value in what pretty much has to be a short-term relationship."

Hallie sighed. "I don't know. I think it would be lovely. A summer romance. I know it's spring, but summer makes it sound more sexy."

"Don't listen to her. She married her first boyfriend and wouldn't go back for anything," Sylvie countered. "Is this all because of your job? A lot of people make long-distance relationships work. I don't see why he couldn't come to see you, or you could come back to Papillon to visit if you really like each other."

"I pretty much work all the time," she admitted.

"Why?" Sera asked.

"Because she's a Hollywood star." Hallie made the pronouncement like it should have been obvious to anyone with half a brain. "She's in demand, and everyone wants to book her for their movies. It's glamorous."

"It sounds exhausting." Sylvie poured herself another drink. "I am a public figure, a small-town mayor, and that's about all the attention I think I can stand right now. I want to spend time with my baby and my husband. I used to work seven days a week and I had to set boundaries. I had to find a balance between my career and my family and myself. That's the hardest part—working yourself in there."

"That's what girlfriends are for." Sera clinked glasses with Sylvie.

"My momma thinks the world is going to fall apart because once a week I meet with my friends and leave the babies with Johnny, but that's only because my daddy actually let us start a fire once because he was too busy watching LSU play Alabama," Hallie said. "Mom was at a church function and the firefighters had to haul my dad out because the game was in overtime. I taught Johnny better than that. Also, he can pause our TV, so that helps. But she still considers our weekly girls' nights a slow slide into chaos. I swear she comes over the next day to make sure my house didn't explode. It's insulting."

"Well, at least your mom is always around for babysitting," Sylvie pointed out. "Mine and Seraphina's are in Vegas right now. They are out there living their best lives and drinking martinis and playing as much blackjack as they can."

Sera grinned. "They're my role models. One day we're going to have raised our babies and the three of us are going to go on crazy cruises and drink fruity drinks and get massages and say anything that comes into our heads."

Sylvie nodded in agreement. "Yes, and embarrass our kids. Fun."

Hallie turned to Brynn. "So now you know what a girls' night looks like here in Papillon. Though sometimes we go out to Guidry's. It depends. Seraphina had a bunch of barbecue left over, so we're here tonight. I bet your girls' nights are way more fun."

She didn't have girls' nights. "Not really."

"Come on," Hallie prompted. "You live in LA. You must get all dressed up with your squad and go to fabulous restaurants and then on to dance at a club with one of those red carpets and a big guy who only lets in the best people."

"Hey, we have clubs," Sylvie pointed out.

"We had Gators and they let everyone in, even teenagers, and that's why it got shut down. And don't let the pastor tell you that his Friday night youth group is as good as a night club. There's no drinking, and he says Jesus is his bouncer," Hallie argued. "I think Jesus is supposed to let everyone in, too. I want a club where some massive guy looks at the long line of people trying to get in and points at me because I'm obviously the one who should be let in."

"Hallie has some very specific fantasies." Sera chuckled. "But it must be fun to be in such a big city. Lots of options."

"Yeah, almost too many," Brynn murmured. The truth was she didn't do girls' nights. She looked forward to nights when she and Ally got to sit in the house, order pizza, and watch a movie. She couldn't remember the last time she'd slept in. "I don't go out much, and I don't have a lot of friends. I have people I hang with when we're filming, but then they go to another set and I go to another set."

"Well, what about the friends you grew up with?" Sera asked.

"I was one of two kids on set from the time I was five until I was a teen and I switched TV shows," Brynn explained.

"Then there were four regulars and a bunch of part-timers and guest stars. We hung out. I was closest to a guy named Stephen."

Hallie slapped her hand on the table. "She's talking about Stephen Cane like he's a regular person."

"He is. Well, as regular as you get in our business. He's a weirdo nerd. That's why we get along." Brynn talked to her old costar on a regular basis. "We used to do our homework together and play board games."

"You didn't get along with the girls?" Sylvie asked.

"I had a couple of them I would spend time with, but we all competed for the same parts. I know we want to believe in this girl-power world, but it's often not like that. We still view each other as competition." Brynn was envious of the bond these three had.

"But *Janie's World* was so female-power oriented," Sylvie said. "I loved that show because of all the positive female friendships. It wasn't a bunch of women looking for men."

"It was about family." She'd figured that out somewhere during year three. "Both blood and the ones we make for ourselves. The actresses who played the adult characters were close. I just never felt comfortable making friends there outside of Stephen."

"Why is that?" Sera asked.

"I think because I didn't understand the world the way they did. I remember filming one episode where the kids were having a slumber party and it was weird because I'd never done that," she replied, a wistfulness overtaking her. "I didn't have playdates. I went to auditions. It wasn't a terrible life, but I'm starting to think it wasn't a childhood. I didn't figure out the things most people do."

"Do you feel like you never got to be you? Like you were always busy being the characters you portrayed? I always thought that must be confusing for a kid. You don't know who you are yet but you spend a lot of time being someone else," Hallie mused.

"I'm not sure about that." She knew herself pretty well. Didn't she? Or was she the creation of those around her? Had she been molded to fit a pretty shape she'd had little decision in? She had to make a few things clear. "My mom didn't force me to act. I liked it."

"You used the past tense," Sylvie pointed out.

She had. "Well, it's a job, and one I've been doing for a long time. I suspect everyone gets to a point where they question their choices. I might be experiencing some burnout."

"I can imagine. You gave ten interviews, and they all asked you the same questions," Sera said. "That would be maddening. I can't imagine all that scrutiny. You're very different than I thought you would be. I expected you to come in and start making all kinds of demands."

"Most actors aren't like that." She knew the stereotype she was fighting. "We have to get along and kind of roll with the punches." She'd been doing it for years. She had to think of the production, of how she would be perceived. "In this business you have to be liked, especially if you're female."

Sylvie huffed. "Don't I know it. If I show one ounce of irritation, I'm an angry black woman. In that way I guess show business is a lot like politics."

"I think all businesses are the same when it comes to that," Sera replied. "But Brynn needs to find her squad. She needs a group of women she can depend on. Even if it's mostly phone calls and FaceTime. I think you're right. You didn't have a normal childhood. You need to start thinking about yourself, too. I know that seems weird coming from a mom. We're supposed to give everything we have to our families, but if our well is empty, then there's not a lot to give."

"My mom took me aside before Marci was born," Sylvie offered. "She told me I needed to pick one thing to be selfish about. One thing that is nonnegotiable and only for me. Rene has his poker nights, and I have my girls' nights. Once a week the other one takes care of the baby and we each get a night to ourselves. My mom was right. It's important to fill that well however it needs to be filled."

Wasn't that what Gavin was offering her? Or was it another ambition trap? Wouldn't the pressure be on if she put herself in another highly competitive venue? She'd thought about it all afternoon. Initially, it had seemed like some glorious, peaceful thing, but it was the Sorbonne. It was elite, and there would be lots of pressure on her all over again.

It seemed nicer to stay here and paint just for herself for a while. Until she was ready and certain she wanted to try doing art seriously.

It seemed like there was never enough time for her.

"I think you should do that *Eat, Pray, Love* thing. It worked real well for Julia Roberts," Hallie offered.

Brynn's cell phone buzzed in her pocket. She wanted to ignore it because it was almost certainly her mom wanting to know when they could meet for dinner to talk about the new contracts. Or the production team wanting to give her a schedule for next week.

It wasn't like either would go away, so she pulled the phone out. "Sorry, I have to take this. You guys have fun tonight."

"We're here most Wednesday nights, Brynn." Seraphina gave her a sympathetic smile. "You're always welcome."

She wished she could join them. She had the feeling they would be good for her. "Thanks."

But she wouldn't. By next Wednesday, she would be working, and she wouldn't see much of these amazing women again. She glanced down at her phone as she started the walk back to her cabin. She would go up and get Duke and make a plan for next week.

Major. Major was calling her. She slid her finger across the screen to accept the call. "Hey. Is everything okay?"

"You told me I could call you." His voice was deep and rich over the line.

"Of course." She wanted to help him if she could. "What can I do? Do you need me to watch Dolly?"

She could dog-sit for him. She turned the corner that led to her cabin and then realized his big truck was in the drive. Her heart felt caught in her throat.

He was standing in front of her door, his back to her. "You told me if I changed my mind, I could call you."

"I did." He was here. She wasn't sure what had happened, but he was here.

"I'm calling you, Brynn."

"Do you want to talk?" She didn't want to talk. She wanted to touch him. She wanted to kiss him. She wanted him to make everything go away for a few hours. But she would slow down her rapidly beating heart and talk to him if that was what he needed. He might only want to be friends. He might be reaching out because it would be hard to talk to someone else.

She watched as his head fell forward and he reached out to lean against the side of the cabin. "I don't want to talk, Brynn. I'm riding the edge of something tonight, and I probably should go home. I'm sorry. It's been a terrible day and all I could think of was getting you underneath me. I wanted to forget about everything but you, and that isn't fair."

She hung up the phone, sliding it back into her pocket, and walked toward him. "I don't care about fair, Major. I want to be with you for as long as I can."

He turned and the look on his face had her running to his arms. He caught her and then his lips were on hers and she didn't think about anything except him.

* * *

Major kissed Brynn and realized what his life had been missing. Her. The last week he'd felt the loss of her, but now he also thought that he'd missed her before he'd even met her. Being around Brynn had made him believe there had been a hole in his heart for years and she was the only one who could fill it.

Her arms wrapped around him as she opened her mouth and let him inside, their tongues tangling, electricity flowing through him like a live wire.

All day, he'd been on the edge, the reality of his father's situation pushing him into a darkness he was afraid he might not come back from, but Brynn was all light.

She might be all the light he needed.

"I'm sorry I pushed you away," he whispered between kisses.

"I understood why." Her hands ran up his back. "What I don't understand is why you changed your mind."

"Because I was reminded today that life is too short. I was trying to protect myself, but I don't want to." It was what he'd decided as he'd talked to his father. He'd figured out that there was no real protecting himself from Brynn. He would miss her either way. He would spend the rest of his time regretting that he'd let her go without adoring her the way she should be adored, or he could ache the loss of her but know he'd given her something of himself.

Memories. He could give her memories.

He was going to start tonight.

"I don't want to, either. I want to spend time with you. Even if it doesn't last very long," she vowed.

"Then take me inside." He needed her so badly, more than he'd ever needed anyone in his life.

Brynn stepped away and pulled her keycard out. Her hands

were trembling, and he realized she needed this, too. She felt the pull the same way he did. She'd likely felt the void of the last week.

The door came open, but he stopped her from walking inside. He pulled her close and stared down into those gorgeous eyes of hers. "I'm sorry. I wasted time. Time we should have had."

She went on her toes so they were nose to nose. "Stop apologizing and let's use the time we have. Make love to me, Major. I won't regret anything except not knowing what it means to go to bed with you."

That was all he needed. "I figured that out today, too."

He reached down and shoved an arm under her knees, his other going around her back so he could lift her up against his chest. He carried her through the door, hearing it slam behind them.

"Are you all right?" She whispered the question as she cuddled against him. "You don't have to talk about it. I just need to know."

Was he all right? He wasn't sure he'd been all right for a long time. "I'm better now that I'm with you. I'll tell you everything you want to know tomorrow. For tonight, let me lose myself. Let me concentrate on you."

He strode through the tiny cabin to where her bedroom was. He knew the layout of the entire place since he often spent his leisure time out here at the B and B helping Harry do small repairs. He found it soothing, but now he was happy that he knew exactly where to take her. He pushed through the bedroom door and set her on her feet, lowering his head so he could kiss her again.

Her hands went straight to his waist, tugging at his shirt. He reached down and pulled it over his head, tossing it aside. He wanted to feel her hands on his skin. His heart thudded in his chest, and he could feel arousal flooding his system.

She'd left a light on, a small lamp next to the bed that was casting a soft light through the room. He allowed her to touch him, drawing her soft palms across his chest. She leaned over and he felt her kiss his shoulder, right below his neck. If he let her continue, this wouldn't last as long as he wanted it to, and he wouldn't give her everything he'd dreamed about. "Take off your shirt for me."

Brynn stepped back, her eyes going wide. There was a gorgeous flush to her skin that told him she was every bit as aroused as he was. She bit her bottom lip and seemed to come to a decision. She reached down and pulled her shirt over her head, tossing it aside with his. She wore a pretty white bra that clung to her breasts in a way that made him think seriously about devouring her. She was gorgeous and so sweet he could barely stand it. "It's been a while for me. I think I mentioned that."

Because she worked all the time. "We can take this as slow as you like."

"And if I want to go fast?" she asked.

"Then we should negotiate because I want to make this last. I want this first time to feel like forever, and I absolutely want to see you naked." He needed to lay out how he wanted the evening to go. He didn't want it to end. "And when we're done, don't expect me to leave. I want to sleep next to you. I want to wake up with you and spend the day with you. I have tomorrow off, and so do you. I know you have to start work next week, but as long as you are physically here in Papillon, I want to sleep beside you."

Her whole body seemed to go soft. "I want that, too."

She reached behind her back and with a twist of her hand, her bra joined their shirts.

He felt every muscle in his body tighten at the sight of her. "You are so gorgeous. Do you have any idea how beautiful you are?"

"Sometimes the idea of being pretty feels like my whole world," she said with a sigh.

He shook his head and let his hands find her waist. "Not pretty. Beautiful. Inside and out. You practically glow for me, Brynn. You're like the sun, and that has more to do with who you are. You talk about how much you love colors, how hard you try to catch them on paper. You chase that art. You are color to me. When you walked into my life, the world seemed more vibrant than it was before, and that's not because you were blessed with a stunning face and a sexy body. That's because you are the woman who stops and helps others, the one who notices things, the one who tries to make the world better for everyone else. I worry that you think about everyone else so much, they forget to think about you."

"How do you always know the right thing to say to me?"

"I don't. I said the wrong thing to you a week ago. I should never have left you to handle all that fallout yourself. I should have been there." He'd known it was a mistake, but he'd had to think of his father. If he could do it all over again, he would find a way to protect them both.

Her hands moved along his back, lighting up his skin everywhere she touched. "It's okay. How about you let me sleep in tomorrow and we'll call it even?"

They wouldn't be even. Not close to it. Still, he kissed the top of her head. "Deal. And I'm going to make you sleep well tonight. I promise."

He kissed her again, but he didn't stop this time. He kissed her forehead and nose and cheeks. He let his mouth play along the curve of her neck and his tongue trace her collarbone. She breathed deep, the act bowing her back and offering her breasts up in an invitation he wasn't about to refuse.

She shuddered when he kissed her breasts, light teasing things right before he sucked the nipple into his mouth and gave her the slightest edge of his teeth.

She gasped and her nails dug into his shoulders. That tiny bite went straight through his system, making him tighten again. He moved to her other breast, lavishing it with as much affection as he'd given the first. Her hands moved to his hair, stroking him like he was some domesticated beast.

She could definitely domesticate him.

She kicked off the sandals she was wearing, and Major helped her out of her jeans until she wore nothing but a silky pair of underwear that already showed signs that Brynn was ready to get into that bed.

He stood and picked her up again.

Brynn gasped and smiled up at him. "You like to do that."

"I do." He crossed to the bed. "When I want to get you alone, I'll pick you up and run away from everyone else. You know I do like a good run. But I promise to be careful where I do it from now on, especially after a rain."

At the time, he hadn't realized how much his life would change simply because she'd shown up to drag him out of the mud.

He laid her out on the bed, her body bathed in the golden glow from the lamp. She was a treasure, and he intended to forget everything but her, at least for one night.

"Kiss me again, Major. I love it when you kiss me." She reached out to him, the gesture asking him to join her.

But if he got on that bed with her, things would be over far too fast, and he needed to show his silver-screen goddess how a small-town guy could worship her. "I'm going to kiss you. All night and all over."

He gently took both of her ankles in his hands and tugged her down the bed until she was in the perfect position before dropping to his knees. She was gorgeous, every inch of her silky skin on display for him.

He started with her feet, kissing his way up one leg, down the other, and back again. He dragged her underwear down her legs and tossed then aside. He breathed her in, the scent of her arousal flooding his senses. He lowered his head to her core and let himself taste her, loving the way she writhed beneath him, whimpering and calling out his name. He didn't stop until he felt her tighten and release, and then it was time for him.

He stood, licking his lips to savor every bit of her sweetness as he kicked off his boots and shoved down his jeans. Before tossing them aside, he extracted the condom he'd pocketed before he'd come over.

She looked up at him with languid eyes. "You were pretty sure of yourself."

He might have felt bad except for the grin on her face. "I was sure I was going to beg. I was sure I was going to try."

She moved back, her head finding the pillow while he took the time to protect them both, then she held out her arms. "I'm so glad you decided to try. I want to stay with you while I'm here. Your place, this cabin, a tent in the woods, doesn't matter, as long as we're together."

He agreed. He would steal every minute he could have with her. Hell, he might take some time off, be selfish for once. He climbed onto the bed, onto her welcoming body, her legs winding around him.

He kissed her as he joined them together, thrusting in gently, and then harder as instinct took over. She matched him, the lazy look coming off her face as his kisses became more passionate, his body driving into hers. He wanted it to last, but she felt too good around him. When she tightened her legs and cried out, he couldn't help it anymore. He let himself go, let himself feel every second of pleasure she had to offer him.

He fell on her, pressing her into the mattress and letting his head rest against hers.

Her arms came around him, holding him tight. "I'm kind of glad I found you out there and not some other woman."

He chuckled. "You like the way I say thank you?"

"It makes me want to save you all over again," she whispered.

"I'll have to see what I can do about that," he vowed. He kissed her and started showing his gratitude all over again.

chapter thirteen

"Brynn is fine. She's sleeping and I'm not going to wake her up."

Too late. Brynn yawned the next morning and realized Major wasn't still in bed with her. There was an indentation in the pillow next to hers, but the covers had been pushed back and she could smell coffee. He seemed to be talking to someone.

"Why don't you allow me to make that observation for myself, Deputy?"

Brynn groaned and let her head find the pillow again. Naturally her mom was here, and she was probably giving Major a hard time. She was surprised her mom hadn't shown up the night before demanding to know what was going on.

She felt something jump onto the bed, and then Duke was nuzzling her. "Hey, buddy. Did you have a good time last night? I bet Mom didn't even make you sleep in a crate, did she?"

When she watched Duke, her mother tended to let him sleep on her bed, snuggled up against her.

Duke's body wiggled in excitement until he looked over

at the pillow beside hers and sniffed all around it. Then he lay right down on it and stared at her, judgment in his doggy eyes.

"Hey, I get a private life, too." Not that she'd had one for the last twenty years. Maybe ever.

"She's sleeping in today," Major insisted. "It's the one thing she asked for, and I'm giving it to her. You can talk to her when she's ready. Don't worry about a thing. I've already picked up breakfast, and I have her coffee brewing right now. She'll be well taken care of. I'll make sure she knows you came by."

And then the door shut. Forcefully.

She heard her mother groan and then the sound of her phone ringing. Of course, it was all the way in the other room. Major had spared her having to deal with her mother so early in the morning. It would be rude to make all that work for naught by answering her phone.

She could take the morning off.

When had she started viewing any interaction with her mom as work?

Despite the fact that she was outside, Brynn could still hear her mother's voice loud and clear. "Brynn, dear, I understand you had an eventful night, but do remember that you have work to do. I brought Duke back, and I expect you to call me the minute you get up."

"She doesn't stop, does she?" Major stood in the doorway, two mugs in his hands.

He was the most delicious-looking man she'd ever seen. He'd put on jeans but nothing else. Those denims rode low on his hips, showing off the notches there. He had a light dusting of dark hair across his muscular chest and the hint of a beard coming in across his chiseled face. The dark look that had been in his eyes the night before was gone, replaced with an expression of satisfied indulgence.

"She's spent much of her life steamrolling through," she replied. She sat up, pulling the sheets around her.

He moved across the room and set the mug down on her side of the bed. "Did she wake you? I promised I'd let you sleep in."

She glanced at the clock on the wall and chuckled. "It's nine thirty. That's the latest I've slept in a very long time. Though I was up pretty late."

They'd made love again and she'd fallen asleep with her head on his chest, listening to the steady beat of his heart.

It was the best sleep she'd had in forever.

He grinned, an adorably arrogant expression. "I won't apologize for that."

"Not many people are willing to take on my mom." Most of her previous boyfriends were involved in the industry, one of them a client of her mother's, so they tended to side with her out of pure fear.

"She is a formidable woman," he allowed. "But she doesn't have any control over my career. She can complain to Armie all she likes and he still won't fire me. It took him long enough to find Landon. Strangely, not everyone wants to work in a town with more critters than people. The people are all eccentric, too."

"I think this place is great. And Mom worked hard for that power." She sipped the coffee, enjoying the rich flavor that came from the chicory Seraphina used. Just the smell brought a smile to her lips.

"She wasn't always so confident?" Major asked, settling on the mattress.

Duke grumbled but nestled down between their pillows.

"She always seemed that way to me." She'd been thinking a lot about her mom lately. Probably because she was thinking about her whole life. Something about this town and this job seemed to bring her to a crossroads. "She was always a force of nature. I've told you about what happened when my dad died, right?"

"You mentioned that he'd passed but not much else."

She generally preferred to listen to Major talk about his family, but she suddenly wanted to talk to him about hers. She wanted him to know her. "My mom was a model. She came from a poor family in Alabama."

A brow arched in surprise over Major's eyes. "Your momma is from Alabama?"

Her mom sounded pure LA, and she'd worked long and hard for it. "She wanted to be an actress, so she took a lot of classes and learned how to change her accent. Sometimes when she gets really worked up a hint of twang will come out."

"I'm having a hard time envisioning your mother in Alabama."

"Rural Alabama," she added. "My grandparents were farmers, but Mom always wanted out. She was on a school trip to Atlanta, and she snuck away and visited a modeling agency. She got suspended from school but booked her first job, and my grandparents forgave her because she got paid well. About two years later, my grandfather had a heart attack, and Mom moved my grandma out to LA. She met my dad, who was a producer, and they got married and for a while everything was great."

"And then he died."

"Yes, he was older than Mom and he had a heart attack, and that was when Mom found out he was leveraged to the hilt and had borrowed against the company." This wasn't something she'd known at the time. She'd pieced it together from things her mom had said and many, many articles on the subject. Her mom hadn't given interviews. She'd tried to keep them out of that particular spotlight, but it hadn't stopped the media from jumping on a juicy riches-to-rags tale. "So he left nothing behind but debt. She thought she'd married well and had secured her future. She'd given up modeling and found herself with a dying mother, two kids, and a couple million in debt at the age of thirty."

"That doesn't sound so old."

"In the modeling world, she was considered way past her prime." Sometimes she wondered if those rejections still affected her mom.

"So she decided to put you to work."

She hated the slight accusation in his tone, but it wasn't anything she hadn't dealt with before. "I had already done a few acting gigs by then. My dad was a producer, and he thought it was fun to put his kids in the films. I liked it, so when I was offered a chance to audition for a TV show, I wanted to take it. The fact that it kept us afloat was a plus."

"You were five," Major pointed out.

"I was, but I also understand why she did what she did. We were a month away from being homeless." She knew one way her mom and Major were alike. "And her mother was so sick. She couldn't take care of her without a roof over our heads. Weirdly enough, that job I got was the TV show with Gavin, and he helped us. He was the reason my grandmother got to stay in our home for as long as she did. Mom didn't understand how to navigate the health care system in California, but Gavin's lawyer did."

Major's expression tightened. "You mentioned your grandmother had dementia."

"She had a host of things wrong with her," Brynn said with a sigh. "But my mom managed to keep her comfortable. We hired an in-house nurse to stay with her. Gavin managed to get us in a government program that offered us a nurse for ten hours a day. When she got worse, we got around-the-clock care."

"Uhm, there's no program like that."

"Maybe it's a California thing," Brynn replied.

"I don't think so. There's nothing that would cover twenty-four-seven care for anything but end-of-life care, and that's only for days or weeks. It's why I had to put my dad in the assisted living center. I could only afford it because of my dad's former employer. They had an excellent health care program but we still had to have me buy the house from him so he wouldn't have any assets or he wouldn't have qualified for any assistance. Trust me. I know the system well. Twenty-four-seven care would cost thousands and thousands of dollars, even if somehow you were only paying the copay."

That didn't make sense, but then she didn't understand the situation. "Well, all I know was my grandma got to stay with us."

"My father is on experimental medication that is probably going to kill him and he wants to stay on it," Major said quietly.

So that was the news he'd gotten yesterday. "What do the meds do?"

"They help with the dementia. I know Lila's explained how it's supposed to work, but I'm still not completely sure I understand. What I do know is the last couple of weeks have been the best my dad has had in a long time. He knows who I am and what year it is. I don't have to explain that Mom died a long time ago and why I'm not still five."

Her heart ached for him. She set the coffee down and moved closer to him, with Duke squeezed in between them. She put a hand on his chest. "I'm so sorry."

"And I have to decide what to do. Do I keep my father on the meds and lose him or do I hold out hope that they'll find some better drug that can help him?"

"Do you know if there are any other drugs in development?"

"I read up on a couple of trials, but I decided to go with

this one because Lila's brother is involved. He's very smart and he's right. The drugs do help, but they hurt Dad's physical condition. I don't know. I have to think about it." He sat there for a moment, looking down where she'd laid her hand over his chest. He placed his own on top of hers. "I'd like you to meet him."

"Of course." She would love to meet anyone in Major's life.

He would be alone when his father was gone. That was what he was truly afraid of. Losing his father was always going to be a part of his life, though he was young to have to go through it. For most people, losing a parent meant leaning on the rest of their family.

Major didn't have any.

Duke's head came up and then he moved closer to Major, as though he knew the man needed some comfort. That was the beauty of a dog. Duke might not like the way Major was intruding on his life, but the pup had never denied comfort to anyone.

His version of comfort meant he started to lick Major.

A brilliant smile crossed Major's face. "Well, now I know how to make him like me. He likes sad guys."

"He's getting used to you." She scooted closer to him and felt more connected to another person than she had in forever.

That was the moment when her mother screamed.

They all sat up, Brynn clutching the sheet around her while Duke took off barking.

There was a flurry of knocks on the door. "Deputy! Deputy! You have to do something. There's been a crime."

Major ran for the door, throwing it open while Brynn pulled on a robe. "What's happening?"

Her mom stood in the doorway and pointed. "My cell phone was stolen and I was assaulted."

"Brynn, call it in." Major pulled on his shirt and started

for his boots. "Tell the dispatcher that I'm on the move. My radio and gun are in my truck."

"Yes, shoot it," her mother said. "I normally am very against killing animals for any reason that doesn't involve high-end dining, but that criminal has to be brought to justice."

Major stopped and took a long breath. "Diane, did a raccoon steal your phone?"

"Yes, and I think he had help. I was walking back to the main house and I tripped over one of them. My phone fell out of my hand and another one ran away with it. I was talking to the head of casting at Universal and now my phone is gone. I didn't even hang it up. What are they going to think of me now?"

Brynn covered her laugh because it was such a Papillon thing to happen. "You're going to require a task force now, Major."

Major sighed. "I'm going to find your mom's phone. I'll be back. Hopefully. Diane, why don't you show me where you lost it?"

Her mother frowned and pointed her well-manicured finger Major's way. "It was stolen. 'Lost it' implies I was negligent. This is victim blaming, and I won't have it. Even now, there is a major player in Hollywood listening to the skittering of overly large rodents and wondering if I've finally lost my mind."

"I think he'll understand." Sometimes her mom got paranoid.

Her mom turned those laser-focused eyes Brynn's way. "Yes, one of the foremost Hollywood casting agents will understand that here in Louisiana, raccoons routinely steal smartphones."

"I would not say routinely," Major offered. "But I would also not not say routinely."

"You know they never leave LA. They believe anything outside of the city is a rampant apocalyptic hellhole where they will likely be eaten by cannibals." Her mom was also excellent at hyperbole.

Brynn couldn't stop her eyes from rolling. "Not everyone is so elitist, Mom."

Major stepped in front of her, giving her his "I'll take care of everything" nod. "I'll find her phone and if I can, arrest the offending party. The good news is the last time they were brought in they didn't appear to have rabies."

"Rabies!" Her mom practically screeched. "And are you saying they've done this before?"

Major winced. "No rabies and yes, ma'am, they aren't first-time offenders, though up to this point they've only stolen trash. Mr. McGovern will tell you they stole his dentures, but I'm almost certain he just doesn't like wearing them."

Her mom's jaw went tight, and the words pressed from her lips with obvious frustration. "I need my phone, Deputy."

Major nodded and reached for the keys to his truck. "I'll get my gear and call animal services out. Why don't you come with me and show me the scene of the crime?" He winked at Brynn. "I'll be back and maybe we can go out to the islands and have another picnic."

That sounded like pure heaven. She went on her toes and kissed him. The morning wasn't going as planned, but the afternoon was looking up.

"Absolutely not. I've got someone coming out to do your manicure and pedicure, and you need a hair treatment," her mother began. "It's getting coarse."

"Her hair is fine." Major started walking out the door.

"And what would you know about it?" Her mom followed.

Major knew because he'd had his hands in it most of the night. He seemed to love stroking her hair and using it to gently twist her this way or that while he kissed her. But he was also a gentleman since he did not respond to her mom's questions.

They were out the door and then she was alone again. Except she didn't feel alone because she knew he would return. She glanced down at her nails. They were fine. She liked them short, and they were only a little chipped.

"Thank god. I thought they would never leave." The powder room door opened and Ally walked out. She was dressed to work out in a tank top and leggings, her sneakers on and hair up in a high ponytail. "Yay. Coffee."

"What are you doing here?" Maybe that wasn't the first question she should ask. "How did you get in? The door was locked."

"Oh, I totally duped your keycard when Seraphina wasn't watching," Ally explained as she poured herself a cup of coffee and eyed the tray of fruit and pastries Major had brought. "Remember when I did that commercial for the hotel app? I learned how to do it then. Method acting comes in handy all the time."

"Okay, why are you here?"

"You try sharing a room with our mother. I went for a jog and then I came here, but I found out you've been all slutty and stuff, so I hid in the bathroom when TW came back. I would have snuck out the bathroom window, but the coffee smelled really good and Mom's on a decaf kick. Also, she doesn't allow carbs near her right now. I tried to explain that just because meno shot her metabolism doesn't mean I can't have a donut every now and then, but apparently that's mean and unsupportive. So you and TW, huh?"

"Don't call him that," she said, walking back into the bedroom, Duke at her heels. "And he wasn't wearing them last night. He wore perfectly respectable boxers, thank you."

Ally followed her, a Danish in her hand. "I bet he didn't wear them long. Come on. I'm living vicariously through you. I haven't had time to be slutty lately. Like in forever. You know how it is when you're working. Well, usually. You were smart and found a friend with benefits right here on set, but not on set."

She turned on her sister. "It's not like that."

Ally sobered. "I know. I know you like him." She brightened up again. "But that doesn't mean you can't tell me all about it. He looks like he would be good in bed. Oh, also, he didn't run around wearing nothing but a pair of low-slung jeans. He got respectably dressed to go to the main house and when he came back here, he took off everything else and made sure those jeans were perfectly placed, if you know what I mean. I think he was planning on showing off for you. Instead he got our mom."

"How long were you in there?"

Ally sat down on the bed, her back against the headboard. "There's a magazine with an article about European politics I was reading."

Brynn stared because she wasn't buying that.

Ally huffed. "Fine. It was about the benefits of collagen, and then I read about the fall shoe trends, okay? I needed some alone time, and I wasn't about to actually go running in these woods. Did you hear about the raccoons?"

That made Brynn smile. "Yeah, I kind of wish someone had gotten that on video."

"Me, too. Mom fighting a raccoon for her precious phone would be a family memory for all time." Ally took a bite of the Danish.

"You would post it on social media."

"I would. I'm terrible like that. But you know I didn't post you and TW on socials until it was already out there, right?" Ally seemed to properly read the look on her face. "I'm sorry. Major. It's a terrible name. Are you sure you don't want to go with TW? We can rebrand him if you want to keep him."

"His name is fine."

"If you insist. But seriously, you know I wouldn't have posted that video without talking to you about it, right? I know I can seem a little callous, but I would have talked to you. It was nothing to be ashamed of. You were smart and quite heroic, and your butt looked good."

"Ally."

"I'm serious. Your glute routine is on point. If it hadn't been for the nosy reporters screwing with Major's dad, it would have been a great thing to have happen. But I barely remember what Grandma was like, and I do feel for him. Don't tell anyone, though. I'm not supposed to have feelings that have nothing to do with acting."

"I promise to keep it between us." She sat down beside her sister, Duke hopping on the bed between them and looking longingly at the Danish that her sister was putting away with gusto. There were a couple of things Ally might be able to clarify. "Hey, Major and I were talking this morning."

"I'm sure you were."

"I'm serious." Something about the conversation was bugging her. Major had seemed very insistent. "We were talking about how expensive it is to keep his dad in the assisted living home. He pointed out that a full-time nurse would be thousands of dollars."

Ally shrugged. "Maybe. I mean when I think about it now, I know that's completely one hundred percent true. Health care is wretchedly expensive, as you will discover when you get the bill for your ankle not-injury. But it was also like a thousand years ago. Maybe it's worse now. Whenever I watch the news, it's always worse. And if you listen to anyone who is over thirty-five, the world is going to hell in something called a handbasket, and not a designer one."

"That's a good point." It had been almost twenty years ago. Health care could have changed a lot in those years. "Thanks. I needed to hear that."

Ally's eyes narrowed. "Why would Grandma's medical bills worry you? Do you think Mom used your money to pay them?"

According to her mom, she hadn't. "At the time I wouldn't have made enough. She would have to have put away fifteen percent by law, and then she had to pay taxes and my tutors and all the other stuff."

"Would it have been so bad? If she had used your money to pay for Grandma's care, would that make you mad? You know I'll pay you back for the tutor."

She'd stepped in it. Ally had a chip on her shoulder. Before she could move, Brynn reached out and held her hand. "You don't ever have to. You couldn't go to regular school because I was working all the time and Mom had to be with me. And honestly, I wouldn't have wanted to be alone. If she paid for Grandma to be comfortable with my money, I would be perfectly happy with that. I wish she'd spent more so we would have had a nicer house."

Ally's lips curled up. "We have a pretty sweet house now."

"Yeah, because I turned eighteen and bought it behind her back," Brynn reminded her sister. "No, I don't regret sharing that bounty with my family. I was just . . . I don't know. Something about it bothered me, but I'm being weird."

"Because your mind is foggy with sex." Ally's grin faded, turning into something akin to horror. "In this bed. Where I'm lying. Ewww."

Her sister jumped up and started yelling about cooties. Brynn threw a pillow her way and prayed Major didn't take too long.

* * *

Major followed Diane Pearson over the big green yard and wished he'd bundled Brynn up and taken her back to his place. Then they would only be dealing with town gossip, which he could handle. His nosy neighbors finding out his girlfriend stayed the night would have been far better than dealing with his girlfriend's freaked-out mom.

It probably wasn't a good thing that he was thinking of Brynn as his girlfriend. He was getting in too deep, but then he'd known he would.

"You know a very important director is going to be staying here next week. The whole crew will be here, and they will bring a lot of technology with them. Do you think the wildlife will band together to steal all of their equipment as well? Should I tell them to up their insurance?"

Yep. He wished Zep was here dealing with this mess instead of him. He'd put in a call to Zep when he'd gone to his truck to get his radio, but it had gone straight to voice mail, which meant he was either sleeping in or on another job. "I'll talk to the animal services department about setting up some traps."

She stopped, turning on him. "Traps? Like bear traps? You know those can be lethal. I didn't ask you to kill the poor creatures."

"You're going to have to be clear about how you want this handled." Not that it would change what he did, but he'd learned that letting people talk out their fears and anxieties often deescalated the situation. Anger was usually about fear or anxiety.

She stopped, obviously surprised by that request. "Well, you should capture the creature and rehabilitate it. Isn't that what you do?"

"That would be a separate department, ma'am. How about

for now I try to get your phone back and we'll worry about future crimes later." He started up the slight hill that led back to the main house.

He heard Diane sigh behind him and then she caught up to him, matching his stride. "I don't always know when you're being sarcastic, Deputy. You've got the stoic thing going on most of the time. It's very confusing."

"I'll try to be more one-dimensional for you."

"See. There. Now, I know that was sarcasm. I was out by the pool. It's a good place to get some steps in," Diane said. "Well, it seemed to be. I would like very much to know what your intentions are with my daughter."

Major stopped because this seemed like a conversation that might take up all of his attention. "Brynn and I are seeing each other."

Diane's deep brown hair was cut in a chic bob, accentuating the angles of her face. It was easy to see the model she'd been all those years ago. There was a classic beauty that would likely cling to her well into her old age. That beauty came with a wealth of judgment as well. "It seems like you're seeing a lot of each other."

He wasn't going into the specifics with her. "I care about your daughter. We've decided to be together for the duration of her time here in Papillon."

"That won't be long. And then what happens?"

"Then she's going to be somewhere else and I'll be here." He didn't want to think about that. He'd told himself he wouldn't think about the inevitable end of their relationship until he had to.

Was it inevitable? Did it have to be? There were phones and planes. There were ways to make long distance work. He couldn't leave Papillon for any real amount of time while his father was alive. Even if he could, what would he do? He couldn't follow her around from set to set. He wasn't sure where he would fit into her world, and he definitely didn't see her staying in his.

"So you're having an affair? Or as you youngsters would say, you're just hooking up." Diane's brow had risen, challenging him.

"I think there's more to it. Like I said. I care about Brynn."

"And she clearly cares about you," Diane allowed. "I've known that since she met you. It was obvious because she's started ignoring my calls."

"I think that was more about needing some time to herself," Major said. From what he could tell, Brynn didn't get much time alone at all.

"Well, she never needed it before."

"Or she couldn't ask you for it," Major countered.

"She can always ask me for anything. I'm not merely her mother. I'm her manager. I work for her," Diane said. "And I know her very well, which is precisely why I worry. She hasn't dated much. She can be a bit naive when it comes to men. I have to watch out for her. If you want to use her to make a career for yourself, you should think again. I can make any jobs you get offered go away. I can make sure you never work in the industry, so anything you gained by hurting her will be taken away."

He started walking again. He should have expected this. Brynn had practically told him this conversation would likely happen. "Then it's a good thing I already have a job. Which I'm going to do now to the best of my ability, despite the insult."

"I wasn't trying to insult you." Diane was like a dog with a bone. "I was trying to protect my daughter. I will continue to try to protect my daughter. Brynn has a history with troublesome dating relationships. When she was sixteen she fell for a young guest star on the show she and Gavin were on.

He was her first real boyfriend. I think she loved him. So it was devastating when she found out he was using her to try to get ahead in the business and had another girlfriend."

"I'm sorry to hear that." Brynn hadn't told him that story. He could only imagine how hard that had been on her. "I'm truly not interested in breaking into show business. I don't act and I don't want that kind of attention. I'm only interested in Brynn and what's best for her."

"And that is my point. You can't possibly know what's best for her because you don't know the business."

"She's more than her job. I do know that."

"Then as was so eloquently stated in a show that earned every actor a lot of money, you know nothing, Deputy Major." Diane's smile was tight as she looked out over the yard. "She *is* her job. This is what you don't understand. Maybe you've never been passionate about something, but when you have a calling, there's nothing more important. We eat, breathe, and sleep our jobs."

She was right about that. He'd never felt like pouring his whole soul into something.

Except, he was starting to feel that way about Brynn. An ache opened in his chest. Was this how his father felt about his mother? She'd been passionate about her work, but his father had viewed his job as nothing more than a way to take care of his family. His father's real passion had always been his marriage and family.

How much did his dad miss his mother? Was that why he was so insistent about continuing the new medication? He didn't want to lose his memories of his wife?

"Are you all right?" Diane's tone had gone softer than before. "I'm sorry. I've had a morning. I fell asleep last night waiting for Brynn to come and get her dog, and when I woke up and realized she hadn't, I was worried. But I shouldn't take it out on you. I'm pushing you when I should be kinder. Did something happen with your father last night?"

That came from out of left field. She'd been needling him one moment, and now she was looking at him like he was something fragile. "Why would you ask that?"

"Because you did a full one-eighty. From what I understood, you and Brynn had decided not to pursue a relationship, and for a solid week you've stayed away from each other. So something happened. You seem to be a stand-up guy. I doubt you simply changed your mind or needed a little sex."

"It wasn't like that."

"Yes, that was what I was saying," Diane agreed. "A man like you only changes course if something shakes you up. Right now, your whole world revolves around your father's health, so it's a good bet. Is he all right? I know that's a foolish question, and I mean it only in the sense of his current health. He's not all right. Nothing feels all right."

If she hadn't been so eloquent in her description of how his world felt, he might have shaken her off. Instead he found himself answering her. "His medication is working."

Diane was silent, as though she knew there was more coming.

"It's also damaging his liver and kidneys."

She sighed, a weary sound. "Yes, I've been there. Though my mother's medications only kept her calm. Her descent was gradual, and she never got back a step she lost."

"The medication is new, and it's helped him enormously."

"But it's not a cure," she said quietly. She put a hand on his arm. "I'm very sorry to hear that. I hope spending time with Brynn is helping you, but you have to understand that she's in a delicate place in her career. I know I'm coming on strong. I do know you have no interest in becoming an actor.

It's a habit because if I show even a moment's weakness in this business, there's trouble. I have to be a ball buster because that's often all the men in this industry understand. You feel like a threat."

He wasn't sure why she would look at him that way. "How?"

Diane seemed to think about the question for a moment. "Brynn is always focused. Always. She has been since she was a child. The only person I know who is more responsible about her work is Allyson, and for some reason she hasn't connected the way Brynn has. But that's not your problem. I think you are a real threat to Brynn's concentration. This movie is important. It's her first real lead dramatic role, and I don't want her focus split."

"I'm not trying to be a threat. I'm not asking her to stay here with me and give up her career," Major pointed out. "I'm spending time with her while we have it. I know she's going to be working long hours, but she's got to sleep. She's got to eat. She's got to shower and change clothes. I'll take what I can get while I can get it. I promise you, I want what's best for her."

She stepped back. "All right, then. I'll back off." She glanced around. "Well, it was somewhere around here."

The door that connected the pool and outdoor dining area to the kitchen came open and Gavin walked out with a mug in his hand. He stopped and stared for a moment before his expression cleared and he gave them the vibrant smile Major was used to seeing on the man's face. "Good morning, Deputy. Diane." He frowned. "What's wrong? Where's your phone?" He set down his mug and rushed over to her. "Are you all right?"

Wow. That woman really loved her phone. She loved it so much that when it wasn't in her hand, her friends knew something was wrong.

Maybe Brian had been doing the world a favor.

He'd just called a raccoon Brian and seriously considered that the critter had pulled off the heist of a cell phone. He was finally truly a citizen of Papillon.

"She lost it," Major said. "I'm trying to help her find it."

"I did not lose it. That rodent stole my phone." Diane was right back to righteous rage.

"She would never lose her phone," Gavin agreed. "It's a part of her soul. She doesn't feel right when it's not with her. You should have seen her when we were all in Central Europe filming a few scenes. Someone knocked out the cell tower and it was three days before we got coverage again. The poor woman runs on 5G. She can make it on four, but anything under that and she's practically nonfunctioning. We have to find it."

"That's what I'm trying to do." The last thing he needed was for Gavin to join the hunt. He and Diane often bickered like an old married couple. It didn't help that the actor had followed Armie for a week and now thought he was an expert on law enforcement. "I'll go check the woods. They can't have gotten too far. I'm surprised they're out at this time of the day. They're nocturnal."

"Well, they're obviously working overtime." Diane sniffled and moved closer to Gavin. "I was talking to the head of casting about a role for Ally in a nighttime drama he's working on. She would be so perfect for the ingenue role."

"Then I'm glad that animal stole the phone from your hand, because you were making a mistake," Gavin said with a righteous huff. "Have you listened to anything I've said? I told you, she should stay away from simpering virginal roles."

"Are you saying my daughter isn't a virgin?" Diane shot back, her spine straightening.

Gavin stared at her.

Diane's eyes rolled. "Well, she can play one on TV. After all, you played a priest in a movie once and we all know you're not exactly saintly."

Major walked away because they were going to be of no help. He should send her into town to buy a new cell, but he was pretty sure she would have to go all the way to Houma.

Maybe all the woodland creatures of the bayou had gathered together and formed their own crime ring. Brian and his cohorts would take the stolen cell phone to Otis, who would find the rougarou and fence the sucker for meat and sweets. Yeah, this was his job. He wasn't sure which was weirder, the fact that he was out here looking for trash panda felons or that he could hear Brynn's parents arguing about whether Ally should have taken a job playing a wisecracking stripper in a buddy-cop movie.

He took a long breath and tried to listen to something other than the argument. The way those two were yelling should have every critter nearby taking shelter.

He should go back and ask for Diane's number. He needed to call it and see if he could hear it ringing. His talk with her had thrown him off, and he wasn't thinking straight. It wasn't like he was going to walk through the woods looking for a raccoon's hideout.

That was when he heard it. A chiming sound in the distance.

He turned, because Gavin must have thought to call the phone.

Instead of Gavin, Brynn was standing there. She'd changed into shorts and a T-shirt, flip-flops on her feet. She held up her phone. "I realized we should probably call it, and you don't have her number. I don't track her phone or I would offer to find it that way. There's no need to track her phone. She's always around. Though you should know that she tracks mine and could show up at any moment. Well, she can do it when it hasn't been stolen by furry bandits."

"Unless we go somewhere there's no cell signal." Major walked toward the dock where Sera and Harry kept a small airboat. The chiming was louder and then stopped.

"I'll call again." Brynn moved closer to him.

The chiming started up again and he switched directions, navigating to a log where the sounds seemed to be coming from. Sure enough, there was the cell phone. He reached in and prayed he wasn't the one who would need to be tested for rabies this time. He pulled the cell phone out and winced.

"I hope your mom has a good disinfectant. I'm pretty sure this has been thoroughly licked."

Brynn's face lit with amusement. "She will clean it like it was her precious baby."

He pocketed it and promised himself he would take a hot shower after touching that thing. Diane would have to figure out how to douse it in antiseptic. "Your mom thinks I'm going to throw your whole career off track."

"Ah, so she decided you aren't some one-night stand, huh?"

"I think she's still wondering if I'm a wannabe actor who laid in wait for you to come along. I planted myself in small-town Louisiana on the off chance that a Hollywood hottie would come into town. Come to think of it, I probably set up the whole mud thing so you would have to save me."

Brynn moved in, tilting her head up so she could look into his eyes. "She's paranoid because of a couple of incidents that hurt me. She doesn't seem to understand that I learned from those incidents. I'm much better at picking out the bad guys now."

"How do you know I'm not using you?" Somehow all that

tension he'd been feeling had evaporated the minute he'd realized she was here.

She grinned up at him. "Because you're my Deputy Major. How do you know I'm not using you for sex?"

"I don't." He felt a smile slide over his face. "I have to hope the gorgeous star wants me for more than my body."

She went on her toes, and the grin on her face made him feel warm, like the world was a softer place with her in it. "It's a pretty nice body. A girl could do worse."

"You are damning me with faint praise, woman." He dipped his head down and kissed her. "I might have to show you what else I can do."

There was a screeching sound, and Brynn screamed and stepped back.

Major turned so he was in front of her. The sound was coming from the log, and he could have sworn he saw a tiny fist bunch up before disappearing inside. "I'll call Zep and let him know we found the hideout."

Brynn's arms wound around his waist. "You do that. I'm going to hide behind you for a while. I think I'm glad I didn't bring Duke with me. He might try to fight the raccoon."

"Dolly would hide from the raccoon." His darling dog wasn't much of a fighter.

"It's okay. Duke would protect her," Brynn promised.

"You should stay out of Ally's career." A loud voice floated down from the pool area.

"And you should understand that you're the reason she doesn't have a career."

Diane and Gavin were going at it again. If Brynn walked through there she would get caught up in it.

"Save me," Brynn whispered.

He could do that. He leaned over and picked her up. "I'll toss this phone your momma's way. I promised when I wanted to get you alone, I'd pick you up and carry you away."

"Oh, well, then we should talk, because my sister is at the cabin. She's been there most of the morning." Brynn's arms went around his neck. "She was hiding in the front bathroom."

He groaned. "We're going to my place. I have a security system."

He was going to need it.

chapter fourteen

Brynn looked out across the park and let the heavenly scent of fried food waft over her. All around, people were mingling, eating food from vendors and drinking beer and wine and strawberry lemonade. She recognized some of the people walking around the fairgrounds as crew who'd come in early.

"Hey, Brynn!" A costumer she'd worked with before waved her way.

"Hi, Pam. It's good to see you again," Brynn returned. "Already hard at work?"

The pretty brunette nodded even as she walked beside another woman, their hands threaded together. "Sure am. Everything looks great. We've got a fitting tomorrow afternoon. See you then."

Brynn smiled but there was a knot in her stomach at the words. Time was moving so fast. She'd already done hair and makeup tests and the initial costume fittings back in LA. This was her final fitting. It wasn't an elaborate costume like some historical film. Her main costume for this movie was awfully close to what Major wore to work every day. Of course, he made khaki sexy. She wasn't sure how good she looked in it.

"Was that Pamela Jackson?" Her mom moved in behind her. She was wearing a designer dress and five-inch heels to a crawfish festival.

"It certainly looked like her." Gavin had driven them all into town when Brynn had asked for a ride to the festival.

She should have called a Guber. At least then she wouldn't have ended up with an escort. Just whiplash and regret because the shock-absorption on that golf cart wasn't the best.

"Good. She's excellent," her mother said approvingly. "Now, what is this party about? Are they welcoming the film crew into town?"

"No, this is a crawfish festival. They're in season from January to July," Gavin replied. "Many local parishes have festivals in late spring because this is when the crawfish have reached maturity. That means they're at their largest and are good to eat." Gavin seemed to realize they were both staring at him. He shrugged. "I study. When Brynn said she wanted to come I used this wonderful thing called the Internet. It's for more than shopping."

"Yes, it's good for researching how to bury a body," her mom shot back, but then winked at Gavin, the corners of her lips turning up slightly. "Show-off."

Brynn frowned, watching the two of them. Did her mom have a crush on Gavin? Ever since Major had talked about the cost of care for his father, she'd had this idea in the back of her head. She'd done a bit of her own research and worried Major was right. Her mom shouldn't have been able to afford the level of care her grandmother had received. She didn't think she could have afforded it even if she'd taken all of Brynn's earnings, which she hadn't.

Had she taken a loan? Had there been money she didn't talk about?

Or had someone else paid the bill? Someone like Gavin. If he had, why wouldn't they talk about it?

Gavin wore a simple outfit of good slacks and a black V-neck shirt that showed off the hint of a sculpted chest. "I am a lifelong learner. Now, Brynn, when should we expect Major to get here?"

Major had offered to give her a ride, but he was coming out after a long shift, and was also picking up his dad. It was easier to meet him here. "Any minute now, so if you and Mom want to get back to the B and B, you can go. I'm fine."

"Now, why would we do that when we can meet your beau's family?"

Only her mother would use the word *beau*. "Or you could not scare him off. Don't you have a deal to make or a whole bunch of phone calls?"

"I can take one night off," her mother replied. "Besides, my recent encounter with sticky-fingered rodents gave me an incredible idea. I'm going to pitch a movie or tv show about a raccoon who can talk. He's an alien and he runs with a group of mercenaries."

"*Guardians of the Galaxy.*" Brynn and Gavin said the title at the same time.

Her mom wasn't big on movies she didn't have a direct hand in.

Her mom huffed. "It already exists? Well, that's unfortunate. Perhaps a possum. They look rather shady. An alien thought he was taking over the body of a human and he ends up in a possum, and he has no idea why he has the constant urge to play dead."

There was nothing to say about that one.

"Duke likes it. Yes, he does. Duke believes in me," her mother cooed at the corgi.

"Duke believes in the insane amount of treats you've been giving him." Brynn held her dog's leash. "And I thought we've all agreed that Major and I are just friends who are enjoying a physical relationship while we can."

"Sure you are. You've practically moved in with the man," her mom countered. "I've barely seen you in days. I'm surprised you were at the B and B this afternoon. Tell me, did you get a chance to sign those contracts?"

She still wasn't sure she wanted to sign those contracts. Gavin's offer had played around in her head, and the days she'd spent with Major had further muddied the waters. It had only been a couple of days they'd spent together and she was already addicted, and not merely to Major. She loved the time they spent together, but the freedom was truly intoxicating. She could walk around town and no one cared who she was. They were all friendly, and in the beginning she'd been asked for autographs, but after the first week, she'd simply been another person. The pressure to achieve, to go higher than she'd gone before, to move into another category of actresses, had disappeared for a little while.

"I haven't yet. I wanted to read them."

Her mom's eyes narrowed. "Why would you do that? Your agent has already vetted the contracts, and I looked through them myself. They are perfectly good contracts in line with SAG. You're getting everything you're supposed to get, and I negotiated a few extra perks including a dog walker when you can't take Duke out yourself."

She could take Duke with her because they were filming in the US. Why couldn't she take Major, too? Why couldn't she find a way to do all the things she wanted to do and explore this relationship with the best man she'd ever met?

"Brynn? Is there a reason you don't want to sign the contracts? I thought this was settled."

She was saved by the dog. Duke barked, standing up and turning his body toward the parking lot, straining at his leash.

Brynn turned and Dolly was doing the same to Major. The dog was wriggling crazily. Walking beside Major was his father.

Brynn turned to her mom. "Please? This is the first time Major's been able to bring his father out in a long time. Can we not fight?"

"I wasn't aware we were fighting at all," her mother whispered in a worried tone. "I suspect we need to have a long talk, but it can wait." She smiled, turning her attention to the newcomers. "Deputy, it's so good to see you. Mr. Blanchard, I'm Diane Pearson, Brynn's mother. It's so lovely to meet you."

Her mom could turn on the charm when she wanted to. Of course, she tended to use it only on those she felt compassion for.

"It's nice to meet you as well." Nelson Blanchard wore khakis and a golf shirt. He held a hand out, introducing himself to Gavin as well before turning to Brynn. His smile widened and he opened his arms. "It's good to see you again, Brynn."

In the days since she and Major had decided to be together while she was here, she'd spent some time with his father and found him as charming and kind as his son. The night before, they'd ordered pizza and played a couple of board games while Nelson had answered all her questions about Major's childhood. He'd been charming and seemed truly in the moment. It had only been late at night that he'd gotten confused. He'd said it was time to go to bed so he could take his meds in the morning and have another lovely day.

She wanted the evening to be perfect for him.

She hugged him. "Good to see you, too. Thanks for letting us crash your festival. Major told me you've always enjoyed the town parties."

Nelson stepped back. "Papillon knows how to throw a

festival. It's one of the best things about small-town living. I know there are bigger festivals, but everyone knows everyone else here. It can be quite amusing."

"He knows all the best booths. Dad's been coming to this festival for years," Major said.

"Though it appears to have grown." Nelson looked out over the fairgrounds, a smile on his face. "Our mayor seems to be working hard to bring new people in. This is the biggest crowd I've seen in a long time."

"The film crew has been trickling in all week," Brynn explained. "They're sure to come out and enjoy the festivities. It's good timing because they'll all have to work next week."

"Sylvie is a shrewd planner," Nelson said. "We usually schedule this festival later in the month. She's a smart one."

Sylvie had talked about the fact that she was using the movie to bring jobs and money into the community. She'd negotiated tax write-offs to make it easy to film here in Papillon, and it seemed to already be paying off for the town.

Major leaned in and kissed her. "I missed you while you were gone."

"I don't see how you could possibly have missed her. She was only gone a few hours. She's spent the last several nights at your place." Her mom managed to make it sound like an accusation. "She won't be able to do that when she starts working. By the way, they're bringing in your trailer tomorrow. I managed to get you one. That way you can take a nap and be comfortable while you have to stay close to the set."

She didn't want to leave Major's place. It was nice and comfy, and she'd even gotten used to his neighbor leaving flyers about the wages of sin on their doorstep. They made for good scratch paper. She kept some in her bag in case she needed to write something down.

Duke and Dolly had even gotten used to each other. She

caught them cuddling down on Dolly's big, fluffy bed from time to time. Would Duke miss the big pup?

Major seemed completely unfazed by her mother. "I guess I'll get used to hanging around your trailer, then."

The dogs seemed to have calmed and were doing the ritual canine greeting of sniffing each other's backsides.

"Trailers aren't so bad. Mine is quite comfortable. Sometimes it's the only place with any kind of air-conditioning." Gavin started leading the group onto the fairgrounds. "And it's got a lock so you can shut out any unwelcome visitors."

Her mom gently slapped at Gavin's chest. "I know you're talking about me, and you should remember that I'm good at breaking down doors that I find unwelcoming."

"Mom." She couldn't take their bickering tonight.

Major's hand found hers, weaving their fingers together and giving her a squeeze. "Everything will be fine once we get your momma a strawberry wine. A couple of glasses and she'll be in a much better mood."

Her mom frowned. "Does it come in a skinny version?"

Nelson chuckled. "Absolutely not. There is very little that is skinny on the bayou. The wine is delicious, and you'll love the food, too. Why don't you allow me to show you around?"

"I would love that." Her mother slid her arm into Nelson's offered one, allowing him the courtly gesture. "Perhaps we can talk about our kids."

"Or you could go back home and get a jump on tomorrow's work." The thought of her mom and Nelson discussing their relationship was not something she wanted to encourage.

"I would definitely like to try the strawberry wine," Gavin announced. "And perhaps something stronger."

"Don't forget, you're driving," her mom admonished.

Gavin shrugged. "There's always Ally's golf cart driver. We could give him a call."

He wandered off.

She prayed the night didn't end in disaster.

"Your girl seems to be getting along with everyone," Zep said after taking a sip of his beer. He leaned over and gave Dolly a pat. The dog rubbed her head against Zep's leg, seeking affection from the man who'd found her on the side of the road and brought her back to his shelter. "Roxie thinks she's far too nice and normal to be in Hollywood."

Major looked across the grounds to where Brynn and his father were currently being strapped into one of the Ferris wheel cabs. The neon-colored lights of the ride lit up the night around them and played across Brynn's skin. Even from here he could see the way her eyes sparkled with pleasure. It should probably worry him, how much he liked the fact that his friends had started calling Brynn *his girl.* "She definitely gets along with my dad. He adores her already."

"And you do, too. You've had a goofy grin on your face for days. I remember that goofy grin. At least your girl can't arrest you twice a day just to get your attention," Zep said on a grumble.

"I so did not do that to get your attention." Roxie walked up with a bag of kettle corn in her hand. She was dressed casually, her hair down around her shoulders. "I did that because you used to be really annoying, and the only time I could stand to be around you was when you were in handcuffs." She leaned over and stroked a hand over Dolly's head as the dog's tail wagged furiously. "Zep needed a leash. Yes, he did."

Zep's lips kicked up in a grin. "Nah, you were definitely trying to get my attention."

A brow rose over Roxie's eyes as she straightened up and gave her husband a knowing grin. "I still have those cuffs, you know."

"I am counting on it, baby." Zep leaned over and brushed his lips against hers. "I was telling our friend how much you like Brynn."

"I never expected her to be so down to earth," Roxie admitted. "Armie and I had made bets on which one would be more obnoxious, but Gavin and Brynn both turned out to be lovely. That will teach me not to stereotype. Though I think she was surprised by me, too. She came down to Louisiana not expecting this New York accent, if you know what I mean. I also think she didn't understand how much of our time goes to making sure people don't kill themselves on ATVs. I'm going to miss spending time with her. She's pretty cool. I will say Gavin can be a bit of a windbag when it comes to lectures on social justice, but he's okay, too. And that coffeemaker they gave us is straight from heaven."

He didn't like the reminder that their time was rapidly running out. Over the course of the last few days with Brynn, he'd come to the conclusion that he needed to stop thinking about the future. He was a planner, but he couldn't be right now. He needed to live in the moment. Major glanced over to see the Ferris wheel turning round and round.

"Your dad seems to be doing well," Zep said. "He remembered who I was. He was surprised to find out I got married though."

Roxie nodded her husband's way. "Yes, because he remembered what an obnoxious, bad-boy player you used to be. I got some stories out of him. Did you actually hit on his ex-wife? I thought I'd heard it all."

"Yeah, I was hoping he would remember less," Zep replied. "And you know I used to flirt with all women. All of them. I'm sorry, Major. I'm joking. It's great that your father seems to be on the mend."

"The medications Lila's been giving him are working well, but I'm afraid he's going to have to come off of them because they're wreaking havoc on his internal organs." He wasn't going to lose his dad. Not now. Not when he'd just gotten him back. He'd made the decision while he'd walked around the grounds this evening, watching his dad charm Brynn's mom. She'd been perfectly pleasant the whole time his father had been around, listening to his every story with interest.

It had been almost like they were a family, his father getting to know Brynn's mom and de facto dad. It felt like they were an everyday, normal couple with a future ahead of them.

His father wouldn't have a future at all if he didn't take him off the meds. They would have to find another way.

"Your dad wants to get off the meds?" Roxie asked, glancing over at the Ferris wheel.

Dolly seemed to grow tired of all the human talking. She laid right down on the grass after a long yawn.

"I'm not sure *want* would be the word I would use." *Want* didn't seem to be a word he could use very often lately. At least not a want that got met. "But Lila's made it clear that the damage will only get worse."

"I'm sorry to hear that," Zep said.

Major tried to shake off the anxiety that came every time he thought about his father getting off the meds. He didn't want to think about it tonight. There would be time enough to deal with that horror later. He kept putting off the time when they had to actually stop giving him the drugs. He wanted his father to get to know Brynn. Or rather, he wanted Brynn to know who his father was when a disease wasn't fogging up his soul and mind. "We'll find some other way. So, Roxie, are you going to be on set at all?"

Roxie brightened. "Yeah, I'm getting paid to hang around in case they have any questions."

"It's called consulting," Zep offered. "I'm thinking about releasing a couple of our long-term residents on the set to see if I can consult on how to deal with critters. I might send Otis walking right through the crew. He won't do anything. He's too lazy, but the sight of him can scare a person."

"Don't you dare." Roxie turned on her husband.

"I wouldn't if I were you. Brynn's mom would probably wrestle Otis and try to turn him into shoes and a handbag if she thought he might harm her precious baby," Major murmured. If there was one thing he'd learned about Diane, it was that she protected Brynn at all costs. At least she protected Brynn's career. "Any news on Brian and his band of merry raccoons?"

By the time Zep had gotten out to the B and B that day, Brian had disappeared, leaving behind an odd mix of things he'd stolen. In the hollowed-out log they'd found two beer bottles, one of Harry's wrenches, a squeaky toy that had to belong to Shep, and most surprisingly, a set of upper dentures that proved John McGovern wasn't merely trying to get out of wearing his teeth. He just wished the man would have at least boiled them before putting them back in. Instead, he'd wiped them off on his shirt and declared he was going in search of a steak.

Lila had been warned she might have a patient soon.

"Well, we've had a couple more reports of trash cans getting knocked over and the contents picked through," Zep said with a sigh. "I expect to see the suckers here sometime tonight."

"Please tell me you're not talking about the raccoons again." Brynn walked up, a smile on her face.

Dolly hopped up to greet her. Her tail wagged, and she looked around as though trying to figure out where her doggy friend was.

"We're not hopeful the threat has passed." Major reached out and brought her in close. "Where's my dad?"

She turned her face up, looking into his eyes. "He's taking

my mom on the Ferris wheel now. He seems to like it a lot. When we got to the top, he pointed out all these places around town and told me stories about them. I know I probably shouldn't have left them alone, but they seem to be getting along nicely. She's going to hang out with him for a while. Don't worry. She's very responsible when it comes to things like this. I know she can seem flighty . . ."

He trusted Diane to watch out for his dad. "Despite your mother's eccentricities, I don't doubt she'll take care of my dad for a second. So are you hungry?"

"I'm starving, and everything smells wonderful," Brynn admitted. "Also, what exactly is a boudin ball?"

"What they are is delicious, and the fact that you've been here for weeks and haven't tried them is a crime." Somehow it was easier to forget all his troubles the minute he saw her face.

"Do you think he'll forget again?" Zep was looking at the Ferris wheel, a thoughtful expression on his face. "Or will he keep some of the memories?"

"Are you talking about Nelson? Why would he forget? He's planning on staying on the medication," Brynn said. "I was talking to him about it tonight. He was saying how excited he was because the meds have a cumulative effect. He's feeling better every day. He hasn't had a single episode all day."

"And every day the meds damage his internal organs more," Major reminded her. "Now, let's grab some food and talk about something more pleasant."

"I think he's more concerned about his mind than his liver." Brynn stepped back, her mouth turning down. Dolly seemed to understand things had taken a turn. She sat down and stared up while Brynn spoke. "Have you talked to him about this?"

"Yes, I have. Of course I have. I've talked about it with

my father, so you and I don't need to have this conversation." He did not need this from her. She was supposed to support him. She was supposed to be the good part of his day, the shiny part.

"We're going to go and see if we can find Zep's mom." Roxie had taken her husband's hand. "I hear she and Marcelle have a booth where they're telling fortunes."

"I bet I know what Major's fortune's about to be," Zep said with a grimace as they walked away.

"Look, I get that you don't want to talk to me about this, but I really think you should discuss this more with your dad. I don't think he understands what your position is. He's got all kinds of plans," Brynn was saying. "He was telling me he's going to meet up with his old Army unit in a couple of months."

"He might not be alive in a couple of months," Major shot back. He'd heard his father talking about all the things he could do now that the meds were helping him. His dad wasn't being realistic. "Not if he stays on those meds."

"He said the damage would take a while, that he's not in danger right now, but it would get worse," she countered. "His eyes are wide open about what's happening to him."

"Yes, it will get worse, but we can stop it." No one seemed to take his father's situation seriously. Certainly not his dad.

"I don't know. He seems very sure that he's going to take the medication."

He hadn't wanted to have this talk with her, but she wasn't backing down, so it was time to point out a few truths to her. "He doesn't get to make that choice. I hold his medical power of attorney. I make the decisions for him because he's not capable of making them himself. Brynn, I've been doing this for several years. I know what I'm doing, and I know what's best for him."

"That medical power of attorney should only be used when

he can't make decisions because he's not in his right mind," Brynn insisted. "He can make decisions for himself right now. He's making his choice very plain."

"His choice is wrong, and I assure you the power of attorney is still in place." He didn't want to fight with her.

But she seemed determined to ruin the evening. "Why would you go against his wishes? More than that, why would you abuse the power he gave you?"

"Abuse? You think I'm abusing my father?"

"That's not what I said. Don't twist my words." She seemed to take a moment to shove down some unnamed emotions. "Major, I understand that you're afraid to lose your dad, but can't you see how much more afraid he is to lose himself? This is a blessing because it doesn't have to be your decision. You can know that this is what your father wants. There's got to be some peace in that."

Dolly was suddenly on her feet, but Major tried to ignore her for the moment.

Peace? There was no peace in any of this. Except those moments when he was with her and he could forget the world. Now she was the one bringing the world in. "I don't need the opinion of someone who won't be around when I have to watch him die."

Now he was the one who needed to take a breath because she'd paled, and the hurt from his words was plain on her face. "Brynn, I . . ."

"Bria Knight, would you like to comment on the news story about your relationship with Gavin Jacks?"

They both stopped and turned in the direction of the cool, collected voice, and immediately Major blinked because someone had turned on a bright light. Camera. A big guy was holding a camera and pointing it at them. It was the woman he'd first met at the assisted living facility. The one from the tabloid show.

Dolly peeked out from her place behind his legs, proving she was the worst guard dog in history.

Brynn put a hand up, trying to shade herself from the light. "Gavin is like a dad to me."

"Then why are there intimate photos of the two of you circulating on the Internet right now?" Jeannie Carbo asked. "Have you not seen the pictures? Is that why Tighty-Whitie is still with you? Are you in relationships with both men?"

"Major, what's going on?" he heard his father ask.

"What the hell is going on here?" Diane stepped forward, moving in front of her daughter. "Jeannie, you've had your interview with my daughter. What is the meaning of this?"

Major moved closer to his dad, but his hand found Brynn's. It didn't matter that they'd been fighting. Something was going on, and he wasn't sure what it was. The reporter had said something about Gavin and Brynn. Which was ridiculous.

"There are pictures of Bria and Gavin Jacks on the web. They appear to support the rumors that have always circulated that they've been in a sexual relationship before. Did it start before she turned eighteen? How long has it been going on?" Jeannie asked.

Diane's mouth hung open for a moment, and for the first time since he'd met the woman, she seemed to have absolutely nothing to say.

"We have no comment beyond the fact that there is absolutely no sexual relationship between Brynn and Gavin. He has always been like a father to her, and if you continue to spread rumors about her, we'll have to get the lawyers involved and you'll be the first one they'll talk to." He wasn't about to let the reporter think she could get away with trashing Brynn's reputation.

She let him lead her away, toward the parking lot, Dolly trotting between them. Diane walked behind her daughter, silent for once.

Gavin jogged up behind them, two drinks in his hand and Duke's leash wrapped around his wrist. Duke was running beside him. "Hey, I thought we were meeting by the games."

Diane grabbed the red solo cup and swallowed it down. "We're leaving."

"I'm not sure what's going on, and for once I don't think it's about my dementia," his dad said. "Why would they say Brynn's seeing Gavin when she's with Major?"

"What?" Gavin stopped, reaching for his phone.

Brynn dropped Major's hand. She reached down and picked up Duke, taking his leash from Gavin and holding him close to her chest. "Don't. Not now. We have to get back to the B and B and then we can figure out what's happening. Please, take us out of here. They already have enough footage of us for one night."

"I'll take you." He hated the blank look on her face. Something had gone wrong, and apparently it was all over the Internet.

She shook her head. "No. Take your father home. Or finish your evening. I'll deal with this problem. Good night, Major."

He stayed where he was, pulling on Dolly's leash when she tried to run after Brynn and Duke. She didn't want him to follow? She didn't want him to help her through this?

"Son, I think she's in trouble," his father said.

She was definitely in trouble, and so was he.

chapter fifteen

Brynn's hands were shaking as she looked at the tablet screen. She'd waited until she'd gotten back to the B and B to try to find the story the reporter had referenced. On the short drive from the fairgrounds to her cabin, she'd simply sat in Gavin's rented SUV and held her dog.

Now she wished that drive had taken longer.

"This is the most ridiculous thing I've ever seen." Her mother paced the living area of Brynn's increasingly crowded cabin. "I thought she was saying someone had doctored photographs of the two of you. You're sitting on a park bench talking."

Oh, but they'd done more than talk that day. She knew exactly which day it had been. Someone had been watching them on the afternoon when Gavin had told her there was a place at the Sorbonne for her after they finished filming. She'd been emotional and grateful to have him around. They'd been very affectionate that day because it had felt natural to lean into him, to hug the man who'd been the father figure in her life.

"That's not what it looks like, and you have to know that, Diane." Gavin sat on the couch, a glass of Scotch in his hands.

He'd taken one look at the photos and the headlines and gone straight for the small bar. "The angle he took that at makes it look like we're kissing."

Brynn's stomach threatened to flip. Would her mother turn and accuse her now? She'd been shockingly calm up to this point.

Her mom stopped pacing and looked Gavin's way. "Perhaps it does, but anyone with half a brain understands that it's only the angle and how Brynn's head is hidden by yours. It doesn't tell the full story. The photographer is obviously hiding behind a tree. That has to count for something."

Brynn needed to make a few things plain. "We didn't kiss. I gave him a hug and he held me for a little while. I was emotional about a lot of things."

Her mom shifted, coming to kneel close to Brynn, her hands pulling the tablet away. "Of course he did. He loves you, Brynn. You've been like a daughter to him, and I've been grateful for his presence in your life. I don't want you to worry. This is nothing. This is some tabloid crap that no one will believe. I'm sure it hurts you, but you know the truth. There's no reason at all for you not to hold your head high."

At least her mom didn't believe it. Her mother had moved the tablet out of Brynn's grasp, but she couldn't take away the memory of those articles.

They played father and daughter on TV, but will they soon have a family of their own?

How long have this TV father-daughter duo been playing house?

It made her sick inside, but it wasn't the only thing that had her gut rolling. She could still hear Major talking about how what his father wanted didn't matter.

He was only scared. That was at the heart of why Major was thinking about making a decision that wasn't his to make. He would wrap his head around the blow and do the right thing. She knew him. Even his reason for why he hadn't wanted to talk to her about it reenforced her belief.

I don't need the opinion of someone who won't be around when I have to watch him die.

Those words were going to haunt her until they talked about them. He was scared and it had made him mean. Like a dog in a shelter who nipped at those initial hands trying to pet him.

She'd sent him away because she'd been numb in that moment, unable to process more than one blow at a time. She'd known something had changed inside her, something fundamental. It was about more than just Major. It was about her whole life, about what she wanted out of it, but he was a part of that.

Would Major see those pictures and believe the tabloids? They'd had a fight and he was obviously angry with her for the stance she'd taken. It would be easier to look at this "evidence" and see something she didn't want him to see. Would he read the headlines and think it was far better to break things off now since she would be dealing with scandal for months?

Maybe that was a question she should think about. Did she really want what could be his last months with his father disrupted with this?

The enormity of the situation threatened to overwhelm her. All that work. All the struggle, and this was what her career might end up being defined by. There were pictures now. Before, it had just been nasty rumors. Now the press could point at a picture that was entirely innocent and twist it.

It wouldn't matter that it wasn't true. Some people would always believe it. Some people would always see her the way the tabloids portrayed her. For a long time that had been as the good girl, the hard-working TV sweetheart.

She feared she was about to see the flip side of the coin.

"It's only a couple of sites," her mother said in a soothing tone. "And they're not popular sites."

"*Entertain America* is covering it." Gavin took another drink. "It'll be on their eleven o'clock show, and that means the larger entertainment and tabloid sites will pick up the story. The fact that they got a camera crew out here so quickly is proof that they think this is going to be big news. They'll bring back all those old rumors. We'll be lucky if the studio doesn't fire us."

"They're not going to fire either of you." Her mom stood back up. "I know one picture looks like you're kissing, but that is easily explainable by the angle of the camera. The studio has too much invested at this point."

"They haven't even started principal photography," Gavin shot back. "It will be easy to replace us."

"You have a contract," her mom countered. "They'll have to pay you whether you do the job or not."

"So they pay me out this time and neither of us gets another job for years." Gavin's jaw tightened. "I don't see how we get through this."

Her mother crossed her arms over her chest, a sure sign she was settling in for a long argument. "The same way we got through it before."

"Before it was one jerk who was angry with me. I got him fired for doing the very thing he went out and accused me of. Everyone in the business knew what he was like. Three other young women came forward to talk about how he'd treated them when he was their director. No one believed it because Brynn was seventeen at the time and there were absolutely no pictures. I know those aren't completely believable, but it's enough. People love a scandal, and they don't care who they hurt. There are people out there who will be thrilled to put me in that hot seat and see if I can come out of it alive." He focused on her mom.

"Unless we change the narrative," said Brynn. "What if we go out and talk about it? We call the producers in the morning, tell them we'll handle it, and then we explain the whole thing. I tell them I have a boyfriend. You can talk about whatever woman you're seeing now. Who are you seeing? I know you tend to keep things casual, but if there's any way she could join us here, that might be helpful."

Oddly, Gavin never took his eyes off her mom, though Brynn thought he was talking to her. "I assure you that the relationship I'm in is far from casual. It's frustrating, and it might cost me everything."

"Gavin, why don't you let me talk to Brynn alone?" Her mom's voice had gone low.

"So you can convince her that this is all going to be all right? So you can tell her all she has to do is keep a stiff upper lip and survive the scandal?" Gavin stood, staring her mother down. "I think I'll stay, because you need to convince me, too. This isn't the same as it was the first time around. She's twenty-five and gorgeous and there are pictures. People will believe it this time, and they won't blame me. You want to know the truth? When I said *we'll* get fired, I meant she's going to get fired."

Tears pulsed behind Brynn's eyes because she thought he might be right.

The door came open and Ally swooped in. She was dressed to kill in a short yellow minidress and high heels, her bag flung over her bare shoulders. Her hair was up in a bun, but it looked like it had seen a lot of wind as tendrils popped out. She had her phone in one hand, and her eyes immediately went for Brynn. "I am so sorry. I was at a bar talking to this hot guy and I ignored the notifications. I got here as fast as the golf cart could take me. By the way, I owe Greg a huge tip because he crossed through some farmland and we apparently started a small war or something. I don't know. There was an old dude in overalls running after us with a gun yelling about his potatoes. It was a whole mood."

Her mother seemed eager to change the topic. "Allyson, we need to sit down and decide how to confront this on Brynn's socials."

Ally shook her head. "This is beyond me. I would tell everyone to screw themselves. We need a fixer."

"A crisis publicist." Her mom nodded. "Yes. You're exactly right. What time is it at home? I might still be able to get one of our lawyers on the phone. Brynn, you are not to talk to anyone until we've got the publicist in place."

The crisis publicist would cost hundreds of thousands of dollars.

Why was she fighting for something she didn't even care about anymore?

"Don't. I'll quit tomorrow," she said, an odd relief coming over her. "I don't care what they think. Gavin's right. He'll weather this and be all right. I'm the one who it's going to follow forevermore. I'll be dealing with every skeevy director who thinks I'll sleep with him. I'm out."

"What the hell does that mean? You're out?" Her mom's eyes had gone wide.

Brynn stood. She felt oddly at peace. "I mean I'm done. I'm retiring. I've got other options, and I'm going to seriously consider taking them."

"Other options?" Her mom asked the question like Brynn had declared she was going on a murderous rampage. "What other options? Are you considering staying here so you can be with that boy?"

This was half the problem. When her mom called Major—a grown-ass man—a boy, it signaled that she also thought of Brynn as a girl who needed guidance. "He's a man, and I'm a woman who can make my own decisions. And yes, I think I might stay here for a while. I need to make a decision about whether I want to go to Paris or if I want some time to myself."

Her mom whirled on Gavin. "Paris? What did you do? I told you the painting is nothing more than a hobby."

"It's a part of who I am," Brynn countered. "It's far more me than acting is. I do that out of habit. I do it because it's the only thing I know to do. I've been doing it since I was a kid and I want out."

Now that she was saying the words, they felt good. They felt right. It was something that had been brewing inside her for years, and to have them out felt like someone had opened a pressure valve and vented for the first time in . . . since she was five and realized it was all on her.

There were tears in her mother's eyes when she looked at Brynn this time. Actual tears. She hadn't seen her mother cry in years. She had joked she didn't have actual working tear ducts because they might cause wrinkles. "Are you trying to punish me? I know he is, but I never expected it from you."

"Why?" Ally stood beyond the small circle, looking like the outsider staring in. "I mean shouldn't you have expected it from her?"

"She doesn't have your anger issues," her mom shot back. "Stay out of this. Go back to our room and I'll be up shortly. We're still calling the lawyer and getting the ball rolling. Brynn is exhausted. She's been through a lot, and maybe we should talk about giving her a brief break."

"It's not going to be brief. It's going to be done for now. I can't say I won't ever want to try again. I'm done limiting myself. I've spent my whole life on a schedule, and that's the only reason I'm not jumping at the chance to go to Paris."

Gavin had put his Scotch down. "We should talk through this. I told you my friend is holding a place for you."

"And if I'm good enough, it'll still be there in the future."

Gavin frowned. "It might not. Anything can happen. Brynn, you know you have to take advantage of any opportunity given to you."

"Why? Why don't I ever get to say I need a break? I need a break to figure out who I am. I've spent my entire life under scrutiny." She pointed to the tablet. "That was inevitable. I'm a child star, and I'm either going to be virtuous and a role model or a train wreck. I don't get to be me. I have to go harder, faster, higher every second of the day or I'm taking the place of someone more worthy, more willing to break themselves for some money and fame. No. I'm done. I'm picking me this time."

"That is the most selfish thing that's ever come out of your mouth," her mom said quietly, the tears falling on her cheeks.

"Out of hers, maybe." Ally stepped in. "But it can barely touch your selfishness, Mother."

"Ally, maybe we should go." Gavin stood up.

Ally laughed, a sound that held not an ounce of humor. "Of course we should. Then Mom can pretend like she's not the problem. Do you two think I'm a moron? Look, I get it. Brynn is perfect."

Brynn huffed.

Ally turned her way. "No, I'm not being a bitch. You really are. You're an amazing sister. You're prettier than me, more likable. I'm a better actress, but you're far easier to deal with. None of that changes the fact that you are genuinely one of my favorite people in the world, and I am often jealous of you. But that's nothing compared to what Mom is doing right now."

"Ally, give her a break." Brynn knew what her mom was feeling. It was fear of the unknown. It was fear of loss. It was becoming the emotional theme of the night. She wasn't going to treat her mom differently than she was Major. They were both capable of saying things they shouldn't if the right pressure was applied. They were both human and so was she. She probably should have found a different way to break this to her mom. "She's got a lot invested in my career."

"Yes, and you should remember that." Her mom seemed willing to jump on any opening she gave her. "You're my biggest client."

"Ally will be bigger if you just let her." Brynn believed in her sister's talent. And she definitely knew Ally was more suited for the business. "Concentrate on Ally. You can make her a superstar. All I was ever going to be was the secondary character, and I don't care enough to try to be more. Mom, I appreciate everything . . ."

"Stop." Ally let her bag clang to the floor. "Don't thank her. Tell me something, Brynn. Did they offer to go public to save you?"

"Allyson." Gavin's voice went hard.

"What do you mean, go public?" She wasn't sure where her sister was going with this. Except she did. Deep inside, hadn't she known for the last couple of years? Hadn't she known why Gavin hung around for months at a time and then seemed to hide from her mom for a while before showing up again?

"Ally, that's not your business." Her mom had paled, but there was still steel in her tone.

"It is because neither one of you has the balls to admit that this is something you could have cleared up a very long time ago. I'm going to tell her the truth because I owe her. I owe her for putting up with my jealous crap. I owe her for all the work she did to keep us not only safe but comfortable. Brynn, they've been off and on for years. Remember that first time these rumors circulated? They could have explained that he's pretty much our stepdad and gotten that heat off you and then we wouldn't be here at all."

"Brynn, it's more complicated than that," Gavin said.

But it wasn't. Her mom had let her take that heat as a barely eighteen-year-old girl. She'd been ready to let her take it this time when all they'd needed was the truth. Oh, some people would still try to make a scandal out of anything, but it would be simpler to say he was her dad and that was why he sometimes held her hand or gave her a long hug.

"How long?" Brynn asked, her voice barely a whisper.

"This is none of your business," her mom insisted.

She'd heard that enough. "As I was about to be the one to spend a hundred K on a crisis publicist when all you had to do is say you're his girlfriend, you'll have to excuse me."

"I'll pay for the publicist," Gavin offered.

"I'm not happy with you, either," Brynn shot back. "And you seem to think you can pay for everything and that makes you innocent. Did you know she told me you got us government funds for my grandmother's care?"

"I didn't want you to think we could go to him every time we had a problem." Her mother put a hand to her face as though checking herself to make sure this was real. "I was grateful, but I knew I had to rely on myself."

"But you didn't, Diane. You relied on Brynn," Gavin argued. "I told you I would take care of you. I asked you to marry me and let me adopt the girls. I did everything I could to be there for you. I loved you. I still do. I would marry you in a heartbeat tomorrow if you would let me."

Her mom pointed his way. "And when I told you no the first time, you went out that night and slept with your costar."

"It was a mistake." He took a step toward her. "I was hurting, and I did the stupidest thing I could. Would it shock you to know I haven't slept with anyone but you in five years? Diane, we're good together. I'm glad this happened because maybe we can all get what we need."

"What we need?" her mom asked.

"Yes." Gavin stood tall. "Brynn needs time to figure out who she is outside of this life she's been in forever. Ally needs you to take her seriously and to find her own damn voice. I need you. I need you to trust that I won't leave you, that you're enough for me."

"And what about what I need?" her mother asked.

It seemed to Brynn that she'd been a servant to her mother's needs for a very long time. "I don't care. Get out."

She was done. She couldn't take this another second longer or she would say something she shouldn't.

"Brynn, I'm not . . ." her mother started.

"Give her some time and leave, or I'll walk out." Ally grabbed her bag. "I'll walk out tonight, hop on a plane, and find another manager. Hell, maybe I'll go on some talk shows. I've got stories to tell."

"Allyson." Her mother breathed her sister's name, a look of pure betrayal in her eyes.

Ally's gaze went hard. "I'm playing hardball. Like you taught me." She turned to Brynn, her expression softening. "I'll lock down your socials and I'll find a way out of this for you. I know you think you know what you want right now, but take some time and think about it. Stay here in this weird town for a couple of weeks and see if you want to make things work with TW."

"It's not about him." Her relationship might have been blown, but she'd made friends here. Even if Major was no longer interested, this place was important to her. She could stay for a few weeks, maybe months, and paint and think and figure out what she wanted to do with her life.

For the first time, she could simply be for a while.

"Of course it is." Her mom slung her bag over her shoulder. "You're a silly girl, giving up everything for a pretty face."

Something nasty had taken root in Brynn, betrayal and anger making her meaner than she would usually be. "I'm not losing everything. I mean I still have the money and the house, after all. The house I bought in LA is worth a couple million if I decide to sell it."

Now Ally gasped. "You would sell our house?"

"I believe your sister is saying it isn't ours at all. Be careful, Allyson. You might still need me." Her mother swept out of the cabin with perfect dramatic flair.

"Ally, I didn't mean that. You have to know I wouldn't kick you out of our home." Shame filled her. "I know how much you gave up so I could work."

Ally sniffled, opening her arms and hugging Brynn. "And that's why I love you despite all the perfection. I'll talk to her. I want you to have options."

"I don't need them."

Ally pulled back. "Okay, then I'll talk to her because I want my family to stay together." She looked back at Gavin. "All of us."

"Brynn, I'm sorry," Gavin said, his tone somber.

She couldn't. Not tonight. "I need to do this tomorrow. I can't even think tonight."

He nodded and picked up the Scotch. "I'm going to take this. I think I'll need it."

Ally rolled her eyes. "Steal an extra glass. If I'm going to drink with my dad, I might as well do it in style. Somehow I don't think I'll be welcome in the suite tonight."

"I'll take care of you," Gavin promised. "It's best to give your mother some time. She can scream quite loudly when she wants to. She reaches this point where I'm sure she can only be heard by dogs. I'll ask Seraphina to bring in a cot."

"Which you'll sleep on," Ally said as she opened the door.

Gavin sighed. "It's not easy being a father."

But he'd been a good one. Of course, a father usually didn't hide his relationship with a mother. How many years had they kept that secret? She felt so betrayed. Why would her mother do this? No one would have questioned their relationship all these years if Gavin had been her stepdad. Or even her mom's boyfriend.

The door closed and she was left with Duke.

She took a long breath. She'd lost so much in the course of a single evening. Gavin was right. She would likely be fired. They would pay out her contract and find a less scandalous actress to play Gavin's daughter. She hadn't signed the other contract, so it would likely be rescinded. It was odd that losing her career wasn't the bad part of the evening. There was something freeing in it.

Losing her mom was much harder.

Losing Major felt bad, too. He hadn't said he wouldn't see her again, but it felt like he was a million miles away. She wasn't sure how they could move forward now, or if he would even want to move forward. Losing Major felt like losing something precious. Something that hadn't quite had a chance to bloom.

She looked down, and Duke had gone into hiding in his crate.

"Sorry, buddy. Tomorrow will be better. I promise." She sniffled and wondered if she should be promising anyone anything. Tomorrow would likely bring new problems. Tomorrow the story would be all over the world, and people would look at her differently. Maybe she should rent a place out on one of the islands and become an isolationist. She could be that crazy dog lady who only came into town for rice and water and canvases. She could be the Van Gogh of the bayou.

There was a knock on the door, and a wave of weariness hit Brynn. "Go away, Mom. I'll talk to you tomorrow."

She wasn't sure what she would say to her mom, but she couldn't do it tonight. Tonight was for sleep so she could try to see things clearly in the morning.

"Brynn, let me in," a familiar voice said. "Please, baby. I'm so sorry we fought earlier."

She knew it was stupid, but she flew across the room. She flung the door open, and Major was there.

"I shouldn't have talked to you the way I did," he said. "I'm so sorry. Can we please talk? I'm worried about you. That story is ridiculous, and you need to know that no one here is going to believe it. Roxie already told that reporter if she comes out here to the B and B, she'll arrest her for trespassing."

He was here. She knew why he'd been short with her, and she'd already forgiven him for that. But she didn't want to talk. She wanted to forget the world and think about nothing but him for a while.

She took his hand, drawing him into her cabin. "No talk. Kiss me. Please kiss me."

He leaned over and picked her up, kicking the door closed behind him. He started for the bedroom, and Brynn let go of everything else.

The sun shone in through the gauzy curtains, and that familiar sense of peace flowed over Major as Brynn curled up beside him, her skin warm against his.

"You sleep okay?" He had to ask because she'd had a hell of a night. After he'd made love to her, she'd told him what she'd learned about her mother and Gavin and talked about the betrayal she'd felt. Then she'd cried, and he'd held her for the longest time until she'd fallen asleep.

She'd trusted him. She'd given him all her trouble and he'd taken it in.

God, he was going to miss her. How much time did they have left? Would she need to go back to LA to handle the fallout of those stupid pictures coming out?

She sat up, stretching, her golden hair draped across her back. "I slept better than I thought I would."

He reached out, running his hand over her cheek. She was the most beautiful woman he'd ever seen. Would ever see. Her beauty was more than her looks. There was practically a glow that came off her. "How do you feel this morning?"

"I don't know. In some ways, it almost feels good that it's over. Do you know what I mean? I mean obviously it's not over. I need to talk to my agent about what the studio is going to do." She picked up her phone. She'd turned it off the night before. Now she pressed the button that would reconnect her with the world.

"They can't fire you, can they?" It didn't make a lick of sense to him. It was a couple of photos that could be easily explained. "You didn't do anything wrong."

"Even the perception of scandal can put the movie's profits at risk," she murmured as she got up and reached for her robe. "This is a film about a father and a daughter. I know it's dumb because it's a story. It's fiction. But a relationship between me and Gavin could make this film have an ick factor that would doom it at the box office."

He watched her, his eyes taking in every inch of that gorgeous body. She was breathtaking, and he knew he was risking more than mere heartache. He was going to miss her the rest of his life.

"Well, my agent called five times," she said with a sigh. "I suppose I should listen to the messages."

"Or you could come back to bed and take a little more time."

She took a long breath. "I think I would rather get it over with so I can move forward with other plans."

He was certain those plans would include going home to LA. "Would it help at all if I did some press with you?"

She put the phone to her ear. "They would simply say I brought you in for cover. You would be my bayou beard, so to speak." She chuckled and then put the phone back down. "Well, that answers that question. Gavin was right. The studio has already reached out to ask me to step back given the bad press around me. Not us. Me. They still think Gavin has box office potential. They're paying my contract, but they would like for me to willingly walk away. For the production's sake. My agent says she'll find another project, but I shouldn't think the rom-com I was supposed to start after this one won't do the same thing. She's talking to them later today."

He didn't understand it at all. "Why would they still want Gavin but not you?"

"Probably because he's got a solid box office record, and they paid him about two million more than me," she replied, putting the phone down again. "No one will care, and in the long run, it'll be one more thing to sell his eventual autobiography. If I don't come out and say he forced me into something—which of course he didn't—it will blow over for him."

"That's not fair."

"Hollywood isn't a fair place." She sat back on the bed.

"Brynn, why won't it blow over for you?"

She shrugged. "It probably would. Eventually. Especially if I stay out of Gavin's life and he stays out of mine, but that seems sad. I don't know when I'll be able to let go of being angry with my mom. I'm angry with him, too, but I can't see myself staying angry forever. I don't want to lose the only family I have. But by the time the scandal blows over, the damage to me will be done. I don't have an established adult career. Watch for it. In the next few weeks there will be lots of stories about how I'm one more damaged child star. It's a narrative that sells."

His heart ached for her. She'd worked all her life and one set of pictures could take it all down? "You can fight it."

She shifted, her back against the headboard. "What if I don't want to?"

"So you've decided to go to Paris?" He wanted to argue with her about her career, but she loved art, too. Maybe it wasn't such a bad idea for her to get away.

"Or I could stay here for a while," she said, a ghost of a smile on her face.

He forced himself to sit up. The idea of her staying here was everything he wanted. And absolutely nothing he could have. He couldn't be the reason she gave up on her dreams. "Brynn, you have the chance to study art. Why would you give that up? Unless they took that away from you, too."

"No. I'm sure the offer is still open, but I think it likely will be open to me next year, too. If I'm good enough now, I'll be better then. And if the offer isn't on the table in a year, I'll know the offer was about Gavin and not me."

He couldn't believe she would turn this opportunity down. "Or you take the chance and prove them all wrong."

"What if I'm tired of constantly proving myself?" Brynn asked, her voice weary.

That weariness was exactly the problem. "Yes. You're tired. You probably shouldn't make any decisions right now."

She shook her head. "No. I think this has been a long time coming. I think it was always going to happen, and I'm going to accentuate the positive. I'm going to stay here in Papillon. I'll let Mom and Ally stay at the house in LA, and

I'll get a place here. I can't stay in the cabin long-term. I'll need some place with a kitchen and maybe a second bedroom I can set up as a studio. Is it weird that I'm kind of excited about buying dishes and stuff? I didn't get to do that when I bought the place in LA. It came fully furnished. I never got to decorate a dorm room. I kind of want to go to Walmart and see how I can do this on the cheap."

What the hell was she thinking? There was a part of him that wanted nothing more than to tell her she didn't have to do anything cheap. He'd already done it. She could move in with him and enjoy all of his cheap stuff. He had three bedrooms. She could pick from the guest rooms and turn one into her studio. He could have her. He could keep her. He could make sure when the time came, she didn't leave him behind. She would stay here with him and . . .

"You can't stay here, Brynn. You aren't meant to be stuck in a small town."

He couldn't let her make this mistake. If he did, she would wake up some time in the next couple of months or even years and she would resent him for keeping her here, for holding her back.

"Why would I be stuck? Do they not let you leave if you stay too long?" She laughed, but there was a wary quality to the sound.

He slid out of bed and reached for his jeans. She wasn't thinking straight. "You know what I mean. You're not meant to be stuck here."

"What's wrong with here?"

There was nothing wrong with Papillon, per se. He loved it here, but she was a big-city girl. She was enchanted with small-town life, but the reality of it hadn't set in yet. "There's no opportunity for you here. What are you going to do? Are you going to get a job at the diner?"

"Maybe. Or maybe I'll volunteer with Zep and hunt down

Brian. I don't know that I'll even get a job, but it's an inter-esting idea. I can't paint all the time." She stood again, watching him with suspicious eyes. "You know I'm not asking to move in with you, right?"

"I wouldn't let you even if you asked." He couldn't. It would be selfish. "You've had a blow. I get that, but you're going to change your mind. You can't change the course of your life because you met a guy."

He watched as her skin flushed, and she seemed to take a steadying breath.

"Well, I suppose I haven't given you a reason not to think this is about you." She made sure the robe was secure around her. "And I was thinking we could see each other, but I'm starting to understand that isn't what you want."

He shouldn't have put it so harshly. He was making a mess of this, but he wasn't sure how to make her understand. "I want it more than anything, but we agreed this would only go on as long as you were here."

"And you didn't think I would be here long."

"That's not it. Don't put words in my mouth, Brynn."

"Then you should say what you mean, Major. Do you want me here or not?"

"Do I want you to stay in Papillon?" He wanted it more than anything in the world, but she would regret it. She would come to resent him for being the reason she gave up every-thing. He loved her. He couldn't do this to her. He'd just fig-ured out he loved her and he had to give her up. This wasn't how he'd wanted to start the morning. "No. I don't want you here."

She shrugged. "That's sad for you, then, because I'm stay-ing. I've made friends here. I think this place could be good for me. I don't want to go back to LA right now. I want some freedom in my life. I'm not taking the place in Paris because I need to not be in a high-pressure position again. I've been in a pressure cooker for twenty years. I want out for a while. I'm making this choice for me."

"But you're not. You're doing this because something bad happened and you don't want to face it. This place seems nice, and you want to hide. How can I let you do that?"

"You don't let me do anything." A brow rose over her eyes, and he caught the moment she went from being sad to angry. "Are you trying to make this decision for me? Because I'm not your father. I'm not signing away some rights to you. You have to be in control, don't you? You seem like a nice guy, and maybe deep down you are, but you also need to control the world around you."

Irritation flared, and he couldn't help himself. He knew he should lower the temperature, but he found himself responding. "Control? You think I have a minute's control? If I did, my mother wouldn't have died. My father wouldn't want to leave me alone. I'm doing this for you. I'm sacrificing what I want so you can have what you deserve."

She sighed, a weary sound. "I'm the only one who gets to decide what I deserve. That's what I've figured out. You don't get to look at my life and decide it's good enough for me and I don't get to change it. My mom has done that for years. She had good reasons for it, and I don't regret working hard to pull us all out of a horrible situation. Although now I look back and realize Gavin would have taken care of all of us anyway. So maybe I shouldn't give her a pass on that." She looked him up and down and then nodded. "All right, then. I hope you have a good day."

She turned and walked into the living area.

"Hey, I know I'm not supposed to break in, but this is important."

Was that Ally? The comment had come from the living room. It seemed they weren't alone.

What the hell had happened? He was trying to fight for Brynn's future and she was accusing him of being controlling? She didn't believe him. She thought he was a liar.

Or maybe he was lying to himself.

He shoved that thought aside and finished dressing, his mind whirling with confusion. How had things gone so wrong? He'd wanted to offer her some comfort. He'd wanted to spend this time with her before she got to go back to her charmed life.

Did anyone truly have a charmed life? Hadn't he learned that about her? Was he doing exactly what she accused him of?

"Oh, hey." Ally looked him over as he walked out. She was as casual as he'd ever seen her. Even when Ally worked out she wore full makeup and had her hair artfully done. She wore no makeup at all today and her hair was in a messy bun. "I shouldn't be surprised you came by. I bet you were good stress relief. Good for you, sis."

"Major was leaving." Brynn opened the crate and Duke jogged out. "What do you need?"

The question was asked of Ally, but Major wasn't about to be dismissed. "I'm not leaving until we talk this out."

"I'm taking Duke out to do his business." She simply leashed her dog and walked out the door, not seeming to care that she was dressed in nothing but a robe.

Ally's eyes were wide as she turned his way. "What did you do? Dude, do you know how hard it is to piss off Saint Brynn? Did you cheat on her? Did you say something bad about dogs?"

He was tempted to walk out after Brynn, but he didn't want a scene. Despite the fact that they were off the main house, he was pretty sure if Brynn started yelling, Seraphina would be able to hear. She was a lovely woman but she liked to gossip.

Brynn had to come back. Right?

"She's got an insane plan to stay here and take some dead-end job."

"She's not going to Paris?" Ally asked. "Gavin told me he got her a place in a super summer program for talented artists."

"She said she didn't want the pressure right now. She wants someplace cheap to stay and find herself or something."

A brilliant smile broke across Ally's face. It was the most open he'd ever seen her. "Good for her."

The door opened and Brynn walked back in with Duke. She let him off the leash. "You're still here."

"I'm staying until I talk some sense into you," he announced.

Ally glanced down at her watch. "Ignore him. So you're staying?"

A peaceful look came across Brynn's face. "I am. I like it here. I think I might be able to think and just be for a while. I'm not saying I won't ever come back to LA. I'm not even saying I don't want to do the Sorbonne classes."

Ally put a hand on her sister's shoulder. "You're choosing you for now. I'm happy for you. And you need to know that I'm going to take care of everything. I'm going to do whatever dumbass parts I have to in order to get my career started so you don't have to worry about me."

"No, she needs to worry about herself. What's going to happen when she runs out of money?" Major pointed out.

"That's going to take some time," Brynn shot back. "I've got a couple million in the bank, and the property I own is worth more, though I'm not selling anytime soon."

"Good, because I have a plan and I think it's going to mean that I can help you out in the future," Ally declared. "Only if you need me. Which you probably won't, but you should know I intend to be crazy rich and very indulgent with my big sister. Now it's time. They had to set this thing up so early in the morning I think Seraphina is going to be thrilled when we leave."

She grabbed the remote and the TV came on. Ally flitted through the channels.

"I'm not trying to push you away." He let his voice go low.

"And yet you're doing a very good job of it."

"Brynn, I only want what's best for you."

"No, you want to feel like you did what's best for me. What you really want is to not have to put any faith in me," she said.

"What does that mean?"

"It means there are only two reasons for you to do what you're doing. The first is weirdly the one I could live with. You don't want a long-term relationship with me. I can handle that. I'm crazy about you but that doesn't mean you feel the same. That's fine. It hurts, but I can get over it."

"I am crazy about you." He wouldn't lie to her about that.

"Then it's the second. You think I'll leave. You think I'll change my mind somewhere down the line and you'll get your heart broken. I've thought about all those women you've dated over the last couple of years. I wondered why I was different. Now I realize I'm not. You were willing to indulge yourself because you knew I was leaving, and you didn't have to take that leap of faith. That's what love requires, and yes, I'm using that word because I thought it was where we were going. Love requires risk, and you can't take it. Love requires you to be out of control, and you won't risk that. You would rather send your father back to hell than lose his physical body."

He felt his gut knot. "Don't bring my father into this."

"But he's part of it, too," Brynn said. "He's told you what he wants, but your needs are greater than his. You wrap it up in sacrifice, but at the heart it's selfish. You can't stand the thought of him dying so you keep him here though it's not his will. You can't stand the thought of losing me so you push me away so you don't have to."

"I'm sorry to interrupt the scene," Ally said. "It's a good one. Like, I kind of wish I was taking notes."

"Ally," Brynn began.

Ally shook her head. "Sorry. But you need to watch this. She wants you to know she's not going to leave you alone this time. Not ever again. No matter how much it hurts."

Brynn gasped as the national morning news shifted to a new story, and her mother was suddenly on the monitor, Gavin beside her. They sat by the pool not a hundred yards away from where they were right now.

"What is she doing?" Brynn whispered the question.

"Coming clean," Ally replied.

Major had the distinct feeling he was no longer needed, but he stood there listening as the anchor in New York laid out the whole sordid tale of the photographers lurking around, taking pictures of Brynn and Gavin. She then asked Gavin if he was in a relationship with Brynn.

That was when he noticed Gavin's hand folded around Diane's.

"I have a very healthy and loving relationship with my fiancée's daughter." Gavin pulled Diane's hand up and kissed it. "Bria Knight has been my costar, and I loved working with her, but what I loved more was being able to be a real father figure to Brynn Pearson and her sister, Allyson. And loving this woman beside me has been the challenge and joy of my life."

"Is she crying?" Brynn's mouth had dropped open.

"I can't get past the fact that I think her forehead moved," Ally continued. "And he called her his fiancée. I didn't hear anything about that."

"I was hesitant to come forward with our relationship

because I work in the industry, and I wanted to be more than Gavin Jacks's girlfriend," Diane was saying. "And honestly, I was afraid to trust again. But I have to come forward because life is too short. I want to live and love openly. And I want to apologize to my daughter."

"We both need to apologize to Brynn," Gavin insisted. "We could have confronted this the first time those nauseating rumors came around, but we valued our privacy over her comfort, and that was wrong of us."

Diane wasn't the only one who was teary now. Brynn was crying, and Ally had linked their arms together.

"Now you won't get fired," he said, trying to find the positive in all of this.

Ally took a step back. "I'm going to talk to them. Can I let them know you'll be by soon?"

Brynn nodded. "I'll get dressed and come up there, but you should prepare Mom that while I appreciate what she did, I'm still sure of what I want to do."

"Okay." Ally opened the door. "Proud of you." She turned Major's way. "You're a dick."

She slammed the door behind her.

He ignored Ally. He'd handled this all wrong. "Brynn, I'm sorry. I should have thought about what I was saying. I am crazy about you, and maybe that's why I fumble so often. The truth is I was already wavering on the idea of letting this relationship be over when you leave Papillon. I was already looking into ways I could come see you."

Brynn sniffled into a tissue and then tossed it aside. "It doesn't matter. As much as I've come to care about you, I can't be in a relationship where you think you can make decisions for me."

A spark of panic started to run through him. "I wasn't trying to . . ." He had been. "I was trying to do what was right for you."

"What you thought was right for me," she corrected. "What you still think is right for me. And you're doing it even after I've told you what I want. Major, I'm still staying. They asked me to walk away and already negotiated how to do it. I'm going to keep that deal and I'm going to do exactly what I said before. I'm going to find a place here and be me for a few months. I don't know how long I'll stay. I don't know when I'll be ready to go to Paris, but I am going to give myself time to figure out what's right for me. I wish you could have cared about me enough to go on that journey with me. I hope we can be polite when we see each other around town."

"Polite?"

She nodded. "Yes, polite. I'm not going to stay in my home and hide. I'm going to volunteer at the animal shelter and have lunch at the diner and sit in the park and paint. We'll see each other, and I need to know you won't give me a hard time."

How could she think for a second he would try to hurt her like that?

Because he'd broken her heart?

Maybe he was the one who needed time to think. She'd asked him to leave, and he wasn't respecting her wishes. He was being everything she'd said he was. "I would never give you a hard time, but I think you're making a mistake."

"It's mine to make."

The words were said with a finality that Major couldn't deny. He stared at her for a moment, regret flowing through him. He wasn't sure where he'd gone wrong, but it was apparent he had. "I'm sorry, Brynn."

"I am, too." She gave him a half smile. "You should go. I need to get dressed and go talk to my mom."

He walked back to the bedroom and quickly got ready. When he walked back out, Brynn was sitting on the couch,

Duke on her lap. The little dog was cuddled close to her, giving her comfort.

"I'll see you around," she said quietly, her hand moving over Duke's back. "And, Major, I hope you know I wish you and your father well."

He could actually feel his heart constrict. "Same."

He walked out, realizing he'd made the biggest mistake of his life.

chapter sixteen

"So you're engaged?" Brynn strode into her mom's suite thirty minutes after Major had walked away.

She felt numb, and that was bad because her mom had taken a big step today and she wasn't ready to celebrate it. She wasn't sure she would be even if Major hadn't turned out to be a mistake.

Her mom was still in the Chanel suit she'd worn for the morning spot. Brynn had passed the film crew the network had sent. They'd been out in the back breaking down their equipment while Seraphina had been showing some of Brynn's would-have-been coworkers around. She'd recognized the director of photography and one of the producers. He'd tried to stop and talk to her, but she'd brushed him off.

They likely would want her back now. Now her relationship with Gavin would be a plus to the film. They could build a whole narrative around it. It would put her right back in the spotlight again. Right where she didn't want to be. However, she was fairly certain that her mom wouldn't understand that. Her mom would want a payoff for what she'd done today.

"Gavin sprung that on me." Her mom shut the door behind her.

The living area of the suite was set up for a celebration. There was a breakfast tray with fruit and pastries and a tray with mimosas and champagne flutes.

"Where is he?" She glanced around but her mom seemed to be alone in the big suite.

"He went to meet the director. He got in this morning. Do you want something to drink?"

Brynn shook her head. "No. I wanted to come by and tell you that I'm still dropping out of the film."

Her mom stopped as though absorbing the blow. "Why would you do that, Brynn?"

"If you did that interview this morning for my sake, you should have talked to me about it. I could have told you I'd already made my decision. I won't let you put me in a position where I go back to work simply because I feel like I owe you."

"You don't owe me anything." Her mom moved around the table and sat down on the couch. "Your sister and I are the ones who owe you. I would say Gavin does, too, but he would have told you a very long time ago."

She was confused. She wanted to understand what exactly had happened. Her mom was perfectly capable of playing out a scene to fix a publicity problem. "When did you start seeing Gavin?"

"We've been off and on for years. More off than on."

"Have you been seeing him while you were here?"

Her mom nodded. "Do you remember when you got this job and he came over to celebrate?"

"I remember he left pretty early that night after the two of you traded barbs the whole evening."

"He came back after you'd gone to bed and we argued

and we ended up in bed," she admitted. "It's kind of what happens between the two of us. Mostly because of me."

"Why? He said he wanted to marry you back when I was a kid. Did you not love him then?"

"I loved him pretty much from the beginning." Her mom sat back, her gaze going soft. "He was so kind to you and me. He was the star of the show, and I was nothing more than a stage mom at that point."

"A gorgeous ex-model stage mom."

A faint smile crossed her mom's lips. "Perhaps, but Gavin is around stunning women all the time. Younger women."

She stared at her mom, trying to understand what she wasn't saying. "Were you insecure?"

A laugh huffed from her mother's mouth. "Oh, my darling girl, I'm always insecure. I simply learned how to shove it all down so no one could use it against me." She took a long breath. "All right. I'm going to tell you the truth, the whole truth. I was afraid to trust anything after your father died. You know that part of the story."

She knew that her dad hadn't told her mom the truth about their financial situation. "You were left with a mess."

"I was left mourning a man I also was so angry with I could barely make it through a day. I was left with two little girls and my own mom utterly dependent on me, and I suddenly had no means to provide for any of you. I sold everything I could, but your father's debts soaked it all up." A flush stole across her mother's cheeks. "I never meant for you to support us. You might not remember this, but you had been in a couple of your father's films and you loved it. Well, I think what you loved was the attention."

"And the cookies from craft services," Brynn admitted. "I never blamed you for that. I still don't. I'm glad I could do it."

"Sometimes I wonder. But I digress. I'd met Gavin when I was married to your father. I wouldn't say they were friends, but they were friendly. He was actually one of the people your father owed money to," her mom admitted. "He'd loaned your father fifty thousand dollars. When you got the part, I was terrified he would reject you because I hadn't offered to pay him back." Her mom blinked, her eyes shining. "I walked right up to his house and I had a big speech prepared threatening to sue him if he dared to get you fired from the show, and he hugged me and asked how I was. No one asked how I was. Certainly not the people William owed money to. He invited me inside and never once mentioned the debt. After you started filming and he found out I was struggling to handle Mom's illness, he offered to help me."

"He paid for the nurses, didn't he?"

Her mom nodded. "He's arrogant and can have the attention span of a gnat, but he's also the best man I've ever known. And I couldn't trust him because I couldn't trust anyone. I couldn't trust the universe. I'd worked so hard to get out of that dreadful town. I worked hard to build something with your father, something you and your sister could count on, and it all went to hell."

"But you started a relationship with him."

She nodded. "I did. I told myself we were friends with benefits. He would come over for dinner with all of us and then I would show him out and he would come back when you and Ally were asleep. He asked me to marry him when the show was ending, and I couldn't. I couldn't trust that it would work." A frown pulled her mouth down. "Then he went and dated that twenty-four-year-old as revenge."

"You turned him down, Mom. You can't dictate who he dated after you left him," Brynn argued. Things were starting to fall into place. "You got back together with him when I got the *Janie's World* role. That was six years. Were you with him the whole time?"

She shook her head. "We saw each other often during that

time, but by then I had established myself as a manager. People took me seriously. I was able to make my own money and to ensure that yours was safe. If I'd married Gavin, I would have ended up dependent on him, and I couldn't do that again."

"I think there's a compromise to be found." She wanted her mom happy. She wanted Gavin happy. Despite the fact that the day had held such heartache, she was already warming to her mom again. "But I need you to understand that you shouldn't marry Gavin because you want to get my job back."

"How about I marry him because I'm tired of being scared and I'm tired of my heart hurting at the thought that I'll never be ready?"

She reached out for her mom's hand. "That sounds like a perfect reason to get married."

"Are you really done acting?" There was an ache in her mother's voice.

She didn't want to let anyone down. It was right there. It would be so easy to change her mind, to let the need to please everyone around her lead her decision-making process. Her whole childhood had revolved around pleasing her director and her costars and her fans. It was time for her to grow up. "I am for now. If I change my mind, then I'll deal with the consequences. I've thought about this a lot. This isn't some rebellion or me trying to punish you."

"That's how it feels."

"That's not the motive. I promise you that I wouldn't hurt myself to hurt you. I wouldn't trash a future I want to punish you."

Her mom sighed and put a hand over hers. "I know that. I truly do. I also know that I'm perfectly capable of thinking the world revolves around me. I am sorry, Brynn. I should have been braver. I should have admitted the relationship when the rumors first circulated, but I was selfish and afraid. Not merely of being taken less seriously. I was afraid of being compared to Gavin's other girlfriends."

"You have to get over that. Or maybe the better way to put it is you have to learn to deal with it." Brynn wasn't sure anyone ever truly got over their insecurities. They simply learned to deal with them.

Like Major would have to learn to deal with his. He could hold on to his father, but eventually time would catch up. Eventually his fear would be made real, and he would be alone because he'd pushed away the person who would have stood by him.

"Yes, I think I will." Her mom squeezed her hand. "Are you going to stay here with Major? Is that one of the things you want to explore?"

"I did, but that's over now." She'd already reconsidered staying here in Papillon. It might be too hard to watch Major stumble and make mistake after mistake. "Depending on how fast the studio replaces me, I can probably stay in the cabin for a couple of days or so. I'll make a decision where to go then."

"I would love to have you back in LA but, darling, if you want to figure out who Brynn Pearson is without the pressure of being Bria Knight, I don't think you should come back for a while." Her mom grimaced. "I hate even saying it, but I think you should stay here. What did Major do?"

"He's not interested in pursuing a relationship."

A brow cocked over her mom's eyes. "He's not?"

"He thinks he is, but he isn't. He basically told me I should go back to LA. That there's nothing for me here."

Her mom sat back with a long sigh. "Did he say you should go back because he doesn't want you here? Or was he doing that all-American male thing of saving you even from yourself? Is he being a self-sacrificing and, quite frankly, controlling idiot?"

"That second thing." It was hard to believe. He'd shown up the night before and he'd tossed out their fight. He'd been everything she'd needed. Warm, loving, caring. He'd wrapped himself around her and she'd felt so safe.

"All right, then you need to decide if he's even worth fighting for," her mother advised.

"He's angry that I disagree with taking his father off the meds. They're working on the dementia but they'll accelerate his physical decline. I think Major is hoping he can keep his dad alive long enough for a miracle cure." It was the only reason she could think of. Major wasn't cruel.

"He's holding on. I understand the impulse. But why would he push you away? It's not because he doesn't care. I've watched the man light up around you." She frowned suddenly. "Have you considered that he's pushing you away because he doesn't think he deserves you or he's afraid he'll lose you the way he's lost everyone else? I know that sounds foolish, but it cost me years of time with Gavin. He probably doesn't even know he's doing it. Self-denial is an easy hiding place. It's warm and comfortable and it feels safer than taking the risk. I would be alone if Gavin hadn't been so tenacious."

"I don't know if I can fight him on this. If he doesn't want to see it, he won't."

"You're tired. It's been a tumultuous few weeks, and you shouldn't make any life-changing decisions right now. Beyond the ones you already have."

Brynn rolled her eyes. "It's not a mistake to take time for myself."

Her mom held up her hands in deference. "No, it isn't. I've pushed you hard all your life. All I'm saying is maybe you follow your original instincts. Maybe you don't write Major off quite yet. Maybe you include your relationship with him in those things you're taking time with."

"I was considering the fact that maybe staying in Papillon wasn't the best idea. I gave him this whole speech about how he better be polite to me."

"I don't think he would ever be impolite unless he was truly hurting. Sometimes even the sweetest puppy can bite when they're in pain. You know that. I know I've been that puppy before. Although I doubt anyone would call me sweet."

"You are very sweet when you want to be, and that's exactly how I like it." Gavin strode in from the front hall, Ally behind him. He walked right to her mom and drew her up so he could wrap his arms around her and give her a long, lingering kiss.

It was weird.

"Gross, huh? Mommy and Daddy need to get a room," Ally whispered.

Gavin finished his sucking of her mom's face. It was really weird. But her mom kind of glowed.

"This is our room," Gavin pointed out. "You are the hangers-on. If you don't like your mother and I showing our deep affection for each other, you'll have to leave. It's not like I haven't caught both of you doing things that embarrassed me. Allyson, most of the time half your butt is hanging out of your shorts."

Ally smiled. "Thanks. It's hard to get exactly the right amount of rear cleavage."

"I believe what your almost-stepfather is saying is he doesn't want to see any of your cleavage. It disturbs him," her mother said, her arm around Gavin.

"But it's a pretty butt," Ally argued. "I work very hard for it. I'm not sure I like having a dad."

The three of them would be living together. Working together sometimes. "You three should do a reality show. I would watch that."

They all went still, sparks in every one of those creative, hustling eyes.

"I was joking." The last thing Brynn needed was her family on a reality show.

Although she honestly would watch it.

"It's not a terrible idea," her mother mused. "A modern Hollywood family. It could highlight Ally's journey as a young artist."

"Mom, you don't want cameras everywhere while you and Gavin are just starting off," Ally said. "Besides, the way you two fight . . . well, that would be good TV."

"I think I would come off pretty amazing," Gavin added. "It might put me in a good position to be a spokesperson in my golden years. I've heard AARP pays well."

"We are not talking about that. We're far too young." Her mother moved to the table and picked up the champagne. "It's something to think about. Now, Gavin, you met with the director. Did he want Brynn back now that she's not the May in your May–December romance? By the way, I'm only August, you understand."

"Absolutely, darling." Gavin didn't point out that they were the same age, and Brynn decided not to, either. They were both Septembers. "And yes, he wants Brynn back. I've also talked to the studio, and they now believe it will help the film to have a true father-daughter team in the leads." He stopped her before she could protest. "I told them you were on sabbatical and might be for a long time."

"Thanks." She didn't want to have to fight them. If there was one thing she was sure of, it was that she needed this time.

Did she have to give up on Major?

Gavin took the glass her mom offered him. "I told them I'm the blessed man who has two incredibly talented daughters. How about it, Ally? You have to screen-test for it, but I know you can do this."

For the first time in forever, her sister was completely speechless.

Her mom looked to Gavin. "Did you really?"

"It's a great role for her. She's a little young, but she's got the grit. She needs parts like this," Gavin insisted. "And we all know she and I can irritate each other. That will come across beautifully on screen."

Ally flew across the room and launched herself at Gavin, hugging him in a wave of affection. "Thank you. I'll get it. I'll be the best."

"I have no doubt of that, whether you get the role or not," Gavin whispered.

How could she stay mad at them? Brynn groaned.

Life was too short. It flew by, and she didn't want to spend it in anger. She didn't want to miss joy and happiness when her mom seemed truly sorry, seemed truly willing to change.

"Well, we should definitely drink to that." Brynn joined her family. No matter what happened, she always had a place to go.

Now it was time to find out who she was on her own.

"I'm not sure I know what I did wrong."

Major sat on the bench next to his father, looking out over the pond that served as the focal point of the assisted living home's green space. It was peaceful, with a fountain in the center that lit up at night and a walking path that the residents used to get some exercise. He'd found his father out here walking around the pond with a friend, talking about the news and some television show they'd watched. He hadn't seen his dad so animated in a long time.

Could he take that away from him? How could he look his father in the eye and tell him he had to go back to hell? His father was perfectly capable of making this decision for himself. He shouldn't try to control something that wasn't his to control.

Wasn't that what Brynn had been trying to tell him?

Wasn't that what he'd tried to do to her?

They were questions he'd been asking himself all day. Since the moment he walked out of her cabin, his mind had been on how he could have handled himself better. He felt like he'd been a zombie, walking through his life but not really living it because all he could think about was her.

"Well, the first thing you did wrong was arguing with her about something you don't know a whole lot about, son. You became the patriarchy in that moment, and these young women have been taught to fight that. Good for them, I say. World would be a better place if men shut up for a moment," his father said. "Honestly, if your mother had been president, we wouldn't have gotten into so many wars and that environment would have been spick-and-span, I tell you."

It appeared that sarcasm had returned along with his father's mental clarity. "I'm serious, Dad."

"So am I," his father insisted. "Did you listen to her or did you plow right on because you knew you were right?"

He'd come out here to talk to his dad because it had seemed more productive than his initial instinct. He'd thought seriously about grabbing a bottle of booze, hopping in his truck, and going to sit by some lake with his dog, bemoaning the fact that his woman done left him like he was in a bad country song. Now he was wondering if he'd made the right choice. "I wouldn't call it plowing."

"Ah, but it was. Do you know how I know what you did?"

his dad asked. "Because I used to be the one plowing on through even when I was in the wrong field. Made your mother crazy. Our marriage got better when I learned to actually listen to her. Not to simply be quiet when she spoke, but to hear her."

"I did hear her." He'd listened, but they'd still had a problem, and he thought he might know what it had been. "Maybe I didn't understand what I heard."

"What did you hear?"

He'd been right to go to her the night before. She'd needed him and he wouldn't have been able to sleep if he hadn't known how she was doing. They shouldn't have fought the way they had. He'd gotten emotional, and his fear had come out as anger. "I heard a woman who'd worked all of her life get kicked, and hard. I heard her wanting to give up."

"Or maybe she's tired and needs a break," his father prompted.

"But she could lose her whole career over this." He groaned because he realized he'd done everything his father was accusing him of doing. "Or maybe she needs to think about whether she wants the career at all. Maybe I've been so mired in my own misery that I can't see straight. Why didn't I jump at the chance to keep her here with me? I want that more than anything. I want a chance to see if we could have a life together, but I sabotaged it."

"You don't want her here when you have to take care of me. You don't want her to have to watch you struggle while I lose my mind again. I only know what it looks like from the inside. It's frightening, but I don't have to constantly think about it. You have to live with it constantly, and you don't want to bring someone you could love into that."

Brynn wasn't the only one who he hadn't been listening to. "Taking care of you isn't misery."

"No, but watching me lose my mind is," his dad said.

"It's not great to go through it, either, but if I had the choice, I'd go through it myself instead of watching it happen to someone I love. And there's some selfishness in there. I know what you're going through is hard, and I know that you struggle to ask for help."

"I shouldn't need it. I have a good life." He didn't have anything to complain about. He had a good job, a house to live in, friends. He'd had great parents.

"That doesn't mean you don't struggle. No one gets out of this life without pain. Sometimes I think the worst thing we did to our kids was teach them they always had to be stoic. We taught you that if someone else had it worse, you didn't have a right to feel bad. That's not healthy, son. You get to feel whatever it is you need to feel. You can have a good life and still have trouble, and if you shove that trouble down without dealing with it, without examining it and finding a solution, that's what will bring you real misery."

"That's what Brynn's doing." He finally understood. His father had found the exact words that made sense to him. "She's trying to figure out what's missing in her life. She's slowing down and giving herself time."

She'd been willing to give them time, too. He'd panicked at the thought. Why?

"I think it's a very mature decision on her part," his father said. "She never had a chance to be a kid. She's never had a chance to sit and think because she was too busy seizing every opportunity she could get. She's been sprinting all her life."

"She talked to you about this?"

His father nodded. "Yes, we had a good conversation at the festival. I know I've told you this before, but I like her a lot. I think she's a good match for you."

"I get a sense of peace when I'm around her. Like we

didn't just meet. Like we've known each other for a long time." It had been an easy relationship until they'd fought.

"Yes, that's what I thought," his dad replied. "And that's a good reason to pursue a relationship, but I think she's the one who can push you. I think she's the one who can get you out of the rut you're in. You've spent years now worried about me, taking care of me. You've done it for so long, it scares you to think about it being over."

"That's not the reason I'm scared of it being over." The words felt choked in his throat.

His father leaned toward him. "I'm going to tell you a secret, Major. I know I've always told you that the best day of my life was when you were born, but that was a lie. There was another day, a day from which all my joy and pain and happiness and heartache flowed. A day I wouldn't take back for anything."

"Your wedding day."

"Yes. It's funny because I thought I knew what love meant that day. I stood there as a twenty-four-year-old kid, and she was so pretty. I married her because she was beautiful and kind, and I didn't know how much she would change who I was. The love I felt for her that day was shallow in the face of how I felt when I held her as she died. Logically I know she wasn't beautiful that day. Cancer had ravaged her, but she was so lovely. She was half of my soul. Loving her, getting to truly know who she was deep inside . . . son, that's what makes life meaningful. You don't have to have some grand purpose. And I don't care what people will tell you. It doesn't have to be one man and one woman. I don't think it even has to involve sex. Love is the important thing. Love is everything. Don't be afraid of it. Don't think it's a weak thing that can't handle adversity."

"She thinks I don't trust her to know her own mind. She

doesn't know how much I want her to be here with me, but beyond that, I want her to be happy."

"And you're worried you can't make her happy."

"She's had the whole world. She's had what most people only dream of."

"Well, now she wants you. Maybe instead of having the whole world looking at her, she wants to be the whole world for the people she loves. Some people have big dreams. Some people need the world at their feet. Most of us build these small worlds where we're loved, where we love. There is nothing wrong with an ordinary life, and I think you'll find there's also no such thing. It's all different. Every story unfolds in its own way. Don't think yours has to play out like the ones around you."

"I guess deep down I was worried that I couldn't be enough for her, that I don't have anything real to offer her. But I do. I can support her. I can love her for who she is even if she's not sure who that is right now." He could give her more. He could stop pretending he didn't need help and treat her like the partner she should be. She wasn't some pretty thing to look at. She was strong. He should have learned that from the moment they'd met. There was no need to save Brynn from herself. She didn't need a knight in shining armor. She needed a hand to hold, a mind to bounce ideas off of, a soul to share her own with.

"Now you are talking sense, son." His father sat back with a sigh.

Major let a moment pass, the silence sitting peacefully between them. His father had put it plainly to him. Time was a gift, but time didn't stop. "Is it time for me to let go?"

His father's hand came out, patting Major's. "It's time for you to ask me the question. You haven't, you know. Not directly. I've been okay with it because I've always known in the end you would make the right decision."

Which was to let him make the decision. "Dad, do you want to keep taking the meds?"

"I do. I would take a few months or even days of being here with you, all of me, over years of my body existing. I would very much like to go and see some old friends. You could come with me. I'd like to spend more time with your Brynn. Share this time with me, Major, and know that I won't regret a second of it. Not even the end because I'll get to see your momma again."

"Okay." Emotion welled inside him, and he didn't fight it this time. He didn't try to stop the tears that fell. He sat with his father, allowing the moment to imprint on his memory. This was one of those times he would always remember, this moment when he accepted that time was not infinite, but his love could be. "So how do I get Brynn back?"

His dad squeezed his hand, a grin coming over his face. "Is the raccoon only a thief or do you think you can talk him into kidnapping?"

He laughed. "I think we'll have to find another way."

But he would. He would find a way to win her back. Even if it meant starting all over again.

chapter seventeen

"You cannot hire that golf cart man as your official driver," her mother said, her hands on her hips. "That is what production assistants are for. Now that you have the job, I'll make sure they assign one to you. You can do it all properly now that you're part of the cast."

The last three days had been a whirlwind of activity, and Brynn was grateful for the distractions. She'd helped her sister prep for her audition. She'd been able to audition for the director and been hired on the spot. Then there was all the press coverage of her mom and Gavin's announcement. She'd agreed to sit for a few spots to talk about how happy she was for her mom.

And she was. But her happiness was tempered by the sorrow she felt at losing Major. She should be excited about taking this time for herself. She should be looking at the world of possibilities and feeling light.

She didn't. She missed him and wondered how long she could really stay here. She hadn't run into him yet. How would that feel? How would it feel when he went back to his serial dating life and she was still pining over him? She knew she'd been right when she'd sent him away, but it didn't make her heart ache less.

"Nope. I want Greg, and I'm paying him myself. He's letting me bedazzle the cart and he bought this little fridge so he can keep my iced lattes on hand. I like it better than a limo." Ally was fresh faced and practically glowing as she poured herself a mug of coffee. "I find normal cars confining now. And a normal, boring limo driver doesn't point out all the fun places. Like we were coming back from the bar last night and Greg showed me where the rougarous meet. That's a Cajun werewolf. I'm pretty sure it was just a bunch of really hairy teens, but it makes a person think."

They'd started this morning ritual the day her mom and Gavin announced their engagement. Every morning she would walk the short distance between her cabin and the main house and join her family for breakfast, where they talked about the industry incessantly and she tried to forget that Major was out there and he and his dad were facing down something terrible.

It hurt that he didn't want her by his side.

"Well, you won't when it's raining or when wind ruins your hair," her mom pointed out.

"That's what hair and makeup are for." Ally had the script in front of her. She'd been working day and night, rehearsing scenes with Gavin. "Don't worry about me, Mom. You don't have to take my Guber. I assure you Gavin's got his own driver, and he'll be happy to share with you."

"You know I will." Gavin strode in from the bedroom, his hair still damp from the shower. He moved in behind her mom and dropped a kiss on her neck. "Imagine the things we can do in that limo."

Brynn and Ally managed to gag at the same time. Some things were still weird and probably always would be.

Gavin ignored them completely. "I'll share everything with you."

"Except my opinion on the wardrobe choices for Ally," her mom shot back.

Gavin stepped away and grimaced. "Yes, that is all your own, my love."

Ally's eyes rolled. "I don't need to change my character's style. It's fine. She's a small-town deputy. She wouldn't wear designer clothes, and I'm not opening the top two buttons of my deputy uniform."

"But it cuts you off," her mom insisted. "You look better with a bit of skin showing."

"What is this about?" Brynn had spent yesterday evening painting and trying to decide if she should stay or go. Somehow she hadn't managed to make herself get on a plane. She was stuck, vacillating between wanting to stay here in Papillon and wanting to insulate herself from the heartache that would come when she saw Major again.

"You know the scene where my character goes to her friend's birthday party?" Ally asked. "Well, we went for the fitting yesterday, and Mom doesn't like what the costumer picked. She was like the worst stage mom ever and I was her precious six-year-old star."

"You should never be in baggy sweats," her mother complained. "You've worked far too hard on your body. I understand that you have to wear those khaki things most of the time, but it's a party. You could wear some tight jeans and a nice top. Maybe some jewelry."

Ally's head dropped back. "My character would be more comfy in sweats. She's not a tight-jeans girl. Have you seen what the deputies around here wear when they're not in uniforms? It's pretty much the uniform without the badge. I did not see Deputy Roxie walking around the fairgrounds in blingy designer jeans and a top that shows off her boobs. Did you have to deal with this?"

So many times. Her mom had very strong opinions on many, many things. "I don't now." The thought actually made her feel lighter. She didn't have to listen to her mom plan things that weren't hers to plan. She didn't have to be her mom's client. She could just be her daughter, and a daughter could leave. "So you guys figure it all out and let me know if you need anything. I'm going to take the day off and paint."

She grabbed her coffee and started for the door, Duke trotting beside her. She heard the three of them start to argue about whether or not Ally's character would wear high heels, which her mom pointed out did amazing things for Ally's legs.

She was so out of that now.

Maybe she would paint this morning and then head to Guidry's for lunch, though she would need to find a ride since the only Guber in town was now permanently attached to her sister.

She was calling it Guber now. She was also constantly on the lookout for criminally minded raccoons, and she'd started to really enjoy Wednesday yoga sessions.

She didn't want to leave. Time would heal the wound, or at least make the pain less sharp.

She needed to get a car. Or a truck. Maybe a Jeep. There were a lot of places out here where a Jeep would be helpful. She wanted to get out and explore, but first she needed to learn a thing or two about how to navigate the bayou. Roxie had offered to show her around in a way that didn't include writing tickets and patrolling. It might be time to take her up on her offer.

Friends. She was going to make friends who knew nothing about Hollywood, who liked her for who she was and not what she or her mom could do for them.

She rounded the corner and stopped.

There was a woman standing in front of her cabin. She was dressed for business in a sensible suit and kitten heels. Her brown hair was up in a bun on her head, and she knocked on the door. Something about the urgency of that knock made Brynn think she'd been there for a while.

"Hello. Is there something I can do for you?"

The woman whirled around, and her eyes widened. "I'm looking for Brynn . . . well, you. You're that TV lady, right? I don't watch much television. I prefer to enhance my mind with books. My name is Miranda Jossart, and I'm the best Realtor in town. I'm also the only Realtor in town, but that doesn't mean I'm not good. Now, I'm here to show you the listings we picked. The deputy explained that you needed some place a little more permanent than this cabin. I told Seraphina the cabins were far too small. Anyway, when I told him there were fifteen homes and/or apartments that might work, he said he didn't want to waste your time, so he went to check them all out yesterday and cut down on what you had to look at. I've got my car ready."

She could talk fast. Way faster than Brynn could keep up. "I'm sorry. I don't understand."

She held up a manilla folder. "I've got properties for you to look at. Four, to be precise. Like I said, there were several more but Major didn't want to bother you with the ones that wouldn't be suitable."

"He chose which places for me to look at." She was confused that he'd chosen anything at all. "We're not together, so he doesn't get to choose anything for me. Even if we were, I wouldn't let him pick where I'm going to live."

What was he trying to do? Was he taking control again? Had he decided if she was staying here, he would make sure she was as far away as possible?

"So you want to look at them all?" Miranda asked, her

brow wrinkling. "I will tell you that I think Major was wrong not to put the old Beyer place on the list. It's five thousand square feet. It's beautiful and comes with all the furnishings. Now, I will tell you that the furnishings are antique, and I know you'll hear that the place is haunted, but I've been told they're very helpful ghosts. Not at all scary. And don't worry about the piano that plays itself from time to time. It's free entertainment, I say."

"Uhm, I probably don't need that much space." Especially if it came with the former residents hanging around.

"Okay, there's a smaller place he wrote off. It's in one of the newer sections of town. Lots of families and kids and energy," Miranda said. "It's even got a decent-sized yard. He said the place had to be dog-friendly. And despite what he said, it's got light. I don't understand why he was so obsessed with light. The sun shines on everyone equally."

"Light?" The implications of that word brought a tear to her eyes.

Miranda waved a hand as though the word itself was silly. "Yes, he went on and on about it. Going through all the rooms saying the light wasn't good. He says you're some sort of artist and you need light. I told him all the electricity works. I don't represent homes without power, and given where I live that's saying something. And the Beyer place sometimes has extra power, if you know what I mean."

She was so not moving into the haunted house. No way. No how.

Major had gone through all the listings and visited them to make sure she would get good light. He knew what it meant. She trusted him to know what light she would need.

"Why would he do this? Why would he spend all that time when he doesn't want me here?"

Miranda shrugged. "He seemed like he definitely wants you here. He talked about you a lot. He walked through all the kitchens, trying to decide if you would like to cook there. I'm also supposed to give you a letter at the end of this. Something about a blind date. So he's also trying to set you up. Which is weird, but I don't ask questions."

He'd written her a letter? "I'd like to read it."

Miranda's lips pursed. "I'm supposed to give it to you at the end."

"But I probably won't go with you if I don't read the letter." She wasn't waiting hours to read what he'd written. What did she mean by blind date? Would the man actually try to set her up with one of his friends as a way to apologize?

"Well, I did my hair and everything, so I suppose I'll have to do it." She handed over a white envelope. "But we should hurry. Your date is supposed to start at noon. I don't know how we'll get through everything and have time to get to Guidry's."

How would she know . . . "You read it?"

The Realtor shrugged as though a spot of spying was nothing between complete strangers. "I took a peek. You see, there's this rumor going around that you broke up with Major probably because you've got all those crazy Hollywood ideas on how men should act. I wanted to see if it was true. My niece needs a date to her best friend's wedding. Her best friend is all hoity-toity because she's marrying some guy who owns a restaurant in New Orleans, and she's not a very good best friend because she picked her New Orleans friend to be her maid of honor, so I think Major taking Kelley Ann to that wedding would show her."

Somehow she didn't see Major doing that anytime soon. "Uh, I think Major is done with blind dates."

"Oh, honey, it's not really a date," Miranda insisted. "Kelley Ann has a boyfriend, but he's a knucklehead. He recently got two teeth knocked out when he tried to join a professional dirt bike team. Did you know they had teams? I want Major there because he's going to look way better in the pictures. And if Kelley Ann can see that there is more out there for her than Joe Bob, then my work here is done."

Miranda was a lot. She was also nosy since she'd opened the letter.

Brynn,

Please forgive me. You were right about everything, including my fear. I couldn't see bringing you into my chaotic world, but now I understand that's what people who care about each other do. I know I blew my chance with you, but I still care. I want you to have a great place to live here in Papillon. I've found a couple of houses and a duplex for you to look at. They have everything you need. I wanted to save you some time and the possibility of getting talked into buying the old Beyer place. Don't. It might not be haunted, but it's creepy as hell.

I want you to know that I'll be looking for you. Every day. If I get to see you, it'll be the best part of my day. I won't merely be polite to you. I'll be kind and always give you anything you need.

In that spirit, I would like to set you up with a man I've recently met. He's going through a lot, but he's ready to be a partner to a woman like you. Don't believe all the rumors about him. Yes, he's dated a lot, but there's really only one woman out there for him. If you would like to meet this man, he'll be at Guidry's at noon, ready to take you to lunch.

And if you're not, that's okay, too. He'll be there every Saturday at noon. Waiting and hoping that you'll show up.

Major

She took a long breath, letting the sweetness of the moment wash over her. He was giving her time. It would have been a mistake to move in together. She needed time and space to figure out who she was without the world watching her. But lunch would be nice. Dates would be nice. More afternoons where they talked and more nights where they held each other. Time. They had some now.

"It sounds like he really screwed up," Miranda said. "You know men don't change, honey."

"Miranda, he's not taking your niece to the wedding. He's going to be busy with me." She reached into her pocket for the key to her cabin. "We should get going. I have a date at noon."

She didn't intend to be late.

"Dear lord, are you dating again?" Lisa Guidry stared at him like he'd grown two heads. "Tell me this is not another blind date set up by one of your nosy neighbors, because I thought the last one went really well."

She was forgetting a lot. "No. The last blind date turned out to have an actual girlfriend. Brynn wasn't a blind date. She just happened to be here when I was dumped and was kind enough to not make me eat by myself."

Though she might today. He'd meant what he'd written to her. He would give her time. He would be patient. He wanted another chance with her, and he would earn it if he needed to.

He stood in the foyer of Guidry's, perfectly prepared to sit on the bench for at least an hour waiting to see if Brynn showed. Maybe he would give her an hour and a half because Miranda could talk a person's ear off and they had four listings to look at. He had a book to read so he was ready to wait. What he hadn't been ready for was the level of scrutiny he would get from the hostess.

He probably should have been.

"And then you did what? I heard the whole movie production is falling apart because you broke that gorgeous actress's heart and now she can't act anymore," Lisa said.

"Oh, I heard he fought with her because he wanted a part in the movie and she wouldn't give it to him," another voice said.

He turned and pointed a finger Mike Hawkins's way. "I did not do that. I never wanted to be an actor."

"I heard she found Josette Trahan in his bed." Sue Nelson worked at the post office, and she delivered far more than the mail.

The grapevine was strong in Papillon. Strong and so wrong.

Lisa nodded. "Now, that I could believe. That woman likes other women's men. You have to show her firm boundaries. I've found snatching a good hunk of her store-bought hair out works."

"Nah, Josette's getting married again," Mike informed them. "She doesn't cheat on her husbands until after she marries them. She's very faithful before."

"It's how she avoids the dreaded prenup, but I heard she's marrying the really old rich ones now," Lisa said with a nod.

"Then who was Major sleeping with?" Sue asked. "Because you cannot tell me that man isn't sleeping with someone. Have you seen him without his shirt?"

"Everyone has. Don't you remember the video that went around where he got caught in his shorts?" Mike asked.

"I don't believe in the Internet," Bernadette insisted. "Though I would watch that show."

"I was not sleeping with anyone except Brynn." He needed to put those rumors down. "And I am trying very hard to sleep with her again, but you weirdos are going to scare her off. Tell everyone that I was a massive ass and that's why Brynn decided to rightly put me in my place. And I would appreciate it if everyone would stay out of my business."

"What fun would that be?"

Major stopped because he knew that voice. That voice haunted his dreams and made his stupid heart leap with excitement every time he heard it. That voice had made her a star, and now it just might make her the center of his whole universe.

He turned and Brynn stood there, a smile on her face.

"You came."

If Brynn noticed that half the town was watching them, she didn't show it. "Of course I came. I'm meeting a blind date." She glanced around. "He's supposed to be here at noon. I hope I'm not late."

Yep, every eye was on him, and he might have made a terrible mistake. "It's me. I'm the date. I'm so sorry if you thought it was someone else."

"Could you talk louder, Major?" Mike asked. "Momma's hearing aid is out." He turned to his elderly mother and started shouting. "The pretty actress lady thought she was on a blind date, but it turned out to be Major, who she already dated. She's probably very disappointed."

Brynn simply moved forward and held out a hand. "Hi. I'm Brynn Pearson. I'm new in town."

Relief flooded his system. She was here and she was ready to try again. He took her hand in his. "Major Blanchard. I can't tell you how nice it is to meet you. I hope you've had a good morning."

She squeezed his hand. "I did. I found a place to live while I'm here. I'm taking half of a duplex. Turns out the other half is owned by some friends of mine. They bought theirs a couple of months ago when the owner moved, but the unit I looked at was still for sale."

"She's taking Darlene Cooper's old place," Mike shouted at his momma.

"Darlene's gone?" Mike's momma shouted back. "Did she die?"

"No. She moved to Beaumont to be with her grandkids," Mike replied.

"You took the one next to Roxie and Zep?" He was going to ignore everyone but her. If they gossiped about them, he was okay with that. It was all part of life here in Papillon.

She nodded. "Yes. It was the best of the bunch, and at least I know I like my neighbors. It's close to town so I can walk to the park, and it's got the loveliest lemon tree in the back. It's a good size for Duke, too. Not to mention the light is beautiful."

He'd thought that would be the one for her. He'd been to Roxie and Zep's place many times, but there was something about the other half of the duplex that had him picturing Brynn and Duke there. "I'm glad."

"She said she likes the lemon tree," Mike announced.

"I'm going to need some help getting my studio ready, though," she said.

He could do that. "I think you'll find me very handy. But you should know I'm going out of town soon. I'm taking my dad to see some of his old friends. He's got a lot of plans, lots of things he wants to see this year."

He couldn't say it. Not yet. He couldn't say *before he dies*. He was going to take it one day at a time, enjoying each for the gift it was.

Brynn moved in, taking her hand back and then wrapping her arms around him. "I'm so glad to hear that."

For the first time in days, the world felt right. He held her for a moment.

"I thought she just met him." Mike's mom was a bit confused. "You know, she looks like that little girl from *Janie's World*."

He felt Brynn chuckle.

"Why don't I take you two to a table?" Lisa hid her smile behind the two menus she held.

He stepped back, offering Brynn his hand again. "Can I get you some of Papillon's best gumbo, Ms. Pearson?"

She took it. "Absolutely, Deputy Blanchard."

They walked into the restaurant, ready to begin again.

epilogue

~

PARIS, FRANCE
Eighteen months later

"Who sent a limo?" Major stared at the well-dressed man holding up a sign indicating that he was waiting for Brynn Pearson and TW.

"Who do you think?" Brynn turned her face up, grinning his way. "That's pure Ally right there. We're lucky she didn't send a Guber."

"I don't think those are street legal in Paris." They weren't legal in Papillon, either, but that hadn't stopped Greg from winding up on the cover of *Vanity Fair* along with Ally Pearson, who'd been named one of Hollywood's hottest actresses. The cover had sported a glamourous Ally in a designer gown hanging on to the side of her now infamous golf cart transport. She carted Greg and his Guber to every shoot she could.

It didn't hurt that she also starred in one of America's favorite reality shows. *Match Made in Hollywood* followed Ally's career and how Diane and Gavin were handling love and fame.

And there was one episode where he and Brynn visited, and he'd hidden behind every bookcase he could when they were filming. Though Dolly and Duke were now famous on the Internet.

One year and a half with this woman, and it had been the best of his life.

One year and a half of getting to know her, falling in love with her, sharing his father's last days with her.

She squeezed his hand and pulled him out of the path of the travelers around them. "Hey, are you all right? Because we can turn around and head back if you're not ready for this. I can defer."

He shook his head and moved his hand to her waist. "No. I'm fine. I was thinking about something your mom told me at the funeral."

His father had had a good year and a couple of months. They'd gone to visit old friends, participated in every crazy Cajun festival they could find, and had one last amazing Christmas. They'd rented an RV and driven out to LA to visit Brynn's parents, stopping at Roswell and the Grand Canyon and the Painted Desert. They'd spent long nights talking, allowing Brynn to really know his dad.

She'd mourned with him, holding him and taking part of his pain.

She'd cried for his past and given him a future.

"What did she say?" Brynn grimaced. "That was two months ago. How bad was it that you didn't mention it until now? You know she doesn't really mean half the things she says."

He wasn't so sure about that, but he knew she'd meant this. "She told me I always have a family with her. She told me she knew she wasn't my mom, but if I needed one, she would always be there for me."

Brynn sighed in obvious relief. "I'm glad. She means that. She adores you."

He rather thought Diane adored how much he loved her

daughter. Brynn had blossomed outside the bright lights. Diane had told him she was happier than she'd ever seen her.

Now they were headed to Paris for six weeks. Gavin had helped them get an apartment close to the Sorbonne, where Brynn would be studying. Armie had given him a two-month sabbatical. If she liked it, they would be moving here for the full two-year program.

"And I adore you." He leaned over and kissed her.

Gavin was also expediting the process of bringing Duke and Dolly over, but it would take a little time. He was sure Duke and Dolly would be getting a lot of *Match Made in Hollywood* screen time over the coming weeks.

"Are you sure you want to do this?" Brynn asked, biting her bottom lip. "I know it's a lot."

"It's an adventure." He would go anywhere with her. And it was time for him to see the world, to make more memories. Papillon would always be home, but it was time to explore with the love of his life before they settled down and raised crazy Cajun kids.

What Brynn didn't know was that he had an engagement ring in his pocket. He was going to ask the woman of his dreams to be his wife right here in the City of Light.

After all, she was his light.

She nodded. "Then let's get going. I'm ready. And I bet that limo has champagne."

He took her hand, ready to start the rest of his life.

author's note

As of this writing the raccoon criminal known as Brian is still at large.

acknowledgments

I'd like to thank Kim Guidroz, Maria Monroy, Kori Smith, Stormy Pate, and Riane Holt for all their hard work. Thanks to my agent, Kevan Lyon, and everyone at Marsal Lyon. Thanks to the whole Berkley team, especially Kate Seaver and Mary Geren. Special thanks to my family for all the support, and to the dogs in my life! To Frodo Waggins, Precious, and Samwise Pupgee—you're always there when I need a smile or to chase away the raccoon who is almost certainly trying to steal my phone.

Look for the next Butterfly Bayou novel

Bayou Beloved

Coming from Berkley in spring 2023!

Ready to find
your next great read?

Let us help.

Visit prh.com/nextread

Penguin
Random
House